Sunshine State EMP Blackout

UNFINISHED BUSINESS

BLOOD IS THICKER SERIES: BOOK FOUR

St. Augustine

Punta Gorda

Miami

BRUNO BRENNAN

Sunshine State EMP Blackout

UNFINISHED BUSINESS

BLOOD IS THICKER SERIES: BOOK FOUR

St. Augustine

Punta Gorda

Miami

BRUNO BRENNAN

SIGN UP FOR MY NEWSLETTER

Be the first to know about new book releases, see behind the scenes content and more.

BrunoBrennan.com

Be sure to check out the entire

Blood is Thicker Series
Sunshine State EMP Blackout

https://www.amazon.com/dp/B0CVFWCWS5

For my family, who despite each of our differences or disagreements,
I know we will always be there for one another because
"Blood is Thicker than Water"

TABLE OF CONTENTS

CHAPTER ONE

The rain fell in a steady drizzle as we gathered around my mother's grave, the gray sky above us matching the somber mood. I stood at the head of the group, my heart heavy with grief as I looked down at the simple wooden casket that held my mother's body. Beside me, Jojo and Taylor clung to each other, their faces streaked with tears. Maria stood a little apart from the rest of us, her head bowed in silent prayer. Even little Parker seemed to sense the gravity of the moment, her tiny face solemn as she clung to her mother's hand.

I cleared my throat, trying to find the words to express the depth of my loss. "My mother was a remarkable woman," I began, my voice thick with emotion. "She was the glue that held our family together, the one who always knew just what to say to make everything better."

I paused, my mind flooding with memories of my mother. "When I was a kid, she used to make me these amazing pancakes every Sunday morning," I said, a small smile tugging at the corners of my mouth. "She'd top them with butter and sugar. That was the way her mother made them for her growing up. I think my grandmother got that from living through the great depression, when they couldn't afford such luxuries like maple syrup. All that sugar always gave me such a sugar rush. I remember spending the night at a friends house and his mom making us pancakes the next morning. I'll never forget the look she gave me when I covered those flapjacks with butter and sugar. Hell I had no idea that's not the way people ate them. When I got home, I told Ma I was so embarrassed. She explained to me that yeah, most people don't eat em' that way. Anyway, she'd always make extra, so I could have some to take to school with me for lunch."

I swallowed hard, fighting back the tears that threatened to spill down my cheeks. "She was always there for me, no matter what. When I got in trouble at school, or when I had my heart broken for the first time, she was the one I turned to. She always knew just what to say to make me feel better."

I looked out at the faces of my family, seeing my own grief reflected back at me. "My mother taught me what it means to be strong," I said, my voice growing steadier. "She taught me to never give up, no matter how hard things got. And she taught me the importance of family, of sticking together no matter what."

I took a deep breath, letting it out slowly. "I will miss her every day for the rest of my life," I said, my voice barely above a whisper. "But I know that she will always be with me, guiding me and giving me strength. And I promise you, Ma, I will make you proud. I will keep fighting, no matter what it takes."

I looked down at the casket one last time, my heart aching with the finality of it all. "Goodbye, Ma," I whispered, my voice cracking with emotion. "I love you."

As Jojo stepped forward, I felt a surge of pride in my chest. He stood tall and strong, his military bearing evident even in his grief.

"Gram was more than just my grandmother," Jojo began, his voice steady despite the tears in his eyes. "She was my friend, my confidante, and my biggest cheerleader."

He paused for a moment, a small smile playing at the corners of his mouth. "When I was a kid, she used to take me fishing down at the lake. We'd sit there for hours, just talking and laughing and enjoying each other's company. She taught me how to bait a hook and cast a line, but more than that, she taught me patience and persistence."

Jojo's voice grew thick with emotion as he continued. "When I enlisted in the Army, Gram was the first person I told. She hugged me so tight I thought she'd never let go. And every time I came home on leave, she'd have a big batch of my favorite cookies waiting for me."

He reached into his pocket and pulled out a small, worn photograph. "This is a picture of Gram and me at my boot camp graduation at Fort Benning. She was so proud of me that day, I thought she might just burst."

Jojo held up the photograph for us all to see. In it, he stood ramrod straight in his crisp new uniform, a beaming smile on his face. And there was Ma, her arm wrapped around his waist, her face glowing with pride.

"Gram always believed in me," Jojo said softly. "Even when I doubted myself, she never did. She saw the best in me, even when I couldn't see it myself."

He took a deep breath, blinking back the tears that threatened to fall. "I will miss you so much Gram. I thank you for everything you taught me in my life, all the lessons I've learned because of your love. But I also always keep this thought in my mind. As long as you're in my mind and in my memories, you will never really be gone. You will always live with each and every one of us. I take great comfort in the knowledge that you will always be by our sides."

Taylor stepped forward, her long brown hair blowing gently in the breeze. She took a deep breath, steadying herself before she began to speak.

"Gram was more than just a grandmother to me," Taylor said, her voice soft but clear. "She was my role model, my confidante, and my best friend."

She paused for a moment, a wistful smile playing at the corners of her mouth. "When I was a little girl, Gram used to take me on these amazing adventures. We'd pack a picnic lunch and head out into the woods, exploring hidden trails and secret clearings. She taught me the names of all the plants and animals we saw, and she always made me feel like I could do anything."

Taylor's eyes shimmered with unshed tears as she continued. "As I got older, Gram was always there for me. When I was struggling in school or feeling lost and alone, she was the one I turned to. She never judged me or made me feel like I wasn't good enough. She just listened and offered her wisdom and love."

She reached into her pocket and pulled out a small, delicate locket. "This was Gram's locket," Taylor said, holding it up for us all to see. "She gave it to me on my wedding day, and I've worn it every day since. Inside, there's a picture of her and Grandpa on their own wedding day. She told me that it was a reminder that true love never dies, that it lives on in the hearts of those we leave behind."

Taylor's voice broke then, and she took a moment to compose herself. "Gram taught me so much about life and love and family. She showed me what it means to be strong and resilient in the face of adversity. And she taught me that no matter what happens, family always comes first."

She looked out at all of us gathered around the grave, her hazel eyes shining with love and grief. "I will miss you every day, Gram. But I know that you will always be with me, guiding me and giving me strength. And I promise to keep your memory alive, to pass on all the lessons you taught me to my own daughter. Because that's what family does. We carry each other's stories forward, even when they're no longer here to tell them themselves."

I watched as Maria stepped forward, her eyes glistening with unshed tears. She took a deep breath, steadying herself before she began to speak.

"I know I only knew Toni for a short time," she said, her voice soft but clear. "But in that time, I found her to be the most wonderful grandmother, mother, and an incredibly strong woman."

Maria paused for a moment, a small smile playing at the corners of her mouth. "From the moment I met her, Toni welcomed me into this family with open arms. She treated me like one of her own, and I will always be grateful for that."

She looked out at all of us gathered around the grave, her warm brown eyes shining with emotion. "Toni had a way of making everyone feel loved and valued. She had such a big heart, and she shared it so freely with all of us."

Maria's voice grew thick with emotion as she continued. "I remember one day, not long after I first met her, Toni pulled me aside and told me how much she appreciated me being there for her son. She said that she could see how happy I made him, and that was all that mattered to her."

She reached up and brushed away a tear that had escaped down her cheek. "In that moment, I knew that I had found not just a wonderful partner in Joe, but an incredible family as well. And Toni was at the heart of it all."

Maria took a deep breath, her voice growing stronger. "Toni taught me so much in the short time I knew her. She taught me about resilience and strength in the face of adversity. She taught me about the power of love and family. And she taught me that no matter what happens in life, we always have each other to lean on."

She looked over at me then, her eyes shining with love and understanding. "I know that losing Toni is an incredible loss for all of us. But I also know that her spirit will live on through each and every one of us. We will carry her memory forward, and we will honor her legacy by continuing to love and support each other, no matter what."

As Maria stepped back, I felt a surge of emotion rising up in my chest. I knew that she was right - Ma may be gone, but she would never truly leave us. She would always be with us, guiding us and giving us strength, just as she always had.

Paulette stepped forward, I felt my breath catch in my throat. I hadn't expected her to speak, and I wasn't sure what she would say.

"I know that many of you may be surprised to see me speak today," Paulette began, her voice shaking slightly. "But I felt that I needed to say a few words about Toni, and the impact she had on my life."

I watched as Paulette took a deep breath, steadying herself before she continued. "When I was married to Joe, Toni was more than just a mother-in-law to me. She was a friend, I always felt I could tell her anything, and she was a source of endless support and advice."

Paulette's eyes shimmered with unshed tears as she spoke. "Toni was always there for me, no matter what. When I was struggling with the challenges of motherhood or feeling overwhelmed by the demands of life, she was the one I turned to. She never judged me or made me feel like I wasn't good enough. She just listened and offered her wisdom and love."

I felt a pang of sadness in my chest as Paulette's voice broke. "But I made mistakes," she said, her words heavy with regret. "And one of my biggest regrets is that I not only disappointed Joe and our children, but I also lost the love and the respect of Toni."

Paulette looked down at the ground, her shoulders shaking with emotion. "I know that Toni was angry with me, and she had every right to be. I betrayed her son and our family, and family was everything to her."

She looked up then, her eyes meeting mine. "Joe, I am so sorry," she said, her voice barely above a whisper. "I was selfish and I made a terrible mistake. I hurt you and I hurt our children in ways that I can never fully make right."

Paulette turned to face Jojo and Taylor, her face streaked with tears. "And to my children, I am so sorry for not being the mother you deserved. I let you both down in so many ways, and I will regret that for the rest of my life."

Finally, Paulette turned to face the casket, her voice trembling with emotion. "Toni, I am so sorry for disappointing you. You were always there for me, and I let you down in the worst possible way. I hope that someday, you can forgive me."

As Paulette stepped back, I felt a rush of emotions washing over me. Anger, sadness, regret - they all swirled together in a dizzying mix. But beneath it all, I felt a glimmer of something else - the possibility of forgiveness, of healing, of moving forward.

I reached down, scooping up a handful of the wet earth. It was more mud than dirt from the steady rain that had been falling all morning. I held it for a moment, feeling the cold weight of it in my palm, before tossing it gently into the grave. It landed with a soft thud on the lid of my mother's casket.

Jojo and Taylor stepped forward next, following my lead. They each took a handful of the sodden soil, their faces tight with grief as they let it fall into the hole. Maria came after, her head still bowed in prayer as she added her own offering to the grave.

One by one, the rest of the mourners approached. Friends, neighbors, people from the community who had known and loved my mother. Each of them took a turn, saying their own silent goodbyes as they added to the growing pile of earth on the casket.

And then, at last, it was Parker's turn. My little granddaughter, barely more than a baby, walked slowly toward the edge of the grave. Her steps were hesitant, unsure, but there was a determined set to her tiny shoulders.

She reached the grave and crouched down, her small hand reaching out to grab a fistful of the muddy earth. As she straightened up, I saw a single tear trickling down her chubby cheek. It broke my heart to see her so sad, so confused by the solemnity of the moment.

"Goodbye, Gwam," she said softly, her little voice quivering. And then she tossed the dirt into the hole, just as she had seen the rest of us do.

A hush fell over the gathered mourners, and I felt a lump rising in my throat. There wasn't a dry eye in the crowd as we all watched Parker, this innocent child, grappling with a loss that was far too big for her to fully understand.

CHAPTER TWO

I gazed at the freshly turned earth of my mother's grave, a dull ache throbbing in my chest like a wound that refused to heal. The garden she had lovingly tended stretched out before me, a bittersweet reminder of her presence that seemed to mock my grief. I could almost see her there, kneeling among the plants, her face etched with concentration as she coaxed life from the soil with her gentle hands. The scent of wet grass and blooming flowers filled the air, a stark contrast to the heaviness in my heart that threatened to pull me under. Jojo placed a hand on my shoulder, his touch a silent offer of support that I both craved and wanted to shrug off. Sam and Miguel stood nearby, their faces somber and watchful, as if they were afraid I might crumble at any moment. I turned to them, my voice low and intense, barely containing the storm of emotions raging within me, threatening to tear me apart from the inside.

"I want to find The Colonel," I said, my words clipped and harsh, each syllable dripping with venom that surprised even me. "I want to make him pay for what he's done. There's no way I can let him get away with this. He's taken too much from us already." The words tasted bitter on my tongue, but they were the only thing keeping me from falling into the abyss of my grief.

Jojo's grip tightened on my shoulder, his fingers digging in slightly as if trying to anchor me to reason, to pull me back from the edge I was teetering on. "Pops, I know you're hurting, but we need to think this through," he said, his voice gentle but firm. "The Colonel is dangerous. Going after him could get us all killed. We can't afford to lose anyone else." The logic in his words stung, but I couldn't bring myself to acknowledge it.

I shrugged off his hand, my eyes blazing with a fury I'd never felt before, a rage that scared me with its intensity. "I don't care," I spat out, the words feeling like fire in my throat. "He needs to answer for his crimes. For what he did to our family. To my mother. To all of us." I could feel the others' eyes on me, their concern palpable in the air.

Sam stepped forward, his expression cautious, his hands slightly raised as if approaching a wounded animal. I knew I must look wild, dangerous even. "Sir... Uhh, Joe, I understand your anger, but Jojo's right," he said, his voice steady despite the tension in his shoulders. "We can't just rush in without a plan. The Colonel has resources, manpower. We need to be smart about this. We've seen what he's capable of." His words were like a bucket of cold water, shocking me back to reality.

Miguel nodded in agreement, his jaw set with determination that matched my own. "We'll get him, Joe. I promise you that, we're all with you," he said, his eyes meeting mine unflinchingly. "But we have to do it the right way. For your mother's sake. She wouldn't want us to throw our lives away in a reckless pursuit of vengeance." The mention of my mother sent another wave of pain through me, but it was tinged with something else - a reminder of her wisdom, her patience.

I looked at each of them in turn, seeing the concern and determination in their eyes. They were my brothers, bound by blood and shared trauma, the family I had chosen. I knew they would follow me to the ends of the earth if I asked them to, and that realization hit me like a punch to the gut, tempering my rage with a flicker of gratitude that threatened to undo me.

But Jojo, Sam and Miguel were right, and I knew it deep in my bones. I couldn't let my emotions cloud my judgment, no matter how much I wanted to lash out, to make someone pay for the ache in my chest. If we were going to take down The Colonel, we had to be strategic. We had to be patient. The thought of waiting made my skin crawl, made me want to scream and break things, but I knew it was necessary.

I took a deep breath, feeling the rage inside me simmering down to a low boil, still there but no longer threatening to consume me whole. My fists clenched and unclenched at my sides as I fought for control, my nails digging into my palms. "Okay," I said finally, my voice rough with barely contained emotion. "We'll do it your way. But one way or another, The Colonel will pay for what he's done. I will not rest until he does. And when we find him, God help him, because I won't show any mercy." The promise felt like a vow, sealed in blood and grief, and I knew that no matter what happened, I would see it through to the end.

I stood aside, deep in my thoughts of revenge over what the Colonel had taken from me and taken from my family. The weight of loss pressed down on my shoulders, a constant reminder of the void left in our lives.

Mourners stood all around me, sharing memories of Toni's strength, wisdom, and love. Their voices were a soft murmur, punctuated by occasional sobs and quiet laughter. Parker, Toni's great-granddaughter, clung to Jojo's leg, her young face streaked with tears. Jojo stroked her hair gently, murmuring words of comfort, his own eyes glistening with unshed tears.

"Remember when Gram taught us how to make her famous peach cobbler?" Taylor said, a wistful smile on her face. "She never measured anything, just threw it all together by feel. But it always turned out perfect. It was like magic, watching her work in the kitchen."

Jake chuckled softly, wrapping an arm around Taylor's shoulders. "She used to say that was the secret - putting love into everything you do. I swear, I could taste the love in every bite of her cooking."

Their words washed over me, memories of my mother's warmth and guidance mixing with the cold fury in my veins. She had been the glue that held our family together, the steady hand guiding us through the chaos of this new world. And now she was gone, ripped away by the cruelty of a man drunk on his own power and ambition.

I clenched my fists, my short nails biting into my palms. The Colonel had no idea what he had unleashed. He thought he could take whatever he wanted, crush whoever stood in his way. But he had never faced the wrath of a Kelly scorned. He had no clue about the storm that was coming his way.

My mother's voice echoed in my head, a lesson she had

drilled into me since childhood. "Never start a fight, Joe," she would say, her eyes stern but loving. "But if someone else starts one, you damn well better finish it." Those words had shaped me, molded me into the man I was today.

Her words kept echoing in my mind as my feelings of guilt for not being there to protect my mother kept gnawing at my gut. I should have been there, should have seen the danger coming. But I had let my guard down, lulled into a false sense of security after we hit the Colonel's forces so hard. That mistake would haunt me for the rest of my days.

I looked around at the gathered mourners, their faces etched with grief and exhaustion. This was the toll the apocalypse had taken, the price we paid for survival. We had lost so much already - homes, livelihoods, friends, family. And now, the one person who had always been our rock, our guiding light, was gone. The weight of that loss was almost unbearable.

Taylor approached me, her eyes red-rimmed but fierce. "We have to do something, Dad," she said, her voice low and urgent. "We can't let him get away with this. Gram deserves justice."

I met her gaze, seeing the same anger and determination that burned in my own heart. "We won't," I promised, placing a hand on her shoulder.

"The Colonel's going to pay for what he's done. To Mom, to all of us. He's going to wish he'd never heard the name Kelly."

Jojo joined us, his jaw set in a grim line. "Don't worry Taylor, we're gonna get him but we need to make a plan first," he said, his military training evident in his calm demeanor. "Whatever it takes. He will pay. We'll make sure of it."

I nodded, feeling a sense of purpose settle over me like a mantle. This wasn't just about revenge, though that was certainly a part of it. This was about justice, about protecting what was left of our shattered world from men like the Colonel who sought to bend it to their will. It was about ensuring that no one else would have to suffer the way we had.

"The Colonel thinks he's untouchable," I said, my voice steady and cold. "He thinks he can take whatever he wants, hurt whoever he wants. But he's about to learn that he's messed with the wrong family. We're going to show him what happens when you cross the Kelly's."

I looked out over the lake, the water rippling gently in the breeze. Somewhere out there, the Colonel was sitting in his fortress, surrounded by his loyal followers, secure in his power. But he had no idea what was coming for him. He had no clue about the storm that was brewing, ready to rain down justice on him.

"Rest easy, Ma," I whispered, my eyes stinging with unshed tears. "We'll take it from here. We'll make you proud."

I looked out over the garden she had worked so hard on getting started, remembering how her face would light up when she talked about her plans for it. Hot tears pricked at my eyes, and I blinked them away roughly. There would be time for grief later. Right now, there was work to be done. We had a mission to plan and execute.

I turned to my children, my resolve hardening into something unbreakable. "We're going to finish this," I said, my voice low and fierce. "For Ma. For our family. The Colonel is going to learn the hard way what it means to cross the Kelly's. And when we're done, he'll wish he'd never set foot in our territory."

CHAPTER THREE

The Colonel sat in his rocking chair on the wraparound porch of the cabin he had now made his new headquarters. The old wood creaked beneath him as he shifted his weight, the sound echoing in the still evening air. He gazed out over the overgrown lawn, his eyes distant and troubled.

He was waiting for reports on his attack on the Kelly compound, an operation he had ordered in a fit of rage and wounded pride. After losing so many men on the bridge ambush, his forces were greatly weakened, and he knew it was a risky move. But he couldn't show any sign of weakness, not now, not after the humiliation of that defeat.

The Colonel reached for the glass of bourbon on the side table, his hand trembling slightly as he raised it to his lips. The liquor burned going down, but it did little to calm his nerves. He had underestimated Joe Kelly, that much was clear. He had been stupid and arrogant, thinking he could crush the man's resistance with a show of brute force.

But Kelly had outmaneuvered him at every turn,

luring his men into a trap and then picking them off like fish in a barrel. The Colonel felt a flush of anger at the memory, his grip tightening on the glass until his knuckles turned white.

He couldn't afford another mistake like that. His position was precarious enough as it was, with whispers of dissent among his ranks and rival factions circling like vultures, waiting for any sign of weakness. He needed a decisive victory, something to remind his followers of his strength and cunning.

The sound of approaching footsteps broke him from his reverie. He looked up to see one of his lieutenants hurrying up the steps, a sheaf of papers clutched in his hand. The man's face was pale and drawn, his eyes wide with fear.

"Report," the Colonel barked, setting his glass down with a thunk.

The lieutenant shifted nervously, avoiding the Colonel's piercing gaze. "Sir, the attack took the Kelly clan completely by surprise. They were scrambling to respond. But..." He hesitated.

"But what?" The Colonel snapped impatiently.

"They had reinforcements, sir. Looked like National Guardsmen."

The Colonel's eyes narrowed. "How many?"

"Not an exact count, sir, but maybe twenty-five or thirty."

The Colonel drummed his fingers on the arm of his chair, his jaw clenched. "And our casualties?"

The lieutenant swallowed hard. "We lost thirteen men, Colonel."

A muscle twitched in the Colonel's cheek. "And theirs?"

"As near as we can tell, only one. An elderly woman."

"An elderly woman?" The Colonel's voice was dangerously soft. "That's it? You bungling fools!"

"Sir, we think..." The lieutenant's voice quavered. "We think it might have been Joe Kelly's mother."

The Colonel sat up straighter, his interest piqued despite himself.

"After the battle, we observed from the tree-line. We saw Kelly kneeling by her body. He was visibly shaken."

The Colonel leaned back in his chair, steepling his fingers thoughtfully.

The Colonel shouted out, "Damn, that's the worst possible news."

The lieutenant looked puzzled by the Colonel's outburst. "Sorry sir, I thought you'd be pleased that we at least gave Kelly something to think about."

The Colonel looked at him sternly. "You would, because you're a damn fool. We've got a huge problem on our hands now."

The lieutenant asked, "You mean because of the Guardsmen?"

The Colonel looked into the man's eyes. "Forget about the Guard, I'm more worried about Joe Kelly now than I was before."

The lieutenant asked, "Why is that, sir?"

"You would be well served to crack open a history book occasionally lieutenant. Those who do not learn from history are doomed to repeat it. This reminds me of Admiral Yamamoto's words after his hugely successful attack on Pearl Harbor."

"What was that, sir?"

"I fear all we have done is to awaken a sleeping giant and fill him with a terrible resolve. In other words lieutenant, we have managed to stir up a hornets nest. Joe Kelly will be coming for us now. We have now become the hunted."

The Colonel stood up from his rocking chair and paced

the length of the porch, his hands clasped behind
his back. He could feel the lieutenant's eyes on him,
watching, waiting for guidance. But for once, the
Colonel didn't have a ready answer, a glib reassurance
to offer.

He stopped at the railing, staring out into the gathering
dusk. In the distance, he could see the flickering glow
of campfires, his men huddled around them for warmth
and comfort. They were looking to him to lead them, to
protect them. And he had failed them.

"Leave me now," he said quietly, not turning around.
"I need to think." He heard the lieutenant's footsteps
retreating, the screen door banging shut behind him.

Alone now, the Colonel let out a heavy sigh. He reached
for the bourbon bottle and poured another generous
shot into his glass. The golden liquid caught the last
rays of the setting sun as he raised it to his lips.

The lieutenant retreated back to where his men
sat around their makeshift campsites, their faces
illuminated by the flickering firelight. The air was thick
with tension and the acrid smell of gunpowder that
still clung to their clothes. One of his men, a grizzled
veteran with a jagged scar across his cheek, looked up

from cleaning his weapon and asked, "What's the good word, lieutenant?"

The lieutenant's eyes darted between the soldier and the Colonel on the porch, his silhouette stark against the warm glow from inside. He hesitated, choosing his words carefully. "The old man is shaken. This was the first time I've ever seen him without an answer. I kinda got the feeling he's a little afraid of this Kelly group. It's like he's seen a ghost or something. His hands were trembling, for Christ's sake."

"Afraid? The Colonel? No way. That group is nothing but a speed bump to us. I know we took a big hit, but we've still got numbers on 'em. We'll crush 'em like bugs," the scarred man scoffed, spitting a glob of tobacco into the dirt. His bravado rang hollow in the stillness of the night.

"That's true, but the old man is worried. He spooked me. He started quoting some guy from history, his voice all quiet and intense. Basically, since we killed Kelly's mother, we stirred up the bees' nest and he'll be coming for us. The Colonel said, now we will be the hunted. Like we've woken up some kind of sleeping giant. He kept muttering about 'the fury of a patient man' or something like that."

"So let them come," the man said with a laugh, though it sounded forced and brittle in the night air. "It'll only make it easier for us. We won't have to travel to him. We can play the home field advantage. Set up some traps, catch 'em off guard. Hell, we might even enjoy it."

The lieutenant's brow furrowed, his unease palpable in the tense set of his shoulders and the way his hand unconsciously tightened on his sidearm. "I sure as hell hope you're right, but the old man is spooked and after listening to him, I am too. I've never seen him like this before. It's... unsettling. It's like he knows something we don't, like he's seen this play out before and it didn't end well."

The men fell silent, the weight of the lieutenant's words hanging heavy in the air like a fog, thick and suffocating. The crackling of the campfire and the chirping of crickets filled the void as each man grappled with the implications of their leader's newfound vulnerability. Some shifted uncomfortably, while others stared blankly into the flames, lost in their own thoughts and fears.

The lieutenant gazed into the fire, his mind racing with possibilities and worst-case scenarios. He had never seen the Colonel like this before - uncertain, unsteady. It was unsettling, like the ground shifting beneath his feet, threatening to upend everything they'd built. The confidence that had carried them through countless battles suddenly seemed as fragile as a house of cards.

He thought back to the battle, the chaos and the carnage that had unfolded like a nightmare. The screams of the dying echoed in his ears, the acrid smell of gunpowder still clinging to his nostrils. And for what? To kill an old woman? What kind of victory was that? It felt hollow, meaningless, and now potentially catastrophic. The image of the old woman's lifeless body flashed before his eyes, and he couldn't shake the feeling that they had crossed a line, one that couldn't be uncrossed.

CHAPTER FOUR

I stood holding Maria in my arms for a long time. Just holding her helped to comfort me and take away some of the pain and guilt I was feeling. The world had gone to hell, and I'd been powerless to stop any of it. But with Maria, for a few moments at least, I could forget about the chaos outside. Could forget about the supplies we so desperately needed, the safety measures I still had to put in place.

Her embrace was warm and solid against the chill that had settled into my bones. I buried my face in her hair, breathing in the scent of her. Wildflowers and sunshine, even now. It amazed me how someone could still smell so damn good in the middle of the apocalypse.

"I'm so glad you're here," I murmured, my lips brushing her ear. "I don't...I don't know what I'd do if..."

I trailed off, unable to finish the thought. Losing Maria was not an option. She pulled back slightly to look at me, her brown eyes soft with understanding.

"I'm not going anywhere, Joe. We're in this together, remember?"

I nodded, not trusting myself to speak around the lump in my throat. I'd never been much for words anyway. Instead, I pulled her close again, letting her steady heartbeat soothe my ragged edges.

For a few more moments, I let myself just be. Let myself draw strength from her presence, her unwavering faith in me. In us.

But reality couldn't be held at bay forever. Reluctantly, I loosened my hold and stepped back, my hands sliding down her arms to link our fingers together.

"We should probably head back," I said quietly. "Got a lot of work to do."

Maria squeezed my hands, a small smile playing about her lips. "Lead the way."

Hand in hand, we walked back to the house, back to the never-ending list of tasks required to keep our people safe. But I felt lighter somehow, better able to shoulder the burden.

Because I wasn't carrying it alone anymore. And that made all the difference.

I nodded at Paulette and Adam as they approached, my hand still linked with Maria's. It was a bit of a surprise to see Adam up and about, but I supposed the man was tougher than he looked.

"Joe, I never had the pleasure of meeting your mom," Adam began, his voice sincere, "but from all that I've heard about her, she seemed to be a pretty fantastic woman."

I felt a pang in my chest at his words, the grief still raw and close to the surface. But I appreciated the sentiment nonetheless.

"Also, just from what I know of you and your family, she clearly raised you right," Adam continued, offering a small smile. "I just wanted to say, I'm sorry for your loss."

He extended his hand, and I reached out to shake it firmly. The man's grip was strong despite his injuries, and I could see the genuine empathy in his eyes.

"Thank you, Adam," I replied, my voice gruff with emotion. "It means a lot."

And it did. In a world gone mad, where so much had been lost and taken from us, these small moments of human connection were more precious than ever.

I glanced at Paulette, noting the way she hovered protectively near Adam, ready to support him if needed. It was a far cry from the woman who had once left her own family behind. But then again, hadn't we all changed in the face of this new reality?

Maria squeezed my hand, drawing my attention back to her. She gave me a soft, understanding smile, and I felt some of the tension ease from my shoulders.

We had a long road ahead of us, one filled with uncertainty and danger. But for now, at least, we had each other. And maybe, just maybe, that would be enough.

The walk back to the cabin was peaceful, a rare moment of tranquility in the midst of the chaos that had become our lives. Maria's hand fit perfectly in mine, her presence a steady comfort at my side.

As we neared the house, a sudden thought struck me and I stopped, turning to face her. "Sweetie, do we have any ministers or reverends here? Maybe a rabbi or a priest? Anyone like that in our group?"

Maria's brow furrowed as she considered the question. "No, I don't think so. Why do you ask?"

I took a deep breath, my heart hammering in my chest. "I know we've talked about it before, but I want to get married. As soon as we can. After everything that's happened, all we've lost...you just never know what tomorrow will bring. And I want you to be my wife, Maria. I don't want to waste another second."

Her eyes widened, a mix of surprise and joy flickering across her face. "Oh, Joe..."

"I know it's sudden," I rushed on, "and maybe it seems crazy, given the circumstances. But I love you. I don't want to face whatever comes next without you by my side, in every way that matters."

Maria's smile was blinding, her eyes shining with unshed tears. "Yes," she whispered, "yes, of course I'll marry you."

I crushed her to me, burying my face in her hair as I fought back my own emotions. She clung to me just as tightly, her laughter muffled against my chest.

After a long moment, she pulled back, her expression thoughtful. "You know, we may not have any clergymen around, but given the big lake over there we do have quite a few boat captains in the group." Her lips twitched with amusement. "They can perform marriages, can't they? Do we have to be at sea, or can they do it on dry land?"

I chuckled, shaking my head. "Honestly? I have no idea. But at this point, I don't really care. This is a whole new world we're living in. I figure we can damn well make our own rules."

Maria grinned, rising up on her toes to kiss me softly. "I like the sound of that."

Hand in hand, we continued on towards the cabin, our hearts full of hope and love and the promise of a future together, come what may.

Sam strode up to Jojo, his brow furrowed with concern. "How's your old man holding up?"

Jojo sighed, the weight of their situation etched on his face. He ran a hand over his close-cropped hair, his gaze distant. "About as well as can be expected, I guess. But we need to keep a close eye on him."

Sam nodded, understanding the unspoken worry in his friend's words. He placed a reassuring hand on Jojo's shoulder, a gesture of solidarity born from their shared military past.

"I know he's hell-bent on revenge." Jojo's voice was low, tinged with a mix of empathy and apprehension. "And I get it, we all are. But I don't want him going off half-cocked, with his mind clouded by emotions."

Sam's grip tightened, his eyes locked on Jojo's. "That's when bad things can happen."

The two men stood in silence, the weight of their responsibility hanging heavy in the air. They had seen firsthand the consequences of unchecked rage, the destruction that could be wrought when pain and grief were left to fester.

Jojo's jaw clenched, his resolve hardening. "We've got to keep him focused, Sam. Keep him grounded. We can't let him lose himself in this fight."

Sam's gaze drifted to the horizon, his mind racing with the challenges that lay ahead. "It won't be easy. Your dad's a force to be reckoned with when he sets his mind to something."

A ghost of a smile tugged at Jojo's lips, a flicker of pride amidst the worry. "Yeah, he is. But that's why we're here, right? To have his back, no matter what."

Sam returned the smile, a glimmer of their old camaraderie resurfacing. "Damn straight. We're in this together, Jojo. We'll keep him on track, keep each other safe. That's what brothers do."

Jojo clasped Sam's hand, their bond reaffirmed in the face of the unknown. They had weathered storms before, and they would weather this one, side by side, united in their purpose.

Sam clapped Jojo on the back, a grin spreading across his face. "Bones, I'm gonna go spend some time with Alicia."

Jojo's eyebrows shot up, a mischievous glint in his eye. "Good for you, Sam. Things getting serious between you two?"

Sam ducked his head, scuffing his boot on the ground. "Yeah, we've got feelings for each other."

"So what's the problem?"

Sam hesitated, his words coming out in a rush. "I'm still a bit nervous and awkward around her. I mean, it's the age thing you know. I've got these feelings, these urges. I'm just not sure if I can control myself when I'm with her, and I wanna wait, you know?"

Jojo chuckled, shaking his head. "Don't even worry about that, man. I've seen the way she looks at you. She's definitely into you, big time."

Sam nodded, a rueful smile tugging at his lips. "Yeah, I know you're right. But I think I still wanna wait. That's the hard part, keeping my hands off of her."

"I get it, Sam. But you're a strong guy."

Sam clasped Jojo's hand, gratitude shining in his eyes. "Thanks, bro. I'm gonna need all the strength I can muster."

With that, he turned and strode off, his heart hammering in his chest as he went to find Alicia. The anticipation was a tangible thing, a mix of excitement and trepidation that set his nerves alight.

He found her by the edge of the camp, her silhouette outlined against the setting sun. She turned as he approached, a soft smile gracing her features.

"Hey, you." Her voice was warm, inviting.

Sam swallowed hard, his mouth suddenly dry. "Hey, yourself."

They stood in silence for a moment, the air between them charged with unspoken longing. Sam's hands itched to reach out, to pull her close and never let go.

But he resisted, the echo of Jojo's words ringing in his ears. He had to be strong, had to take this slow. Alicia deserved better than a moment of unbridled passion.

She deserved everything.

Sam stood staring into Alicia's eyes, his heart racing as he tried to find the right words. Her gaze was soft, questioning, a hint of vulnerability shining through.

"Sam, I know you have feelings for me," she said, her voice barely above a whisper. "And I have strong feelings for you as well. Why do you always seem so distant, so hesitant?"

The question hung in the air between them, heavy with unspoken emotions. Sam turned away, his hands clenching and unclenching at his sides. He took a deep breath, steeling himself for what he needed to say.

"I do have very strong feelings for you, Alicia." His

voice was rough, thick with emotion. "I guess I just want to take it slow. I know that sounds a little old-fashioned, but as much as I want to, you know, go further..." He trailed off, his eyes searching hers for understanding.

Alicia stepped closer, her hand coming to rest on his arm. The warmth of her touch sent a shiver down his spine, and he had to fight the urge to pull her into his arms.

"I really would just like taking our time and enjoying each other's company for now," he continued, his gaze locked on hers. "The last thing in the world I would want to do is to rush you or take advantage of you."

Alicia's eyes widened, a flicker of surprise and something else, something deeper, dancing in their depths. Sam swallowed hard, his heart in his throat.

"I guess what I'm trying to say is that I imagine you in my life for a long time, or at least I certainly hope so. And I don't want to do anything to jeopardize that." His words came out in a rush, a desperate plea for her to understand. "I'm in this for the long haul, sweetie, not for a quick roll in the hay. I want you to know that, and I can wait."

Alicia looked into Sam's eyes, reaching out to grasp his hands. A tear of appreciation formed in her eye, glistening in the fading light.

"Sam, I understand what you're saying, and I am willing to move at whatever speed you're comfortable with, as long as we're together." Her voice was soft, filled with understanding. "As far as going further, yeah, I've thought about it too, and I'm fine with waiting. You know, I have had concerns about the same exact thing that's been bothering you. I even discussed it with the girls."

Sam's eyes widened, a look of shock crossing his features. "What? You talked about it with other people?"

Alicia raised a hand, a reassuring gesture. "Calm down, Sam. Yes, I shared my feelings with Paulette, Claire, and Toni. Toni was so funny but really made me think."

Sam's brow furrowed, curiosity mingling with apprehension. "What did she say?"

Alicia ducked her head, a blush creeping up her cheeks. "She asked if I had had my first period. I was mortified by her question but I told her yes, I had."

Sam's eyes bulged, his face reddening. "Oh my God, too much information. What did she say?"

Alicia met his gaze, a newfound confidence in her eyes. "She said if you've had your first period, you're a woman. I guess what I'm saying to you, Sam, is I'm more than willing to go at whatever speed you want."

Sam couldn't help himself. He reached out and embraced Alicia in a tight hug, his strong arms enveloping her, pulling her close to his chest. She melted into his embrace, her own arms wrapping around his waist, her head nestling into the crook of his neck.

"Thank you for understanding, sweetie," Sam murmured, his voice thick with emotion. "I just want to do what's right for you, for us. Like I said, we have a long life ahead of us to, well, you know." He chuckled softly, his breath stirring her hair. "For now, let's just take it one day at a time."

Alicia nodded against his chest, her heart swelling with love and gratitude. She had never felt so cherished, so respected, so seen. Sam's willingness to put her needs first, to prioritize their emotional connection over physical desire, only made her love him more.

Sam pulled back slightly, his hands coming up to cup her face. His thumbs brushed over her cheekbones, wiping away the tears that had begun to fall. "But know this, Alicia," he said, his gaze intense, unwavering. "My heart aches for you when I'm not near you. I love you."

The words hung in the air between them, a declaration,

a promise. Alicia's breath caught in her throat, her own heart threatening to burst with the force of her emotions.

"I love you too, Sam," she whispered, her voice trembling. She reached up, her hands covering his, holding him close. More tears spilled from her eyes, tears of joy, of relief, of pure, unadulterated love.

They stood there, wrapped in each other's arms, lost in the moment. The world around them faded away, the challenges they faced, the uncertainties of their future, all of it receding into the background.

For now, there was only this - the warmth of their embrace, the beating of their hearts, the love that bound them together. And for now, that was enough.

CHAPTER FIVE

I carefully extracted myself from Maria's warm embrace, trying not to wake her. She looked so peaceful, her dark hair fanned out on the pillow, her face relaxed in sleep. For a moment, I let myself imagine a different life, one where we could linger in bed, make love, enjoy a lazy breakfast together. But that wasn't our reality, not anymore.

I pulled on my jeans and a flannel shirt, laced up my boots. The familiar routine grounded me, prepared me for the day ahead. There was so much to do, so many people counting on me.

I leaned down and brushed a kiss against Maria's cheek. She stirred slightly but didn't wake. "I love you," I whispered, the words catching in my throat. I didn't say it often enough, always holding back, afraid to be vulnerable. But if there was one thing this new world had taught me, it was that every moment was precious, every connection worth cherishing.

I slipped out of the room, quietly closing the door behind me. The compound was already stirring to life - I could hear the distant clatter of dishes from the kitchen, the low murmur of voices. I nodded to the people I passed, my mind already jumping ahead to the tasks before me.

First on the list was finding Captain Rodriguez. The guardsmen's arrival had been a godsend, but it also meant a major shift in our dynamics, our resources. Rodriguez and I needed to get on the same page, figure out how to integrate our two groups into a cohesive whole.

I found him in the armory, already inventorying our weapons and ammo.

"Good morning, Captain," I called out as I entered the armory. "Glad to see you're an early riser too."

Rodriguez looked up from the rifle he was cleaning, a brief smile flickering across his face. "Good morning to you, Joe. Yeah, I like to get an early start to the day. I've been busy taking stock of exactly what we have and what we don't have as far as weapons and defenses."

I stood in the doorframe. "And how are we looking?"

The Captain let out a long breath, setting the rifle aside. He rubbed a hand over his close-cropped hair. "Well, we're not too bad off, but I'd sure as hell feel a lot better if we had more guns and a lot more ammunition."

An idea sparked in my mind, a memory of our recent

misadventure. "Captain, do you have any mechanics, auto mechanics in your group?"

Rodriguez's brow furrowed as he considered the question. "Yeah, a couple of the guys are pretty handy with a wrench. Why?"

I pushed off from the doorframe, pacing a few steps as I gathered my thoughts. "Recently, we made a trip to rescue one of our guys. He was a prison guard at Raiford."

The Captain's eyebrows shot up. "You went to Raiford?"

I held up a hand. "Yeah, it's a long story. I'll tell you later when we have more time. But we used an old van we had, and on the way back it died on us. We hoofed it back the rest of the way." I paused, meeting his gaze. "The point is, that van was loaded up with gear. Guns, ammo, quite a bit of valuable, useful stuff. I didn't want to just leave it in the van, so we hid some caches in the woods. We could sure use that stuff now, and I'd love it if we could somehow revive that van as well."

I could see the wheels turning in Rodriguez's head, his interest piqued. "How far away is that van?"

I scratched my beard, trying to picture the route in my mind. "I'm not exactly sure, but I figure about twenty-five, maybe thirty miles."

Rodriguez thought for a moment. "Well, we do have some vehicles that could get us there in a short time. I'm not sure about working on the van out there off the side of the road though. Do you think we could tow it back here if need be?"

I considered his question. "When we left the van, it was in drivable condition. The only thing was the engine wasn't running, so I don't see why we couldn't tow it back here to work on it. We'll just need a large enough vehicle to carry those caches back and big enough to tow the van. Along with some rope or chains to hook it up."

The Captain smiled, his dark eyes sparking with determination. "We've got you covered there. Let me get a few of our guys and we'll gear up. We'll take two vehicles, one for providing cover and a bigger show of force. You get who you need to go and let's meet up in about thirty minutes and hit the road."

I grinned back at him, feeling a surge of energy and purpose. "Captain, I like your thinking. I'll see you in thirty."

I turned to leave, my mind already racing ahead. I'd need to let Maria know where I was going, make sure Jojo and Miguel could hold down the fort while I was away. And I wanted to bring along Jake, Sam and Dave on this mission. They were there when we hid the gear.

I figured between the four of us we would be able to find our hidden assets once again.

But even with the risks, I felt good about this mission. Those supplies could make a real difference for our community, help us fortify our defenses and keep everyone fed for just a little bit longer. And working alongside Captain Rodriguez and his men, I felt a sense of camaraderie, of shared purpose.

We were in this fight together, all of us. And together, we just might have a chance of surviving, of building something worth living for in this crazy new world.

I burst into the cabin, my heart pounding with excitement. Maria was in the kitchen with Taylor, the two of them chatting as they prepared breakfast. The smell of frying bacon and fresh coffee filled the air, making my stomach growl.

Maria looked up as I entered, her brow furrowing at the sight of my flushed face and hurried movements. "Joe? What's going on?"

I crossed the room in a few long strides, pulling her into a hug and planting a kiss on her cheek. "I have good news," I said, grinning down at her. "Remember those supply caches we had to leave behind when the van broke down? Captain Rodriguez and I are putting together a team to go retrieve them."

Taylor looked up from the stove, her hazel eyes wide. "Really? That's great news!"

I nodded, already moving towards the bedroom to grab my gear. "It is. Those supplies could make a real difference for us." I started shoving items into my backpack - extra ammo, a first aid kit, some protein bars. "I'm taking Dave, Jake, and Sam with me. They were there when we hid the stuff, so they'll be able to help locate it."

Maria followed me into the bedroom, her arms crossed over her chest. I could see the worry in her eyes, the way she chewed on her bottom lip. "Joe, are you sure about this? It could be dangerous."

I paused in my packing, turning to face her. I took her hands in mine, running my thumbs over her knuckles. "I know," I said softly. "But it's a risk we have to take. We need those supplies, Maria. And I'll have Captain Rodriguez and his men with me. We'll be careful, I promise."

She searched my face for a long moment, then nodded. "Okay," she whispered. "Just... come back to me, alright?"

I pulled her into a tight hug, breathing in the scent of her hair. "Always," I murmured. "We have a date to get married, remember, don't think you're gonna get rid of me that easily. That's a date I refuse to miss, trust me."

With a final squeeze, I released her and slung my backpack over my shoulder. "I'll be back before you know it," I said, forcing a confident grin.

She managed a small smile in return. "I'll hold you to that."

I gave her one last quick kiss, then headed for the door. "Love you," I called over my shoulder.

"Love you too," she replied, her voice trailing after me as I jogged out into the morning sun.

Dave, Jake, and Sam were already waiting by the vehicles, geared up and ready to go. Captain Rodriguez was there too, along with a handful of his men.

"Ready?" the Captain asked, eyeing me appraisingly.

I nodded, feeling the familiar thrill of adrenaline starting to hum through my veins. "Let's do this."

We climbed into the vehicles, the engines rumbling to life. As we pulled out of the compound, I glanced back at the cabin, catching a glimpse of Maria watching from the window.

"I'll be back," I whispered, a promise to her and to myself. "I'll always come back to you."

We drove along slowly and cautiously, keeping a sharp

eye out for any hidden dangers, any signs of trouble or the Colonel's men. The last thing we needed was to run into an ambush or get caught off guard. I gripped the steering wheel tightly, my eyes scanning the road ahead.

As we drove, Captain Rodriguez turned to me, his expression serious. "Joe, we need to have a long talk real soon about security around that compound."

I glanced over at him, nodding in agreement. "Yeah, I know. We've done a pretty good job up to now, but I know there's room for improvement."

The Captain leaned back in his seat, his gaze thoughtful. "I've got some training in that area. I'd like to talk to you about some things we can do to upgrade security, make sure we're as prepared as possible for any threats."

I let out a long breath, feeling a weight lift off my shoulders. "Absolutely. Frankly, we've been so busy managing one crisis after another, and with more and more people showing up looking for sanctuary, it's just gotten out of control." I shook my head, the exhaustion of the past few weeks catching up to me. "I would love your expertise and help. After all, it's your home now too. And thanks again for coming. It is surely appreciated."

Rodriguez clapped me on the shoulder, a small smile tugging at his lips. "Of course. We're in this together now. We'll get that compound fortified and secure, make sure everyone is safe. That's a promise. I just wish we could've done more before, well you know."

I looked at the Captain, my jaw clenched tight. "I know, and I appreciate it, but what's done is done and we can only focus on the future. We can't dwell on the past." I turned my gaze back to the road, my knuckles white gripping my rifle. "Right now, my focus is firmly on the Colonel."

Rodriguez nodded, his dark eyes studying my face. "What are your thoughts on the Colonel, Joe, if you don't mind me asking?"

I took a deep breath, the rage simmering just beneath the surface. "My thoughts are of his death," I said, my voice low and hard. "As much as I want him dead as soon as possible, I think I would also like to make him suffer as much as possible."

I could feel the Captain's gaze on me, but I kept my eyes on the road, the landscape blurring past. "I think I would love to shrink his world slowly but surely. I want him to feel hunted, to make him feel nervous and unsure of what's coming next."

A humorless smile twisted my lips. "They say revenge

is a dish best served cold. Those are my thoughts on the Colonel."

Rodriguez was silent for a long moment, the only sound the rumble of the engine and the crunch of gravel beneath the tires. Finally, he spoke, his voice thoughtful. "I understand the desire for vengeance, Joe. Believe me, I do. But we have to be smart about this. The Colonel is a dangerous man, and he has a lot of resources at his disposal."

I nodded, my grip on the steering wheel loosening slightly. "I know. And I'm not going to do anything reckless or stupid. But I also know that as long as the Colonel is out there, as long as he's a threat, none of us will ever be truly safe."

I turned to look at Rodriguez and asked, "Now let me ask you some questions."

The Captain nodded. "Sure, what's on your mind?"

My mind was racing with questions, "Do you have any information on just what the hell happened to take down the grid? How big is this? With your position in the Guard, do you have any inside intel?"

Rodriguez's brow furrowed as he considered my questions. "Honestly, Joe, I don't have a lot of solid information. When the grid went down, it was chaos. Communication was spotty at best, and a lot of what we heard was just rumors and speculation."

He shifted in his seat, his gaze distant. "From what I could gather, it was some kind of coordinated attack. Multiple power stations hit simultaneously, some kind of cyber attack maybe. But who was behind it, or how far-reaching it was? I just don't know."

I digested this information, my mind racing. A coordinated attack. Multiple power stations. The implications were staggering.

"What about the government? The military? Surely they have some kind of plan in place for something like this?" I asked, a note of desperation creeping into my voice.

The Captain shook his head, his expression grim. "If they do, I haven't heard about it. Last I heard, the government was in disarray. The President, the Vice President, most of the cabinet - they were all in D.C. when it happened. No one knows if they made it out."

I felt a chill run down my spine. The thought of our country's leaders, the people meant to guide us through a crisis, being taken out in one fell swoop... it was almost too much to comprehend.

"So what do we do now?" I asked, my voice barely above a whisper.

Rodriguez met my gaze, his dark eyes intense. "We survive, Joe. We protect our own. We build something worth living for in this new world. And we never, ever give up hope. That's all we can do."

I nodded, a grim determination settling over me. He was right. We had to keep going, keep fighting. For our families, for our community, for the future.

"Okay," I said, squaring my shoulders. "Let's go get those supplies. One step at a time, right?"

The Captain clapped me on the shoulder, a small smile tugging at his lips. "One step at a time," he agreed. "We've got this, Joe. Together."

CHAPTER SIX

Jojo adjusted his faded tan beret, a remnant of his Army days, as he and Miguel set out on another scrounging mission. The sun beat down on the cracked asphalt, the heat rising in shimmering waves. Miguel's tousled hair and unruly beard gave him a wild appearance, but Jojo knew the man's skills were indispensable.

"We're gonna have to go further out this time," Jojo said, his hazel eyes scanning the desolate landscape. "Pickings are getting slim closer to base."

Miguel grunted in agreement, his weathered hands gripping the straps of his backpack. "Ain't gonna be easy. But we don't have much choice."

They walked in silence for a while, their boots crunching on the debris-strewn road. Jojo's mind wandered to his family—his father Joe, sister Taylor, and little niece Parker. They were the reason he pushed himself, the reason he risked his life on these missions.

As they trudged onward, the relentless sun sapping their energy with each step, a glimmer of hope appeared on the horizon. Jojo squinted, trying to make out the distant shape. It looked like a farm, a small oasis amidst the barren landscape.

"Miguel, do you see what I see?" Jojo asked, a hint of excitement in his voice. "I wonder if they would be open to some good old-fashioned bartering?"

Miguel, ever the cautious one, narrowed his eyes as he studied the distant property. "Could be trouble," he muttered, his hand instinctively reaching for the gun at his hip. "We should watch the place for a while before approaching."

Jojo nodded, acknowledging the wisdom in his companion's words. They veered off the road, seeking cover behind a cluster of trees. Jojo unslung his rifle, using his binoculars to get a better view of the farm.

The place looked well-maintained, a rarity in these times. The fields were lush with crops, and Jojo could make out the shapes of chickens pecking in the yard. A curl of smoke rose from the chimney of the farmhouse, suggesting someone was home.

"Looks peaceful enough," Jojo murmured. "But appearances can be deceiving."

Miguel hummed in agreement, his dark eyes scanning the surrounding area for any signs of danger. "We'll wait until dusk," he said, his voice low and gruff. "See if we can spot any movement, get a sense of how many people we're dealing with."

Jojo settled in, his back against a tree trunk. He reached into his pack, pulling out a battered canteen. The water was warm and stale, but it soothed his parched throat.

As the sun began its slow descent, painting the sky in hues of orange and pink, Jojo's thoughts turned to his family. He wondered how they were faring back at the base, if little Parker was driving everyone crazy with her endless energy. A smile tugged at his lips at the thought of his niece's infectious giggles.

"We'll find something good," he said, as much to himself as to Miguel. "Something to make this trip worth it."

Miguel just nodded, his eyes never leaving the farm. They had a long evening ahead of them, but Jojo was determined to make it count. For his family, for their future, he would do whatever it took.

Jojo blinked against the first rays of sunlight filtering through the trees. He and Miguel had spent the night in shifts, one keeping watch while the other snatched a few precious hours of sleep. It had been an uneventful night, with no signs of activity from the farmhouse.

As the sun climbed higher, Jojo's stomach grumbled. He reached into his pack, pulling out a strip of jerky. The tough meat was a far cry from a hearty breakfast, but it would have to do.

Miguel stirred beside him, rubbing the sleep from his eyes. "Anything?" he asked, his voice rough from disuse.

Jojo shook his head. "Quiet as a graveyard."

They settled in, eyes trained on the farmhouse. Jojo adjusted his position, trying to ease the stiffness in his muscles.

Jojo squinted through the dusty binoculars, his jaw tightening as he observed the unfolding situation. Six miles out from their compound, a once-thriving farm stood as an oasis amidst the barren landscape. Cattle grazed lazily in a fenced corral, a rare sight in their post-apocalyptic world.

"We got company," Miguel muttered, his gruff voice low as he scanned the area with a practiced eye.

Four figures approached the main house, rifles slung over their shoulders. Jojo's grip tightened on the binoculars as three women emerged, confronting the armed men. Tension crackled in the air, palpable even from their vantage point.

"Damn raiders," Jojo growled, his military instincts kicking in. He watched with growing unease as the men harassed the defenseless women, their intentions clear as they started moving towards the corral.

Miguel's hand hovered over the handgun holstered at his hip, his jaw set in a grim line. "We can't let them take those cattle."

Jojo knew he was right. In their world, livestock represented more than just sustenance; it was a lifeline, a source of hope in the midst of scarcity. He weighed their options, his mind racing through tactical scenarios.

Jojo lowered the binoculars, his hazel eyes hardening with resolve. He turned to Miguel, his voice low but firm. "We need to stop those men from robbing those women. We could use some cattle, and we could at least trade for them. These guys are just gonna take what they want."

Miguel nodded, his weathered face set in a determined scowl. "I'm with you, brother. What's the plan?"

Jojo's mind raced, his military training kicking into high gear. "We'll approach from the south, use the tree line for cover. I'll take the lead, you watch my six. We'll try to diffuse the situation peacefully, but be ready for anything."

They moved swiftly and silently, their boots barely making a sound on the dry, cracked earth. As they drew closer, the voices of the men grew louder, their tones menacing and cruel.

"Please, just take what you need and go," one of the women pleaded, her voice trembling.

"Oh, we'll take what we need, alright," one of the men sneered, his hand reaching for the woman's arm.

Jojo stepped out from the trees, his rifle raised. "That's enough," he called out, his voice steady and commanding. "Let the women go."

The men whirled around, their own weapons drawn in an instant. "This ain't none of your business, boy," the leader snarled, his eyes narrowing. "Walk away now, and we'll forget we ever saw you."

Jojo stood his ground, his gaze unwavering. "I'm afraid I can't do that. These women are under our protection now. We're willing to trade for some of their cattle, but we won't let you just take what isn't yours."

The leader scoffed, his finger tightening on the trigger. "You and what army boy?"

As if on cue, Miguel stepped out from cover flanking the men, his own weapon at the ready. "This army asshole," he growled, his dark eyes glinting with a dangerous light.

For a tense moment, no one moved. The air crackled with the promise of violence, the slightest twitch likely to set off a deadly chain reaction. Jojo's heart pounded in his ears, but his hands remained steady on his rifle.

Then, slowly, the leader lowered his weapon. "Fine," he spat, his voice dripping with venom. "We'll go. But don't think this is over."

Jojo kept his rifle trained on the men as they slowly backed away, his finger poised on the trigger. His heart raced, but his voice remained steady as he spoke.

"Trust me, this is over," he said, his hazel eyes hard as flint. "We do have an army, and the next time you come around, you will surely die."

The leader's face twisted into a sneer, but he said nothing as he and his men began to retreat down the dusty road. Jojo watched them go, his jaw clenched tight. He didn't lower his weapon until they were mere specks on the horizon.

"You alright?" he asked, turning to the women. They nodded, their faces pale but relieved.

"Thank you," the eldest said, her voice trembling slightly. "I don't know what we would have done if you hadn't shown up."

Jojo shook his head. "No need to thank us, ma'am. We're just glad we could help."

Jojo turned to the women, his brow furrowed with concern. "We came across your place yesterday and we've been watching it over night. We were hoping to maybe do some trading with you for some cattle or whatever you have here. But I now think you've got bigger problems. Those men will be back, and they will come in force."

The eldest woman, her grey hair pulled back in a tight bun, nodded grimly. "We've had trouble before," she said, her voice heavy with worry. "We've been able to handle it so far. But now...lately it's just been getting tougher."

She trailed off, her eyes glistening with unshed tears. Jojo felt a pang of sympathy. He knew all too well the fear and uncertainty that came with living in this new world.

"Listen," he said, his voice gentle but firm. "We have a group, a safe place. We can help you, protect you. But we need to act fast."

The women exchanged glances, a silent conversation passing between them. Finally, the eldest spoke again.

"What did you have in mind?" she asked, her voice tentative but hopeful.

Jojo took a deep breath, his mind racing with possibilities. He knew they had stumbled upon something valuable here, not just in terms of resources, but in the lives they could save. He looked at the women, their faces etched with worry and hope, and made his decision.

"Well, we could certainly benefit from what you have here, and you all could certainly benefit from a protected environment," Jojo began, his voice steady and reassuring. "My thought is to get you ladies and your livestock and whatever we can back to our compound. We have a lot of people there and even some National Guardsmen for protection."

He paused, making sure to meet each woman's eyes. "It's up to you, of course. We would never take anything that wasn't ours. But I'll be real honest with you, we've got a couple of babies due soon and milk from those cows might come in real handy."

Jojo watched as the women exchanged glances, their expressions a mix of uncertainty and cautious hope. He understood their hesitation – in this world, trust was a rare commodity, often more valuable than any material goods.

"I know it's a big decision," he continued, his tone gentle but urgent. "But those men will be back, and next time, they might not be so easily deterred. At our compound, you'd have safety, community, and a chance to start over."

The eldest woman stepped forward, her eyes searching

Jojo's face. "And what would be expected of us in return?" she asked, her voice wavering slightly.

Jojo smiled, appreciating her directness. "We all contribute what we can," he explained. "Your skills, your knowledge – they'd be invaluable. And of course, we'd work out a fair arrangement for sharing the resources you bring."

Jojo watched as the women's expressions shifted, a glimmer of hope replacing the fear in their eyes. He could see the gears turning in their minds, weighing the risks and benefits of his offer.

"My immediate thought is that you ladies know how to deal with animals and what they need. That's invaluable," Jojo continued, his voice steady and reassuring. "I'm thinking you just continue to do what you're doing here, but do it there and let us protect you. We certainly would love the milk and I assume you breed this cattle so there could be the possibility of meat in the future?"

The eldest woman nodded slowly, a small smile tugging at the corners of her mouth. "Yes, we do breed them. It's been a challenge, but we've managed to keep the herd going."

Jojo felt a surge of excitement. This could be a game-changer for their community. Fresh milk for the children and expecting mothers, the possibility of sustainable meat production - it was more than he had dared to hope for when they set out on this mission.

"That's fantastic," he said, unable to keep the enthusiasm from his voice. "Your expertise would be incredibly valuable to our community. We have people with various skills, but animal husbandry isn't one of our strong suits."

He glanced at Miguel, who gave a subtle nod of approval. Turning back to the women, Jojo continued, "We could learn from you, and in return, you'd have the safety and support of our entire group. It's a win-win situation."

The women huddled together, speaking in hushed tones. Jojo waited patiently, knowing that this decision couldn't be rushed. After what felt like an eternity, the eldest woman stepped forward again.

Jojo felt a wave of relief wash over him as Betty introduced herself and her daughters, Pam and Tracy. He extended his hand, shaking each of theirs in turn.

"I'm Joe Kelly Jr., but everyone calls me Jojo," he said, offering a warm smile. "And this is Miguel. We're glad you're willing to come with us."

Jojo's mind was already racing, formulating a plan to get the women and their livestock safely back to the compound. He glanced at the cattle grazing in the nearby field, then back at Betty and her daughters.

"Alright, we need to move quickly," he said, his voice taking on a more authoritative tone. "Those men could come back at any time. Do you have a truck or any vehicles we could use to transport the cattle?"

Betty nodded. "We have a very old pickup that's still running and a small trailer. It's not much, but it's been reliable."

Jojo nodded, relief evident on his face. "That's perfect. We'll use that to transport as many of the cattle as we can."

He turned to Miguel. "Can you help them start loading up the most essential items from the house? We'll need to prioritize - food, water, medical supplies, and anything else that's crucial."

Miguel nodded and headed towards the farmhouse with Pam and Tracy.

Jojo turned back to Betty. "I gotta be real honest with you Betty, I know nothing about raising cows. I'm not even sure that we have what will be needed to do it back at our compound. What I do know is you, your daughters and these animals are not safe here. How many cattle do we need to move?"

"We have twelve head, ten cows and two very happy bulls." Betty replied. "It's not a large herd, but it's been enough to keep us going. The trailer can only hold six at a time though."

Jojo ran his hand through his hair letting out a long breath. "Okay, we should be able to move them in two trips. We'll take six in the first load, along with you and your daughters. Miguel and I will bring a few of our guys back with us for the rest. I'd love to get those chickens as well, it looks like that chicken coop could be lifted up put on that trailer if we have enough guys."

Betty glanced back to the chickens. "It can be done, it's been moved before. I'll leave Pam and Tracy at your place and come back with you and your men. I can help with rounding up the chickens and of course the roosters, plus there's a lot of supplies in that barn that would sure come in handy taking care of these animals. There are also several gas cans in there for the pickup."

He paused, looking Betty in the eye. "Looks like this may take several trips but we'll get it done. We just have to move fast before those men come back with reinforcements. Look, I know this is a lot to take in, and it's happening fast. But I promise you, we're going to do everything we can to keep you and your daughters and your animals safe."

Betty nodded, her eyes shining with a mix of gratitude

and determination. "We appreciate that, Jojo. We're ready to do our part too. Just tell us what you need us to do."

CHAPTER SEVEN

The Colonel's polished white shoes clicked against the worn wooden floorboards as he paced back and forth in the dimly lit cabin. Every few steps, he paused to peer out a window, his piercing blue eyes scanning the dense forest beyond. The trees swayed gently in the breeze, their leaves rustling softly, but it was the silence that unnerved him most. The eerie quiet seemed to press in on him from all sides, making the cabin feel smaller with each passing moment.

He tugged at his impeccable white suit, smoothing out non-existent wrinkles. His fingers twitched towards the antique silver pocket watch in his vest, but he resisted the urge to check the time again. The ticking of the watch, usually a comforting rhythm, now felt like a countdown to some unseen disaster.

"Gentlemen," he called out, his voice carrying a hint of strain beneath its usual smooth drawl. "A moment of your time, if you please." The words echoed in the empty room, emphasizing his isolation.

The cabin door creaked open, and three men filed in. They were a motley crew - a former sheriff still clinging to his badge, an ex-military man with haunted eyes, and a wiry youth who'd proven himself surprisingly ruthless. Each man carried the weight of their past and the uncertainty of their future in their posture and wary expressions.

"Take a seat," the Colonel gestured to the mismatched chairs around a battered table. As they settled in, he remained standing, unable to keep still. His restlessness was palpable, filling the room with an electric tension that set everyone on edge.

"Now, I declare we've got ourselves a bit of a--" A twig snapped outside, and the Colonel's head whipped towards the sound. His hand flew to the revolver at his hip before he caught himself, forcing a chuckle. "Pardon me, gentlemen. These woods do play tricks on a man's ears." The laugh sounded hollow, even to his own ears, and did nothing to dispel the growing unease in the room.

He turned back to his lieutenants, noting their confused expressions. The Colonel opened his mouth to continue but faltered as a floorboard groaned under his weight. His eyes darted to the corner of the room, muscles tensing. For a moment, he could have sworn he saw a shadow move, but when he blinked, it was gone.

"Sir?" the ex-sheriff ventured, his voice tinged with concern. "You were saying?"

"Yes, yes," the Colonel waved a hand dismissively, struggling to regain his composure. The gesture, usually so authoritative, now seemed frantic and uncontrolled. "We've got ourselves a situation that requires our immediate attention. It seems our little paradise is--"

A bird call pierced the air, sharp and sudden, and the Colonel nearly jumped out of his skin. His carefully cultivated image of calm control cracked, revealing a man on edge. Sweat beaded on his forehead, and his eyes darted wildly around the room.

"Sakes alive!" he exclaimed, pressing a hand to his chest. His heart raced beneath his palm, a staccato rhythm that matched his ragged breathing. "These blasted birds will be the death of me."

His lieutenants exchanged worried glances. They'd never seen their leader so rattled. The man who had always exuded confidence and control now seemed to be unraveling before their eyes.

The Colonel's demeanor shifted abruptly, his face hardening as he slammed his palm on the table. The sudden noise made everyone jump, including himself. "Enough of this dilly-dallying. We're doubling patrols, effective immediately. I want fortifications strengthened along the perimeter. No one sleeps until it's done, you hear?"

The ex-sheriff frowned, lines deepening on his weathered face. "Sir, we're already spread thin. The men are exhausted, and our supplies--"

"Did I ask for your opinion, Sheriff?" The Colonel's voice cracked like a whip, his southern drawl becoming more pronounced in his agitation. "Last I checked, you wear that tarnished star because I allow it, not because you have any real authority here." His words dripped with venom, a stark contrast to his usual charm.

The cabin fell silent, tension thick in the air. The young lieutenant cleared his throat, his adam's apple bobbing nervously. "Colonel, maybe we should--"

"Kelly!" The Colonel exploded, spittle flying from his lips. His face contorted with rage, eyes bulging. "That's what this is about. Joe Kelly is out there, plotting, scheming. He thinks he can outsmart me? Ha!" He jabbed a finger at each man in turn, the gesture more threatening than emphatic. "I want daily reports on Kelly. Sightings, rumors, whispers - I don't care how small. If someone so much as dreams about Joe Kelly, I want to know about it. Hell, if a squirrel looks at you funny, I want to know if it's working for Kelly!"

The ex-military man shifted uncomfortably, his chair creaking under his weight. "Sir, we haven't had any confirmed sightings in days. Are you sure--"

The Colonel's eyes narrowed dangerously, his voice dropping to a menacing whisper. "Are you questioning me, soldier? Or perhaps you're in league with Kelly? Is that it?" He leaned in close, studying the man's face. His breath, sour with fear and whiskey, washed over the ex-soldier. "How do I know you're not feeding him information right now? How do I know you're not Kelly in disguise?"

"That's absurd," the ex-military man protested, recoiling from the Colonel's intense scrutiny. But the Colonel had already moved on, his paranoia finding new targets.

"New security measures, effective immediately," he barked, pacing frantically around the table. "Passwords change daily. No, hourly! No one moves between sectors without my express permission." He glared at each man in turn, his eyes wild and unfocused. "Dismissed!"

As his lieutenants filed out, confusion and concern etched on their faces, the Colonel sagged against the table. With trembling hands, he poured himself a large glass of whiskey, sloshing amber liquid onto the scarred wood. He downed half of it in one gulp, grimacing as it burned its way down his throat.

He stumbled to the window, peering out into the darkness. Shadows seemed to dance at the edge of his vision, and he flinched at every rustle of leaves. The forest, once a sanctuary, now felt like a prison closing in around him.

"Kelly," he muttered, taking another swig. The whiskey did nothing to calm his nerves. If anything, it amplified his paranoia, making the shadows deeper and more menacing. "You won't get me, Kelly. I'm too smart for you. Too smart..." His words slurred together, a mantra repeated over and over as he stared into the night, seeing enemies in every shadow and hearing threats in every whisper of wind.

The cabin door creaked shut behind them as the Colonel's lieutenants stepped out into the cool night air. They exchanged wary glances, the tension from the meeting still thick between them, like a heavy fog settling over their shoulders. The scent of pine and damp earth filled their nostrils, a stark contrast to the stuffy atmosphere they'd just left.

"Over here," the ex-sheriff muttered, jerking his head towards a cluster of trees away from the cabin. They followed, boots crunching softly on fallen leaves and twigs. The darkness seemed to close in around them, broken only by slivers of moonlight filtering through the canopy above.

Once out of earshot, the ex-sheriff let out a low whistle, his breath visible in the chilly air. "What in tarnation was that about? I ain't never seen the Colonel so... unhinged. It was like watching a man come apart at the seams."

The young lieutenant ran a hand through his hair, his fingers trembling slightly. "You think he's losing it? I mean, jumping at bird calls? Accusing us of conspiring with Kelly? It's like he's seeing enemies in every shadow."

"Keep your voice down," the ex-military man hissed, his eyes darting around nervously. "We need to tread carefully here. The Colonel's always been... intense. But this is different. It's like he's teetering on the edge of something dangerous."

"Different? It's downright dangerous," the ex-sheriff grumbled, his weathered face creased with worry. "How're we supposed to double patrols when we're already running on fumes? And hourly password changes? That's just asking for confusion. Our people are stretched too thin as it is."

The young lieutenant nodded vigorously. "Not to mention strengthening the fortifications. We barely have enough supplies to keep things patched up as it is. Half our tools are rusted or broken, and we're running low on nails and lumber."

"And all this fuss over Joe Kelly," the ex-military man added, his voice low and tense. "We haven't had a confirmed sighting in days. It's a waste of resources to have everyone on high alert for ghosts. For all we know, Kelly's long gone or..." He didn't finish the thought, but they all knew what he meant.

They fell silent for a moment, the weight of their situation settling over them like a heavy blanket. The only sounds were the rustling of leaves and the distant hoot of an owl.

The ex-sheriff sighed, his breath forming a small cloud in the cool air. "Look, we can't just ignore orders. But maybe we can... prioritize. Focus on the most critical tasks, do what we can with what we've got. We've got to be smart about this, or we'll run ourselves into the ground."

"Agreed," said the ex-military man, nodding grimly. "We'll have to be smart about it. Rotate patrols to give the appearance of increased presence without burning out our people. Maybe implement the password changes every few hours instead of hourly. It's not ideal, but it's better than nothing."

The young lieutenant nodded, his brow furrowed in thought. "I can work on the fortifications, but I'll focus on the most vulnerable areas first. We'll have to get creative with materials, maybe salvage what we can from abandoned buildings nearby. As for Kelly... well, we'll keep our ears open, but I'm not about to waste manpower on wild goose chases. We've got enough real problems to deal with."

"Good," the ex-sheriff said, his voice gruff but approving. "Now, about the Colonel himself..." He trailed off, leaving the unspoken concern hanging in the air between them.

They exchanged uneasy glances, each man's face a mirror of the others' worry and uncertainty.

"His behavior tonight was erratic, to say the least," the ex-military man said quietly, his words barely above a whisper. "We need to keep a close eye on him. Each of us should monitor different aspects - his decision-making, interactions with the group, any more... episodes like tonight. We can't afford to be caught off guard if things take a turn for the worse."

The young lieutenant shifted nervously, his fingers fidgeting with the hem of his jacket. "And if he gets worse? What then? We can't exactly stage an intervention in the middle of all this chaos."

The ex-sheriff's face hardened, his jaw clenching visibly. "Let's hope it doesn't come to that. For now, we present a united front. Keep the group stable, shield them from any... instability at the top. But we need to be prepared for the worst. If push comes to shove, we might have to make some tough decisions for the good of everyone."

They nodded grimly, the unspoken weight of their new responsibility settling on their shoulders like a physical burden. The air around them seemed to grow colder, as if nature itself sensed the gravity of their situation.

"Alright," the ex-military man said, squaring his shoulders. "Let's get to it. We've got a long night ahead of us. Stay alert, stay focused, and above all, stay quiet about this conversation. The last thing we need is for word to get back to the Colonel."

As they dispersed, each man felt the tenuous balance of their situation. They'd weathered storms before, but this one was brewing from within, and none of them were sure how it would break. The darkness of the forest seemed to close in around them as they made their way back to their respective posts, each lost in thought about the challenges that lay ahead.

CHAPTER EIGHT

Maria, Claire, Abby, and Robbin strolled through the compound, their footsteps in sync as they enjoyed a rare moment of peace. The late afternoon sun cast long shadows across the well-worn paths, and a gentle breeze rustled through the nearby trees.

"I swear, this little one's doing somersaults today," Abby said, rubbing her swollen belly with a mixture of affection and exasperation.

Claire chuckled. "Mine's been pretty active too. I think they're having a dance party in there."

"Just wait until they start kicking your ribs," Maria added with a knowing smile. "That's when the real fun begins."

Robbin, the quietest of the group, spoke up softly. "I felt a huge kick yesterday. It was... amazing."

The others turned to her, their faces lighting up with shared joy.

"That's wonderful, Robbin," Maria said warmly, giving the younger woman's shoulder a gentle squeeze. "It really makes it feel real, doesn't it?"

Robbin nodded, a small smile playing on her lips. "It does. I never thought I'd be excited about this, but... I am."

"We all are," Claire affirmed. "These babies are hope, you know? A future we're fighting for."

They continued walking, their conversation flowing easily between them.

"So, any weird cravings yet?" Abby asked, her eyes twinkling with mischief. "I've been dying for pickles dipped in peanut butter."

Claire made a face. "Ugh, no thanks. But I'd kill for some spicy food. The hotter, the better."

"I've just been craving fresh fruit," Maria admitted. "Oranges, especially. Guess the Florida girl in me is coming out."

Robbin hesitated before adding, "I... I've been wanting my mom's homemade chicken noodle soup. She used to make it whenever I was sick."

The mood sobered slightly, each woman acutely aware of the loved ones they'd lost or been separated from.

"We'll have to swap recipes sometime," Maria said gently. "Maybe we can recreate some of those comfort foods for our little ones someday."

The conversation shifted to their hopes and fears for the future.

"I worry about raising a child in this world," Claire confessed. "It's so different from what we knew."

Abby nodded. "But maybe that's not all bad. They won't take things for granted like we did."

"And they'll be strong," Maria added. "Survivors, like us."

Robbin looked thoughtful. "I hope they'll still know kindness and compassion. That's important, maybe now more than ever."

The others murmured in agreement.

As they rounded a corner, their talk turned to more practical matters.

"We should start thinking about a nursery," Claire suggested. "Maybe we can convert one of the empty rooms?"

Maria nodded. "Good idea. We'll need to start gathering supplies too. Diapers, clothes, blankets..."

Robbin smiled, feeling a sense of belonging she hadn't experienced in a long time. "We've got this," she said softly. "Together."

The women's conversation was suddenly interrupted by a distant rumble. They all paused, their bodies tensing as they listened intently.

"Is that...?" Abby started, her eyes widening.

"A vehicle," Claire confirmed, her hand instinctively moving to the knife at her hip.

Maria stepped forward, shielding the others slightly. "Let's not jump to conclusions. It could be friendly."

They moved quickly towards the compound's main gate along with others carrying rifles, their earlier relaxed demeanor replaced by cautious alertness. As they approached, the sound grew louder, the unmistakable growl of an engine drawing closer.

"There!" Robbin pointed, her voice barely above a whisper.

In the distance, a plume of dust rose from the road leading to their sanctuary. As it neared, they could make out the shape of an old pickup truck, its once-shiny paint now dulled and scratched. Behind it, a small trailer bounced along the uneven terrain.

"Should we alert the others?" Abby asked, her hand protectively cradling her belly.

Claire squinted, trying to make out any details. "Wait... is that...?"

As the truck drew closer, features became clearer. The familiar outline of the driver in the cab, the tan beret tilted to one side - it was a figure they knew well.

Maria's breath caught in her throat. "It's Jojo," she said, her voice a mixture of relief and surprise.

Sure enough, as the pickup truck slowed its approach, they could see Jojo behind the wheel, his familiar profile unmistakable. His eyes were focused on the road, his jaw set in concentration as he navigated the final stretch to the compound.

"He's back," Robbin whispered, a small smile tugging at her lips.

The group watched as Jojo brought the truck to a stop just outside the gate. He sat there for a moment, his hands still gripping the steering wheel, before turning to look at them through the dusty windshield.

As Jojo stepped out of the truck, a grin spread across his face. He stretched his arms wide, as if embracing the entire compound. "Thought you might need some milk for those babies!" he called out, his voice filled with pride and excitement.

The women exchanged puzzled glances, their confusion evident. It was then that they noticed the trailer hitched to the back of the truck. As if on cue, a low, rumbling moo emanated from within.

Claire's eyes widened. "Are those...?"

Jojo strode over to the trailer, his movements filled with purpose. "Yes, they are exactly what you think they are. Five cows and one bull and we've got another load to go back and get just like this one."

"Oh my god," Abby gasped, her hand flying to her mouth.

Maria stepped forward, her face a mixture of disbelief and joy. "Jojo, where on earth did you find them?"

Robbin, usually quiet, couldn't contain her excitement. "Real cows! I can't believe it!"

The women moved closer, their earlier caution replaced by wonder. The cows, seemingly unfazed by the attention, continued to chew contentedly.

"Found them on a farm about five or six miles up the road." Jojo explained, patting one of the cows on its flank. "Let me introduce you to their owners. This is Betty and her two daughters Pam and Tracy. They were being harassed by some men trying to take what wasn't theirs when Miguel and I stepped in. These ladies have agreed to move in with us and we are so thankful to have them."

Claire reached out tentatively, running her hand along the cow's soft coat. "This is... incredible. Fresh milk, maybe even cheese..."

"And butter," Abby added dreamily. "God, I've missed butter."

Robbin hung back slightly, her eyes shining with unshed tears. "It's like a piece of the old world," she murmured.

Maria turned to Jojo, her face serious despite the joy in her eyes. "This is a game-changer, Jojo. For the babies, for all of us. Thank you and thank you ladies. You are so welcomed here."

The impact of Jojo's discovery rippled through the group like a stone cast into still water. Claire was the first to vocalize what they were all thinking.

"This changes everything," she said, her voice filled with awe. "Fresh milk for the babies... it's more than we could have hoped for."

Abby nodded vigorously, her hand still resting on her belly. "And for us too. The extra calcium, the nutrients... it's exactly what we need."

Robbin, usually reserved, spoke up with enthusiasm. "It's not just about the milk. This is a renewable resource. We can use the manure for fertilizer, maybe even make cheese and yogurt."

Maria's eyes sparkled with excitement. "You're right.

This is going to improve our nutrition significantly. And for the little ones on the way, it's a godsend."

As the news spread, more people began to gather around the truck and trailer. Excited chatter filled the air, punctuated by the occasional moo from their new bovine residents.

"Is it true? Real cows?" someone called out from the back of the crowd.

Jojo grinned, clearly pleased with the reaction. "It sure is. And there's more where these came from."

The excitement was palpable as people began to discuss the possibilities. One of the older men in the group, a former farmer, stepped forward to inspect the animals.

"These ladies look healthy," he announced. "With proper care, they could provide milk for years to come."

Claire turned to the others, her mind already racing with plans. "We'll need to set up a milking station, figure out storage..."

"And we'll have to allocate more resources to growing feed," Maria added thoughtfully. "But it's worth it."

As the discussion continued, it became clear that this unexpected windfall would have far-reaching effects on their community. The prospect of fresh dairy products was just the beginning.

"We could trade milk with other settlements," someone suggested. "It would give us a valuable bargaining chip."

Abby's eyes lit up. "And butter! We could make butter. I can't even remember the last time I had real butter."

The conversation flowed freely, with people offering ideas and suggestions. It was clear that Jojo and Miguel's find had injected a new sense of hope and possibility into the community.

As the initial excitement settled, the group began to focus on the practical aspects of welcoming their new additions.

"Alright, folks," Jojo called out, clapping his hands to get everyone's attention. "Let's get these ladies settled in. We'll need some strong arms to help with the unloading."

Several volunteers stepped forward, eager to assist. Betty directed them to the trailer, showing them how to guide the cows down the ramp safely. The animals were surprisingly cooperative, perhaps sensing the positive energy around them.

As they worked, Jojo began to explain how he had come across this unexpected treasure. "Miguel and I were on a routine scouting mission," he said, wiping sweat from his brow. "We heard some commotion coming from an old farmstead. Turned out, a group of raiders was trying to steal these beauties from Betty and her daughters."

Claire, who was helping guide one of the cows, looked up with interest. "What happened then?"

Jojo grinned. "Well, we couldn't just stand by and watch. Miguel and I stepped in, managed to scare off the raiders. Betty and her girls were grateful, but they knew they couldn't protect the herd on their own anymore. That's when we struck a deal – they'd come back with us, bringing the cows, in exchange for safety , by the way, we've got another little surprise for you as well."

Claire looked up at Jojo. "I don't think there's any way you could possibly top this Jojo."

Jojo laughed. "Maybe not top it, but how would you feel about having real eggs for breakfast tomorrow morning?"

Claire froze in her steps. "Are you friggin' kidding me, don't even think about teasing me. Are you saying what I think you're saying, you're bringing back chickens as well?"

Jojo's smile widened. ""Chickens and roosters my love."

Claire wrapped her arms around Jojo and whispered in his ear. "You are going to be so rewarded for this later, count on it."

As the last cow was unloaded, the group's attention turned to the logistics of caring for their new charges.

Maria, ever practical, spoke up. "We'll need to set up a proper shelter for them. Something sturdy that can protect them from the elements and any potential threats."

The former farmer nodded in agreement. "And we'll need to establish a regular milking schedule. These ladies need to be milked twice a day, every day."

"What about feed?" Robbin asked, her voice tinged with concern. "Do we have enough to sustain them?"

Jojo nodded. "Betty's bringing seeds for feed crops in the next load. We'll need to allocate some land for growing it, but it'll be worth it in the long run."

As the group discussed the care and maintenance of the cattle, it became clear that this would be a community effort. People began volunteering for various tasks – from building the shelter to establishing a milking rotation.

As the initial excitement settled, the women found themselves gathered near the newly arrived cows, their conversation turning reflective.

"Can you believe it?" Abby said softly, her hand resting on her belly. "Just this morning, I was worried about how we'd manage to feed our babies. I mean I'm still planning on breast feeding but this gives us nutrition after the breast feeding is done. Now...I know our kids have a real shot at being healthy for a long time."

Claire nodded, her eyes bright. "It's like a miracle. Real milk, maybe even cheese and butter. Our kids won't have to grow up without knowing these things."

"It's more than just food," Maria added thoughtfully. "It's a piece of the world we lost, something normal in all this chaos."

Robbin, who had been quiet, spoke up. "I never thought I'd be so excited about cows," she said with a small laugh. "But it feels like... like we're building something real here. Something that can last."

The women fell silent for a moment, each lost in their own thoughts about the future. It was Claire who broke the silence.

"You know, I've been so focused on just surviving," she admitted. "But this... this makes me think about actually living. About giving these kids a real childhood, not just teaching them how to survive."

Maria smiled warmly. "That's right. We're not just surviving anymore. We're building a future for them."

Abby rubbed her belly gently. "I want my baby to know joy, to have favorite foods, to experience simple pleasures. Maybe now they can."

As they talked, more people from the community gathered around, drawn by the excitement. The conversation expanded, with everyone sharing their hopes and dreams for the future.

"We could have community dinners again," someone suggested.

"And maybe even ice cream in the summer," another added wistfully.

The mood was infectious, spreading through the group like wildfire. People who had been strangers just months ago were now planning and dreaming together, united by this unexpected blessing.

Robbin looked around at the animated faces surrounding her. "You know," she said softly, "I think this is about more than just the cows. It's about us. All of us, coming together, making something good out of all this bad."

The others nodded in agreement, feeling the truth of her words. In that moment, surrounded by the gentle sounds of the cows and the excited chatter of their community, the future seemed a little brighter, a little more hopeful.

CHAPTER NINE

J oe wiped the sweat from his furrowed brow as he surveyed the abandoned van, its rusted frame and shattered windows a stark reminder of the desolate world they now inhabited. The vehicle sat like a forgotten relic, a testament to the life they once knew. "Alright, let's get this show on the road," he called out to the group, his voice carrying a mix of determination and urgency, tinged with a hint of weariness that seemed to seep into his very bones.

Captain Rodriguez nodded, his keen eyes methodically scanning the area as he gestured to his men. The captain's posture was rigid, his movements precise – a man who never truly left the battlefield. "Miller, Jones, start hooking up the tow line. We need to get this van back to the compound ASAP. And keep your eyes peeled, gentlemen. We can't afford any surprises out here. This isn't a drill anymore; it's life or death."

As the soldiers worked diligently on securing the van, their movements precise and efficient, a well-oiled machine born of necessity and survival, Joe turned to Sam, Dave, and Jake, his trusted companions in this post-apocalyptic nightmare. The bond between them was palpable, forged in the fires of adversity. "You boys remember where we stashed those caches? Every bit of supplies counts now, more than ever. We can't leave anything behind. Our families are counting on us."

Sam nodded, his face set with grim determination as he was already moving towards a nearby copse of trees, his hand resting on the holster at his hip. His eyes, once filled with laughter, now held a haunted look that never quite faded. "I've got the first one. Dave, you take the second. Jake, you're with me. Let's move quickly and quietly. In and out, no unnecessary risks. We've come too far to lose anyone now."

The men split up, carefully retracing their steps through the overgrown terrain to uncover the hidden weapons and supplies they had strategically placed weeks ago, when the world still held a glimmer of hope. The landscape had changed, nature reclaiming what was once civilization with alarming speed. Joe kept watch, his weathered hands gripping his rifle tightly, knuckles white with tension as his eyes scanned the surrounding area for any signs of trouble, be it human or otherwise. The eerie silence was broken only by the occasional rustle of leaves and the distant call of an unfamiliar bird, a haunting melody in this new, dangerous world.

Dave grunted as he lifted a heavy crate from its hiding spot, leaves and dirt falling away to reveal the precious cargo within. His muscles strained under the weight, a reminder of how far they'd come from their comfortable lives before. "Damn, I forgot how much we left behind. It's like Christmas, but with more ammunition and less holiday cheer. Never thought I'd be so happy to see a box full of canned beans and bullets. Funny how priorities change when the world goes to hell."

Jake appeared from behind a fallen log, his arms full of medical supplies that glinted in the fading light, a stark contrast to the grime and decay surrounding them. His youthful face was etched with a seriousness that belied his years. "Better safe than sorry, right? These might just save a life one day. God knows we've needed them before, and we'll need them again. I just hope we have enough to last us through whatever comes next."

As they began loading the retrieved items into the van, a twig snapped in the nearby underbrush, the sound cutting through the eerie silence like a gunshot. Everyone froze, hands instinctively moving to their weapons as adrenaline surged through their veins, hearts pounding in their chests. The camaraderie of moments before vanished, replaced by the razor-sharp focus of survival.

"Hold," Captain Rodriguez whispered, raising his fist in a silent command, his body tense and ready for action. The soldiers immediately took defensive positions around the van, their training kicking in as they prepared for potential threats, eyes scanning the tree line for any sign of movement. Each man became a statue, barely breathing, every sense heightened to painful acuity.

Joe's eyes narrowed as he peered back and forth from left to right, the bright sunlight making him squint, playing tricks on his tired mind. The tension was palpable, each man barely breathing as they waited for whatever was out there to reveal itself, friend or foe. The weight of their weapons felt reassuring in their hands, a lifeline in this unpredictable world. Joe's finger rested lightly on the trigger, muscle memory from countless encounters ready to spring into action.

Seconds ticked by, feeling like hours in the oppressive silence. Then, a small deer emerged from the brush, its delicate form a stark contrast to their battle-ready stance. It paused to look at them with wide, startled eyes before bounding away into the safety of the forest, leaving behind a trail of rustling leaves and relieved sighs. The graceful creature seemed almost surreal, a fleeting reminder of the beauty that still existed in their harsh reality.

A collective exhale of relief rippled through the group, the tension draining away as quickly as it had come. "False alarm," Joe muttered, but the incident had put everyone on edge, a stark reminder of the constant dangers that lurked in this new world. His hands still shook slightly as he lowered his weapon, adrenaline slowly ebbing away. He could feel his heart hammering against his ribs, a reminder of his own mortality.

"Let's finish up and get moving," Sam said, his voice tight with lingering anxiety. "There's something about this place that gives me the willies." His eyes darting around searching for any lurking danger. "I do not want to be out here after the sun goes down. Especially with the Colonel and his men unaccounted for. Too many things that go bump in the night these days, and not all of them are as harmless as deer. We've seen what happens to those who linger too long."

They worked quickly and efficiently, loading the last of the supplies into the van with practiced ease, each man acutely aware of being exposed and vulnerable to any threat that may arise. The clanking of metal and the rustle of supplies being stowed away seemed unnaturally loud in the stillness of the afternoon. As they prepared to depart, Captain Rodriguez approached Joe, his face etched with concern, the lines around his eyes deeper than ever, telling tales of sleepless nights and constant vigilance.

"We're all set. But that little scare... it's a reminder we can't let our guard down, not even for a second. This world isn't forgiving anymore. One mistake could cost us everything we've fought so hard to protect. We've lost too many good people already to carelessness." The captain's words hung heavy in the air, a somber truth they all knew too well.

Joe nodded grimly, the weight of responsibility heavy on his shoulders, feeling every one of his years. The burden of leadership seemed to physically press down on him, bowing his back ever so slightly. "Agreed. Let's get this caravan rolling. It's going to be a long thirty miles back to the compound, and who knows what we might encounter along the way. Keep your wits about you, everyone. We're not home yet. And in this world, home is the only safe place left... if there is such a thing anymore."

The convoy rumbled down the cracked asphalt, a small dust cloud trailing behind them like a ghostly tail. Joe sat in the passenger seat of the lead vehicle, his weathered hands gripping the dashboard, eyes constantly scanning the horizon for any sign of trouble. The radio crackled with periodic check-ins from the other vehicles, their voices tense and clipped, each word carrying the weight of their precarious situation.

"All clear on the rear," came Sam's voice from the last truck, towing the van. The extra weight made their progress slower, more vulnerable, like a wounded animal limping through predator-infested territory.

Captain Rodriguez gripped the steering wheel, his knuckles white with tension. "Keep sharp, people. We're not home yet," he barked, his voice a mixture of authority and barely concealed anxiety.

The afternoon sun beat down mercilessly, creating shimmering mirages on the road ahead that danced and wavered like heat-induced hallucinations. Thick stands of trees lined both sides of the highway, their shadows offering perfect cover for potential ambushes. Joe's calloused hand never strayed far from his weapon, fingers twitching with anticipation.

Suddenly, a flicker of movement caught Joe's keen eye. "Three o'clock, about 200 yards out," he said quietly, raising his scratched and battered binoculars to get a better look.

Rodriguez eased off the accelerator, slowing the vehicle to a crawl. The rest of the convoy followed suit, engines idling nervously. Through the lenses, Joe spotted a small group of men moving stealthily through the trees parallel to the road. His stomach dropped like a stone as he recognized their distinctive armbands, a sight that had become all too familiar in recent weeks.

"It's the Colonel's men. Scouting party, looks like," Joe reported grimly, his mouth suddenly dry.

A moment of tense silence filled the cab as Rodriguez considered their limited options, the air thick with unspoken fear. "We could try to slip by..." he began, his voice trailing off uncertainly.

Before he could finish his thought, a sharp crack split the air like a thunderbolt. The windshield spiderwebbed as a bullet impacted just inches from Joe's head, showering him with tiny fragments of safety glass.

"Contact right!" Joe shouted into the radio as he ducked down, heart pounding in his ears. "The Colonel's men are engaging!"

The air erupted with gunfire as both sides opened up, the peaceful afternoon shattered by the cacophony of battle. Joe could hear the ping of bullets striking their armored vehicle, the shouts and curses of his people as they returned fire, and the sickening thud of rounds finding flesh. The acrid smell of cordite filled his nostrils as he fumbled for his weapon, knowing that the next few minutes would determine whether they lived or died.

The world narrowed to a chaotic blur of gunfire and shouted orders. Joe's ears rang from the deafening cacophony of automatic weapons and the sharp crack of rifle shots. Bullets whizzed past, thudding into trees and kicking up sprays of asphalt. The air grew thick with acrid gun smoke and the metallic tang of spilled blood.

"Keep them pinned down!" Joe bellowed, his voice barely audible over the din. He squeezed off controlled bursts from his rifle, forcing the Colonel's men to duck behind cover.

Despite the initial ambush, Joe's group held a significant tactical advantage. Their vehicles provided mobile cover, and they boasted superior firepower. Years of military training kicked in as they responded with disciplined volleys, their aim true and devastating.

Sam's voice crackled over the radio, "Two tangos down on the left flank!"

Captain Rodriguez, cool under fire, saw an opportunity. He keyed his mic, "Jones, take your team and sweep right. We'll draw their fire."

Joe nodded grimly, pride swelling in his chest as he watched this unfold in front of him. Their small group moving in unison into a flanking maneuver. Rodriguez coordinated suppressing fire, keeping the enemy's heads down as Jones team maneuvered through the trees.

The tide of battle shifted suddenly. A panicked shout erupted from the Colonel's forces as Jones team caught them in a deadly crossfire. Their cohesion broke, and the organized assault devolved into a desperate scramble for survival.

"They're retreating!" Sam called out, the excitement clear in his voice.

Joe allowed himself a moment of grim satisfaction as he watched the remaining attackers melt into the forest, leaving their fallen comrades behind. The sudden silence was almost deafening after the chaos of combat.

As the echoes of gunfire faded, Joe scanned the tree line, his senses still on high alert. Suddenly, movement caught his eye – a lone figure darting between the trees, separated from his retreating comrades.

"Sam, Jake – on your three o'clock!" Joe barked into the radio. "We've got a straggler."

Without hesitation, Sam and Jake sprang into action. They moved with practiced efficiency, fanning out to flank the isolated scout. Joe watched as they closed in, their movements fluid and coordinated.

The scout, realizing he was cut off, spun wildly, his rifle

swinging from Sam to Jake and back again. His eyes were wide with panic, chest heaving as he gasped for breath.

"Drop it!" Sam's voice rang out, firm and commanding. "You're surrounded. It's over."

For a tense moment, Joe thought the man might try something foolish. But then, slowly, the fight seemed to drain out of him. The scout's shoulders slumped, and his rifle clattered to the ground.

"Hands where we can see them," Jake ordered, moving in cautiously.

As Sam secured the prisoner, Joe's mind raced. This was an unexpected opportunity – one they couldn't afford to waste.

"Captain," Joe called out to Rodriguez, "we've got ourselves a prisoner. Could be valuable intel."

Rodriguez nodded grimly. "Good thinking. Get him secured in one of the rear vehicles. We'll question him once we're clear of the area."

Joe watched as Sam and Jake escorted the captured scout back to the convoy. The man's SS-SA armband stood out starkly against his dirty uniform – a chilling reminder of the enemy they faced.

As the prisoner was secured in one of the trucks, Joe

scanned the forest one last time. In the distance, he could hear the fading sounds of the Colonel's remaining forces in full retreat. They had won this skirmish, but Joe knew the war was far from over.

Joe's group quickly regrouped, assessing the aftermath of the intense firefight. "Anyone hit?" Joe called out, his eyes scanning anxiously for signs of injury among his people. The acrid smell of gunpowder hung heavy in the air, mixing with the metallic tang of blood and the sharp scent of fear.

A few minor wounds were reported – mostly cuts from flying debris and glass, with one or two grazes from near misses – but miraculously, no one had taken any serious fire. The vehicles, while peppered with bullet holes and sporting shattered windows, remained operational. Joe silently thanked whatever higher power might be listening for their good fortune.

"We got lucky," Captain Rodriguez muttered, running a hand through his sweat-soaked hair, his face etched with a mixture of relief and concern. "But we can't count on that holding out. Next time, we might not be so fortunate."

As they patched up the wounded and performed hasty repairs on the vehicles, using whatever materials they had on hand, Joe pulled Rodriguez and Sam aside. "That prisoner could be a game-changer," he said in a low voice, glancing towards the truck where the captured scout was secured, his hands bound tightly behind his back.

Sam nodded grimly, his eyes hard. "If we can get him to talk, we might finally get some solid intel on the Colonel's operations. It could give us the edge we've been looking for."

"It's a double-edged sword," Rodriguez warned, his brow furrowed in thought. "Having one of their men could make us an even bigger target. The Colonel doesn't strike me as the type to leave loose ends. He'll come at us harder than ever now."

With repairs complete and the prisoner secured, the convoy resumed its journey, the engines rumbling to life with a sense of urgency. The mood was tense, everyone on high alert after the ambush. Joe found himself constantly scanning the tree line, his hand never far from his weapon, half-expecting another attack at any moment. Every rustle of leaves, every snapping twig, set nerves on edge.

As they drove, speculation about their captive buzzed through the group, voices crackling over the radio. "Think he knows where the Colonel's main base is?" Jake asked, his tone a mixture of hope and apprehension.

"Even if he does, getting that information won't be easy," Joe replied, his voice grim. "But any insight into their numbers, supply lines, or future plans could give us a real advantage. We need to be smart about how we handle this."

The miles rolled by, each one bringing them closer to the relative safety of the compound. There was a palpable sense of accomplishment among the group – they had faced a direct assault from the Colonel's forces and come out on top. But with that victory came an acute awareness of the increased danger they now faced. The stakes had been raised, and everyone knew it.

"We've bloodied their nose," Sam said quietly to Joe, his voice barely audible over the rumble of the engine. "You can bet the Colonel won't take that lying down. He'll be out for revenge, and he won't care who gets hurt in the process."

Joe nodded, his jaw set in grim determination, his knuckles white on the steering wheel. The compound was still miles away, and a lot could happen before they reached its protective walls. Every moment until then was fraught with danger, and Joe knew that this small victory might just be the prelude to an even greater conflict.

The convoy rolled through the gates of the compound,

a collective sigh of relief rippling through the group. Joe's eyes widened as he took in an unexpected sight – a small herd of cows grazing peacefully in a makeshift pasture.

"I'll be damned," he muttered, rubbing his eyes in disbelief. "Are those... are those cows?"

Captain Rodriguez chuckled, the tension of the journey finally easing from his shoulders. "Looks like the scavenging teams have been busy while we were gone. Fresh milk and beef will be a game-changer for our supplies."

As the vehicles came to a stop, the compound burst into activity. People rushed to greet the returning team, faces a mix of joy and concern as they took in the bullet-riddled vehicles and weary expressions of the travelers.

Joe's focus quickly shifted to their captive. "Sam, Jake," he called out, his voice low but authoritative. "Get our 'guest' secured in the holding area. We need to make sure he's under constant guard until we're ready for questioning."

Sam nodded grimly, moving to the truck where the prisoner was held. "On it, Joe. We'll make sure he's locked down tight."

As Sam and Jake led the bound scout away, whispers rippled through the gathering crowd. The sight of an

SS-SA uniform in their midst sent a shiver of unease through the compound.

Joe turned to Rodriguez, his voice barely above a whisper. "We need to be smart about this, Cap. That man could be our key to getting ahead of the Colonel's next move."

Rodriguez nodded, his eyes following the prisoner. "Agreed. But we can't rush this. He'll be expecting us to come at him hard. We need to be strategic."

The anticipation of the upcoming interrogation hung heavy in the air. Joe could feel the weight of expectation from the compound's residents, their eyes filled with a mixture of hope and fear. They all knew what was at stake – the information this man held could mean the difference between survival and annihilation.

Joe pulled Captain Rodriguez aside, his voice low and urgent. "Cap, I've been thinking about our prisoner. We should keep him up all night, wear him down. It'll make him more susceptible to questioning in the morning."

Rodriguez nodded slowly, a glimmer of approval in his eyes. "That's good thinking, Joe. Sleep deprivation can be a powerful tool. It might just give us the edge we need to crack him."

"Exactly," Joe agreed, feeling a surge of relief at the

captain's support. "We'll have our best chance if we hit him when he's exhausted and off-balance."

"Alright, let's make it happen," Rodriguez said, his voice firm with decision. "I'll arrange for rotating guard shifts to keep him awake. We'll start the interrogation at first light."

Joe clapped Rodriguez on the shoulder, a rare grin breaking through his usual stoic expression. "Awesome, Cap. Now that we're in agreement on that, there's something else I've got to take care of."

Without waiting for a response, Joe turned and jogged towards the cabin where he knew Maria would be. His mind was buzzing with questions about the unexpected addition to their compound.

"Maria!" he called out as he approached the cabin. "Maria, you've got to tell me about these cows!"

CHAPTER TEN

The battered convoy of SS-SA vehicles limped into camp, their arrival marked by the screech of damaged metal and the hiss of punctured tires. Bloodied and dejected soldiers stumbled out, drawing concerned stares from their comrades. The acrid smell of gunpowder and burnt rubber filled the air, a stark reminder of the violence they had just endured. Smoke still curled from the engines of several trucks, adding to the apocalyptic scene.

"What in tarnation?" muttered a sentry, his eyes wide as he took in the bullet-riddled trucks. He unconsciously tightened his grip on his rifle, scanning the horizon for any signs of pursuit. His gaze lingered on the treeline, half-expecting to see enemy forces emerging from the shadows.

The commotion spread through the camp like wildfire. Whispers and pointed fingers followed the defeated soldiers as they made their way towards the Colonel's quarters. Women clutched their children close, while off-duty guards reached for their weapons, tension thick in the air. Some of the younger recruits looked ready to bolt, their faith in the SS-SA's invincibility shaken to its core.

Inside his opulent cabin, the Colonel sat behind an antique desk, his fingers steepled beneath his chin. The polished wood gleamed in the lamplight, a stark contrast to the chaos outside. A half-empty tumbler of whiskey sat at his elbow, evidence of his growing unease. The door opened with a creak, admitting a group of haggard men who stood at uneasy attention, their uniforms caked with dried blood and dirt. The stench of fear and failure clung to them like a second skin.

"Well?" the Colonel drawled, his piercing blue eyes taking in their battered appearance. A hint of disdain crept into his voice as he added, "I trust you have good news for me?" His Southern charm had an edge to it now, sharp enough to draw blood.

The soldiers exchanged nervous glances, shifting their weight from foot to foot. Their leader, Pernell, a stout man with a fresh gash across his cheek, stepped forward, wincing as he did so. Blood still oozed from the wound, a testament to the ferocity of the recent battle.

"Sir," he began, his voice hoarse from shouting orders and breathing in smoke, "we encountered a convoy, it was definitely Joe Kelly, but... things didn't go as expected. Not at all." He swallowed hard, struggling to maintain eye contact with his imposing leader.

The Colonel's eyes narrowed, his jaw tightening imperceptibly. "Go on Bobby," he commanded, his tone brooking no argument. The temperature in the room seemed to drop several degrees.

"They had National Guard troops with them, sir. Professional soldiers, not just ragtag survivors. We were outgunned and outmaneuvered from the start. It was like they knew we were coming." The soldier's voice trembled slightly as he recounted the battle, the memories still fresh and painful.

As the soldier recounted the encounter and the fierce firefight that followed, the Colonel's face darkened. His fingers drummed an impatient rhythm on the desk, the sound echoing in the tense silence of the cabin. The ticking of an ornate grandfather clock in the corner seemed to grow louder with each passing moment, marking the seconds until the Colonel's inevitable explosion.

"So you're telling me," he interrupted, his voice dangerously soft, like the whisper of a blade being drawn, "that not only did you fail in your mission, but you also lost one of our own? Is that what I'm hearing?" His eyes glittered with barely suppressed rage, promising swift retribution.

The soldier swallowed hard, Adam's apple bobbing visibly. "Yes, sir. They... they captured Jenkins. We couldn't get to him in time. We tried, sir, we really did, but..." His voice trailed off, knowing that no excuse would be good enough.

The Colonel exploded from his chair with surprising speed for a man his age, his face contorted with rage. "Incompetent fools!" he roared, sending papers flying in all directions. The sudden outburst made his men flinch back instinctively, some raising their arms as if to ward off a physical blow. "Do you have any idea what that man could reveal under interrogation? The damage he could do to everything we've built?"

His men flinched, exchanging worried glances as their leader paced the cabin like a caged animal, muttering under his breath. His carefully cultivated image of Southern gentility had cracked, revealing the ruthless, paranoid man beneath. The mask of civility slipped away, leaving only the raw, dangerous core of the SS-SA's leader exposed.

"Kelly," the Colonel muttered, his eyes wild and unfocused. "Always Kelly. What game is he playing? What does he want? How does he always seem to be one step ahead?" His hands clenched and unclenched at his sides, as if itching to wrap around Joe Kelly's throat.

He whirled on his subordinates, causing them to take

an involuntary step back. "Double the patrols!" he barked. "No, triple them! No we need to move to a new location completely! I want a new location for our base of operations scouted out and on our way to it my midday tomorrow. Make it happen and remember we can't trust anyone now. Anyone! For all we know, we could be infiltrated already." Spittle flew from his lips as he ranted, his face growing redder by the second.

The soldiers stood frozen, unsure how to respond to their leader's increasingly erratic behavior. They glanced at each other, silently debating who should speak up. The air in the cabin grew thick with tension, making it difficult to breathe.

"Well?" the Colonel snapped, spittle flying from his lips. "What are you waiting for? Get out! Out! And God help you if you fail me again!" His voice cracked on the last word, a hint of desperation creeping in beneath the anger.

As the men scrambled to leave, nearly tripping over each other in their haste, the Colonel sank back into his chair. He ran a trembling hand through his thinning white hair, his mind racing with paranoid thoughts about Joe Kelly and his growing threat to the SS-SA's power. The once-pristine white suit was rumpled now, his carefully crafted image in tatters.

Outside the Colonel's cabin, Pernell huddled with the Colonel's top men, his face grim. "You heard the man," he growled, voice low to avoid being overheard. "We need a new base of operations by midday tomorrow."

The men exchanged shocked glances, their faces a mix of disbelief and concern.

"Midday tomorrow?" Garcia hissed. "That's impossible. We can't possibly scout a secure location, plan logistics, and move our entire operation in less than 24 hours."

Reeves nodded in agreement. "We're talking about relocating hundreds of people, tons of supplies, weapons caches... It's a logistical nightmare."

"Not to mention the security risks," Thompson added, running a hand through his salt-and-pepper hair. "Moving in broad daylight? We might as well paint targets on our backs."

Pernell held up a hand to quiet the murmurs of dissent. "I know it sounds crazy, but you saw the Colonel. He's not in a mood to be reasoned with right now."

"But surely we can talk some sense into him," Wilson protested. "Once he calms down-"

"And risk his wrath?" Pernell cut him off. "No, our best

bet is to at least look like we're following orders. Start scouting potential locations immediately."

The group fell into a tense silence, each man lost in thought as they grappled with the impossible task before them.

Finally, Reeves spoke up. "What about the old missile silo complex to the north? It's defensible, hidden, and we've had our eye on it for a while."

Thompson shook his head. "Too far. We'd never make it by the deadline."

"The abandoned mall in Clearwater?" Garcia suggested.

"Too exposed," Pernell countered. "We need something more secluded."

The debate continued, voices rising and falling as they argued the merits and drawbacks of various locations. The weight of their impossible task hung heavy in the air, along with the unspoken fear of what would happen if they failed to meet the Colonel's demands.

Thompson's jaw clenched, his patience finally snapping. He turned back toward the Colonel's cabin abruptly, his feet straining to begin moving. "This is ridiculous," he growled, eyes flashing with frustration. "I'm going back in there to talk some sense into the Colonel. We need at least two days for proper reconnaissance, and another three to execute the move safely at the very least."

The other officers exchanged alarmed glances. Reeves reached out, grabbing Thompson's arm. "Think about what you're doing. The Colonel's not in a state to be reasoned with right now."

Thompson shook off Reeves' hand. "Someone has to tell him the truth. We can't keep bowing to his every whim, especially when it puts our people at risk."

Garcia stepped in front of the door, blocking Thompson's path. "Sir, please. This isn't the way. You know how the Colonel gets when he's challenged."

"Get out of my way," Thompson growled, his voice low and dangerous.

Pernell moved to Thompson's side, speaking in a hushed, urgent tone. "Hey, I understand your frustration. We all feel it. But storming in there... it's not going to end well for you or for us."

"He needs to hear the reality of the situation," Thompson insisted, though his resolve was wavering slightly.

"And he will," Pernell assured him. "But not like this. Not when he's in one of his moods. Give it time. We'll find a way to present our concerns that won't set him off."

Thompson's fists clenched and unclenched at his sides as he wrestled with his decision. The air fell silent, tension thick in the air as they waited to see what he would do.

Thompson opened the cabin door, went inside, and closed the door behind him.

The other men stood out front waiting for him. They quietly chatted as they waited, tension thick in the air. Pernell paced back and forth, his boots crunching on the gravel. Garcia leaned against a nearby tree, arms crossed tightly over his chest. Reeves stood stock-still, eyes fixed on the cabin door.

"You think he'll actually get through to the Colonel?" Garcia whispered.

Reeves shook his head. "Doubt it. But maybe he can buy us some time at least."

Pernell stopped pacing, opening his mouth to respond when suddenly a gunshot rang out.

The shot came from inside the Colonel's cabin.

For a split second, the men froze, eyes wide with shock. Then, as one, they sprang into action. Pernell reached the door first, shouldering it open with a loud crack. The others piled in behind him, hands instinctively reaching for their weapons.

The scene that greeted them sent a chill down their spines. The Colonel stood calmly in the center of the room, a thin wisp of smoke curling from the barrel of his pistol. At his feet lay Thompson's body, a growing pool of blood spreading across the worn wooden floorboards.

The Colonel looked up at the men, his face a mask of eerie calm. His piercing blue eyes swept over them, taking in their shocked expressions without a hint of remorse.

"Get this filthy carcass out of my quarters," he drawled, gesturing dismissively at Thompson's body with his free hand. "And please do get busy carrying out my orders."

CHAPTER ELEVEN

J oe sprinted up the path to the cabin, his heart
racing with excitement. The sight of those cows at
the compound had sparked a glimmer of hope he hadn't
felt in months. As he approached, he called out eagerly,
"Maria! Maria, you won't believe what I saw!"
The cabin door swung open, and Maria rushed out to
meet him. She threw her arms around him in a tight
embrace, her relief palpable. "Joe! Thank God you're
safe. We were so worried."

Joe hugged her back, then pulled away slightly, his eyes
bright with enthusiasm. "Maria, there were cows at the
compound. Actual, living cows! How is that possible?"

Maria's face broke into a wide smile. "Oh, Joe, you
won't believe what's happened. Jojo and Miguel made
an incredible discovery." She took his hand, leading
him towards the cabin. "Come inside, I'll tell you
everything."

Once they were seated, Maria recounted the tale. "Jojo
and Miguel were out scouting when they stumbled
upon this farm. A group of men were trying to steal
the cows but Jojo and Miguel were able to fend them

off. A woman named Betty ran the farm with her two daughters Pam and Tracy and they've agreed to join us here."

Joe listened, awestruck, as Maria continued. "They brought back five cows and a bull on their first trip. Can you believe it?"

"That's incredible," Joe breathed, shaking his head in disbelief. "But you said first trip? There's more?"

Maria nodded excitedly. "Jojo and Miguel are out there right now with a few others. They're planning to bring back five more cows, another bull, and even some chickens and roosters. Betty's been incredibly generous - she's letting us take supplies from her farm too."

Joe leaned back, his mind reeling with the possibilities. "This changes everything, Maria. With livestock, we could start rebuilding some semblance of normalcy. It's more than just food - it's hope."

Joe leaned forward, his mind racing with the possibilities. "Maria, do you realize what this means for us? Fresh milk for the community. That alone is a game-changer."

Maria nodded, her eyes bright. "I was thinking the same thing. It's not just about having something to drink. It's about nutrition, especially for the most vulnerable among us."

"Exactly," Joe agreed. "Pregnant women, growing children - they'll benefit the most. And it's not just the milk. We're talking about a sustainable food source."

"And don't forget about the chickens," Maria added. "Fresh eggs will be a huge boost to our diet."

Joe stood up and began pacing, his excitement palpable. "You know, this could open up possibilities we haven't even considered yet. What if we could start trading with other settlements?"

Maria's eyebrows shot up. "Trading? You really think that's possible?"

"Why not?" Joe replied. "We've got something valuable now. Milk, eggs, maybe even meat eventually. Other groups might have things we need - medical supplies, tools, seeds for planting. This could be the start of rebuilding some kind of economy."

"It's almost hard to believe," Maria said softly. "After everything we've been through, to think we might be able to start rebuilding..."

Joe sat back down next to her, taking her hand in his. "I know it seems overwhelming, but think about it. With a steady food supply, we can focus on other things. Maybe we can even start thinking about expanding our community, bringing in more people."

Maria squeezed his hand. "You're right. This changes everything. But Joe, we need to be careful. Having something this valuable could make us a target."

Joe nodded gravely. "You're absolutely right. We'll need to step up our security measures. But that's a problem for tomorrow. Right now, let's focus on the good news."

Joe gazed at Maria, his eyes softening with affection. The lines around his eyes crinkled as he smiled, a testament to the years of laughter and worry that had shaped his face. "You know, with all this excitement, I almost forgot how much I missed you while I was gone. It felt like a piece of me was missing."

Maria's lips curved into a gentle smile, her warm brown eyes meeting his. She reached out, her fingers lightly brushing his arm. "I missed you too, Joe. More than I can say. The days feel so much longer without you here."

He stood up, stretching slightly before offering her his hand. His palm was rough and calloused, but his touch was gentle. "Why don't we go somewhere a little more private? I'd like to properly celebrate our reunion. Just you and me, away from all the chaos for a bit."

Maria took his hand, her touch sending a familiar warmth through him. Her fingers intertwined with his, fitting perfectly as always. "I'd like that," she said softly, her voice filled with anticipation and love.

They made their way to their room, their footsteps in sync as they walked. Joe opened the door for Maria, ever the gentleman, before following her inside and closing it behind them. The small space felt like a sanctuary, a place where they could shut out the chaos of the world for a little while. The faint scent of Maria's lavender soap lingered in the air, a comforting reminder of home.

Joe pulled Maria close, wrapping his strong arms around her waist. He breathed in deeply, savoring her familiar scent. "I can't believe how much has changed in such a short time," he murmured, his breath warm against her ear. "It feels like a lifetime ago that I left. Hell, this has been a whole new lifetime since the grid went down."

Maria reached up, running her fingers through his salt-and-pepper hair. She loved the texture, the mix of rough and soft strands. "Some things haven't changed though," she said, her voice barely above a whisper, filled with emotion. "Like how I feel about you. If anything, it's only grown stronger."

Joe's heart swelled at her words, a lump forming in his throat. He leaned in, pressing his forehead against hers, their noses almost touching. "Maria, you're the best thing that's happened to me in this crazy new world. No, in my entire life. You know that, right? You're my anchor, my home."

Instead of answering, Maria closed the distance between them, capturing his lips in a tender kiss. Her lips were soft against his, conveying all the words left unsaid. Joe responded eagerly, his hand moving to cup the back of her head as he poured all his love and relief into the embrace. The kiss deepened, speaking of longing fulfilled and promises renewed.

As they parted, both slightly breathless, Joe cupped Maria's face in his hands. His thumbs gently caressed her cheekbones as he gazed into her eyes. "I love you," he said simply, his voice rough with emotion. The words felt inadequate to express the depth of his feelings, but they were all he had.

Maria's eyes shimmered with unshed tears, the brown depths filled with warmth and affection. "I love you too, Joe. So much. More than I ever thought possible." Her voice quivered slightly, betraying the intensity of her emotions.

They stood there for a moment, savoring the closeness, the quiet intimacy of being together. Joe's arms tightened around Maria, pulling her closer as if he could merge their very beings. In that moment, the worries of their uncertain world faded away, leaving only the warmth of their connection. The room around them seemed to disappear, and for a brief, precious time, it was just the two of them, lost in their own private universe of love and belonging.

CHAPTER TWELVE

J oe stirred as the first hint of dawn crept through the window, casting a soft, ethereal glow across the room. He blinked away the remnants of sleep, his eyes slowly adjusting to the dim light that filtered through the threadbare curtains. Beside him, Maria's warmth radiated through the thin blanket, a comforting presence in the quiet morning. He turned, drinking in the sight of her peaceful face, relaxed in slumber, her features softened by the gentle caress of dawn.

As if sensing his gaze, Maria's eyes fluttered open, long lashes brushing against her cheeks. A sleepy smile curved her lips, transforming her face with a gentle radiance. "Mornin'," she murmured, her voice husky with sleep and tinged with affection.

Joe's heart swelled, a familiar warmth spreading through his chest. He reached out, his calloused fingers brushing a stray lock of hair from her forehead with a tenderness that belied his rugged exterior. "Morning, beautiful," he whispered back, his voice low and intimate in the stillness of the room.

Maria nestled closer, fitting herself against the contours

of his body as if they were two pieces of a puzzle finally coming together. "What time is it?" she asked, her words muffled against his chest.

"Early," Joe replied, wrapping a strong arm around her and pulling her even closer. "Sun's not up yet. We've got a little while before the world comes knocking."

They lay in comfortable silence, savoring the quiet moment that felt stolen from the chaos of their new reality. Joe's fingers traced lazy patterns on Maria's arm, mapping constellations on her skin, while she nuzzled into the crook of his neck, her breath warm and steady against him.

"I wish we could stay like this forever," Maria sighed, her words carrying a wistful longing that echoed Joe's own feelings. Her breath was warm against his skin, a gentle reminder of the intimacy they shared.

Joe pressed a kiss to her forehead, his lips lingering for a moment. "Me too," he admitted, his voice gruff with emotion. "But we've got work to do. The world won't rebuild itself."

Maria propped herself up on an elbow, looking down at him with an intensity that made his breath catch. Her eyes, warm and brown like rich earth after a spring rain, held a mix of love and concern that spoke volumes. "Promise me you'll be careful today," she said, her voice barely above a whisper.

Joe cupped her cheek, his thumb caressing her cheekbone with a gentleness that contrasted with his weathered hands. "Always am, darlin'," he assured her, his eyes never leaving hers. "Got too much to come back to."

Their lips met in a tender kiss, slow and deep, conveying all the words left unspoken between them. Joe's hand slid down Maria's back, pulling her closer, feeling the curve of her spine beneath his palm. She responded eagerly, her fingers threading through his salt-and-pepper hair, nails lightly scraping his scalp in a way that sent shivers down his spine.

As the kiss intensified, their bodies moved together with practiced familiarity, yet each touch felt new and electric. With unhurried movements, hands exploring well-known paths with renewed wonder. They made love slowly, savoring each touch, each sigh, each shared breath. The world outside faded away, leaving only the two of them, connected in the most intimate way.

Afterward, they lay tangled together, hearts racing in tandem, skin flushed and glistening in the growing light. Joe pressed his forehead against Maria's, their noses touching, breaths mingling in the small space between them. "I love you," he murmured, his voice rough with emotion, the words carrying the weight of everything they'd been through together.

Maria's eyes shimmered with unshed tears, a smile playing on her lips. "I love you too, Joe," she whispered back, her voice thick with feeling. "More than life itself. You're my anchor in this storm."

The room gradually lightened as the sun peeked over the horizon, painting the walls with hues of gold and pink. Joe sighed, a mix of contentment and resignation, knowing their moment of peace was coming to an end. He kissed Maria once more, soft and lingering, before reluctantly pulling away.

"I've got to get ready," he said, sitting up and swinging his legs over the side of the bed. The cool air hit his skin, a stark contrast to the warmth they'd shared moments ago.

Maria sat up too, the blanket pooling around her waist as she wrapped her arms around him from behind. She rested her chin on his shoulder, her presence a comforting weight against his back. "Be safe out there, okay?" she murmured, her words carrying a weight of worry and love.

Joe turned his head, meeting her concerned gaze. He saw in her eyes all the fears she tried to hide, all the love she held for him. "I will," he promised solemnly, reaching up to cover her hand with his own. "I'll always come back to you, Maria. Always."

Joe approached the old shed that held their captive, the gravel crunching beneath his boots. The battered shed loomed before him, its weathered exterior a stark reminder of their new reality. He took a deep breath, steeling himself for what lay ahead.

Captain Rodriguez emerged from the shadows, his face etched with fatigue. "Joe," he nodded, extending a hand.

"Cap," Joe replied, clasping the offered hand firmly. "How's our guest?"

Rodriguez's lips tightened. "Stubborn as hell, but we've kept him awake all night. I think he's ready to crack."

They fell into step, moving towards the building's entrance. Joe's voice lowered. "What's our play?"

"Good cop, bad cop?" Rodriguez suggested, a hint of dark humor in his tone. "You've got that whole stern father figure thing going on."

Joe snorted. "And you've got the intimidating military man down pat." He paused, considering. "Let's start easy, build some rapport. Then we'll turn up the heat."

Rodriguez nodded, his expression grim. "We need answers, Joe. Whatever it takes."

They reached the door. Rodriguez pulled it open with a groan. They stepped inside and dismissed the guard that was keeping Jenkins awake.

Rodriguez, then turned to Joe. "Ready?"

Joe squared his shoulders. "Let's do this."

In the center of the shed sat Jenkins, slumped in a chair, his wrists bound. He looked up as they entered, his bloodshot eyes darting between them.

Joe pulled up a chair, its legs scraping against the concrete floor with a harsh grating sound. He sat down deliberately, leaning forward with his elbows resting on his knees, his weathered hands clasped together. "Jenkins, we're not here to hurt you," he said, his voice low and steady. "We just want to talk. That's all."

Jenkins glared at them defiantly, then spat on the ground, a glob of saliva landing inches from Joe's boot. "I ain't tellin' you shit," he snarled, his eyes darting between Joe and Rodriguez.

Rodriguez stepped forward, his face hardening into a mask of stern authority. The faint light glinted off his captain's bars as he loomed over Jenkins. "That's not how this works," he said, his voice cold and unyielding.

"You will talk. It's just a matter of time."

For hours that stretched into an eternity, they alternated between gentle coaxing and stern warnings. Jenkins held firm at first, his jaw clenched and eyes blazing with defiance. But as exhaustion began to set in, his resolve slowly started to crumble. Dark circles formed under his eyes, and his shoulders slumped with fatigue.

Joe offered him a plastic cup of water, his voice softening to a gentle, almost fatherly tone. "Look, we know you're not the big fish here," he said, holding the cup just out of reach. "Help us out, and we'll make sure you're taken care of. You have my word on that."

Jenkins' eyes darted between them, uncertainty creeping into his expression for the first time. He licked his dry lips, considering. "The Colonel..." he began, his voice barely above a whisper. "He'll kill me if I talk. You don't know what he's capable of."

"He can't touch you here," Rodriguez assured him, his tone firm but not unkind. "You're under our protection now."

Finally, like a dam breaking, Jenkins cracked. Words spilled out of him in a torrent, as if he'd been holding them back for an eternity. "The main base," he gasped, "it's in an old theme park near Ocala. They've fortified it, turned the rides into watchtowers. It's like a fortress now."

Joe and Rodriguez exchanged meaningful glances. This was big, potentially game-changing information.

"What about supply routes?" Rodriguez pressed, leaning in closer.

Jenkins nodded wearily, resignation etched on his face. "They use the old highways, move everything at night. Got checkpoints set up every twenty miles or so. Armed to the teeth, those boys."

As Jenkins continued to talk, a clearer picture emerged of the SS-SA's operation. He spoke of internal power struggles, of ambitious men constantly vying for the Colonel's favor, each trying to outdo the others in displays of loyalty and cruelty.

"The Colonel..." Jenkins muttered, shaking his head. "He ain't right in the head no more. Keeps ranting about you, Joe Kelly, says he's gonna be the one to take us down. He is obsessed with you Joe Kelly."

Joe stiffened involuntarily at the mention of his name but fought to keep his face neutral. His mind raced with the implications of this revelation.

"Where are they keeping their weapons?" Rodriguez asked, his voice sharp with urgency.

Jenkins hesitated for a long moment, then sighed

heavily, seeming to deflate. "Got caches all over
the place. Big one's in an abandoned mall outside
Gainesville. Another in a warehouse in Lake City.
They're stockpiling like crazy, getting ready for
something big."

As Jenkins continued to divulge information, spilling
secrets he'd held onto for so long, Joe and Rodriguez
realized they had struck gold. The intelligence they
were gathering could change everything in their fight
against the SS-SA. It was more than they had dared to
hope for when they began this interrogation.

As the interrogation concluded, Joe and Rodriguez
stepped outside the shed, leaving Jenkins slumped in
his chair. The breeze outside was a stark contrast to the
stuffy interior they'd just left.

"Well, that was... illuminating," Joe said, rubbing his
chin thoughtfully.

Rodriguez nodded, his face grim. "More than we
expected. The theme park base, the supply routes, those
weapon caches... This could change everything."

"And the Colonel's obsession with me," Joe added, his
brow furrowing. "That's... unsettling."

They walked a short distance from the shed, speaking
in low voices.

"We need to verify this information," Rodriguez said. "But if it's true, we might finally have a chance to strike back effectively."

Joe agreed, then hesitated. "What about Jenkins?"

Rodriguez's expression hardened. "He's a security risk. We can't just let him go."

Joe was quiet for a moment, then surprised Rodriguez with his next words. "I think we should release him."

"What?" Rodriguez exclaimed, his eyes widening. "Joe, you can't be serious. He knows too much about us, our location-"

Joe held up a hand, cutting him off. "Hear me out, Cap. For one, the Colonel already knows where we are. Jenkins is no longer a threat to us. He can't go back to the SS-SA - Like he said himself, the Colonel would kill him in a heartbeat. And keeping him prisoner indefinitely... beside the fact keeping him a prisoner would be a drain on our manpower guarding him as well as feeding him, that's just not who we are."

Rodriguez opened his mouth to protest, but Joe continued.

"By showing him mercy, we might gain an ally. Someone who knows the inner workings of the SS-SA. And it sends a message about who we are, what we stand for."

Rodriguez frowned, clearly conflicted. "It's a risk, Joe. A big one."

"Life's full of risks these days," Joe replied with a wry smile. "But sometimes, a little faith in humanity can go a long way."

After a long moment, Rodriguez nodded reluctantly. "Alright, we'll do it your way. But I hope you know what you're doing."

"So do I Cap," Joe muttered. "So do I."

Joe and Cap returned to the shed, finding Jenkins slumped in his chair, fast asleep. His chin rested on his chest, soft snores escaping his lips.

"Jenkins," Joe called softly, shaking the man's shoulder. "Wake up, son."

Jenkins startled awake, his eyes wild and unfocused. "No, please," he begged, voice hoarse. "Just let me sleep. I can't... I can't take anymore."

Joe's expression softened. "It's alright, Jenkins. We're not here to interrogate you anymore. We're taking you to a real bed where you can sleep comfortably."

Jenkins blinked, confusion etched across his haggard face. "What?"

"You heard right," Rodriguez added, his tone surprisingly gentle. "When you wake up, you'll be fed and free to go wherever you want."

Jenkins stared at them, disbelief clear in his bloodshot eyes. "You're... you're letting me go? Just like that?" His voice trembled. "This is a trick. You'll shoot me in the back as soon as I leave."

Joe shook his head, meeting Jenkins' gaze steadily. "Hey, I promised you we'd take care of you, and that's just what we'll do. We don't run things around here like the Colonel does."

Jenkins' eyes darted between Joe and Rodriguez, searching for any sign of deception. Finding none, his shoulders sagged, a mix of relief and exhaustion washing over him.

"Come on," Joe said, helping Jenkins to his feet. "Let's get you to that bed."

CHAPTER THIRTEEN

Joe and Rodriguez carefully guided Jenkins out of the shed and across the compound. The exhausted man stumbled between them, his legs weak from hours of sitting.

"Easy there," Joe murmured, supporting Jenkins' weight. "We're almost there."

They led him to a small, windowless room with a simple cot against one wall. Joe lit a candle that cast a soft glow over the sparse furnishings.

"Here we are," Rodriguez said, helping Jenkins sit on the edge of the cot. "It's not much, but it's quiet and it's safe."

Jenkins looked around, his eyes wide with disbelief. "I... I don't understand," he whispered. "Why are you doing this?"

Joe crouched down to meet Jenkins' gaze. "Because it's the right thing to do. Get some rest, son. You're safe here."

Tears welled up in Jenkins' eyes. "Thank you," he choked out. "I don't deserve this kindness, but... thank you."

Joe patted his shoulder gently. "Everyone deserves a second chance. Now lie down and get some sleep."

Jenkins didn't need to be told twice. He was asleep almost as soon as his head hit the pillow, his body finally surrendering to exhaustion.

Joe watched him for a moment, then turned to Rodriguez. "I'll leave him a note. Can you grab some paper and a pen?"

Rodriguez nodded and left, returning moments later with the requested items. Joe scribbled out a quick note, his brow furrowed in concentration.

"What are you writing?" Rodriguez asked, peering over Joe's shoulder.

"Just letting him know he's welcome to join us for food when he wakes up," Joe replied. He added a simple map to the bottom of the note, showing the path from the room to the makeshift mess hall. "And giving him directions so he doesn't get lost."

Joe placed the note on a small table next to the cot, where Jenkins would easily see it when he woke. They took one last look at the sleeping man before quietly exiting the room.

Joe and Rodriguez stepped out of the warehouse,

blinking in the bright sunlight. They had barely taken a few steps when the sound of approaching vehicles caught their attention. Joe tensed at the sound, but his heart leapt as he finally recognized the familiar tan beret on the head of the driver.

"They're back," he said, a grin spreading across his face.

As the small convoy rolled into view, Joe's eyes widened. Behind Jojo's truck trailed a makeshift caravan of livestock. One of the National Guards trucks brought up the rear, packed with supplies.

Joe couldn't contain his excitement. He broke into a run, his feet pounding the dusty ground as he made his way towards his son. Jojo had barely stepped out of the truck when Joe reached him, grabbing him by the shoulders.

"Son, this is... this is incredible!" Joe exclaimed, his voice thick with emotion. He looked over the animals, then back at Jojo, his eyes shining with pride. "Do you realize how important this find is? These animals, they're not just food - they're a future. A way to sustain ourselves long-term."

Jojo nodded, a tired but satisfied smile on his face. "We got lucky, Dad. Found an old farm that had somehow managed to keep going. The family there... they were struggling and being threatened daily. We worked out a trade - we brought them, their animals and supplies to continue their farming but they'll just do it here and share the fruits of their work in exchange for the safety we can provide."

Joe shook his head in amazement. "You did good, son. Real good." He pulled Jojo into a tight hug, his voice dropping to a whisper. "I'm so proud of you."

Jojo returned the embrace, allowing himself a moment to relax in his father's arms. The two men stood there for a long moment, the chaos of unloading the vehicles fading into the background as they shared this quiet moment of connection.

As Joe and Jojo separated from their embrace, an older woman with short grey hair and a determined expression approached them. Jojo placed a hand on her shoulder, guiding her forward.

"Dad, I want you to meet Betty," Jojo said, his voice warm with admiration. "She's the one who really made this happen. Her knowledge of livestock and farming is invaluable."

Joe's eyes lit up as he extended his hand to Betty. "It's a pleasure to meet you, Betty. I can't thank you enough for what you've done here."

Betty shook his hand firmly, a slight blush coloring her cheeks. "It's nothing, really. I'm just glad I could help."

Joe shook his head, his expression serious. "No, it's not nothing. What you've done here... it's given us hope. A real chance at building something sustainable." Without warning, he pulled Betty into a bear hug. "Thank you," he said, his voice thick with emotion.

Betty stiffened for a moment, surprised by the sudden display of affection, but then relaxed and returned the hug. "You're welcome, Mr. Kelly," she said softly.

As they separated, two more women approached the group. One was tall with long dark hair, while the other was shorter with curly locks.

Jojo gestured towards them. "Dad, these are Betty's daughters Pam and Tracy. They are all gonna join our group here and kinda take charge of running our new farm. They were getting harassed by folks at their farm, men trying to take what they had. So I suggested they just move their operations here, where they can be safer and in return we can all share in what they brought."

Joe shook hands with both women, his smile warm and genuine. "It's great to meet you both. Thank you for everything, this is truly a godsend."

Pam tucked a strand of her long dark hair behind her ear and nodded towards a makeshift structure visible in the distance. "We worked through the night to set up a temporary corral for the livestock," she explained. "It'll do for now, but we'll need to reinforce it soon."

Joe squinted in the direction she indicated, impressed by the quick work. "That's a hell of an effort. We'll get a team on strengthening it right away."

"Appreciate that," Pam replied. "Now, about those chickens..."

As if on cue, a cacophony of clucks and squawks erupted from one of the trucks. Joe raised an eyebrow, and Jojo grinned.

"Yeah, we've got quite a few of them," Jojo said. "Figured we should start unloading the coop before they get too riled up."

The group made their way to the truck, where several people were already gathered around a large, wire mesh structure filled with agitated chickens.

"Alright, let's do this carefully," Betty instructed, taking charge of the situation. "We don't want to stress them out any more than necessary."

With slow, deliberate movements, they began lifting the coop from the truck bed. Joe and Jojo took one end, while Pam and Tracy handled the other. The chickens inside fluttered and squawked in protest at the movement.

"Easy does it," Joe muttered, his muscles straining

under the weight. They shuffled towards the area designated for the new coop, a cleared space near the edge of the compound.

As they set the coop down, Betty and Rodriguez quickly moved to secure it, making sure none of the chickens could escape in the transfer.

"Okay, now we need to set up their new home," Tracy said, wiping sweat from her brow. She pointed to a pile of lumber and wire mesh nearby. "We brought materials to build a more permanent structure."

The group worked efficiently, following Tracy's instructions to construct a larger, more secure coop. Joe couldn't help but feel a sense of pride as he watched everyone come together, working towards a common goal.

As the day wore on, the compound buzzed with activity. People from all corners of their community pitched in to help with the new arrivals. Some worked on reinforcing the temporary corral, while others assisted in setting up shelter for the chickens and roosters. The air was filled with the sounds of hammering, sawing, and the occasional moo from the livestock.

Joe stood back for a moment, taking in the scene before him. A smile tugged at the corners of his mouth as he watched the flurry of activity. There was an undeniable energy in the air, a sense of purpose and hope that had been missing for far too long.

"It's something, isn't it?" Jojo said, coming to stand beside his father.

Joe nodded, his eyes still scanning the busy compound. "It sure is, son. This... this is what we've been working towards. A real chance at building something sustainable."

As they watched, Betty's voice rang out, giving instructions on how to properly care for the chickens. A group of eager listeners hung on her every word, their faces a mix of concentration and excitement.

Joe's mind drifted to the recent developments. The livestock acquisition was a game-changer, no doubt about it. It wasn't just about the immediate food source; it was about long-term sustainability. With proper care and management, these animals could provide food, fertilizer, and even trade goods for years to come.

His thoughts then turned to Jenkins and the information he had provided. The intel on the Colonel's operations could prove invaluable in keeping their community safe. They would need to verify and act on that information soon.

Looking out over the bustling compound, Joe felt a

mix of pride and apprehension. They had come so far, accomplished so much, but he knew there were still challenges ahead. Integrating the new members, managing resources, defending against potential threats – these were all hurdles they would need to overcome.

But as he watched his people work together, their faces alight with purpose and hope, Joe felt a surge of confidence. They had faced adversity before and come out stronger. Whatever challenges lay ahead, they would face them together, as a community.

CHAPTER FOURTEEN

As the bustling activity continued around the compound, Captain Rodriguez made his way through the crowd, his eyes scanning for Joe and Jojo. He spotted them standing together near the makeshift armory, observing the scene with a mixture of pride and contemplation. With purposeful strides, he approached the father-son duo, his boots crunching on the gravel beneath his feet.

"Joe, Jojo," Rodriguez called out as he neared them, raising a hand in greeting. "Got a minute? There's something important we need to discuss."

Joe turned, nodding at the Captain, his weathered face etched with curiosity. "What's on your mind, Rodriguez? You look like you've been chewing on something."

Rodriguez glanced around, ensuring they had a modicum of privacy before speaking in a low, serious tone. He leaned in closer, his voice barely above a whisper. "I've been thinking about the information Jenkins provided during his interrogation. I believe we need to act on it quickly before it becomes stale or the situation changes."

Jojo's posture straightened, his military training kicking in as he sensed the gravity of the conversation. His hand instinctively moved to rest on the holster at his hip. "What are you proposing, Captain? You've got that look in your eye."

Rodriguez took a deep breath before continuing, his words measured and deliberate. "I think we should send a small recon group to the theme park near Ocala. It's only about 50 miles from here, and based on what Jenkins told us, it could be a significant outpost for the Colonel's operations. We can't afford to ignore this potential threat."

Joe's brow furrowed as he considered the suggestion, his eyes narrowing as he processed the implications. "That's not too far, but it's still risky. We'd be venturing into unknown territory. What exactly are you thinking? This isn't just a spur-of-the-moment idea, is it?"

"A quick, in-and-out operation," Rodriguez explained, his voice steady and confident as he laid out his plan. "I want to stress that this would be for reconnaissance only. No engagement unless absolutely necessary. We gather intel, assess their defenses, and get out without being detected. It's crucial we know what we're up against."

Jojo nodded slowly, seeing the merit in the plan. His tactical mind was already running through potential scenarios. "A small team would have a better chance of staying undetected. We could get valuable information about their numbers, resources, and maybe even their future plans. It could give us a significant advantage."

Joe rubbed his chin thoughtfully, the stubble rough against his calloused fingers as he weighed the potential benefits against the risks. His eyes darted between Rodriguez and Jojo, gauging their resolve. "It's a bold move, but I can see why you think it's necessary. We can't just sit here and wait for the Colonel to make his next move.

Joe nodded, his decision made. "Alright, Rodriguez. I agree with your plan for the theme park recon. It's a risk, but one we need to take. Knowledge is power, especially in these times. We can't afford to be caught off guard again."

Jojo chimed in, his military training evident in his tactical thinking. "I'm on board too, Captain. But while we're at it, I think we should consider an additional mission. Something that could give us a significant edge."

Rodriguez raised an eyebrow, intrigued by the younger Kelly's suggestion. "What do you have in mind, Jojo? I'm all ears for any strategic advantage we can get."

"Weapon caches," Jojo said, his voice low and determined, leaning in slightly as if sharing a secret. "Jenkins mentioned that the Colonel has several buried caches in the immediate area. I think we should locate and secure them before he has a chance to use them against us."

Joe's eyes lit up at the suggestion, a mix of pride and excitement evident in his expression. "That's not a bad idea, son. It could serve a dual purpose. We'd be killing two birds with one stone, so to speak."

Rodriguez nodded, understanding dawning on his face as he considered the implications. "Acquiring weapons for ourselves while depriving the Colonel of his resources. It's a smart move, Jojo. It could potentially shift the balance of power in our favor."

"Exactly," Jojo confirmed, his confidence growing with the support of the older men. "We focus on the caches closest to us first. It'll strengthen our position and weaken the Colonel's at the same time. Plus, it might give us insight into his overall strategy and supply lines."

Joe stroked his beard thoughtfully, weighing the pros and cons in his mind. "It's riskier than just reconnaissance, but the payoff could be significant. We'd need to be careful though. The Colonel's men might be monitoring those caches, and we can't afford to walk into an ambush."

"We'll need to plan carefully," Rodriguez agreed, his tactical mind already working on potential scenarios. "But I think it's worth the risk. We can't pass up the opportunity to arm ourselves better and hit the Colonel where it hurts. It could be the advantage we need to turn the tide."

Joe looked between Rodriguez and Jojo, a grim smile on his face as he made his decision. "Alright, let's do it. We'll set up two teams - one for the theme park recon and one for locating these weapon caches. We'll need to choose our people carefully for both missions. These operations could make or break our resistance against the Colonel."

Rodriguez nodded, his posture straightening as he shifted into planning mode. "Agreed. We'll set up two separate teams for these operations. I'll personally lead the theme park reconnaissance, while we'll need someone experienced to head up the cache recovery team."

Joe rubbed his chin thoughtfully. "Jojo, I think you should lead the cache recovery team. Your military experience and local knowledge will be crucial for that operation."

Jojo nodded, a determined look in his eyes. "I'm on it,

Dad. I'll start putting together a list of potential team members."

Rodriguez pulled out a worn notebook from his pocket and began jotting down notes. "Alright, let's break this down. For the theme park recon, we'll need a small, agile team. No more than four people. We'll focus on stealth and observation."

"For the cache recovery," Jojo added, "we'll need a slightly larger team. Maybe six to eight people. We'll need muscle for digging and carrying, but also eyes and ears for security."

"What about timing?" Jojo asked. "Do we launch both operations simultaneously, or stagger them?"

Rodriguez considered for a moment. "I think we should stagger them slightly. The recon team will leave first, under the cover of darkness. The cache recovery team can head out at first light. That way, if something goes wrong with the recon, we can abort the cache mission if necessary."

Joe nodded, seeing the logic in the plan. "Agreed. We'll need to brief both teams thoroughly. Everyone needs to understand the importance of these missions and the potential risks involved."

"I'll start drafting the operation plans immediately," Rodriguez said, his pen moving quickly across the

paper. "We'll need to allocate resources carefully
- weapons, vehicles, supplies. We can't leave the
compound understaffed or underdefended either."

Joe listened intently as Rodriguez and Jojo discussed
the details of their upcoming missions. As they finished,
he cleared his throat, drawing their attention.

"These operations are good first steps," Joe began, his
voice low and thoughtful. "But we need to think bigger
picture here. We can't just react to the Colonel - we
need a long-term strategy."

Rodriguez and Jojo exchanged glances, then turned
back to Joe, giving him their full attention.

"What are you thinking, Dad?" Jojo asked.

Joe's eyes narrowed as he laid out his vision. "We need
to slowly tighten the noose around the Colonel. We're
not strong enough for a direct confrontation - not yet.
But we can chip away at his power base."

He paused, making sure his words were sinking in.
"I'm proposing a strategy of attrition. We gradually
reduce his forces, starting with the most vulnerable
targets."

Rodriguez nodded slowly, understanding dawning on
his face. "Like remote supply line checkpoints?"

"Exactly," Joe confirmed. "We hit those first. They're

likely to be lightly defended, and taking them out will disrupt his operations. Plus, there's potential to acquire supplies while we're at it, further weakening his position while strengthening ours."

Jojo's eyes lit up with comprehension. "So we're not just defending ourselves, we're actively working to undermine the Colonel's power structure."

"That's right," Joe said, a grim smile on his face. "It won't be quick, and it won't be easy. But if we're patient and strategic, we can wear him down over time. Make him vulnerable for when we're finally ready to take him on directly."

Joe leaned against a nearby crate, his voice low and intense as he continued outlining his strategy. "These supply line checkpoints are our best bet for early success. They're likely to be in remote locations, which works to our advantage. We can strike quickly and disappear before they know what hit them."

Rodriguez nodded, his tactical mind already churning. "Remote locations mean fewer witnesses, less chance of reinforcements arriving quickly. We could potentially hit and run before they even realize what's happened. It's a classic guerrilla tactic, and it's effective for a reason."

"Exactly," Joe agreed, running a hand through his

graying hair. "And given our current resources, these smaller targets are more feasible than trying to take on one of the Colonel's main strongholds. We need to be smart about this, conserve our strength for when it really counts."

Jojo chimed in, his eyes narrowed in concentration. "Plus, disrupting his supply chain could have far-reaching effects. We cut off fuel, food, ammunition - it'll cripple his operations bit by bit. It's like death by a thousand cuts. Each raid might seem small, but they'll add up quickly."

"Not just practically, but psychologically too," Rodriguez added, his voice grim. "Every successful raid will chip away at the Colonel's image of invincibility. His men will start to doubt, maybe even desert. It could even hamper his recruitment effort as well. Fear and uncertainty can be powerful weapons if we use them right."

Joe nodded, a determined glint in his eye. "That's the idea. We're not just fighting a physical battle here, but a mental one too. We need to show the Colonel and his forces that we're a real threat, that they're not as untouchable as they think. It's about breaking their will as much as their supply lines."

"It'll be a delicate balance," Jojo cautioned, absently fingering the worn edge of his beret. "We need to be effective enough to cause real damage, but not so aggressive that we provoke a full-scale retaliation before we're ready. One wrong move and we could bring the full force of the Colonel's army down on us."

"Agreed," Joe said, his tone serious. "We'll start small, test the waters. Each successful operation will give us more intel, more resources. We'll use those to plan bigger, more impactful strikes. It's a snowball effect - each victory makes the next one easier."

Rodriguez nodded, already jotting down notes in a small, battered notebook. "We'll need to be careful about which checkpoints we target first. We don't want to expose our strategy too early. We should probably mix up our targets, keep them guessing about where we'll strike next."

"Right," Joe confirmed, straightening up from the crate. "We'll need to gather more intelligence, map out his supply routes. But this gives us a framework to start with. It's not much, but it's a plan. And right now, that's what we need most."

Captain Rodriguez's eyes lit up with unbridled enthusiasm as he absorbed the full scope of Joe's strategy. He nodded vigorously, a rare smile breaking across his usually stern features, transforming his face into one of genuine excitement.

"This is exactly what we need, Joe," he said, his voice filled with approval and a hint of admiration. "A long-term plan that plays to our strengths and exploits the Colonel's weaknesses. I'm fully on board with this strategy. It's brilliant in its simplicity and potential effectiveness."

Rodriguez clapped his hands together, his energy palpable and infectious. "Alright, gentlemen. Let's get this show on the road. We've got work to do, and time is of the essence. Every moment we delay is another moment the Colonel strengthens his grip on the region."

Without missing a beat, Rodriguez began barking out orders, his military training kicking into high gear. His voice carried the weight of years of command experience. "Jojo, I need you to start assembling your team for the cache recovery mission. Choose your people carefully - we need a mix of strength and stealth. Look for those who can think on their feet and adapt to unexpected situations."

He turned to Joe, his voice crisp and authoritative, but tinged with respect for the older man's experience. "Joe, can you gather our best scouts? We need detailed intel on the Colonel's supply routes and checkpoint locations. The more information we have, the better we can plan our strikes. Pay special attention to any patterns or vulnerabilities we might exploit."

Rodriguez himself moved with purpose, heading towards the makeshift command center, his stride purposeful and determined. "I'll start drafting detailed operation plans for both the theme park recon and our first supply line raid. We'll need to coordinate our resources carefully, making sure we're not stretching ourselves too thin."

As the three men dispersed to their tasks, there was a palpable sense of anticipation in the air, electric and invigorating. The compound buzzed with activity as word spread of the upcoming missions. People moved with renewed purpose, a spark of hope igniting in their eyes, replacing the dull resignation that had settled over the community in recent weeks.

For the first time since the Colonel's rise to power, it felt like they were taking control of their own destiny. The tide was turning, slowly but surely, against the tyrannical rule of the Colonel. There was a sense that this could be the beginning of something momentous, a chance to reclaim their freedom and build a better future.

CHAPTER FIFTEEN

Maria spotted Paulette sitting alone by the lake, her gaze fixed on the rippling water. Something about Paulette's hunched shoulders and distant expression tugged at Maria's heart. The older woman looked lost in thought, her fingers absently tracing patterns in the dirt beside her. Taking a deep breath, Maria approached, her footsteps crunching softly on the gravel path. The late afternoon sun cast long shadows across the ground, and a cool breeze rustled through the nearby trees, carrying with it the scent of pine and damp earth.

"Mind if I join you?" Maria asked gently, her voice barely above a whisper. She tucked a stray strand of hair behind her ear, suddenly feeling a bit nervous about intruding on Paulette's solitude.

Paulette looked up, startled. Her eyes were red-rimmed, as if she'd been crying, and there was a vulnerability in her expression that Maria had never seen before. "Oh, Maria. I didn't hear you coming." She gestured to the empty space beside her, brushing away a few fallen leaves with a trembling hand. "Please, sit. I could use some company, I think."

Maria settled down, feeling the coolness of the ground seep through her jeans. She let the silence stretch between them for a moment, listening to the soft lapping of the water against the shore and the distant call of a bird. "Is everything alright? You seem... preoccupied," she finally ventured, her tone laced with concern. She watched Paulette's profile, noticing the way the fading sunlight highlighted the lines of worry etched around her eyes and mouth.

Paulette sighed heavily, her fingers fidgeting with a loose thread on her sleeve. She seemed to be struggling with whether to open up or not, her internal conflict visible in the way she bit her lower lip and furrowed her brow. "I... I've been thinking about Adam," she admitted reluctantly, her voice barely audible over the gentle rustling of leaves.

"Adam?" Maria prompted softly, tilting her head in curiosity.

"Yeah. It's... complicated." Paulette's voice wavered, thick with emotion. She swallowed hard before continuing, her gaze fixed on the horizon where the sun was beginning to dip below the tree line. "You already know, he's the reason my marriage to Joe fell apart. But there's so much more to it than that."

Maria's eyebrows rose, but she remained silent, allowing Paulette to continue. She sensed that the other woman needed to unburden herself, and she was determined to be a supportive listener.

"I was unhappy and selfish, I was looking for excitement in my life. That's when I met Adam and we began our affair," Paulette admitted, her voice barely above a whisper. The words seemed to pain her as she spoke them, each syllable heavy with regret. "I left Joe and the kids for him. God, what was I thinking?" She shook her head, eyes glistening with unshed tears. Her hands clenched into fists in her lap, knuckles turning white with the force of her grip.

"That must have been a difficult time," Maria offered, her tone free of judgment. She resisted the urge to reach out and comfort Paulette, sensing that the other woman wasn't quite ready for that. Instead, she picked up a small pebble and rolled it between her fingers, giving Paulette a moment to collect herself.

Paulette nodded, a bitter smile twisting her lips. "The worst part is, Adam left me not long after. I threw away everything for a man who didn't even want me in the end. And now, seeing him again..." She trailed off, struggling to find the words to express the turmoil of emotions she was experiencing. A lone tear escaped, tracing a silvery path down her cheek.

"It's stirring up old feelings?" Maria guessed, her voice gentle and understanding. She watched a pair of ducks glide across the lake's surface, leaving ripples in their wake.

"Yes, but also pain and so much guilt. I hurt Joe so badly. The kids, too." Paulette's voice cracked, and another tear slid down her cheek. She brushed it away impatiently, leaving a smudge of dirt on her face. "And now, with everything that's happened, I find myself drawn to Adam all over again. He seems to be interested in me as well. How can I say this, we actually had an intimate encounter the other day. A physical encounter. But I'm so terrified of causing more pain. Haven't I done enough damage already?"

Maria listened attentively, finally offering a supportive hand on Paulette's arm. She could feel the tension in the other woman's muscles, the way she seemed to be holding herself together through sheer force of will. "It's a complex situation," she acknowledged, choosing her words carefully. "But we're all trying to navigate this new world, aren't we? Maybe this is a chance for healing, for all of you. Sometimes, life gives us second chances when we least expect them."

Paulette looked at her, hope and doubt warring in her eyes. The late afternoon sun caught the silver strands in her hair, giving her an almost ethereal appearance. A flock of birds flew overhead, their calls echoing across the water. "Do you really think so? After everything

I've done? How can I even begin to make things right?"

"We've all made mistakes, Paulette," Maria said softly, her own eyes clouding with memories. "Hell, I can certainly attest to that, remember who I was married to. The things I endured, the choices I made... What matters is how we choose to move forward. You can't change the past, but you can shape your future. It's never too late to try and make amends, to be better."

Paulette nodded slowly, absorbing Maria's words. She took a deep breath, as if a weight had been lifted from her shoulders. The tension in her body seemed to ease slightly, and she unclenched her fists, flexing her fingers. "Thank you for listening," she said, a small smile tugging at her lips. "It feels good to finally talk about this. I've been carrying it around for so long, I forgot how heavy it was."

Maria returned the smile, feeling a new understanding blossom between them. The air seemed lighter somehow, filled with possibility. The setting sun painted the sky in brilliant hues of orange and pink, reflecting off the lake's surface. "Anytime, Paulette. We're all in this together now. And who knows? Maybe this new world is giving us all a chance to start over, to be the people we always wanted to be. I almost feel guilty with all the misery all around these days, I have found so much joy finding Joe. Like I said, all things happen for a reason Paulette. Maybe there's a reason you've found Adam again."

CHAPTER SIXTEEN

The Colonel stood at the window of his makeshift command center, his piercing blue eyes scanning the horizon. The setting sun cast long shadows across the landscape, painting the world in shades of orange and red. He drummed his fingers on the windowsill, his mind racing with calculations and possibilities.

"Damn it all," he muttered under his breath. "I'm tired of waiting for these fools to find a new base. We're sitting ducks here."

He turned abruptly, his white linen suit a stark contrast to the dimly lit room. Maps and charts littered every available surface, each one marked with scribbled notes and circled locations.

"Pernell!" he barked, his voice carrying easily through the thin walls.

Pernell with a nervous demeanor scurried into the room, nearly tripping over his own feet. "Yes, Colonel?"

The Colonel's eyes narrowed. "Get me everything we have on Dunnellon. Now."

As Pernell rushed to comply, the Colonel paced the room, his footsteps echoing in the silence. He paused at a large map of Florida, tracing his finger along the path of two rivers.

"The Withlacoochee and Rainbow Rivers," he mused aloud. "Now that's an opportunity if I ever saw one."

Pernell returned, arms laden with papers and folders. The Colonel snatched them from him, spreading them across his desk with feverish energy.

"Look here," he said, jabbing his finger at a point on the map. "Dunnellon. It's perfect. We'd have access to not one, but two major waterways. Think of the possibilities, Pernell. Improved mobility, easier supply routes..."

His voice trailed off as he lost himself in thought, envisioning the potential of this new location. Pernell stood awkwardly, unsure if he was dismissed or not.

The Colonel's head snapped up, his eyes gleaming with a mixture of excitement and calculation. "We're moving. Start making preparations immediately. I want a detailed plan on my desk by morning. And Bobby?"

"Yes, Colonel?"

"Not a word of this to anyone outside our inner circle. Understood?"

Pernell nodded vigorously and hurried out of the room. The Colonel turned back to the window, a small smile playing on his lips. In the fading light, he could almost see the future he was crafting, a future where the Sunshine State Sovereign Alliance would reign supreme.

The sun had barely peeked over the horizon when the SS-SA members gathered in the clearing, their faces etched with a mixture of excitement and trepidation. Murmurs of anticipation rippled through the crowd as they waited, eyes fixed on the makeshift stage constructed from salvaged lumber and draped with faded American flags. The air was thick with tension and the earthy scent of damp grass.

Suddenly, the crowd fell silent, as if a switch had been flipped. The Colonel strode in, his white suit immaculate despite the dusty surroundings, every step purposeful and measured. He ascended the platform with the grace of a seasoned performer, pausing at the top to survey his followers before speaking. His piercing blue eyes seemed to make contact with each person in the crowd.

"My friends," he began, his voice soft yet commanding, carrying easily across the hushed gathering. "We've weathered storms together, faced hunger and fear. We've endured sleepless nights and days of uncertainty. But we're still standing, aren't we? Still fighting for a better tomorrow."

A chorus of agreement rose from the crowd, punctuated by shouts of affirmation and nods of determination.

"Now, I bring you news that will shape our destiny," the Colonel continued, his southern drawl more pronounced with emotion. "We're moving to Dunnellon." He paused, letting the announcement sink in, watching as confusion turned to curiosity on the faces before him. "Two rivers, my friends. The Withlacoochee and the Rainbow. Think of the possibilities that lie before us in such a place."

He paced the stage with measured steps, gesturing expansively to paint a picture with his words. "Water for crops, fish to nourish our bodies and spirits. Water for transport, to connect us to the world beyond. Water for power, to light our homes and fuel our ambitions. It's the key to our future, the lifeblood of the new world we'll build together. Dunnellon will be our new capitol city."

The Colonel's eyes narrowed suddenly, his voice dropping to a growl that sent a shiver through the crowd. "But make no mistake, there are those who would see us fail. There is a group of people that would very much like to stop us from realizing our grand vision. Joe Kelly and his ragtag band of malcontents would like nothing more than to see us annihilated, ground into the dust of this broken world. Joe Kelly, that self-righteous fool, would like nothing more than to rule over you like a king, imposing his narrow-minded will on us all."

Boos and jeers erupted from the crowd, faces contorting with anger at the mention of their enemy.

"They're power-hungry fools," he spat, his disgust palpable. "They see only the opportunity for power over the weak, for petty tyranny. We, my friends, we see something far greater. We see the foundation of an empire, a beacon of hope in this dark new world."

He raised his voice, passion blazing in his eyes as he leaned forward, gripping the edges of the makeshift podium. "From Dunnellon, we'll expand. North to Gainesville, where knowledge once flourished. To Jacksonville, gateway to the Atlantic. To Tallahassee, where we'll reclaim the seat of power. East to Daytona, where the sun rises over endless possibilities. West to the Gulf, rich with resources waiting to be tapped. South to Palm Beach, to Miami, and beyond to the Keys. We'll bring order to this chaos, piece by piece, county by county, until the Sunshine State Sovereign Alliance controls it all!"

Cheers echoed through the clearing, growing in volume until they seemed to shake the very ground beneath their feet.

"But it won't be easy," the Colonel cautioned, his tone softening as he held up a hand to quiet the crowd. "The road ahead is long and fraught with danger. We'll need every one of you. Your strength to build our new home. Your skills to forge a new society. Your unwavering loyalty in the face of adversity. I ask you now, are you with me? Will you stand beside me as we march towards our glorious future?"

The response was deafening, a wall of sound that seemed to push back the encroaching wilderness. Fists pumped the air as the crowd chanted with one voice, "SS-SA! SS-SA! SS-SA!"

The Colonel raised his hands, a benevolent smile spreading across his face as he basked in the adoration of his followers. "Then let's move out, my friends. Our future awaits in Dunnellon. Together, we'll build a paradise from the ashes of the old world."

As the Colonel's impassioned speech echoed through the clearing, four shadowy figures crouched low in the dense underbrush at the edge of the SS-SA encampment. Rodriguez, the leader of the recon team, pressed a finger to his lips, signaling for silence as they strained to catch every word. The humid Florida air clung to their skin, mosquitoes buzzing incessantly around them, but they remained motionless, focused entirely on their mission.

The men exchanged meaningful glances as the Colonel revealed his plans for Dunnellon. Rodriguez's eyes widened at the mention of the two rivers, recognizing the strategic importance immediately. He scribbled furiously in a small notebook, his hand barely visible in the pre-dawn gloom. The weight of this information settled heavily on his shoulders, understanding all too well the implications for their own community.

Beside him, Martinez shifted uncomfortably, leaves rustling softly beneath him. Rodriguez shot him a warning look, and Martinez froze, hardly daring to breathe. The cheers of the crowd masked any small sounds they made, but they couldn't risk detection now. The consequences of discovery would be dire, and they all knew it.

As the Colonel's speech reached its crescendo, Rodriguez motioned for his team to start pulling back. They crawled backward on their bellies, inch by agonizing inch, until they were far enough from the camp to risk standing. Every movement was calculated, every sound scrutinized as they retreated from the enemy's territory.

"Move," Rodriguez whispered urgently, his voice barely audible over the continued chanting from the SS-SA gathering. "We need to get this intel back to Joe

ASAP." The gravity of their discovery weighed heavily in his tone, spurring his team to action.

The four men melted into the shadows of the forest, their movements swift and silent. Years of training and experience guided their steps as they navigated the treacherous terrain, always alert for any sign of pursuit. The forest was alive with sounds, providing cover for their retreat but also masking potential threats.

After what felt like hours but was likely only minutes, they reached the hidden spot where they'd stashed their gear and transportation. Rodriguez did a quick headcount, ensuring all his men were accounted for before they mounted up. The familiar weight of their packs and weapons provided a small measure of comfort in this uncertain territory.

"Alright, boys," he said, his voice low but intense. "We've got vital information. Joe needs to know about this Dunnellon plan immediately. It could change everything." The men nodded grimly, understanding the gravity of their mission. As they set off into morning light, each of them silently vowed to see this crucial intelligence safely delivered, no matter the cost.

As the Colonel's speech concluded, a wave of excitement rippled through the crowd. Followers clapped each other on the back, their faces alight with renewed purpose. The air buzzed with enthusiasm, conversations erupting in every corner of the camp. The energy was palpable, as if the Colonel's words had breathed new life into the weary souls gathered before him. Laughter and cheers punctuated the night, a stark contrast to the somber mood that had prevailed just hours before.

"Did you hear that? We're heading to Dunnellon!" A young woman exclaimed, her eyes shining with a mixture of hope and anticipation. "Finally, a place we can call home! A real chance to build something lasting!" She clutched her partner's arm, practically bouncing with excitement as she spoke.

"The Colonel's vision is incredible," an older man nodded sagely, stroking his salt-and-pepper beard. "Two rivers, defensible position - it's perfect! It's like he's found the Garden of Eden in this godforsaken wasteland." He paused, his weathered face softening as he added, "Reminds me of the stories my granddaddy used to tell about the pioneers."

Groups began to form, discussing their roles in this grand plan with animated gestures and raised voices. Carpenters and builders huddled together, already sketching rough plans in the dirt with sticks and pebbles. Some argued over the best materials to use, while others debated the merits of various architectural styles. Farmers debated the best crops for the region, their hands mimicking the act of sowing seeds. A heated discussion broke out over whether to prioritize quick-growing vegetables or invest in long-term fruit orchards. Those with military experience talked strategy, using makeshift models to demonstrate potential defensive positions. They moved rocks and twigs around, simulating various scenarios and countermeasures.

However, not everyone shared in the jubilation. In the shadows cast by the flickering campfires, doubts began to surface like unwelcome guests at a celebration. The firelight danced across worried faces, highlighting the lines of concern etched deep into their skin.

"Another move?" A weary mother whispered to her husband, her voice tinged with exhaustion and worry. "How many times are we going to uproot ourselves? The children are barely over the last journey." She glanced at their sleeping kids, huddled together in a makeshift bed of blankets and coats.

"Dunnellon's not exactly empty," a former sheriff muttered to his companion, his weathered face creased with concern. "What happens to the folks already living there? Are we really prepared to fight for this 'promised land'?" His hand unconsciously moved to the empty holster at his hip, a habit from a life long past.

These whispers of doubt were quickly hushed, drowned out by the louder voices of true believers. But the seeds of uncertainty had been planted, taking root in the minds of a few like stubborn weeds in a well-tended garden. Those with misgivings exchanged meaningful glances, silently acknowledging their shared concerns.

Despite these hidden misgivings, the camp burst into action with an almost manic energy. The Colonel's words had lit a fire under them all, spurring them into a flurry of activity. Tents were quickly dismantled, the sound of canvas flapping and poles clanking filling the air. Children, awakened by the commotion, were quickly put to work rolling sleeping bags and gathering personal belongings. Supplies were packed with practiced efficiency, each item carefully accounted for and stowed. Those with scouting experience gathered around worn maps, their fingers tracing possible routes as they plotted the safest path to their new promised land. They argued over the merits of different routes, weighing the risks of exposure against the need for water and potential scavenging opportunities.

A group of the Colonel's most trusted men huddled

around him, receiving more detailed instructions in hushed tones. They nodded solemnly, their faces set with determination, then dispersed to oversee various aspects of the move like generals commanding their troops. Each carried themselves with an air of importance, puffed up by their proximity to power.

"I want an advance team ready to move out within the hour," one barked, his voice carrying authority. "We need eyes on Dunnellon before the main group arrives. Scout the area, assess any potential threats, and report back immediately. And for God's sake, be discreet. We don't want to tip our hand too soon."

"Medical supplies are our priority," another called out, her voice rising above the din. "We can't afford to lose anyone on this journey. Double-check our inventory and make sure we're prepared for any emergencies. I want extra antibiotics and bandages packed, just in case." She turned to a young assistant, adding in a lower voice, "And see if you can scrounge up any more pain meds. We're running dangerously low."

The camp, so recently filled with celebration, now hummed with purposeful activity. It was like watching a giant machine spring to life, each person a cog working in perfect harmony. Vehicles were loaded, weapons were distributed, and provisions were carefully rationed. The air was thick with a mixture of dust, sweat, and anticipation. The Colonel stood at its center, a small smile playing on his lips as he watched his vision begin to unfold. His eyes gleamed with satisfaction, reflecting the firelight and something deeper - a hunger for power that seemed to grow with each passing moment. He straightened his impeccable white suit, a beacon of order amidst the controlled chaos, and began to make his rounds, offering words of encouragement and gentle guidance to his flock.

CHAPTER SEVENTEEN

The distant rumble of engines caught Joe's attention, piercing through the calm. He squinted into the afternoon light, his weathered hand shielding his eyes as he spotted a cloud of dust billowing on the horizon. As the vehicles drew closer, their outlines sharpening against the darkening sky, he recognized Rodriguez's team returning from their scouting mission. A mixture of anticipation and unease settled in his gut. "Open the gates!" Joe bellowed, his gruff voice carrying across the compound with an authority honed by years of leadership. The sentries scrambled to obey, the creaking of metal echoing through the air.

The battered trucks rolled in, their tires kicking up gravel and sending small stones skittering across the packed earth. Rodriguez, his face etched with urgency and fatigue, leapt from the lead vehicle before it came to a full stop, his boots hitting the ground with a thud.

"Kelly! We need to talk. Now." Rodriguez's eyes darted around the compound, his voice low and tense, laden with the weight of whatever news he carried.

Joe nodded, instantly sensing the gravity of the

situation. His jaw set in a grim line as he replied, "My office. Five minutes." He turned on his heel, already mentally preparing for whatever storm was brewing on the horizon.

Inside the makeshift command center, a repurposed shipping container that smelled of sweat and metal, Joe settled behind his desk. The worn leather of his chair creaked as Rodriguez paced the room, his restless energy palpable. The rest of the team filed in, their expressions grim and bodies tense, filling the small space with an air of foreboding.

"Spill it, Rodriguez. What'd you find out there?" Joe's voice was steady, but there was an edge to it that betrayed his concern.

Rodriguez took a deep breath, his chest expanding as if he were preparing to dive into murky waters. "It's the Colonel. He's on the move." The words hung in the air, heavy with implication.

Joe leaned forward, his calloused hands flat on the desk, his jaw tightening. "Where to?" he asked, though a part of him already dreaded the answer.

"Dunnellon. He's gathered a sizable force. They're calling it the 'Promised Land'." Rodriguez's words were clipped, each one carrying the weight of their potential consequences.

One of Rodriguez's team members, a former cop named Martinez with a scar running along his jawline, chimed in. His voice was gruff, tinged with a mix of disgust and worry. "It's not just about finding a new home, Joe. The Colonel's got bigger plans. This ain't no simple relocation."

Rodriguez nodded, his eyes meeting Joe's. "He's talking about expanding his control across Florida. Dunnellon's just the start. It's like he's building his own little empire out there."

Joe's brow furrowed, deep lines etching themselves into his forehead. "What kind of numbers are we looking at?" He dreaded the answer, but knew he needed every scrap of information they could gather.

"At least a few hundred," Rodriguez replied, his voice tight. "But he's charismatic, drawing more people in every day. They see him as some kind of savior. It's like he's got them under a spell or something."

Martinez snorted, a sound of derision and barely contained anger. "A savior with a mean streak. We saw how he deals with dissenters. It ain't pretty. The man's got a cruel streak a mile wide."

Joe stood, his chair scraping against the floor as he walked to the large map pinned on the wall. It was worn and creased, marked with various notations and symbols. He traced the route to Dunnellon with his finger, feeling the texture of the paper beneath his skin. "Tell me about their defenses, their supplies. I want to know everything you saw, everything you heard."

As Rodriguez began to detail the Colonel's preparations, Joe's mind raced, processing the information and its implications. The threat was clear, looming like a storm on the horizon, but so were the opportunities. They had information the Colonel didn't know they possessed. It was time to plan their next move, to turn this potential disaster into an advantage. Joe felt the familiar rush of adrenaline, the challenge of outmaneuvering a dangerous opponent. It was time to show the Colonel that he wasn't the only one who could play this game.

Joe rubbed his chin, the stubble rough against his palm, a mix of concern and grudging respect crossing his weathered face. "Gotta hand it to the Colonel, he knows how to pick 'em. Dunnellon's a smart choice. The man's always had an eye for strategy."

Jojo, who had been silently absorbing the information from his corner of the room, his posture tense and alert, nodded in agreement. His military training was evident in the way he analyzed the situation. "Strategic location, access to water, defensible terrain. He's not just thinking about survival, he's planning for expansion.

It's a textbook move for establishing a power base."

"Exactly," Joe said, turning to face the group, his eyes scanning each face in the room. "The Colonel's always been a step ahead. But this time, we might have an edge. We've got something he doesn't expect."

Jojo stepped closer to the map, his eyes scanning the familiar landscape with the intensity of a predator sizing up its territory. "Dad, remember those fishing trips we used to take? Withlacoochee and Rainbow rivers? All those summers we spent out there?"

A faint smile tugged at Joe's lips, a momentary softening of his stern expression as memories flooded back. "How could I forget? Spent half my life on those waters. Feels like another lifetime now."

"We know that area like the back of our hands," Jojo continued, his voice gaining enthusiasm, the tactical wheels in his mind clearly turning. "Every bend in the river, every hidden cove. The sandbars, the deep pools, the best spots for ambush..."

Joe's eyes lit up with understanding, the spark of a plan igniting in his mind. "The local terrain, the backroads, the best spots for cover... We've got a home-field advantage he can't match."

"And the weak points," Jojo added, his tone becoming more urgent. "We've got intel the Colonel doesn't even know exists. The old flood plains, the seasonal changes in the river levels, the areas prone to sinkholes..."

Joe turned to Rodriguez, a new energy in his movements. "What about the old phosphate mines? Are they using those? They could be a game-changer."

Rodriguez shook his head, his brow furrowed in concentration as he recalled what they'd seen. "Not that we could see. Looks like they're focusing on the town itself. The mines seem to be off their radar."

"That's our in," Joe said, his mind already formulating a plan, the possibilities unfolding before him like a map. "Those mines are a maze of tunnels and caverns. Perfect for moving unseen, for staging supplies, for launching surprise attacks."

Joe's eyes gleamed with a mix of nostalgia and determination as he continued, "And as far as the river is concerned, Jojo and I have been up and down the Withlacoochee from Dunnellon to Lake Rousseau which leads right to the Gulf and back towards the south. We know that terrain like the back of our hands."

Jojo nodded, a hint of a smile playing at the corners of his mouth. "Every bend, every shallow, every deep pool. We've fished it, swam it, camped along its banks."

"Remember that hidden cove just past the old railroad bridge?" Joe asked, his voice taking on a wistful tone.

"Perfect spot for laying low, watching river traffic without being seen."

"And the limestone outcroppings near the confluence with Rainbow River," Jojo added, his military training evident in the way he assessed the tactical advantages. "Natural high ground, excellent vantage point for surveillance."

Joe traced his finger along the river's path on the map. "The seasonal flooding patterns, the changes in current... We know when that river's going to be our friend and when it might turn against us."

Rodriguez leaned in, his interest piqued. "What about access points? Places where we could move in and out undetected?"

"Plenty of em'," Joe replied, his confidence growing. "There's an old boat ramp about a mile south of town, overgrown now. Most folks have forgotten it exists. And the network of small creeks feeding into the main river? They're like secret highways if you know how to navigate them."

Jojo stepped closer to the map, pointing out specific locations. "All of these offshoots, small creeks that come off the river are perfect spots to hide some weapons caches. We're gonna have to build our own Navy. We're gonna have to get boats, lot's of boats to move up and down those rivers and they're gonna need motors. No way you can row against those currents."

Joe nodded approvingly. "Good thinking, son. Old outboards should have survived the EMP just fine, but you're right we are indeed going to need as many as we can get our hands on."

The room buzzed with a new energy as the team began to see the possibilities unfolding before them. Their intimate knowledge of the river and surrounding terrain was more than just fond memories of fishing trips past - it was a strategic advantage that could tip the scales in their favor against the Colonel's forces.

Jojo nodded, already on the same wavelength, his military training meshing seamlessly with his father's experience. "And there's that old railway bridge over the Withlacoochee. Abandoned now, but it could be a key crossing point if we need it. Most people have forgotten it exists, but it should still be solid enough to use."

Joe's expression grew serious, the weight of the situation settling on his shoulders like a familiar burden. "We've got the lay of the land, boys. Now we need to figure out how to use it. The Colonel thinks he's got the upper hand, but we're about to change the game. It's time to show him what real strategy looks like."

CHAPTER EIGHTEEN

As the Colonel's forces began to tighten their grip on Dunnellon, unforeseen complications started to bubble beneath the surface. The relocation of his troops from their previous strongholds had stirred up resentment and discontent among the ranks, creating a volatile atmosphere that threatened to undermine the entire operation.

"This ain't what I signed up for," grumbled a burly soldier named Hank, his voice low but filled with frustration as he sat cleaning his rifle. "We had a good thing going back in Ocala. Why'd we have to uproot everything? Feels like we're chasing ghosts out here."

His companion, a wiry man called Slim, nodded in agreement, spitting a wad of tobacco onto the dusty ground. "Yeah, and now we're stretched thin. Feels like we're sittin' ducks out here. One good push from the locals and we could be in real trouble."

The whispers of dissent spread through the camp like wildfire, growing louder with each passing day. Soldiers huddled in small groups, their conversations hushed but intense, eyes darting around suspiciously.

The Colonel's inner circle struggled to maintain order, their usual tactics of intimidation less effective on their own battle-hardened troops who had seen too much and endured too many hardships to be easily cowed.

Meanwhile, the local survivors of Dunnellon were proving to be a tougher nut to crack than anticipated. The Colonel's scouts had reported a docile population, ripe for subjugation. Instead, they found a community hardened by post-apocalyptic living, fiercely protective of their independence and well-versed in the art of survival against all odds.

"You think you can just waltz in here and take over?" spat an elderly woman, her weathered face contorted with defiance as she stood before a group of the Colonel's men. Her gnarled hands gripped a gnarled walking stick, brandishing it like a weapon. "We've been surviving just fine without your 'protection.' We've faced worse than you lot, and we're still standing. You'd do well to remember that."

The soldiers shifted uncomfortably, caught off guard by the unexpected resistance. They were used to dealing with desperate, malleable survivors, not this brand of stubborn self-reliance. The fire in the old woman's eyes spoke of a determination that couldn't be easily extinguished, and it was clear she wasn't alone in her sentiments.

As night fell, a series of small but coordinated acts of sabotage struck the Colonel's outposts. Supply caches were found emptied, their contents spirited away into the darkness. Vehicles were mysteriously disabled, fuel lines cut and engines sabotaged beyond easy repair. The local resistance moved like ghosts, striking and vanishing before the Colonel's forces could mount an effective response, leaving confusion and frustration in their wake.

In his command cabin, the Colonel paced furiously, his carefully crafted image of calm control slipping with each step. Beads of sweat formed on his brow, his pristine white suit now rumpled and stained. "How is this happening?" he demanded, rounding on his lieutenants with blazing eyes. "You assured me this town was ripe for the taking! Instead, we're being made fools of by a bunch of backwater hicks!"

One of his men, a man named Jackson, struggled to find an explanation, his usual confidence shaken. "Sir, it seems we underestimated the locals. They know the terrain better than we do, and they're using it to their advantage. Every alley, every hidden path is a potential ambush site. We're fighting blind out here."

The Colonel's eyes narrowed dangerously, a vein pulsing at his temple. "Then it's time we showed them the consequences of defiance. Prepare for a show of force. We'll make an example of these... resistors. Burn out their hiding spots if we have to. Let's see how brave they are when their precious town is going up in flames."

But as he turned to issue his orders, a commotion erupted outside the cabin. The sounds of shouting and scuffling filled the air, growing louder by the second. The clash of metal on metal and the unmistakable pop of gunfire cut through the night, shattering the Colonel's illusion of control. Whatever was happening out there, it was clear that the situation in Dunnellon had just escalated beyond anyone's expectations.

The Colonel burst from his cabin, his once-pristine white suit now disheveled and stained with sweat, the fabric clinging uncomfortably to his lean frame. Before he could fully assess the chaos erupting around him, a group of shadowy figures emerged from the darkness, their faces obscured by makeshift masks fashioned from scraps of cloth and bits of scavenged materials.

"Now!" one of them shouted, their voice muffled but urgent, and they rushed at the Colonel from all sides, feet pounding against the dry Florida earth.

For a moment, it seemed the Colonel would be overwhelmed by the sheer number of attackers converging on him. But as the first assailant reached him, something changed in the older man's demeanor.

His eyes hardened, taking on a steely glint, and a cruel smile twisted his thin lips, transforming his genteel façade into something far more sinister.

With surprising speed and agility that belied his years, the Colonel ducked under a wild swing and drove his fist into his assailant's solar plexus with pinpoint accuracy. The man crumpled with a wheeze, gasping for air. Another resistor lunged forward, brandishing a rusty pipe that glinted dully in the moonlight. The Colonel sidestepped with fluid grace, grabbed the man's wrist in an iron grip, and used his momentum to send him sprawling face-first into the dirt.

"Is this the best you can muster?" the Colonel taunted, his voice dripping with disdain and barely concealed amusement. "I expected more from the brave resistors of Dunnellon."

He moved with deadly precision, each strike calculated and brutally effective, his body remembering skills honed long ago. His men, initially caught off guard by the sudden attack, now rushed to assist their leader, quickly subduing the remaining attackers with a flurry of punches, kicks, and the occasional gunshot.

Within minutes, the ambush had been thoroughly crushed, leaving a scene of groaning bodies and scattered weapons. The Colonel stood amid his would-be assassins, barely winded, straightening his jacket with a contemptuous flick of his wrists. He surveyed the carnage around him with a mixture of satisfaction and disappointment.

"Bring them to the square," he ordered, his voice cold and filled with menace, carrying easily over the sounds of the aftermath. "It's time we remind these people of the natural order of things. Let them see what happens to those who dare to challenge my authority."

The resistors were roughly hauled to their feet by the Colonel's men, some barely conscious, others defiant even in defeat. They were marched through the streets of Dunnellon, a grim procession that drew curious and fearful onlookers from their homes. Word spread quickly through the small town, traveling on whispered voices and hurried footsteps, and soon a crowd had gathered in the town square, their faces a mixture of fear, anger, and morbid curiosity.

The Colonel strode to the center of the square, his white suit now a stark contrast to the grime and desperation surrounding him. The crowd parted before him, no one daring to meet his piercing gaze. He pulled a gleaming revolver from his holster, its polished surface catching the light of the moon. With practiced ease, he checked the cylinder, the soft click of metal on metal audible in the tense silence.

"People of Dunnellon," he began, his voice carrying

across the hushed crowd with the practiced cadence of a seasoned orator. "It seems some among you have forgotten their place in this new world. They cling to outdated notions of freedom and rebellion, failing to understand that such luxuries no longer exist. Allow me to offer a reminder of the consequences of defiance."

Without warning, he raised the gun and fired. The sharp crack of the shot echoed through the square, followed by a collective gasp from the onlookers. The first resistor fell, a look of shock frozen on his face as crimson bloomed across his chest. The crowd recoiled, but the Colonel continued, his face an impassive mask as he methodically executed each captured attacker with a single, well-placed shot.

The Colonel placed his revolver back in its holster with a practiced motion, his fingers lingering for a moment on the worn grip. He meticulously straightened his pristine white suit, brushing away an imaginary speck of dust from his lapel. With an air of calculated nonchalance, he turned to face the crowd that stood in stunned silence, still reeling from the brutal executions they had just witnessed. The Colonel's piercing blue eyes swept over the assembled townspeople, his thin lips curving into a smile that never quite reached his gaze.

"People of Dunnellon," he began, his soft Southern

drawl carrying easily across the square, "we are here to help you, we are here to build a better society for all of you. A society free from the chaos and lawlessness that has plagued our great state since the fall." He paused, letting his words sink in before continuing, his voice taking on a harder edge. "I certainly hope there will be no further... unpleasantness. For your sakes."

His words hung in the air, heavy with threat and promise, like storm clouds pregnant with lightning. The crowd remained frozen, their faces a kaleidoscope of emotions - horror, fear, and barely suppressed rage warred for dominance. Some averted their eyes, unable to look at the bodies still lying in the square, their blood seeping into the cracks of the pavement. Others stared defiantly at the Colonel, their jaws clenched and fists balled at their sides, a spark of rebellion still burning in their eyes despite the grim display of power they had just witnessed.

With that, the Colonel turned on his heel and walked back to his cabin, surrounded by his top men like a king with his royal guard. His polished shoes clicked against the pavement, the sound unnaturally loud in the eerie silence that had fallen over the square. It was as if the very air held its breath, waiting to see what would happen next. His men formed a tight perimeter around him, their hands resting on their weapons, eyes constantly scanning the crowd for any sign of trouble or resistance.

As they retreated, the spell of silence seemed to break, shattering like thin ice on a spring morning. Hushed whispers began to ripple through the gathered townspeople, growing louder with each passing moment. The murmur swelled like a wave, filled with fear, anger, and disbelief. Some rushed to the fallen resistors, falling to their knees beside the bodies and checking for any signs of life despite the futility of the act. Sobs and anguished cries punctuated the air as the reality of their loss set in.

Others huddled in small groups, their faces etched with worry and despair as they contemplated their new reality under the Colonel's rule. Parents clutched their children close, as if their embrace could shield them from the horrors they had just witnessed. Elderly residents shook their heads in dismay, muttering about how they never thought they'd see such times again.

The Colonel's procession disappeared into the night, swallowed up by the shadows cast by their own flickering torches. They left behind a town forever changed by the events that had unfolded, a community whose innocence had been violently stripped away. The air was thick with the acrid smell of gunpowder and the metallic tang of blood, a grim reminder of the price of defiance in this new world order. As the last echoes of the Colonel's footsteps faded, the people of Dunnellon were left to grapple with the harsh truth of their situation and the difficult choices that lay ahead.

CHAPTER NINETEEN

The sun had barely crept over the horizon when Joe Kelly heard a soft knock on his cabin door. He opened it to find Rodriguez, his face etched with worry, eyes darting nervously.

"Joe, we need to talk," Rodriguez said, his voice barely above a whisper.

Joe nodded, stepping aside to let Rodriguez in. They moved to the kitchen table, where a map of the area lay spread out, marked with various notations and scribbled notes. Coffee mugs and half-eaten protein bars littered the edges, testament to long nights of planning.

Rodriguez didn't waste time. "I've been doing some recon, gathering intel from our scouts. The situation's worse than we thought. Much worse."

Joe's brow furrowed, deep lines etching across his weathered forehead. "How bad?"

"The Colonel's forces," Rodriguez paused, his voice dropping, eyes locked on Joe's, "they're pushing a thousand strong. Maybe more."

Joe felt his stomach drop, a cold weight settling in his gut. He'd known they were outnumbered, but this... this was beyond his worst fears. "Christ," he breathed, "You're sure about that number?"

Rodriguez nodded grimly, his fingers tapping a nervous rhythm on the table. "As sure as I can be. We've had three separate confirmations. And us? We've got just over a hundred. Maybe one-twenty if we push it, scrape the bottom of the barrel. I mean we've got to leave a decent sized force here to guard the compound"

Joe leaned back in his chair, the wood creaking under his weight. He ran a calloused hand through his salt-and-pepper hair, feeling every one of his fifty-nine years. The weight of the odds settled on his shoulders like a physical burden, threatening to crush him.

"Joe, I gotta be honest with you," Rodriguez continued, his voice tight with barely contained panic. "I'm not sure we can do this. The odds... they're not just against us. They're damn near impossible. We're talking about a slaughter."

Joe met Rodriguez's gaze, seeing the doubt and fear that the man was trying hard to mask. He understood it all too well - the same emotions churned in his own gut, a maelstrom of anxiety and dread.

"We knew it wasn't going to be easy," Joe said, his

voice low and steady, more to convince himself than Rodriguez.

"Easy? This ain't about easy anymore, Joe. This is suicide," Rodriguez shot back, his frustration evident in the way he slammed his palm on the table. "We're talking about going up against an army with what amounts to a large hunting party. It's David versus Goliath, except David forgot his slingshot."

Joe didn't respond immediately. He stood up, joints protesting, and walked to the window to look out at the awakening camp. People were starting to stir, going about their morning routines, unaware of the grim conversation taking place in his cabin. Children laughed, chasing each other between tents. Smoke rose from cooking fires. It all seemed so normal, so peaceful.

"What are you thinking, Joe?" Rodriguez asked, breaking the heavy silence that had fallen between them.

Joe turned back to face him, his expression resolute, jaw set in determination. "I'm thinking we need to get creative. We may be outnumbered, but we've got home field advantage. We know this land better than they do. Every hill, every stream, every hidden cave. It's time we use that knowledge."

Joe moved back to the table, his eyes scanning the map

before him. He traced a finger along the winding paths, dense forests, and meandering rivers that surrounded Dunnellon. The topography was familiar to him, each contour and landmark etched into his memory from years of hunting and exploring these lands.

"Look, Rodriguez, I hear you. The numbers are bad, real bad. But we can't just roll over and die. We've got families to protect, a community to defend. These people are counting on us," Joe said, his voice filled with resolve.

Rodriguez nodded, his expression a mix of resignation and hope. He understood the gravity of their situation all too well.

Joe continued, his voice taking on a tone of grim determination. "We're not going to win this in a straight-up fight. That's for damn sure. But we don't have to. What we need is to do is stick with our plan, a war of attrition. It's our only shot at coming out of this alive."

Rodriguez furrowed his brow, "Well, I do know that if we just sit here and wait, the Colonel's strength will only grow and they will eventually come for us, that's for sure. So, I see the merits in your plan. It just seems like a monumental task ahead of us, that's for sure.

"I know it seems daunting right now, but remember the

journey of a thousand miles begins with the first step,"
Joe explained patiently. "We wear 'em down, bit by bit.
Make every step they take towards us cost them dearly.
We don't need to wipe them out all at once. We just
need to bleed them dry, slowly but surely. It's about
playing the long game, making them regret ever setting
foot in our territory."

Joe's calloused finger traced a circle around Dunnellon
on the map, encompassing the surrounding wilderness.
"We use guerilla tactics. Hit and run. Ambushes. Traps.
We know these woods and waterways like the back
of our hands. Every hill, every stream, every hidden
cave. We use that to our advantage. They may have the
numbers, but we've got home field advantage."

Rodriguez leaned in, his interest piqued. The wheels in
his head started turning as he began to see the potential
in Joe's strategy. "Go on," he urged, eager to hear more.

"We set up small teams. Mobile, quick-striking units.
They hit the Colonel's forces when they least expect
it, then melt back into the forest before they can
respond. We target their supply lines, their scouts, their
stragglers. We make them jumpy, paranoid. Make them
waste resources and manpower just trying to stay safe.
Every night, they'll go to sleep wondering where we'll
strike next."

Joe's eyes lit up with a fierce intensity, the fire of a

man who'd found his purpose. "And every day, every engagement, we chip away at their numbers. Maybe it's just one or two at a time, but it all adds up. We make them bleed for every inch of ground they take. No easy victories, no moment of peace. We'll be like ghosts, always there but just out of reach."

Rodriguez nodded slowly, beginning to gain more confidence as he could see the strategy unfold in his mind's eye. "And while they're dealing with all that..."

"Exactly," Joe finished for him, a grim smile playing at the corners of his mouth. "While they're out there, getting picked off and worn down, we sit back, retreat, stay Safe. Conserving our strength. And when the time is right, when we've whittled them down enough..."

"We strike," Rodriguez said, a glimmer of hope igniting in his eyes.

Joe nodded grimly, his jaw set with determination. "We strike. And by then, maybe those impossible odds won't look so impossible anymore. It won't be easy, and it sure as hell won't be pretty. But it's our best shot at survival, at protecting everything and everyone we care about."

As Joe and Rodriguez continued to ponder their strategy, a commotion outside drew their attention. Urgent footsteps approached, and the cabin door burst open. Maria stood in the doorway, her chest heaving from exertion.

"Joe, Rodriguez," she gasped, her eyes wide with concern. "It's Abby. She's gone into labor."

Joe's brow furrowed. "Labor? But it's too early."

Maria nodded grimly. "That's the problem. She's only at, we think about eight months, but we're really not sure. We're worried about complications."

Rodriguez muttered a curse under his breath. "Of all the times..."

Joe held up a hand, silencing him. He turned to Maria. "Where is she now?"

"Claire's with her in the medical tent. But Joe, we're not equipped for a premature birth."

Joe's mind raced, weighing their limited options against the gravity of the situation. Finally, he nodded, decision made. "Alright, we need to halt preparations for now. This takes priority."

He strode out of the cabin, Rodriguez and Maria following close behind. The camp was fully awake now, people milling about with worried expressions, news of Abby's condition spreading quickly.

Joe raised his voice, addressing the gathered crowd.

"Listen up, everyone. We've got a situation here. Abby's gone into premature labor, and she needs our support. I know we're all scared, and we've got a hell of a fight ahead of us. But right now, we need to come together."

He paused, looking around at the faces of his community. "I'm calling for a group prayer. For Abby, for her baby, and for all of us."

A hush fell over the crowd as people began to gather closer, forming a loose circle around Joe. He bowed his head, and others followed suit.

"Lord," Joe began, his voice carrying across the now-silent camp, "I'm not really good at this but we come to you in a time of need. We ask for your protection and guidance for Abby and for her unborn child. Grant them strength and health in this difficult hour."

He took a deep breath before continuing. "And Lord, we ask for your blessing on our upcoming mission. Guide our hands, steady our hearts, and give us the courage to face what lies ahead. Amen."

A chorus of "Amens" rippled through the crowd.

Maria turned to Joe, her eyes filled with a mix of concern and uncertainty. "What should we do?" she asked, her voice barely above a whisper, her hand trembling slightly as she reached for his arm.

Joe met her gaze, his weathered features softening as he looked at her. He reached out and gently took her hand in his, giving it a reassuring squeeze. The warmth of his touch seemed to calm her nerves. "We have no experts in the area of birthing, Maria," he said, his voice low and steady, carrying the weight of experience. "That's why I turned to the only place I knew to turn to. It's in the Lord's hands now."

He paused, taking a deep breath before continuing, his thumb gently caressing the back of her hand. "All we can do is keep Abby comfortable and trust that God knows what's best." Joe's eyes never left Maria's as he spoke, his words carrying the weight of his conviction. The lines around his eyes crinkled with a mixture of concern and determination. "Have faith, sweetie. We've come this far together, and we'll see this through too."

Maria nodded slowly, drawing strength from Joe's calm demeanor. She squeezed his hand back, grateful for his presence and leadership in this challenging moment. A small smile tugged at the corners of her mouth, a silent acknowledgment of the comfort he provided.

The camp around them had grown quiet, the earlier commotion settling into a tense anticipation. People moved about with hushed voices and worried glances toward the medical tent where Abby lay. The air was thick with unspoken fears and whispered prayers.

Joe looked around at the gathered community, seeing the fear and uncertainty etched on their faces. He knew they were all thinking the same thing - that this premature birth was just one more challenge in a world that seemed determined to test them at every turn. The weight of their collective anxiety pressed down on him, but he stood tall, a beacon of strength in the midst of uncertainty.

But as he stood there, hand in hand with Maria, Joe felt a sense of resolve wash over him. They had faced adversity before, and they would face it again. Together, as a community, they would weather this storm just as they had weathered others. He squeezed Maria's hand once more, drawing strength from her presence, and prepared himself for whatever challenges lay ahead.

Joe and Maria made their way to Abby's bedside, their footsteps muffled on the worn floor of the medical tent. The air was thick with tension and the sharp smell of antiseptic, mingled with the earthy scent of sweat and fear. Claire stood beside Abby, her hand clasped tightly around the younger woman's, murmuring words of encouragement. Her blue eyes were filled with determination, a stark contrast to the worry etched on everyone else's faces.

As they approached, Joe's eyes swept over the

makeshift medical setup. It was basic at best, a stark reminder of their limited resources in this post-apocalyptic world. A few scavenged instruments lay on a nearby tray, glinting dully in the dim light. Abby lay on a narrow cot, its metal frame creaking slightly with her movements. Her face was pale and glistening with sweat, her usually vibrant blonde hair matted against her forehead, clinging to her skin in damp tendrils.

"How you holding up, Abs?" Joe asked, his gruff voice softening with concern. He fought to keep his own anxiety at bay, knowing that Abby needed strength now more than ever.

Abby's blue eyes, wide with fear and rimmed with exhaustion, locked onto Joe's. "I'm scared, Joe," she admitted, her voice barely above a whisper, cracking slightly with emotion. "What if... what if something's wrong? I want my baby to be healthy. I can't... I can't do this alone."

Joe's weathered features softened, a reassuring smile tugging at the corners of his mouth. The lines around his eyes deepened with compassion as he reached out, patting Abby's arm gently. His calloused hand felt rough against her clammy skin. "Now, don't you worry. I'm sure that child of yours is gonna be a fighter, just like its momma. You've got more strength in you than you know, Abby. And remember, you're not alone.

We're all here for you."

A weak smile flickered across Abby's face at Joe's words, a glimmer of hope lighting up her eyes. For a moment, she looked more like her old self, the vibrant young woman they all knew. But the moment was short-lived. Her smile suddenly contorted into a grimace, her body tensing as another contraction gripped her. She squeezed Claire's hand tightly, her knuckles turning white with the effort. A low moan escaped her lips, building into a pained cry that echoed through the tent, a stark reminder of the challenging hours that lay ahead.

CHAPTER TWENTY

As the group gathered to discuss their plans, the tension in the air was palpable. Joe, Captain Rodriguez, Jojo, Miguel, Jake, Dave and Sam formed a tight circle with the National Guard troops and compound men, their faces etched with determination. The weight of their decisions hung heavy in the humid Florida air, each man acutely aware of the stakes involved.

Joe cleared his throat, his weathered features creased with concern. The lines around his eyes deepened as he spoke, betraying the worry that had been gnawing at him. "Cap, I've been negligent not even thinking about fuel for those trucks we've been using. That trip to Dunnellon while it ain't a long way away, it's a good sixty miles or so. That's gonna eat up a lot of gas travelling back and forth. We can't afford to be stranded out there."

Captain Rodriguez's eyes gleamed with a hint of pride as he responded, his posture straightening almost imperceptibly. "Don't worry, Joe. We're way out in front on that matter. I've had some of my men going out siphoning fuel from abandoned vehicles for days now. We've been able to get a pretty good stockpile of both regular and diesel fuel. It's not an endless supply, but it should keep us mobile for a while. Plus we'll need gas for any outboard motors we can get our hands on."

Relief washed over Joe's face, his shoulders visibly relaxing. "Thank God you were thinking about it 'cause it slipped my mind completely. I've been so focused on other things, I overlooked something so crucial."

The Captain continued, his voice steady and reassuring, a calming presence in the group. "On that front, a couple of my guys have been working on your van. Good news, they got it running. It was shot up pretty bad, but they patched it up and it's good to go now. For how long I can't say, but maybe if we just use that close to home for now and not risk any long trips with it. We need to be smart about our resources."

Joe's face lit up at the news, his eyes crinkling at the corners, a spark of hope igniting in his gaze. "Thanks again, Cappy. You are on the ball. Your eye for detail is phenomenal. I don't know what we'd do without you."

Rodriguez smiled, reaching into his pocket to pull out a well-worn notebook, its pages dog-eared and filled with cramped handwriting. "That's why you always see me writing in this notebook. It's what keeps me on track at all times. In times like these, we can't afford to let anything slip through the cracks."

For the next few hours, the group huddled together in the dimly lit room, their voices low but intense as they hammered out their strategy. Ideas flew back and forth like rapid-fire, each man contributing his unique perspective to the plan. The air was thick with tension and the smell of stale coffee, but there was also an undercurrent of excitement, the thrill of finally taking action against their common enemy.

Rodriguez leaned forward, his weathered hands clasped tightly on the table, his eyes glinting with determination. "We can't take 'em head-on, boys. We gotta be smart about this. We hit 'em fast, hit 'em hard, and disappear before they know what hit 'em. Like ghosts in the night."

Joe nodded, stroking his salt-and-pepper beard thoughtfully before adding, "Exactly. We'll wear them down bit by bit. Death by a thousand cuts. It's not glamorous, but it's effective."

A ripple of chuckles spread through the group, the grim humor a welcome break from the tension. Sam cracked a rare smile, his hand unconsciously moving to the scar on his shoulder.

As the sun began to dip low on the horizon, painting the sky in hues of orange and purple, they finally settled on a plan. They'd make the journey to Dunnellon, setting up camp for several days, maybe even a week. Their primary goal: reconnaissance. They needed eyes on the Colonel's operation, to understand his strengths and weaknesses, to find the chinks in his armor.

"We'll need to be smart about this," Jojo chimed in, his military training evident in his precise tone. "We should set up caches along the river. Weapons, food, fuel. That way, we're never too far from supplies. It could mean the difference between success and failure."

Miguel nodded in agreement, his dark eyes narrowed in concentration. "And we should keep our eyes peeled for boats. We'll need 'em to move quickly and quietly. The river could be our best friend or our worst enemy."

Joe's eyes hardened as he added, his voice low and dangerous, "If we get the chance, we take out as many of his men as we can. Every soldier we eliminate weakens his hold. But remember, we're not murderers. We're fighting for our freedom, for our families."

The group murmured in agreement, the gravity of their mission settling over them like a heavy blanket. Each man felt the weight of responsibility on his shoulders, knowing that their actions could determine the fate of countless innocent lives.

"Alright," Joe said, straightening up and looking each man in the eye. "Tomorrow, we load up. Everything we need for an extended stay. We move out before first light the day after. Any questions? This is your last chance to back out. Once we're in, we're all in."

The men shook their heads, their faces set with grim determination. The die was cast. The fight against the Colonel was about to begin in earnest, and they were ready to risk everything for a chance at freedom.

As the sun began to rise the following morning, the compound buzzed with a frenetic energy. Nearly everyone had gathered to help load the gear for the crucial Dunnellon mission. Bodies moved in a well-orchestrated dance, passing supplies and equipment from hand to hand with practiced efficiency. The air hummed with purpose and determination, a palpable sense of urgency permeating the scene.

"Watch that crate, it's got the ammo," Jojo called out, his voice carrying over the controlled chaos. His military training was evident in the way he directed the operation, ensuring every item was properly secured and accounted for.

Within a few hours, the loading was complete. The vehicles stood ready, packed to the brim with everything they'd need for the dangerous journey ahead. Weapons, medical supplies, food, and ammo were all carefully stowed away, a testament to the group's meticulous planning.

As the flurry of activity died down, Joe found himself with a rare moment of quiet. His feet carried him almost instinctively to the familiar bench in front of his mother's grave. He sank down onto the worn wood, the weight of responsibility settling heavily on his shoulders like a physical burden.

Joe's mind raced, replaying countless scenarios of what might unfold in the coming days. The risks were enormous, but the stakes were even higher. He spoke softly, as if his mother could hear him from beyond the veil.

"We're heading out tomorrow, Ma. Gonna try to put an end to this madness." His voice cracked slightly, betraying the emotion he usually kept tightly controlled. "I swear I'll make that bastard pay for what he did to you. For everything he's done to all of us."

He fell silent, head bowed and eyes closed. The gentle breeze rustled the leaves around him, a stark contrast to the turmoil in his thoughts. For a moment, he allowed himself to feel the full weight of his grief and anger.

Suddenly, the sound of racing footsteps shattered the stillness. Joe's head snapped up to see Maria sprinting towards him, her face etched with worry and fear. Her ponytail whipped behind her as she ran, adding to the sense of urgency.

He leapt to his feet, meeting her halfway across the grass. "What's wrong, sweetie?" he asked, his heart already beginning to race with renewed adrenaline.

Maria's eyes brimmed with tears, her breath coming in short gasps. "Follow me, quickly," she gasped, already turning to run back the way she'd come. The panic in her voice sent a chill down Joe's spine.

They raced across the compound, Joe's heart pounding in his chest. As they neared the medical tent, a cold dread settled in his stomach like a block of ice. His mind immediately went to Abby, heavily pregnant and vulnerable. Had something gone wrong with the baby?

"Oh God, no," he muttered, following Maria into the tent. The canvas flap whipped shut behind them as they rushed inside, bracing himself for whatever crisis awaited.

As Joe's eyes adjusted to the dim light in the tent, he saw Abby lying on the cot, holding a tightly wrapped newborn close to her chest. Abby's face was aglow with an uncontrollable smile, her eyes sparkling with a mixture of exhaustion and pure joy. The air in the tent was thick with the pungent smell of antiseptic and the metallic tang of blood, but there was also an undeniable sense of hope and new beginnings.

Joe looked to Maria, his heart pounding with a mixture of relief and lingering concern. "So everyone is okay? Abby, the baby?" His voice was hoarse with emotion, barely above a whisper.

Maria, still with tears shedding down her cheeks, nodded emphatically. "Yes Joe, they're both doing just fine. It was touch and go for a while, but Abby was so strong." She reached out and squeezed Joe's arm reassuringly.

Joe was awash with relief, his shoulders sagging as the tension drained from his body. "Thank God for that. Is it a boy or a girl?" He found himself holding his breath, waiting for the answer.

Abby looked up at Joe, her eyes shining with pride. "It's a girl. Would you like to hold her?" She adjusted the bundle in her arms, preparing to pass the precious cargo.

Joe reached down to pick up the newest member of their group, his hands trembling slightly. "Absolutely, it's been a long time since I've held a baby." As he cradled the infant, his voice softened with wonder, his rough features melting into a gentle smile. "Oh my God, Abby, she's... she's so beautiful. You are adorable little baby, you're gonna bring a lot of joy around here little..." He paused, realizing he didn't know what to call her. "What do I call her? Does she have a name yet?"

Abby smiled, her voice barely above a whisper. "Yes Joe, you can call her Toni."

Joe began to sob, his body shaking with emotion. "Oh my God, Abby, I'm at a loss for words. I am so honored." He cradled the baby closer, as if trying to shield her from the harsh world outside.

Abby also began to shed tears, her voice thick with emotion. "I miss her too, Joe. Not many people knew this, but she spent a lot of hours counseling me. She changed my life in so many ways, and I'll always love her for that. This is just one small way I can honor her memory." She reached out and touched Joe's arm, a gesture of shared grief and understanding.

Joe reached down, carefully handing Toni back to Abby and gave Abby a kiss on the cheek. "Thank you, Abby. It truly means the world to me." He stepped back, wiping his eyes with the back of his hand, overwhelmed by the mix of joy and sorrow that filled the tent. In that moment, despite all the hardships they had faced and would continue to face, there was a sense of hope and renewal that seemed to radiate from the tiny bundle in Abby's arms.

CHAPTER TWENTY ONE

The next morning dawned crisp and clear, a deceptively beautiful day for such a grim mission. Joe stood by the lead truck, watching as his team made their final preparations. The air was thick with a mixture of determination and trepidation, the weight of their task hanging heavy over the group. The sun cast long shadows across the compound, highlighting the tense faces of those preparing to leave and those staying behind.

"Alright, folks. It's time," Joe called out, his voice steady despite the churning in his gut. He ran a hand through his salt-and-pepper hair, eyes scanning the faces of those he'd come to rely on. His gaze lingered on each member of his team, silently acknowledging the trust they'd placed in him and the dangers they were about to face together.

One by one, the members of his group approached those staying behind. Tears were shed, hugs exchanged, and whispered promises made. Joe's heart clenched as he watched Abby cradle baby Toni close, her fingers gently stroking the infant's cheek. The sight was a stark reminder of what they were fighting for - a future for the next generation. Abby's eyes met Joe's for a moment, a silent understanding passing between them.

"Take care of yourself Joe," Maria said, her voice breaking. "And come back to me, to all of us." Her warm brown eyes searched his face, memorizing every line and contour. The worry etched in her features was unmistakable, but there was also a fierce determination that Joe had come to admire.

Joe approached her, wrapping Maria in his arms. "We will. You stay safe here as well, you hear?" He pressed a gentle kiss to her forehead, inhaling the familiar scent of her hair. His arms tightened around her, savoring the moment and drawing strength from her presence.

As the goodbyes concluded, Joe took a moment to survey their convoy. Two olive-drab National Guard trucks stood ready, their diesel engines rumbling with barely contained power. Behind each truck, a supply trailer was hitched, loaded with provisions, weapons, and medical supplies. The vehicles looked formidable, a stark contrast to the peaceful community they were leaving behind. Joe couldn't help but feel a twinge of pride at how far they'd come, how prepared they now were for the dangers that lurked beyond their walls. The sight of their well-equipped convoy was a testament to their resilience and resourcefulness.

Joe climbed into the lead truck, settling into the driver's

seat. As he gripped the steering wheel, he allowed himself a moment of reflection. The Colonel's influence had spread like a cancer, corrupting everything it touched. This mission wasn't just about taking down one man; it was about cutting out the rot that threatened to consume them all. Joe's jaw clenched as he thought of the lives already lost, the communities torn apart by the Colonel's twisted vision. The faces of those they'd lost along the way flashed through his mind, fueling his resolve.

The convoy lurched forward, tires crunching on gravel as they began their journey to Dunnellon. As they passed through the gates of their compound, Joe's mind raced with the challenges that lay ahead. The Colonel was cunning, ruthless, and had no shortage of devoted followers. This wouldn't be a simple in-and-out operation. They would need to be smart, adaptable, and above all, united. Joe mentally ran through their plan once more, considering every possible contingency.

But as Joe glanced in the rearview mirror at the determined faces of his team, he felt a surge of hope. They were strong, they were prepared, and most importantly, they were fighting for something bigger than themselves. Whatever the Colonel threw at them, they would face it together. Joe's grip tightened on the wheel as they hit the open road, the Florida landscape stretching out before them. The familiar sights of their home state took on a new significance, reminding them of all they stood to lose if they failed. Come hell or high water, they would see this through to the end. The fate of their loved ones, their community, and perhaps all of Florida rested on their shoulders, and Joe was determined not to let them down.

The convoy crawled along the highway, their progress painstakingly slow. Joe's eyes darted constantly between the road ahead and the rearview mirror, watching for any signs of trouble. The landscape was a graveyard of abandoned vehicles, silent reminders of the chaos that had engulfed the world. Rusted hulks of cars and trucks littered the shoulders, some overturned, others stripped bare by desperate scavengers. The eerie stillness of the scene was broken only by the low rumble of their engines and the occasional creak of metal shifting in the breeze.

"Damn," Joe muttered, swerving to avoid yet another car left haphazardly across the lanes. "This is like threading a needle." His knuckles whitened as he gripped the wheel, carefully maneuvering around the obstacle. Sweat beaded on his forehead as he concentrated on navigating the treacherous path.

Beside him, Jojo nodded grimly. "Yeah, Pop. But better slow than sorry. We can't afford to damage the trucks." He scanned the horizon, alert for any movement that might signal danger. His hand rested on the butt of his pistol, ready for action at a moment's notice.

The journey stretched on, the tension in the vehicles palpable. Every mile brought them closer to danger, to the heart of the Colonel's territory. Joe's hands ached from gripping the steering wheel so tightly, but he couldn't bring himself to relax. The weight of responsibility for the entire group pressed down on him like a physical force. He could feel the eyes of his family and friends on him, trusting him to lead them safely through this perilous mission.

As they approached the outskirts of Dunnellon, Jojo studied his map intently, tracing their route with his finger. "Dad, I think I see a good spot to pull over," he said, his voice tinged with cautious optimism. "There's an abandoned road about a quarter mile ahead on the right." He pointed ahead, indicating a barely visible turn-off, almost hidden by overgrown vegetation.

"Copy that," Joe responded, relief flooding through him. They'd made it this far without incident, but he knew the real challenges were yet to come. He signaled to the vehicles behind them, preparing for the turn. The convoy moved as one, a testament to their coordination and shared purpose.

The convoy turned onto the deserted road, the trucks' tires crunching on loose gravel. Weeds sprouted between the cracks in the pavement, nature slowly reclaiming the forgotten stretch of asphalt. Branches from encroaching trees scraped against the sides of the vehicles, leaving thin scratches in the paint. Joe brought the lead vehicle to a stop, the others falling in line behind him. As the engines quieted, the sudden silence felt oppressive, broken only by the occasional creak of cooling metal and the distant call of a bird.

Joe climbed out of the truck, stretching his stiff muscles. The others followed suit, gathering around him in a tight circle. Their faces were a mixture of determination and apprehension, mirroring Joe's own emotions. The air was thick with unspoken tension and the weight of their impending mission. The smell of hot engines mingled with the scent of wild vegetation, creating an odd juxtaposition of man and nature.

"Alright, folks," Joe began, his voice low but firm. He looked each member of the group in the eye, conveying both confidence and the gravity of their situation. "We made it here in one piece. Now comes the hard part. Let's go over the plan one more time." He took a deep breath, preparing to outline the dangerous task that lay ahead of them. The group leaned in closer, their faces set with resolve as they prepared to face whatever challenges awaited them in the Colonel's territory.

Joe nodded to the group, his voice low and steady, carrying the weight of their mission. "Alright, time to split up. Remember your teams and objectives. Stay alert and maintain your stealth. We can't afford any slip-ups now. Set up your camps and let's meet back here at sunrise tomorrow."

The men moved with quiet efficiency, gathering their gear and forming into their assigned groups. They double-checked their weapons, exchanging determined glances that spoke volumes about their shared resolve. Joe, Jojo, and Sam headed west, their footsteps barely audible on the forest floor, each step carefully placed to avoid snapping twigs or rustling leaves. Dave and Jake paired up to go north, their movements synchronized after years of working together, a testament to their unspoken trust. Miguel and Captain Rodriguez led a team of National Guardsmen east, their military training evident in their precise formations and disciplined approach. The remaining compound men split into two groups covering the southern approaches, their faces set with grim determination, fully aware of the gravity of their task.

As Joe's team made their way through the dense underbrush, Sam held up a hand, signaling them to stop. His eyes, keen from years of survival training, scanned the area methodically. He pointed out a small clearing nestled between two rocky outcroppings. "There," he whispered, his voice barely audible above the gentle rustling of leaves. "Natural cover on three sides. Perfect for what we need. We couldn't ask for a better spot."

They set to work with practiced efficiency, using fallen branches and leafy boughs to construct a low-lying shelter. Jojo expertly wove smaller branches and vines to create a canopy that blended seamlessly with the surrounding foliage, his nimble fingers working quickly and silently, a skill honed from countless similar operations. Joe spread a layer of leaves and moss over the top, carefully arranging them to mimic natural patterns, further obscuring their hideout from aerial view. His experienced eye caught every detail, ensuring no telltale signs of human presence remained visible. They worked in comfortable silence, each man focused on his task, their movements fluid and purposeful.

Meanwhile, Dave and Jake found a suitable spot in a thicket of tall grass and scrub brush. They dug shallow trenches, their hands working tirelessly in the soft earth, using the excavated soil to build up natural-looking berms. The rhythmic sound of their digging was muffled by the surrounding vegetation. Jake gathered armfuls of dried grass, his movements slow and deliberate as he carefully arranged it over their position to break up any man-made lines. His patience was evident in every placement, ensuring their hideout would withstand even the most scrutinizing gaze. Dave kept watch, his keen eyes constantly scanning their surroundings for any sign of movement, his hand never far from his weapon.

Miguel's team utilized a cluster of fallen trees, incorporating the natural debris into their camouflage with impressive ingenuity. They strung up camouflage netting between the logs, creating shadowy spaces that could conceal both men and equipment. The netting rippled slightly in the breeze, blending seamlessly with the forest's natural movements, creating an illusion of undisturbed wilderness. Captain Rodriguez supervised the placement of their gear with a critical eye, ensuring clear lines of sight while maintaining cover. He moved from position to position, offering quiet suggestions and adjustments, his years of military experience evident in every calculated decision.

The southern teams took advantage of the rolling terrain, setting up in shallow depressions that offered natural concealment. They used local vegetation and soil to create ghillie-style coverings for their shelters, meticulously attaching leaves, twigs, and grass to break up their outlines. Their efforts made them nearly invisible from a distance, blending into the landscape like chameleons. Each man worked with painstaking attention to detail, knowing that their lives could depend on the quality of their camouflage.

As the sun began to set, painting the sky in hues of orange and purple, each team had established a well-hidden base of operations. They settled into their positions, weapons at the ready, prepared to begin their surveillance of the Colonel's territory. The forest grew quiet around them, save for the occasional rustle of leaves or call of a night bird. The men remained vigilant, their senses attuned to any sign of approaching danger as they waited for darkness to fully envelop them. The air was thick with tension and anticipation, each man acutely aware that the success of their mission – and their very survival – hinged on the coming hours.

As dawn broke, the four teams converged at the rendezvous point, their movements cautious and alert. Joe nodded to each group as they arrived, his eyes scanning the surrounding area for any signs of trouble or potential threats. The air was thick with tension, and the only sounds were the soft rustling of leaves and the occasional call of a distant bird.

"Alright," he said in a low voice, his tone serious and focused, "time to split up and get to work. We've got a lot to accomplish today, and every minute counts. Stay sharp and watch each other's backs."

The teams quickly divided their tasks, each group understanding the gravity of their mission. Joe, Jojo, and Sam headed towards the river, their steps purposeful as they sought out usable watercraft. They moved silently along the riverbank, eyes peeled for anything that could aid their mission, their senses heightened by the potential danger lurking around every bend. The damp earth beneath their feet muffled their footsteps, and they communicated mostly through hand signals and meaningful glances.

At an abandoned marina, they struck gold. Sam's keen eye spotted several small fishing boats partially hidden under overgrown vegetation, their outlines barely visible beneath the tangle of weeds and vines. Jojo worked quickly to clear the debris, his muscles straining as he pulled away the stubborn growth, sweat beading on his forehead despite the cool morning air. Joe assessed their condition with a practiced eye, running his hands along the hulls and checking for any signs of damage or weakness.

"These'll do nicely," Joe murmured, running his hand along the hull of a sturdy pontoon boat, checking it closely to ensure it was seaworthy. "These appear to be seaworthy. It's not perfect, but it's a damn sight better than nothing. We need to check the outboards on these."

As they made minor repairs on the boats and checking engines, Sam discovered a sizable cache of rope hidden beneath a tarp, its presence a welcome boon for their plans. The thick coils felt reassuring in his hands, a tangible asset in their dangerous mission. He quickly began sorting through the ropes, separating the usable ones from those that had rotted or frayed beyond repair.

Joe crouched beside the first outboard motor, his weathered hands moving with practiced efficiency. He primed the engine, adjusted the choke, and gave the pull cord a sharp tug. The motor sputtered, coughed, then roared to life, sending a ripple of excitement through the group. The sudden noise seemed deafening in the quiet marina, and they all instinctively ducked lower, scanning the area for any signs that the sound had attracted unwanted attention.

"One down," Joe muttered, a hint of satisfaction in his voice. He quickly moved to silence the engine, not wanting to risk discovery.

Moving to the pontoon boat, he repeated the process. The larger engine caught almost immediately, its steady purr a welcome sound in the quiet marina. Joe nodded approvingly, his eyes gleaming with cautious optimism. He allowed himself a small smile, knowing that each working engine increased their chances of success.

Two jon boats, however, refused to cooperate. Joe frowned, leaning in to examine them more closely. After a moment, he straightened up, wiping his hands on his pants, leaving dark smudges on the worn fabric.

"Fuel's probably stale," he said, glancing at Jojo. "We might be in luck if that's all it is."

Jojo didn't need to be told twice. He reached for the small gas can they'd brought along, anticipating this very situation. Unscrewing the cap, he carefully poured a measure of fresh gasoline into each jon boat's tank, the strong smell of fuel filling the air around them.

Joe returned to the stubborn engines, his movements deliberate and focused. He primed them again, adjusted the settings, and pulled the cords. This time, both jon boats sputtered to life, their engines joining the chorus of the others. The sound of all four engines running simultaneously filled them with a sense of accomplishment and hope.

A smile spread across Joe's face, a rare sight these days. He turned to Jojo and Sam, his eyes alight with renewed determination. The lines of worry that usually creased his forehead seemed to soften for a moment.

"We're in business, boys," he said, his voice low but filled with resolve. "Now we just have to get these boats to a more secure location. Sam, start scouting a route.

Jojo, help me get these engines covered up. We don't want to advertise what we've found here."

Meanwhile, Dave and Jake set out to search abandoned buildings for supplies, their footsteps echoing in the empty streets. They moved from structure to structure, their movements swift and efficient, always on guard for any sign of hostiles. The eerie silence of the once-bustling town weighed heavily on them, broken only by the occasional creak of a door or the scuttling of small animals in the debris.

In an old clinic, Jake's face lit up as he pried open a locked cabinet, the metal groaning in protest. The sound made them both wince, and they paused, listening intently for any response to the noise. When nothing stirred, Jake resumed his efforts.

"Dave, check this out," he whispered excitedly, his voice barely containing his enthusiasm. Inside lay a treasure trove of medical supplies - bandages, antibiotics, and various medications that could prove invaluable in the days to come. The sight of the neatly stacked boxes and bottles filled them both with a surge of hope. Jake began quickly inventorying their find, while Dave kept watch, his eyes constantly scanning their surroundings.

The third group, led by Captain Rodriguez and Miguel, cautiously made their way towards Dunnellon, their bodies tense with anticipation. They used every scrap of cover available, ducking behind abandoned cars and crumbling walls, their military training evident in their stealthy approach. The sun climbed higher in the sky, casting long shadows that they used to their advantage, moving from one patch of darkness to another.

As they neared the town, they could see the first signs of the Colonel's presence - makeshift barriers of twisted metal and wood, and patrolling guards with weapons at the ready. The once-peaceful streets now resembled a war zone, with sandbags piled high and crude fortifications blocking major intersections.

Rodriguez pulled out a pair of binoculars, his eyes narrowing as he surveyed the scene, taking in every detail of the enemy's defenses. He noted the patrol patterns, the placement of lookouts, and any potential weak points in their perimeter. "Looks like they've fortified the main street," he murmured to Miguel, his voice low and grave. "We'll need to be careful with our approach. One wrong move, and this whole operation could go south fast. Let's fall back and regroup. We need to come up with a solid plan before we go any further."

As the group began to fall back, Miguel's keen eyes caught movement in the periphery. He held up a hand, his voice low and urgent. "Hold up, Cap. What's going on over there?" He pointed towards a cluster of abandoned buildings, his body tensing instinctively.

Rodriguez raised the binoculars to his eyes, focusing on the area Miguel indicated. Through the lenses, he saw three figures moving with purpose, their bodies low and quick as they approached one of the Colonel's vehicles. The captain's breath caught in his throat as he watched the scene unfold, his mind racing with possibilities.

One of the men produced what appeared to be a long rag, setting it ablaze with a quick flick of a lighter. The flame danced in the early morning light, casting eerie shadows on the man's face and illuminating the determination in his eyes. Beside him, a second figure worked swiftly to remove the gas cap from the truck, his movements precise and practiced. With practiced efficiency, they inserted the burning rag and immediately turned to flee, their footsteps barely audible in the stillness of the dawn.

Rodriguez's grip on the binoculars tightened as he watched the men sprint away from the vehicle, his knuckles turning white with tension. Seconds later, the truck erupted into a fireball, the explosion shattering the relative quiet of the morning and sending a shockwave through the air. The Colonel's men, caught off guard, scrambled in confusion, their shouts carrying across the distance as they futilely attempted to extinguish the rapidly spreading flames. The acrid smell of burning fuel and rubber reached Rodriguez's nostrils, a stark reminder of the violence unfolding before them.

Lowering the binoculars, Rodriguez turned to Miguel, a rare smile playing at the corners of his mouth. "Interesting," he mused, his voice tinged with newfound hope and a hint of excitement. "Looks like the good folks of Dunnellon are not fans of the Colonel. Resistance fighters, and I'll bet there's more than just those three. This is the best news we've had yet." His mind was already whirring with potential strategies and alliances.

Miguel nodded, his eyes still fixed on the chaos unfolding before them. The implications of what they'd just witnessed were not lost on him, and a spark of optimism flickered in his chest for the first time in weeks.

Rodriguez clapped a hand on Miguel's shoulder, the gesture both reassuring and energizing. "Let's get back, tell the others. This changes things." As they turned to leave, the sound of distant shouting and the crackle of flames followed them, a reminder of the unexpected allies they might have just discovered in their fight against the Colonel's tyranny.

CHAPTER TWENTY TWO

J oe, Jojo, and Sam spent the next couple of hours shuttling and hiding their newfound boats to two different spots off the main river. The work was strenuous, but they moved with practiced efficiency, their muscles straining as they maneuvered the vessels into secluded alcoves. Sweat beaded on their foreheads and trickled down their backs as they carefully concealed each boat under a canopy of overhanging branches and dense foliage, ensuring they were invisible from both the river and the shore. The humid Florida air clung to their skin, making their clothes stick uncomfortably as they worked in silence, communicating mostly through nods and hand gestures.

As they worked, Jojo's keen eyes caught sight of movement on the main river. He paused, squinting against the glare of the sun reflecting off the water, his hand instinctively moving to shield his eyes. "Dad, Sam," he called out softly, his voice barely above a whisper, "take a look at this." His body tensed, years of military training kicking in as he assessed the potential threat.

The three men crouched low, their bodies tense and alert as they peered through the dense foliage. A pontoon boat cruised slowly in the distance, its engine a low hum barely audible over the natural sounds of the river - the gentle lapping of water against the shore and the rustle of leaves in the breeze. Four men stood aboard, their black uniforms unmistakable even from afar, the sun glinting off what appeared to be weapons at their sides. The sight sent a chill down their spines, a stark reminder of the dangerous new world they were navigating.

Sam's voice was low and grim, his expression hardening as he assessed the situation. "Looks like a patrol boat. I bet it makes regular runs up and down the river. Probably keeping an eye out for any survivors or resisters." His fingers twitched involuntarily, as if itching to reach for a weapon.

Jojo nodded, his mind already racing with possibilities, a familiar glint of strategic planning in his eyes. "You know, that gives me an idea. A way we could turn their patrols against them." His voice held a mix of excitement and determination, the same tone he'd used countless times during mission briefings in his military days.

Joe turned to his son, curiosity etched on his weathered face, lines deepening around his eyes as he raised an eyebrow. "What kind of idea, son? I can see those gears turning in your head." He leaned in closer, intrigued by the spark of inspiration he recognized in Jojo's eyes.

A slow smile spread across Jojo's face, his eyes gleaming with a mix of excitement and determination. The same look Joe had seen countless times before when his son was onto something big. "If we could stop that boat, those dudes would be sitting ducks. And I think I know just how to stop any boat we'd like to. It's simple, but it could be devastatingly effective." His voice dropped even lower, barely audible above the ambient sounds of the river.

Joe raised an eyebrow, intrigued by his son's confidence. "How do you propose to do that, son? We're all ears." He shifted his weight, leaning in closer to hear the plan, his own mind already racing with possibilities.

Jojo's gaze fell on the rope Sam had found earlier. He picked it up, running it through his hands as he explained his plan, the coarse fibers catching on his calloused palms. "What I propose, Dad, is that we stretch this rope across the river. Tie it around a tree on the other side and keep it hidden under the water until a boat comes by. Then we lift the rope up just enough to catch under it. We could probably snag it on the outboard. The prop is on the back side, so it wouldn't cut the rope. The boat will stop, and the men won't even know why." His fingers worked the rope as he spoke, demonstrating the technique with practiced ease.

His voice grew more animated as he continued, gesturing with his hands to illustrate his points. "While they're trying to figure it out, we pick 'em off one by one from cover. They'll never know what hit 'em. Then we dump their bodies in the river and take the boat, easy as pie. We'd have their vessel, their weapons, and any intel they might be carrying." The excitement in his voice was palpable, his military training evident in the precision of his plan.

Joe's face broke into a proud grin, his eyes crinkling at the corners. "Jojo, I've said it before, and I'll say it again. You're a goddamn genius. That mind of yours never ceases to amaze me." He clapped his son on the shoulder, a gesture of both pride and approval.

Sam clapped Jojo on the back, his eyes shining with admiration and a hint of excitement at the prospect of action. "I'll second that, sir. It's a brilliant plan. Simple, effective, and it plays to our strengths. Those bastards won't know what hit them. Not to mention the psychological effect it'll have on the rest of the Colonel's men when their patrols keep disappearing. Men, boats and all." His voice held a note of grim satisfaction at the thought of striking back at their oppressors.

Joe chuckled, a low, rumbling sound that held both humor and determination. "Absolutely, a few patrols go missing and the Colonel's men will think the Withlacoochee River is the Goddamn Bermuda Triangle. And we'll be the unseen force behind it all, chipping away at their control bit by bit." His eyes glinted with a mixture of pride in his son's plan and anticipation of the battles to come.

CHAPTER TWENTY THREE

The sun dipped low on the horizon, casting long shadows across the compound. A gentle breeze rustled through the trees, carrying with it the scent of pine and the faint aroma of dinner cooking. The day's heat slowly faded, replaced by the cool embrace of evening.

Residents trickled into the main courtyard, their faces etched with the weariness of another long day of survival. Some carried tools, others baskets of freshly picked vegetables. They gathered in small groups, voices mingling in a low hum of conversation.

The atmosphere was one of cautious relaxation, a rare moment of communal peace in their harsh new reality. Laughter occasionally punctuated the air, a welcome sound in these trying times.

As the last rays of sunlight painted the sky in hues of orange and pink, Jack emerged from one of the buildings. He sauntered towards the gathering, a mischievous grin playing on his lips. His hands were behind his back, concealing something from view.

"Hey, folks!" Jack called out, his voice carrying across

the courtyard. Heads turned, conversations paused. "I've got a little surprise for y'all."

With a flourish, Jack revealed two large jugs from behind his back. The cloudy liquid inside sloshed enticingly. "Homemade moonshine, courtesy of yours truly!"

A ripple of excitement spread through the crowd. Eyes widened, smiles broke out on tired faces. The promise of a rare treat, a moment of normalcy and celebration, was a powerful lure.

"Well, I'll be damned," Claire chuckled, rising from her seat. "Jack, you old dog. When did you manage this?"

Jack's grin widened. "Been working on it for weeks. Figured we all could use a little pick-me-up."

The news spread quickly, drawing more people from the edges of the compound. Soon, the courtyard was filled with eager faces, the earlier weariness replaced by anticipation.

Claire approached Jack, her eyes sparkling with curiosity. "How the hell did you make this?"

Jack's grin widened, pride evident in his stance. He set the jugs down carefully on a nearby table and leaned in conspiratorially.

"Well, darlin', it all started with those orange and

grapefruit trees we found growin' wild on the old Johnson property," Jack began, his voice low and excited. "Figured they'd make a mighty fine base."

Claire nodded, impressed. "Smart thinking. But that's not all, is it?"

"You bet your boots it ain't," Jack chuckled. "Took myself on a little foraging expedition in the woods. Found some blackberries and wild raspberries. Thought they'd add a nice kick to the flavor."

By now, a small crowd had gathered around them, listening intently to Jack's explanation.

"But here's the real secret," Jack continued, lowering his voice further. "Remember that beehive we found last month? Well, I sweet-talked Sarah into lending me some of that honey. Makes for one hell of a sweetener."

A murmur of appreciation rippled through the group. Claire whistled low, shaking her head in admiration.

"Damn, Jack. You really thought this through, didn't you?"

Jack nodded, clearly pleased with himself. "Sure did. Took about two weeks to ferment properly. Had to keep it hidden away in that old root cellar. Checked on it every day, making sure the temperature was just right."

The residents exchanged impressed glances. In a world where survival often meant focusing solely on necessities, Jack's initiative to create something purely for enjoyment was a welcome surprise.

"Well, I'll be," muttered Tom, an older man with weathered hands. "Never thought I'd see the day when we'd have our own distillery."

"It's not just about the drink," Sarah chimed in, her eyes bright. "It's about what it represents. Ingenuity, resourcefulness, making something good out of what we have."

Claire nodded in agreement. "You're right, Sarah. Jack, you've done more than just make moonshine. You've given us all a reminder that life can still be sweet, even in these tough times."

Maria stepped forward, her warm brown eyes twinkling with a mix of amusement and concern. She placed a gentle hand on Jack's shoulder, her voice carrying a note of admiration.

"Jack, you never cease to amaze me," she said, shaking her head. "Your creativity and resourcefulness are truly remarkable. In times like these, it's heartening to see someone think beyond mere survival."

Jack beamed at the praise, but Maria's expression turned serious. "However," she continued, her tone shifting to that of a concerned nurse, "we need to remember the importance of moderation. This isn't exactly regulated spirits we're dealing with here."

A few chuckles rippled through the crowd, but Maria pressed on. "I'm not trying to be a killjoy, but we need to be careful. Our bodies aren't used to alcohol anymore, and we can't afford to let our guards down completely."

She scanned the faces around her, her gaze steady and earnest. "We've worked hard to build this safe haven. Let's enjoy Jack's creation, but let's also remember to stay vigilant. We don't know what's out there, and we need to be ready for anything."

The crowd nodded solemnly, acknowledging the wisdom in Maria's words. But the mood quickly lightened as Jack raised one of the jugs.

"Alright, who's brave enough to be our first taster?" he challenged, a mischievous glint in his eye.

Tom, the older man with weathered hands, stepped forward. "Hell, I'll give it a go," he declared, reaching for the jug.

All eyes were on Tom as he took a hearty swig. His eyes widened, and he let out a whoop that startled nearby birds into flight. "Whoo-ee!" he exclaimed, coughing and laughing at the same time. "That's got some kick to it!"

Encouraged by Tom's reaction, others stepped forward.
Claire was next, taking a more cautious sip. Her face
contorted into a mix of surprise and delight. "Oh
my," she gasped, her voice slightly hoarse. "It's like...
sunshine and fire had a baby in my mouth!"

The unique flavor of Jack's creation sparked animated
discussions. "I can taste the citrus," Sarah mused,
smacking her lips. "But there's something else...
berries?"

"And a hint of sweetness," added another resident. "Is
that honey?"

As the moonshine made its rounds, the reactions
ranged from exuberant praise to comical grimaces.
Laughter filled the air, punctuated by coughs and
exclamations of surprise at the potency of Jack's brew.

As the evening unfolded, the compound's courtyard
transformed into a lively gathering. The initial
tension melted away, replaced by an atmosphere
of camaraderie and mirth. Residents sprawled on
makeshift seats, their faces flushed and eyes bright with
laughter.

Claire, perched on an overturned crate, regaled the
group with a tale from her park ranger days. "So there
I was, face to face with this massive grizzly," she said,

gesticulating wildly. "And all I had was a can of bug spray!"

The crowd erupted in laughter, their spirits lifted by both Claire's storytelling and Jack's potent brew.

Tom chimed in, his weathered face creased with mirth. "That's nothin'! Let me tell you 'bout the time I wrestled an alligator with nothin' but a pool noodle and a rubber duck!"

As the night wore on, the effects of the moonshine became increasingly apparent. Sarah, usually reserved and practical, giggled uncontrollably at the slightest provocation. Jack's words began to slur, his trademark grin wider than ever.

Suddenly, Paulette sprang to her feet, swaying slightly. "I've got an idea!" she announced, her eyes sparkling. "Let's dance!"

With exaggerated flourish, she attempted a twirl. Her foot caught on a loose stone, sending her stumbling. She windmilled her arms, trying to regain balance, only to topple backwards into Adam's lap.

The courtyard erupted in good-natured laughter as Paulette, red-faced but grinning, scrambled to her feet. "Okay, maybe dancing isn't my strong suit," she admitted sheepishly.

Inspired by Paulette's attempt, Tom decided to showcase his own talents. "Who wants to hear a song?" he bellowed, puffing out his chest.

Before anyone could object, Tom launched into a painfully off-key rendition of "Sweet Home Alabama." His voice cracked on the high notes, and he forgot half the lyrics, substituting with creative humming.

Not to be outdone, Sarah jumped in with her own version of "I Will Survive." Her enthusiasm far outweighed her musical ability, resulting in a cacophony that sent nearby wildlife scurrying for cover.

As the impromptu singing contest continued, each performance more comically disastrous than the last, the storytelling took on a life of its own.

Claire, her inhibitions lowered by Jack's concoction, began spinning an increasingly outlandish tale. "Did I ever tell you about the time I single-handedly fought off a pack of velociraptors?" she asked, her eyes wide with mock seriousness.

"Velociraptors?" Jack sputtered, nearly choking on his drink. "In Florida?"

Claire nodded solemnly. "Oh yes, they were part of a top-secret government experiment. Escaped from a lab in the Everglades. Used my trusty Swiss Army knife to take 'em all down!"

As the night wore on, Maria, ever the voice of reason, began to gently encourage people to turn in for the night. She moved through the crowd, her warm brown eyes filled with a mixture of amusement and concern.

"Alright, folks," she called out, her voice firm but kind. "It's been a wonderful evening, but we've got work to do tomorrow. Let's start wrapping things up."

Her words were met with a chorus of good-natured groans and protests. Sarah, still giggling, attempted to stand up, only to plop back down on her makeshift seat.

"I think... I think the ground is moving," Sarah mumbled, her eyes wide with confusion.

Maria chuckled, helping Sarah to her feet. "That's just the moonshine talking, honey. Come on, let's get you to bed."

As people began to disperse, the true effects of Jack's potent brew became apparent. The usually graceful Claire stumbled over her own feet, ricocheting off a nearby tree like a pinball.

"Whoa there!" Jack called out, reaching to steady her. "You okay, darlin'?"

Claire nodded vigorously, then immediately regretted the action as the world spun around her. "I'm fine," she slurred. "Just... just need to find my way back to my...

uh... where do I sleep again?"

Tom, determined to prove he was perfectly capable of walking, set off towards his quarters with exaggerated care. Each step was a comical display of concentration, his arms outstretched for balance as if he were walking a tightrope.

Meanwhile, a small group huddled around the remaining jug of moonshine, determined to see it through to the end. Paulette, her cheeks flushed, raised the jug triumphantly.

"We can't let this go to waste!" she declared, her words slightly slurred. "It'd be... it'd be downright disrespectful to Jack's hard work!"

Adam nodded enthusiastically, nearly losing his balance in the process. "Agreed! We have a... a moral obligation to finish this!"

Maria sighed, shaking her head with a mixture of exasperation and fondness. "Just... try not to overdo it, okay? And make sure you drink some water before bed."

As she turned to help another unsteady resident to their quarters, she couldn't help but smile. Despite the challenges they faced, moments like these reminded her of the resilience of the human spirit. Even in the darkest times, people found ways to come together, to laugh, to celebrate life.

The morning sun crept over the horizon, its rays piercing through the makeshift shelters of the compound. Groans and muffled curses filled the air as the residents slowly stirred from their alcohol-induced slumber.

Claire emerged from her room, squinting against the harsh light. Her head pounded like a jackhammer, and her mouth felt like it was stuffed with cotton. She stumbled towards the communal area, desperate for water.

"Morning, sunshine," Tom croaked, his voice rough as sandpaper. He sat slumped against a tree, looking like death warmed over. "You look about as good as I feel."

Claire managed a weak chuckle. "What happened last night? Everything's a blur after Sarah's... was that singing?"

Tom winced at the memory. "I think so. Though 'caterwauling' might be a more accurate description."

Nearby, Paulette was attempting to piece together

the events of the previous night. "Did I... did I try to dance?" she asked, her face a mixture of confusion and horror.

Adam nodded, then immediately regretted the motion. "Oh yeah. It was quite the performance. You even gave us an encore when you fell into my lap."

Paulette buried her face in her hands, groaning. "Oh god. I'm never drinking again."

Despite the collective misery, there was an undercurrent of good humor in the camp. People exchanged sheepish grins and playful jabs as they recounted snippets of the night's escapades.

As the morning wore on, a steady stream of residents made their way to Jack's shelter. Some came bearing gifts - extra rations, handmade trinkets, promises of future favors - all in hopes of securing a spot on the list for the next batch of moonshine.

Jack, looking surprisingly chipper, greeted each visitor with a knowing smirk. "Seems like my little concoction was a hit," he drawled, clearly enjoying his newfound popularity.

Maria watched the proceedings with a mixture of amusement and concern. She couldn't deny the positive impact the gathering had on the group's morale. The air of camaraderie was palpable, a stark contrast to the tension that had been building in recent weeks.

As she helped distribute water and herbal remedies for the hangovers, Maria reflected on the delicate balance they needed to maintain. These moments of joy were crucial for their survival, a reminder of what they were fighting for. But they couldn't lose sight of the harsh reality of their situation.

CHAPTER TWENTY FOUR

J oe Kelly led his group through the dense Florida woods, his senses on high alert. The agreed meeting point was just ahead, a small clearing barely visible through the thick foliage. As they approached, Joe signaled for his team to spread out and secure the perimeter, his hand moving in a series of practiced gestures.

"Keep your eyes peeled," he muttered, scanning the treeline with practiced vigilance. "We don't know what—or who—might be out here. Stay frosty."

Minutes ticked by in tense silence, the only sounds the soft rustling of leaves and the occasional call of a distant bird. Then, a rustling from the east caught their attention. Joe's hand instinctively went to his holster, his fingers brushing against the cool metal of his sidearm, but he relaxed when he saw Jake and Dave emerge from the underbrush.

"Glad you made it," Joe said, clasping Jake's hand firmly, feeling the calluses that had formed over months of hard survival.

Dave nodded grimly, his eyes darting around the

clearing. "Ran into some trouble on the way, but nothing we couldn't handle. Had to take a detour through some swampy terrain."

The two groups merged, exchanging quick updates and wary glances at their surroundings. The atmosphere was thick with anticipation, everyone acutely aware that their rendezvous wasn't complete. Each person stood ready, weapons at hand, ears straining for any sign of approaching danger.

Nearly an hour passed before they heard the telltale signs of another group approaching. Captain Rodriguez's team materialized from the shadows, moving with military precision, their movements fluid and coordinated.

"Captain," Joe acknowledged, stepping forward to meet him, his posture straightening almost unconsciously in the presence of the military man.

Rodriguez's eyes swept over the assembled group, quickly assessing their condition with the practiced eye of a seasoned commander. "Looks like we all made it in one piece," he said, his voice low and controlled, betraying no hint of the relief he felt at seeing them all alive.

The three leaders huddled together, speaking in hushed tones while their respective groups maintained a cautious distance. The air crackled with tension as everyone realized the gravity of their situation, the weight of their mission pressing down on them like a physical force.

Joe couldn't help but notice the haggard appearance of Rodriguez's men. Their uniforms were torn and dirty, their faces etched with fatigue and marked with small cuts and bruises. It was clear they had been through hell to get here, fighting their way through who knows what dangers.

Similarly, Rodriguez took in the makeshift weapons and determined expressions of Joe's group. They had a fire in their eyes that spoke volumes about their will to survive. He saw the way they held their weapons, the alertness in their postures, and knew they were ready for whatever came next.

As the initial greetings subsided, an uneasy quiet settled over the clearing. Each person present knew that this meeting was just the beginning of a dangerous journey ahead, a first step on a path that could lead to freedom or destruction.

Captain Rodriguez cleared his throat, drawing everyone's attention. "We've got intel," he said, his voice low but clear, carrying easily across the hushed clearing. "There's resistance activity in Dunnellon."

Joe's eyebrows shot up, a spark of hope igniting in his chest. "Resistance? Against the Colonel?"

Rodriguez nodded, a hint of excitement breaking through his professional demeanor. "Seems like it. We watched a group take out one of the Colonel's trucks, blew it to bits. Looks like there's an organized group pushing back against his control. They appeared a bit rag tagged but seemed to know what they we're doing. They were in and out like ghosts"

The news sent a ripple of excitement through the gathered survivors. Jake stepped forward, hope glimmering in his eyes, his voice barely containing his enthusiasm. "This could be huge. If we could join forces with them... we might actually have a much better chance at taking down the Colonel's operation."

"Hold on," Dave interjected, always the voice of caution, his brow furrowed in concern. "We don't know anything about these people. What if it's a trap? The Colonel's been known to use false flags before."

Joe rubbed his chin, considering, feeling the rough stubble beneath his fingers. "Dave's got a point. But potential allies could be a game-changer. We can't afford to ignore this opportunity, but we need to approach it carefully."

The group broke into a heated debate, voices rising and

falling as different opinions were voiced. Some, like Jake, were eager to make contact immediately, seeing it as their best chance at victory. Others, including Dave, urged caution and more reconnaissance, wary of walking into an ambush.

"We can't rush into this," Rodriguez said, his military training evident in his measured tone. "But we can't ignore it either. A local resistance group could provide invaluable support – supplies, intel, manpower. They might have information about the Colonel's operations that we desperately need."

Joe nodded, weighing the risks against the potential benefits, his mind racing through possible scenarios. "Alright, let's break it down. What are our options for making contact? We need to consider every angle here."

The discussion continued, with various plans proposed and dissected. Send a small team to scout? Try to identify a contact and reach out? Wait and gather more information? Each option was carefully considered, its pros and cons debated with intensity.

As they debated, Joe couldn't help but feel a glimmer of hope growing in his chest. If there really was an organized resistance in Dunnellon, it could tip the scales in their favor. But he also knew the risks were immense. One wrong move could expose them all to the Colonel's wrath, bringing down the full force of his army on their heads.

The clearing buzzed with nervous energy as they hashed out the pros and cons. It was clear that this discovery had changed everything. Now, they just had to figure out how to play it, how to turn this unexpected development to their advantage without getting themselves killed in the process.

As the debate wound down, a consensus began to emerge from the chaos of conflicting opinions. Joe cleared his throat, drawing everyone's attention with the authority he had come to command.

"Alright, folks. We've got two clear objectives here. We need to make contact with this resistance group, and we need to disrupt the Colonel's operations. I think our best bet is to split into two main groups. We'll hit them from multiple angles, keep them off balance."

Captain Rodriguez nodded in agreement, his military mind already formulating strategies. "My team can handle the resistance contact. We've got the training for covert ops, and we can approach carefully. We'll use standard recon techniques, establish a secure line of communication before revealing ourselves."

"Good," Joe said, feeling a sense of relief at having a solid plan taking shape. "While you're doing that, my group will focus on disrupting the river patrols. We've got local knowledge that'll come in handy. We know the waterways like the back of our hands."

Jake leaned in, curiosity piqued, his eyes bright with anticipation. "What's the plan for that, Joe? You said earlier they have patrol boats moving up and down the river. What's your plan for dealing with those patrols?"

Joe's eyes lit up with a hint of mischief, a grin tugging at the corners of his mouth. "Ah, glad you asked about that Jake. Jojo came up with a stroke of genius. We're gonna string a rope across the river, just below the water line. When a patrol boat comes by, we lift the rope just enough to catch the boat and force it to stop. While they're trying to figure out what the hell happened, we pick 'em off and retrieve their boat, weapons, supplies and any intel they might be carrying."

Dave let out a low whistle, impressed despite his usual caution. "Simple but effective. I like it. Low-tech solution to a high-tech problem."

"Exactly," Joe continued, his excitement building as he laid out the plan. "We'll need to set up the rope, and then wait under cover on the shoreline for the patrols to fall into our trap. We'll have to be patient, but when it works, it'll be worth it."

Captain Rodriguez looked impressed, nodding his

approval. "That could work. It'll certainly throw a wrench in their operations. Disrupt their patrols, gather intel, and maybe even score some much-needed supplies. Not bad, Joe."

The group spent the next hour hashing out the details, voices overlapping as they worked through every aspect of the plan. Roles were assigned based on each person's strengths and experience, with Joe making sure everyone understood their part in the operation.

"What about risks?" Dave asked, ever cautious, his forehead creased with worry. "If they catch on to what we're doing... if they spot us before we're ready..."

Joe nodded grimly, acknowledging the valid concern. "It's dangerous, no doubt. We'll need lookouts and an escape route planned. And if things go south, we abort immediately. No heroics. The mission isn't worth dying for if we can't complete it."

They discussed potential countermeasures, from emergency signals to backup meeting points. As the plan took shape, a sense of nervous excitement filled the air. It was risky, but it felt good to be taking action, to be doing something proactive instead of just reacting to the Colonel's moves.

As the final details of their plan fell into place, Joe and Captain Rodriguez oversaw the distribution of supplies and equipment. Weapons were checked and double-checked, ammo counted and divided among the team members, and supplies stowed away in waterproof bags. Joe handed out detailed maps of the area to key team members, going over the terrain one last time.

"Remember," Joe said, his voice low but firm, carrying the weight of command, "conserve your resources. We don't know how long this operation might last. Every bullet, every scrap of food could make the difference between success and failure."

Captain Rodriguez added, his tone equally serious, "And stay alert. The Colonel's men could be anywhere. Don't let your guard down for a second, even if you think you're in a safe area."

The groups huddled together for some last-minute advice, tension and anticipation thick in the air. Dave stressed the importance of stealth, reminding everyone to move quietly and stay out of sight. Jake went over the designated roles one more time, making sure everyone knew their part in the plan inside and out. They set a time and location for their next rendezvous, choosing a secluded spot upstream that offered good visibility and multiple escape routes.

As the moment of departure drew near, a somber mood settled over the clearing. Joe looked around at the faces of his brothers in arms, acutely aware of the dangers that lay ahead. He saw determination in their eyes, but also fear, hope, and resolve.

"Listen up, everyone," he said, his voice thick with emotion, struggling to find the right words for the moment. "What we're about to do... it's not going to be easy. We're going up against a well-armed, ruthless enemy. But remember why we're doing this. For our families, for our future. For a chance to live free from the Colonel's tyranny."

Captain Rodriguez stepped forward, his posture straight and proud, embodying the strength and discipline of a seasoned soldier. "You've all shown incredible strength to make it this far. Trust your training, trust each other, and we'll get through this. Remember, we're fighting for something bigger than ourselves. Stay focused, stay alert, and watch each other's backs."

Nods of agreement rippled through the group, faces set with determination. There were no long goodbyes – just quick hugs, firm handshakes, and meaningful looks exchanged between comrades. Words seemed inadequate in the face of what they were about to undertake.

With a final nod to Joe, Captain Rodriguez led his team back towards Dunnellon, disappearing swiftly into the dense Florida undergrowth. The rustling of leaves and snapping of twigs faded quickly, leaving an eerie silence in their wake.

Joe turned to the remaining group, his jaw set with resolve. "Alright, folks. Let's move out. Stay low, stay quiet, and remember the plan. We've got a long night ahead of us."

As they set off towards the river, a palpable sense of determination settled over the group. Despite the weight of their mission, there was a spark of hope in their eyes, a fire that burned bright in the face of adversity. They moved with purpose, each step taking them closer to their goal of undermining the Colonel's control. The dense Florida wilderness swallowed them up, concealing their passage as they ventured forth into the unknown, ready to face whatever challenges lay ahead.

CHAPTER TWENTY FIVE

Joe led the group through the dense Florida underbrush, their footsteps muffled by years of fallen leaves and pine needles. The air hung heavy with humidity, clinging to their skin like a second layer as they moved silently towards their hidden boats. The scent of damp earth and decaying vegetation filled their nostrils. As they approached the concealed location, Joe raised his fist, signaling the group to halt with a gesture honed by years of experience.

"Alright, let's go over the plan one more time," Joe whispered, his voice barely audible above the gentle lapping of the river and the distant chorus of cicadas. The group huddled close, their faces etched with determination and a hint of nervous anticipation.

Jojo stepped forward, his eyes scanning the far bank with the practiced gaze of a seasoned soldier. "Sam and I will cross the river. We'll use the jon boat to set up the rope, making sure it's secure and hidden from view."

Sam nodded, adding, "We'll tie it off to a sturdy tree on the other side, preferably an oak or cypress. Should give us a good anchor point and enough strength to hold."

"Once they're back, we'll secure this end," Joe
continued, his voice low but firm. "Remember, we need
to work fast and stay alert. In and out in 30 minutes,
tops. Any longer, and we risk exposure."

The group murmured their agreement, a collective
determination settling over them like a shroud. Joe
looked at each of them in turn, seeing the resolve in
their eyes and the tension in their postures. "Alright,
let's move. Stay sharp and watch each other's backs."

Jojo and Sam wasted no time, their movements fluid
and practiced from countless drills and real-world
operations. They slipped into the jon boat with barely
a sound, their weight distributed evenly to prevent
rocking. Sam fired up the outboard, keeping the revs
low to minimize noise as he expertly steered the boat
to the opposite bank. Jojo kept watch, his eyes alert for
any sign of movement on either bank, his hand resting
lightly on his weapon.

As they reached the far side, Jojo leapt out, rope in
hand, his feet finding purchase on the slippery bank.
He moved swiftly through the undergrowth, pushing
aside hanging vines and ducking under low-hanging
branches, seeking out the perfect tree. Finding a sturdy
oak with a trunk as thick as a man's torso, he quickly
secured the rope, his fingers working deftly as he tied
a series of complex knots. He tested it with a firm tug,

satisfied when it held fast.

Meanwhile, Sam kept the boat steady, his muscles tense as he scanned their surroundings with the heightened awareness of a trained operative. The only sounds were the gentle lapping of water against the boat's hull and the distant calls of birds hidden in the canopy above.

With the rope secured, Jojo returned to the boat, his movements quick but controlled. They crossed back to their side of the river, where Joe and the others waited anxiously, their bodies taut with tension. As soon as they touched the bank, Jojo quickly threw the rope to his dad, the coil unfurling in a graceful arc. He and Sam then guided the jon boat back to its place of hiding, concealing it beneath a camouflage net and a layer of branches.

Joe took the rope from Jojo, quickly finding a suitable anchor point. With practiced efficiency, born from years of experience in the wilderness, he carefully wrapped it twice around a thick tree, his calloused hands working the rope with precision. He positioned it just below the waterline, where it would remain hidden from casual observation. When it came time, all that would be needed was to pull the rope slowly to raise it and hopefully snag their prey in a trap as old as warfare itself.

"Time?" Joe asked, his voice low and gruff, barely

above a whisper.

"Eighteen minutes," came the whispered reply from Dave, who had been keeping a watchful eye on his watch.

Joe nodded, a flicker of satisfaction evident in his eyes despite the gravity of the situation. "Good work, everyone. Now we wait. Stay alert and remember your training."

The group melted into the shadows of the riverbank, finding cover among the thick vegetation with the skill of seasoned hunters. Joe crouched behind a fallen log, its bark rough beneath his weathered hands. Moss and lichen clung to the decaying wood, providing additional camouflage. To his left, Jojo and Sam positioned themselves behind a cluster of saw palmettos, their military training evident in their silent, efficient movements. The sharp-edged fronds provided excellent cover while allowing them a clear view of the river.

Joe's eyes never left the river, scanning the murky water for any sign of movement. The gentle current carried debris downstream - leaves, twigs, the occasional plastic bottle, a stark reminder of the world that once was. Each new shape on the water's surface sent a jolt of anticipation through the group, only to fade as it passed harmlessly by. The tension was palpable, a living thing that seemed to pulse with each passing moment.

Minutes crawled by, feeling like hours in the oppressive heat and humidity. The air grew thick with tension, broken only by the occasional buzz of an insect or the distant call of a bird. Sweat beaded on Joe's forehead, trickling down his temples, but he dared not move to wipe it away. Every muscle in his body screamed for movement, for release, but he remained as still as the ancient trees surrounding them.

Jojo shifted slightly, adjusting his grip on his rifle, the metal warm beneath his palms. He caught his father's eye, a silent question passing between them. Joe gave an almost imperceptible shake of his head. Not yet. The waiting game continued, each second stretching into eternity.

The wait wore on, testing the limits of their endurance and patience. Sam's muscles ached from holding still for so long, but he remained motionless, his eyes fixed on the far bank. Every rustle in the undergrowth, every ripple on the water's surface, demanded their full attention. The weight of their mission, the lives depending on their success, pressed down on them like a physical force.

As the sun climbed higher in the sky, the heat became oppressive, seeming to suck the very air from their lungs. The group's breathing grew shallow, their bodies tense with anticipation. Joe felt his heart pounding in his chest, each beat seeming to echo in the stillness. Sweat trickled down his back, his shirt clinging uncomfortably to his skin.

A fish jumped nearby, the splash shattering the silence like a gunshot. Everyone flinched, muscles coiling instinctively, then quickly settled back into their positions, eyes wide and alert. The anticipation was palpable, a living thing that hung in the air between them, thick enough to cut with a knife.

The silence was shattered by the distant hum of an engine, the sound carrying clearly over the water. Joe's hand tightened on his weapon, his eyes narrowing as he scanned the river with renewed intensity. The sound grew louder, unmistakable now - a boat was approaching, its engine thrumming with purpose.

"Heads down," Joe whispered, his voice barely audible but carrying the full weight of command. The group pressed themselves lower into their hiding spots, hearts pounding in their chests. The rustle of leaves and the soft creak of branches were the only signs of their movement.

Jojo's keen eyes, honed by years of military service, caught the first glimpse of movement on the water. "Visual," he breathed, his body tense as a coiled spring, ready to unleash at a moment's notice.

The boat came into view, its outline growing clearer with each passing second. Joe squinted, studying its profile with the practiced eye of a seasoned veteran. The sleek lines, the telltale shape of a pontoon - there was no mistaking it. This was what they had been waiting for, the moment of truth.

"Patrol boat," Sam confirmed, his voice a low rumble, barely audible above the approaching engine. "Five men on board. Armed."

Joe nodded grimly, a mixture of anticipation and determination etched on his weathered features. This was what they'd been waiting for, the culmination of weeks of planning and preparation. He glanced at Jojo and Sam, seeing the same mix of anticipation and steely resolve in their eyes that he felt himself.

The patrol boat drew closer, its wake lapping against the shore in gentle waves. Joe could make out the figures on board now - five men in black uniforms, their eyes scanning the riverbanks as they passed. The sun glinted off their weapons, a stark reminder of the danger they posed.

"Get ready," Joe murmured, his fingers flexing on his weapon, muscle memory taking over. The group tensed, ready to spring into action at his signal. Every sense was heightened, every nerve on edge as they prepared for what was to come.

The boat was almost upon them now, close enough for Joe to hear the low conversation between the men on board, their words indistinct but their tone alert and professional. He could see the sunlight glinting off their weapons and the insignia on their uniforms. His breath caught in his throat as the boat neared the submerged rope, the moment of truth rapidly approaching.

Jojo shifted slightly, his rifle at the ready, his finger resting lightly beside the trigger. Sam's hand moved to the rope, prepared to pull it taut at Joe's command. The air crackled with tension as the group waited, poised on the knife's edge between hiding and action.

Joe's eyes never left the approaching boat, tracking its progress with laser focus. His mind raced, calculating distance and timing with the precision of a chess master. They would only get one shot at this, one chance to turn the tables and gain the upper hand. He drew in a deep breath, steadying himself for what was to come, the weight of leadership and responsibility settling heavily on his shoulders.

As the boat entered the kill zone, Joe's muscles tensed, ready to give the signal that would unleash chaos on the unsuspecting patrol. The fate of their mission, perhaps even their very survival, hung in the balance of the next few seconds. The jungle held its breath, as if nature itself was waiting to see what would unfold on this humid Florida morning.

CHAPTER TWENTY SIX

C aptain Rodriguez's men approached the outskirts of Dunnellon. The group coming to a halt in a secluded clearing, hidden from prying eyes by dense foliage.

Captain Rodriguez stepped out in front of his men, his sharp gaze sweeping the area. "Alright people, let's move. We need to set up a perimeter and establish our base camp."

As the group bustled into action, Miguel approached the Captain, his face etched with determination. "Cappy, we need to discuss our next move."

Rodriguez nodded, gesturing for Miguel to follow him to a makeshift command post. "What's on your mind, Mig?"

"We need intel on the town's defenses, supply routes, and key locations," Miguel said, his voice low and urgent. "But we can't risk sending in a large team. It'd draw too much attention."

The Captain's brow furrowed as he considered Miguel's words. "You're right. We need someone to infiltrate, blend in with the locals. Get a feel for the lay of the land."

Miguel's eyes lit up with a mix of anticipation and resolve. "I can do it, sir. With my appearance, I could pass for a drifter or a day laborer. No one would look twice."

Rodriguez studied Miguel for a long moment, weighing the risks and potential rewards. Finally, he nodded. "Alright, Miguel. You're our best shot at this. But remember, this is strictly reconnaissance. No heroics, understood?"

"Yes, sir," Miguel replied, a hint of a smile tugging at his lips.

As the sun began to dip towards the horizon, Miguel set out towards Dunnellon, his gait relaxed and unhurried. He'd swapped his usual attire for more worn, nondescript clothing that would help him blend in with the town's working-class residents.

Approaching the town limits, Miguel took a deep breath, settling into his role. He hunched his shoulders slightly, adopting the weary posture of a man down on his luck. As he entered Dunnellon proper, he kept his eyes low but alert, taking in every detail of his surroundings.

The streets were busy with people going about their daily lives, a facade of normalcy that belied the tension

Miguel could feel thrumming beneath the surface. He shuffled along, just another face in the crowd, all the while cataloging potential weaknesses in the town's defenses and noting the locations of important buildings.

Miguel meandered through Dunnellon's streets, his keen eyes taking in every detail. The Colonel's influence was palpable. The atmosphere was a strange mix of order and unease, as if the town was balanced on a knife's edge.

Spotting a bustling marketplace, Miguel decided it was the perfect place to gather information. He approached a weathered fruit stand, running his calloused hands over an apple.

"Quite the selection you've got here," he remarked casually to the vendor.

The old woman behind the stand eyed him warily. "The Colonel makes sure we're well-supplied. You new in town?"

Miguel nodded, adopting a sheepish grin. "Just passing through, looking for work. Any leads?"

She softened slightly. "Check the marinas on the river. They're always short-handed."

Miguel thanked her and moved on, filing away the

information. He made his way to a group of laborers taking a break near the docks.

"Mind if I join you fellas?" he asked, settling down without waiting for an answer. "Heard there might be work here."

One of the men, a burly guy with a thick beard, grunted. "If you don't mind breaking your back for the Colonel's scraps."

Miguel raised an eyebrow. "That bad, huh?"

The group exchanged glances before another worker, younger and more nervous, spoke up. "It's not all bad. We've got food, protection. Better than being out there."

"Yeah, if you don't mind trading your soul," the bearded man muttered.

Miguel listened intently as the conversation flowed around him, picking up snippets of discontent. There were whispers of unfair rationing, of people disappearing in the night. But also grudging admissions of the Colonel's organizational skills, how he'd brought a semblance of order to the chaos.

As the day wore on, Miguel engaged with various groups - marina workers, shopkeepers, even a few of the Colonel's lower-ranking men. He pieced together a picture of Dunnellon under the Colonel's rule - a place of relative safety and stability, but at a steep cost.

As dusk settled over Dunnellon, Miguel's wanderings led him to a dimly lit alleyway behind a row of dilapidated warehouses. The sound of hushed voices caught his attention, and he slowed his pace, straining to hear.

"The Colonel's gone too far this time," a woman's voice hissed. "Taking food from children? It's inhuman."

"Shh!" another voice warned. "You want to end up like old man Carmichael?"

Miguel's interest piqued. He edged closer, careful to keep his footsteps silent.

"We can't just sit back and do nothing," a third voice chimed in, deep and gravelly. "The Colonel's chokehold on this town is getting tighter every day."

Heart racing, Miguel realized he'd stumbled upon something significant. These people were openly criticizing the Colonel - a dangerous act in a town under his control. Could they be part of an organized resistance?

Taking a deep breath, Miguel stepped out of the shadows and approached the group. "Couldn't help but overhear," he said softly, raising his hands in a non-threatening gesture. "Sounds like you folks aren't too fond of the Colonel."

The conversation died instantly. Four pairs of eyes snapped to Miguel, filled with a mix of fear and suspicion. The group consisted of two men and two women, all bearing the weathered look of people who'd seen hard times.

"Who the hell are you?" the large man with the gravelly voice demanded, stepping protectively in front of the others.

Miguel kept his posture relaxed, but he could feel the tension crackling in the air. "Name's Miguel. I'm new in town, just looking for work. But I'm starting to think this might not be the best place to settle down."

The woman who'd spoken first, a wiry redhead with sharp eyes, scoffed. "You got that right, stranger. Best keep moving if you know what's good for you."

"Unless," the other man said, his voice low and dangerous, "you're one of the Colonel's spies. Come to root out dissent?"

Miguel shook his head emphatically. "No, nothing like that. I've got no love for tyrants, believe me."

The group exchanged glances, their suspicion palpable. Miguel could see them weighing their options, trying to decide if he was a threat or a potential ally.

"How do we know we can trust you?" the second woman asked, her hand hovering near her hip where Miguel suspected she had a concealed weapon.

Miguel held up his hands placatingly. "Look, I understand your caution. In times like these, trust is hard to come by. But I've seen what men like the Colonel can do to good people. I've got my own reasons for opposing him."

The group exchanged glances, their suspicion softening slightly.

"Alright," the gravelly-voiced man said. "I'm Jim. This here's Gina, Mack, and Diana. What's your story?"

Miguel nodded, choosing his words carefully. "I've seen communities torn apart by men drunk on power. Families separated, resources hoarded. It ain't right."

Gina, the redhead, stepped forward. "You don't know the half of it. The Colonel, he talks a good game about protection and order, but the cost..." Her voice trailed off, eyes distant.

Jim's face darkened. "They took my wife," he said, his voice barely above a whisper. "Said she was 'needed for special duties.' Haven't seen her in weeks."

The others murmured sympathetically, and Diana spoke up. "My son questioned one of the Colonel's new policies. Next day, he was gone. Just... vanished."

Mack nodded grimly. "It's the same all over town. You toe the line or you disappear."

Miguel listened intently, his heart heavy. These were the stories Captain Rodriguez needed to hear, the human cost of the Colonel's regime.

Taking a deep breath, Miguel decided to take a risk. "I'm going to be honest with you folks. I'm not just some drifter. I'm here to gather information, to find out what's really going on in Dunnellon."

The group tensed, hands moving towards concealed weapons.

"Wait," Miguel said quickly. "I'm not working for the Colonel. I'm with a group that wants to help. We're planning to take him down, but we need to know what we're up against."

Miguel took a deep breath, his eyes scanning the wary faces around him. "I'm part of a group based out of Leesburg. We've got National Guard troops with us, led by Captain Rodriguez. Our mission is to take down the Colonel and put an end to his reign of terror. He's been causing trouble all over the state."

The group exchanged glances, a mix of hope and skepticism on their faces.

"National Guard?" Jim asked, his gravelly voice tinged with disbelief. "Thought they were all gone."

Miguel shook his head. "Not all. We've got a solid core of trained soldiers, plus civilians who've learned to fight. We're organized, and we've got a plan."

Gina stepped forward, her eyes narrowed. "If that's true, why come here alone? Why the subterfuge?"

"We needed intel," Miguel explained. "Can't mount an assault without knowing what we're up against. The Colonel's got this place locked down tight."

Mack nodded slowly. "That he does. But if what you're saying is true..."

Miguel saw the spark of hope in their eyes and pressed on. "Look, we could use people like you. Folks who know the lay of the land, who understand how the Colonel operates. I'm proposing an alliance."

Diana spoke up, her voice cautious but intrigued. "What kind of alliance?"

"Join forces with us," Miguel said, his voice low and urgent. "Help us take down the Colonel. You know this town, its people. With your knowledge and our firepower, we stand a real chance."

The group huddled together, whispered conversations flying back and forth. Miguel waited, tension coiling in his gut. This could be the break they needed.

Finally, Jim turned back to him. "We'll need to verify your story, of course. But if what you're saying is true..." He paused, a fierce light in his eyes. "Count us in."

Miguel nodded, relief washing over him. "I understand. We'll need to be careful about how we communicate, but I can arrange a meeting with my superiors."

As they began to discuss the logistics of their newfound alliance, Miguel felt a surge of hope. They had taken the first step towards liberating Dunnellon from the Colonel's iron grip.

The resistance fighters huddled together, their voices low and urgent as they discussed Miguel's proposal. After several tense minutes, Jim turned back to Miguel, his weathered face set with determination.

"Alright, we're willing to meet your group," Jim said, his gravelly voice barely above a whisper. "But we need to be smart about this. How do you suggest we proceed?"

Miguel nodded, relief washing over him. "I'll take three of you to meet Captain Rodriguez. We'll use a secure location outside town. You can verify our claims and resources for yourselves."

Gina stepped forward, her eyes sharp. "I'm in. Someone needs to make sure this isn't a trap."

Mack and Diana quickly volunteered as well. Jim agreed to stay behind and coordinate with the rest of their network.

As night fell, Miguel led the three resistance fighters through the outskirts of Dunnellon. They moved silently, sticking to the shadows, every sense alert for any sign of the Colonel's patrols.

The group's tension was palpable as they approached the meeting point. Miguel could feel the weight of their scrutiny, their lingering doubts about his story.

"We're almost there," Miguel murmured, gesturing towards a clearing ahead.

As they entered the clearing, Captain Rodriguez stepped out from behind a tree, his posture alert but non-threatening. "Welcome," he said, his voice low and steady. "I'm Captain Rodriguez."

Gina, Mack, and Diana tensed, their eyes darting between the Captain and the other soldiers emerging from the treeline.

"Easy," Miguel said softly. "Remember why we're here."

Captain Rodriguez held up his hands, palms out.

"We're not here to cause trouble. We want to help liberate Dunnellon from the Colonel's control."

Gina stepped forward, her chin lifted defiantly. "Prove it. Show us you're really National Guard, not just some other group looking to take over."

The Captain nodded, understanding their caution. He began explaining their mission, detailing their resources and plans. As he spoke, the resistance fighters' postures gradually relaxed, hope beginning to replace suspicion in their eyes.

Captain Rodriguez finished outlining their resources and initial strategy. The resistance fighters listened intently, their expressions a mix of hope and cautious optimism.

Gina spoke up first. "Alright, let's say we believe you. How do you propose we work together?"

The Captain nodded, appreciating her directness. "We need your local knowledge and connections. You know the town, its people, and the Colonel's operations better than we ever could."

Mack leaned forward. "We've got a network of about thirty people we trust. Some in key positions - the Colonel's staff, guards, supply managers."

"That's excellent," Rodriguez said. "We'll need detailed

information on the Colonel's defenses, patrol schedules, and any weaknesses in his security."

Diana chimed in. "We can provide that, but what about the civilians? We can't risk a full-scale assault with innocent people caught in the crossfire."

The Captain's expression softened. "Agreed. Our primary objective is to remove the Colonel with minimal collateral damage. We'll need your help to evacuate key areas when the time comes."

Miguel, who had been quietly observing, added, "We could also use your network to spread disinformation. Create confusion in the Colonel's ranks before we strike."

The group nodded, warming to the idea. Gina's eyes lit up. "We could stage a few small incidents, draw his forces to the wrong areas."

"Good thinking," Rodriguez agreed. "Now, let's talk about communication. We'll need a secure way to share information."

They spent the next hour hashing out details - code words, dead drops, and emergency protocols. As the meeting wound down, there was a palpable sense of purpose in the air.

"We'll need a few days to get everything in place,"

Mack said. "But we're in. It's time the Colonel learned he's not untouchable."

Captain Rodriguez extended his hand. "Welcome aboard.

I believe together, we'll bring freedom back to Dunnellon."

As they shook hands, sealing their alliance, the first glimmer of dawn began to lighten the eastern sky. A new day was coming - for Dunnellon and for the fight against the Colonel's tyranny.

CHAPTER TWENTY SEVEN

J oe crouched in the dense undergrowth along the riverbank, his heart pounding in his chest. He glanced at Sam and Jojo, their faces taut with concentration, beads of sweat forming on their brows. The rest of their team was spread out nearby, hidden among the lush foliage and waiting with bated breath. The low rumble of the approaching engine broke the stillness, growing louder with each passing second. Sam's grip tightened on the rope in his hands, his knuckles turning white with the tension.

"Get ready," Joe whispered, his voice barely audible above the gentle lapping of the water against the shore.

The patrol boat rounded the bend, cutting through the mist that clung to the water's surface like a ghostly shroud. Joe could make out five of the Colonel's men aboard, their eyes scanning the shoreline with practiced vigilance. Their weapons glinted in the early morning light, a stark reminder of the danger they faced.

Joe waited, counting the seconds as his pulse quickened. The boat drew closer, closer... The anticipation was almost unbearable.

"Now!" he hissed, his voice sharp and urgent.

Sam began to pull on the rope with all his might, his muscles straining with the effort. It moved upward right under the pontoon patrol boat, the rough fibers catching on the propeller with a satisfying jerk.

The boat began to slow, its momentum gradually ebbing away until it finally came to a dead stop in the middle of the river. The sudden halt sent ripples across the water's surface, disturbing the mist and creating an eerie, dreamlike scene.

Confusion erupted among the Colonel's soldiers as their boat lurched to an abrupt halt. They stumbled, grabbing onto railings and each other to keep their balance, their curses echoing across the water.

"What the hell?" one of them barked, steadying himself against the helm, his eyes wide with surprise and growing concern.

The five men scrambled around the deck, peering over the sides into the murky water. Their movements were frantic, eyes darting from the river to each other and back again, searching for any explanation for their sudden predicament.

"Check the engine!" the leader shouted, his voice tinged with panic and a hint of frustration. His hand instinctively moved to the weapon at his hip, ready for any potential threat.

Two men rushed to the rear of the boat, fumbling with the engine cover, their fingers clumsy with urgency. The others continued to search the water's surface for any sign of what might have stopped them, leaning dangerously far over the railings.

"I don't see anything," one called out, leaning precariously over the side, his voice laced with confusion and a touch of fear.

"Be careful, you idiot," another snapped, yanking him back by his collar with surprising force. "You want to fall in? Who knows what's in these waters."

The two at the engine emerged, shaking their heads in bewilderment. "It's still running, sir. Nothing wrong that we can see. It just... won't move."

Frustration and fear mingled on the leader's face as he scanned the shoreline, his eyes narrowed suspiciously. The dense foliage revealed nothing, but he couldn't shake the feeling they were being watched. His instincts screamed danger, but there was nothing tangible to act upon.

One of the soldiers, a lanky man with a patchy beard, suddenly shouted, "We must've run aground!" His voice carried a note of desperate hope, clinging to any rational explanation.

The others turned to him, hope and skepticism warring in their expressions. The idea seemed to offer a lifeline of normalcy in an increasingly tense situation.

"In the middle of the river?" the leader questioned, but there was a note of desperation in his voice. He wanted to believe it, wanted any explanation that didn't involve an ambush or some other nefarious plot.

"Could be a sandbar," the bearded man insisted, gaining confidence in his theory. "River's always changing, right? Currents shift, bring in new sediment. It happens."

The leader nodded slowly, latching onto the idea like a drowning man grasping at a life preserver. "Alright, let's check the hull. If we're grounded, we need to know where. Maybe we can push ourselves off."

As the Colonel's men leaned over the sides of the boat, their attention fully focused on the murky waters below, Joe gave a sharp whistle. The sound cut through the air like a knife, signaling the moment they'd all been waiting for.

In an instant, the riverbank erupted with gunfire. Joe, Jojo, Sam, Jake, and Dave opened fire simultaneously, their weapons trained on the exposed soldiers. The sudden cacophony shattered the stillness, sending birds scattering from nearby trees in panicked flight.

The sudden barrage caught the patrol completely off guard. Two men fell immediately, their bodies slumping over the railing with sickening thuds. The others scrambled for cover, but in the confined space of the boat, there was nowhere to hide. Their shouts of alarm and pain mingled with the relentless gunfire.

"Take 'em all down!" Joe shouted over the din, his voice hoarse with adrenaline. "Don't let any of them escape!"

The remaining three soldiers managed to return fire, but their shots went wide, thudding harmlessly into the trees and kicking up sprays of water. The element of surprise had robbed them of any real chance to mount an effective defense. Within seconds, they too had fallen, their bodies sprawled across the deck in grotesque poses.

As the echoes of gunfire faded, replaced by an eerie silence, Joe signaled to Jojo and Sam. The two men quickly pushed their small jon boat back into the river and began moving toward the patrol boat with swift, practiced efficiency.

Sam clambered aboard, his eyes scanning for any signs of movement, his weapon at the ready. "Clear!" he called back to the others, his voice tinged with a mixture of relief and grim satisfaction.

Methodically, Sam began to search the bodies, collecting

weapons and ammunition with efficient movements. He tossed each item to Jojo, who stowed them in the jon boat, arranging them carefully to maintain balance.

"Good haul," Sam muttered, hefting a high-powered rifle with an appreciative whistle. "The Colonel keeps his boys well-armed. This'll come in handy."

As they worked, Jake and Dave stood vigilant on the shoreline, weapons ready for any further trouble. Their eyes scanned the river and the surrounding forest, alert for any sign of reinforcements or other patrols.

"Let's make this quick," Joe called from the shore, his voice taut with urgency. "We don't know when another patrol might come by. We need to be long gone before anyone realizes what's happened here."

One by one, they rolled the bodies over the side, their movements grim but determined. The river's dark waters swallowed them without a sound, leaving no trace of the ambush behind. The current would carry the evidence far downstream, buying them precious time.

Sam surveyed the patrol boat one last time, his experienced eye ensuring they hadn't missed anything valuable. Satisfied, he moved to the stern and waved his arm in a circular motion, signaling the all-clear.

Joe nodded, understanding the signal. He began to

lower the rope that had snagged the boat's propeller, allowing it to sink back into the murky water. The simple yet effective trap had served its purpose perfectly.

As the rope disappeared beneath the surface, Sam fired up the engine. The patrol boat lurched forward, free from its unexpected tether. With practiced ease, Sam guided the vessel towards their predetermined hiding spot, a secluded inlet shrouded by overhanging trees and thick vegetation.

Jojo followed close behind in the jon boat, his eyes constantly scanning the shoreline for any signs of trouble. The two boats moved silently through the water, leaving barely a ripple in their wake. Years of experience had taught them the value of stealth.

As they approached the inlet, Joe and the others emerged from their hiding spots, grins spreading across their faces. The mission had gone off without a hitch, a rare moment of unqualified success in their ongoing struggle.

Sam expertly maneuvered the patrol boat into the concealed area, cutting the engine as Jojo tied off the jon boat. The team gathered on the shore, clapping each other on the back and exchanging triumphant looks. The adrenaline of the ambush was still coursing through their veins, lending an extra edge to their celebrations.

"Nice work, everyone," Joe said, his voice low but filled with pride. "We just dealt a significant blow to the Colonel's operations. This'll set him back, no doubt about it."

Dave chuckled, shaking his head in disbelief. "I still can't believe how smooth that went. Those bastards never knew what hit 'em. It was like taking candy from a baby."

Jake nodded in agreement, but his expression remained cautious. "The element of surprise was definitely on our side. But we can't count on that every time. We got lucky today."

"Jake's right," Joe said, his expression turning serious as the reality of their situation reasserted itself. "We need to plan our next move carefully. The Colonel won't take this lying down. He'll be out for blood once he realizes what's happened."

The group huddled closer, their voices dropping to whispers as they discussed potential targets and strategies. Ideas flew back and forth – sabotaging supply lines, disrupting communication networks, maybe even a raid on one of the Colonel's outposts. Each option was weighed carefully, considering both potential gains and risks.

As they talked, Sam and Jojo began the task of securing the captured patrol boat. They covered it with camouflage netting, their movements quick and efficient. Layer by layer, they blended it seamlessly into the surrounding foliage. Any passing boat would be hard-pressed to spot it, even if they knew exactly where to look.

The successful ambush had provided them with valuable resources and a morale boost, but Joe knew they couldn't afford to become complacent. The war against the Colonel was far from over, and each victory only raised the stakes. As he listened to his team's ideas, Joe's mind was already racing ahead, planning their next move in this deadly game of cat and mouse.

CHAPTER TWENTY EIGHT

T he Colonel paced back and forth in his opulent office, nestled in the heart of Dunnellon. The room, once a quaint city hall chamber, now exuded an air of menace and power. His polished white shoes clicked against the hardwood floor, a sharp counterpoint to the tense silence. The antique grandfather clock in the corner ticked away the seconds, each sound like a hammer blow in the oppressive atmosphere.

"Get in here, now!" he barked, his southern drawl tinged with barely contained rage. The words echoed off the wood-paneled walls, making even the portraits of long-dead politicians seem to flinch.

One by one, his top men filed into the room. They arranged themselves around a large oak table, their faces a mixture of apprehension and forced stoicism. The Colonel's fury was legendary, and none wanted to be its target. Each man tried to make himself as small and inconspicuous as possible, a feat made difficult by their imposing physiques.

He stopped his pacing, planting both hands on the table and leaning forward. His eyes, normally twinkling with calculated charm, now blazed with an intensity that made even his hardened followers flinch. The veins in his temples throbbed visibly, a testament to his barely contained fury.

"Would someone care to explain," he began, his voice deceptively soft, "why everything seems to be going to hell in a handbasket?" The words dripped with venom, each syllable carefully enunciated for maximum effect.

No one dared speak. The Colonel's close-lipped smile grew wider, more predatory. It was the smile of a shark circling its prey, promising imminent violence.

"No takers? Well then, allow me to illuminate our current predicament." His tone was almost conversational, but the underlying threat was unmistakable.

He pushed off from the table, resuming his pacing. The floorboards creaked under his weight, punctuating each step with an ominous groan. "In the past week alone, we've had three supply trucks explode. Poof!" He gestured expansively, his hands painting a picture of destruction in the air. "Gone, just like that. Along with all the food and ammunition they were carrying. Months of careful planning and resource allocation, up in smoke."

The Colonel's voice began to rise, his carefully

cultivated southern charm giving way to raw fury. "Then there's the matter of our patrols. Men vanishing into thin air, leaving not so much as a boot print behind. Trained soldiers, armed to the teeth, disappearing without a trace. And let's not forget the fires. Oh, the fires!" He slammed his fist on the table, making everyone jump. The sound reverberated through the room like a gunshot. "Our grain stores, our fuel depots – all up in smoke! The very lifeblood of our operation, reduced to ashes!"

He whirled to face his men, his carefully cultivated image of genteel charm completely shattered. His face was a mask of rage, eyes bulging, spittle flying from his lips as he shouted. "And now, the cherry on top of this shit sundae – we've lost contact with three of our river patrols. Three damn boats and their crews, just gone! Vanished into the murky waters of the Withlacoochee like they never existed!"

The Colonel's chest heaved as he fought to control his breathing. His piercing blue eyes swept the room, pinning each person in turn with their intensity. The silence was deafening, broken only by the ragged sound of his breathing and the relentless ticking of the grandfather clock.

"So I ask you, my trusted advisors," he hissed, leaning in close. His breath, hot and smelling faintly of bourbon, washed over their faces. "What in tarnation is happening to my operation?"

The room remained silent for several agonizing moments. The tension was palpable, thick enough to cut with a knife. Then, a stocky man with a salt-and-pepper beard cleared his throat. The sound was like a thunderclap in the oppressive silence.

"Colonel, if I may," Gonzalez began, his voice steady despite the tension. He straightened his shoulders, meeting the Colonel's gaze with a mixture of respect and trepidation. "We believe there's an organized resistance movement operating in the area. This isn't just random acts of sabotage or isolated incidents of rebellion."

The Colonel's eyes narrowed, his gaze boring into Gonzalez like a laser. "Go on," he growled, his voice low and dangerous.

Gonzalez took a deep breath, steeling himself. He could feel the weight of the Colonel's attention, as well as the nervous glances of his fellow lieutenants. "They're well-equipped, sir. And they seem to have insider knowledge of our operations. The timing of these attacks, the precision... it's not random. These people know what they're doing, and they know us. Our routines, our vulnerabilities."

The Colonel's face contorted with rage, transforming his usually handsome features into something monstrous. In a flash, he grabbed a crystal decanter from a nearby sideboard and hurled it across the room. It shattered against the wall with a resounding crash, sending shards of glass and droplets of expensive bourbon flying. The smell of alcohol filled the air, mingling with the scent of fear and tension.

"Insider knowledge?" he roared, rounding on Gonzalez. His voice was a thunderous bellow that seemed to shake the very foundations of the building. "Are you telling me we have a rat?"

Gonzalez swallowed hard, his Adam's apple bobbing visibly. He could feel sweat beading on his forehead, but he held his ground. "It's... it's possible, sir. We can't rule it out. The level of information they seem to have... it's troubling."

The Colonel's chest heaved as he glared at each person in the room, his eyes wild with fury. "I built this organization from nothing!" he snarled, spittle flying from his lips. "I gave you all purpose in this godforsaken wasteland. I took you from the gutter, made you into something! And this is how I'm repaid?"

His hand moved with lightning speed, drawing a polished Colt .45 from a shoulder holster. The sound of the gun clearing leather was unnaturally loud in the tense silence. Before anyone could react, he leveled it at Gonzalez's forehead. The barrel gleamed in the light, a promise of swift and merciless judgment.

"You know what happens to rats, don't you?" The Colonel's voice was eerily calm now, a stark contrast to his earlier fury. It was the calm of a predator about to strike, all the more terrifying for its suddenness.

Gonzalez's eyes widened in terror, the color draining from his face. He raised his hands slowly, palms out in a gesture of supplication. "Colonel, please... I'm loyal. I swear-"

The gunshot rang out, deafening in the enclosed space. The sound seemed to hang in the air, a physical presence that pressed against the eardrums. Gonzalez slumped forward, a neat hole between his eyes, blood pooling on the polished oak table. The acrid smell of gunpowder filled the room, mingling with the metallic scent of fresh blood.

The Colonel lowered the smoking gun, his face a mask of cold fury. He swept his gaze across the stunned faces of his remaining lieutenants. Some looked away, unable to meet his eyes. Others stared, transfixed by the violence they had just witnessed.

"Let this be a lesson," he said, his voice low and menacing. Each word was carefully enunciated, dripping with threat. "I will not tolerate failure. I will not tolerate disloyalty. And I most certainly will not tolerate rats."

The Colonel holstered his weapon, his movements precise and controlled. The room remained deathly silent, the smell of gunpowder hanging heavy in the air. The only sound was the soft ticking of the grandfather clock, counting away the seconds of Gonzalez's life.

"Now," he said, straightening his pristine white suit, smoothing out invisible wrinkles. His voice was calm, almost conversational, as if he hadn't just executed a man in cold blood. "I expect results, not excuses. This resistance needs to be crushed, and I mean yesterday. I want them found, I want them broken, and I want them made an example of."

He fixed each of his remaining lieutenants with a piercing stare. His eyes, cold and calculating, seemed to look right through them, judging their very souls. "I want you to deal with any trouble swiftly and mercilessly. Make examples of those who dare oppose us. Let the people of Dunnellon know the price of defiance. I want them to tremble at the mere mention of our name."

The Colonel's voice dropped to a dangerous whisper, forcing the men to lean in to hear him. "Your orders are simple. Take control of this town. Every street, every building, every whispered conversation. I want eyes and ears everywhere. No stone unturned, no shadow left unexplored. I want to know what these people are thinking before they think it."

He leaned forward, his hands splayed on the table, careful to avoid the growing pool of blood. The crimson liquid crept across the polished surface, a stark reminder of the price of failure. "And let me make myself crystal clear gentlemen. If you fail me in this, your fate will make poor Gonzalez here look positively blessed. I have a wealth of creativity when it comes to dealing with disappointments."

The threat hung in the air, as tangible as the acrid smell of gun smoke. The Colonel's eyes glittered with malice as he surveyed the room, taking in the pale faces and trembling hands of his lieutenants.

"Do I make myself understood?" The question was rhetorical, delivered in a tone that brooked no argument.

A chorus of mumbled agreements filled the room, each man eager to affirm their loyalty and understanding. The Colonel's lips curled into a cold smile, satisfaction gleaming in his eyes.

"Good. Now get out of my sight. I expect hourly updates on your progress. Don't disappoint me, gentlemen. You've seen the consequences."

The lieutenants scrambled to their feet, eager to escape the oppressive atmosphere of the room. Chairs scraped against the floor as they rose, a cacophony of movement after the tense stillness. As they filed out, the Colonel called after them, his voice dripping with menace.

"Remember, gentlemen. I didn't get where I am today by accepting failure. Don't disappoint me. Your lives quite literally depend on it."

The door closed behind the last of them with a soft click, leaving the Colonel alone with the cooling body of his former lieutenant. He stood there for a long moment, staring at Gonzalez's lifeless form, a contemplative expression on his face.

In the wake of Gonzalez's execution, a palpable tension gripped the Colonel's compound. The once-bustling corridors fell eerily quiet, save for the occasional nervous shuffle of feet. Men spoke in hushed whispers, casting furtive glances over their shoulders. The air was thick with fear and suspicion, every interaction fraught with potential danger.

In the barracks, a group of soldiers huddled around a makeshift table, their faces drawn and pale. The usual banter and camaraderie were notably absent, replaced by a somber, anxious silence.

"Jesus, did you hear what happened?" one of them muttered, his voice barely above a whisper. His eyes darted nervously to the door, as if expecting the Colonel himself to burst in at any moment.

Another soldier nodded, his hands shaking as he lit a cigarette. The flame from his lighter cast flickering shadows on the wall, adding to the tense atmosphere. "Gonzalez. Just like that. Boom. One minute he's one of the Colonel's right-hand men, the next minute he's cooling on the floor with a bullet in his brain."

"The Colonel's lost it," a third chimed in, his eyes darting nervously to the door. His voice was thick with fear and barely suppressed panic. "We're all walking on eggshells now. One wrong word, one misstep, and we could be next."

The first soldier leaned in closer, his voice dropping even lower. "You think there really is a rat? Someone feeding info to the resistance?"

Silence fell over the group, each man eyeing the others suspiciously. Trust, once the bedrock of their operation, had crumbled in an instant. The camaraderie that had bound them together through countless missions and hardships now felt like a distant memory.

Outside, patrols moved with heightened vigilance, jumping at shadows. The resistance, once a minor annoyance, now loomed large in their minds. Every civilian became a potential threat, every whispered conversation a possible plot. The streets of Dunnellon, once firmly under their control, now felt hostile and alien.

In the command center, the remaining lieutenants scrambled to implement the Colonel's orders. Maps were spread out across tables, covered in hastily scrawled notes and markings. Strategies were drawn up and discarded in rapid succession, each man desperate to find a solution that would appease their volatile leader.

"We need to double the patrols," one lieutenant insisted, his voice strained. Sweat beaded on his forehead as he jabbed a finger at the map. "Cover every inch of this town, day and night."

Another shook his head, frustration evident in his voice. "We don't have the manpower. We're stretched thin as it is. If we double the patrols, we leave ourselves vulnerable elsewhere."

"Then we make do!" the first snapped back, slamming his fist on the table. "It's that or face the Colonel's wrath. You saw what happened to Gonzalez. Do you want to be next?"

The implications of their new reality settled heavily

on everyone. The resistance, emboldened by their recent successes, would likely step up their attacks. But now, the Colonel's men faced enemies on two fronts - the external threat of the resistance, and the internal paranoia sown by the possibility of a traitor in their midst.

Resources, already strained, would be further taxed as they attempted to fortify their position. Trust between units, crucial for effective operations, had been severely undermined. Every setback, every minor failure, now carried the weight of potential execution. The pressure was immense, and cracks were beginning to show in the once-unshakeable facade of the Colonel's organization.

As night fell over Dunnellon, an uneasy quiet settled over the town. The Colonel's men, once swaggering with the confidence of unchallenged authority, now moved like hunted animals. Their eyes darted from shadow to shadow, hands never far from their weapons. In the darkness, every rustle of leaves, every creaking floorboard, became a potential threat.

In the shadows, the resistance watched and waited, sensing the shift in the balance of power. They saw the fear in the eyes of their oppressors, noted the increased patrols and the nervous energy that permeated the air. They whispered among themselves, planning their next move, emboldened by the knowledge that their actions had struck fear into the heart of the Colonel's operation.

The stage was set for a confrontation that would determine the fate of Dunnellon and its people. As the night deepened, both sides prepared for the battles to come, each knowing that the coming days would be a test of will, cunning, and ruthlessness. The Colonel's iron grip on the town was slipping, and in the ensuing chaos, anything was possible.

CHAPTER TWENTY NINE

J oe and Captain Rodriguez crouched low in the abandoned warehouse on the outskirts of Dunnellon. The air was thick with tension as they faced the small group of resistance fighters gathered before them. The musty scent of decay and neglect hung heavy in the air, a stark reminder of the world they now inhabited.

"Alright, listen up," Joe whispered, his voice barely audible above the gentle lapping of the river outside. His calloused hands gripped his rifle tightly, knuckles white with anticipation. "Tonight, we hit 'em where it hurts."

Captain Rodriguez unrolled a crude map on the dusty floor, the paper crinkling loudly in the silence. "The Colonel's fleet is their lifeline. We take that out, we cripple their operation. Joe and his crew have already hit 'em pretty hard, taking out a bunch of their patrol boats, but I wanna see if we can finish their little navy off once and for all." His eyes gleamed with determination as he traced their planned route along the river.

A wiry man with a scraggly beard leaned in, his breath reeking of stale cigarettes. "How we gonna do that? They got guards crawling all over the docks." His voice trembled slightly, betraying his nervousness.

Joe's eyes glinted in the dim light, a predatory smile playing at the corners of his mouth. "That's where these come in." He gestured to a pile of glass bottles and rags, neatly arranged in the corner. "Molotov's. Quick, dirty, and damn effective."

The group spent the next hour preparing their improvised weapons, carefully filling bottles with a mixture of gasoline and oil. The acrid smell filled the warehouse as they worked in silence, each lost in their own thoughts about the night ahead. The clink of glass and the soft rustle of cloth were the only sounds that broke the tense quiet.

Captain Rodriguez divided them into small teams, assigning each to a different boat. His voice was low and steady as he outlined the plan. "We've now grown our own collection of boats to twelve, thanks to the Colonel. We'll use the motors until we get close, then we cut the engines and drift in silently. When we are on top of them, we heave these babies onto their boats and docks. Then we light up our engines and get the hell out of Dodge and pray we were successful. Remember, stealth is key. We get in, light 'em up, and get out. No heroics." His gaze swept over the group, making sure each fighter understood the gravity of their mission.

As the sun began to set, painting the sky in hues of orange and purple, they made their way to the hidden assortment of pontoon and jon boats that they had scavenged and captured. They had them stashed along the riverbank, concealed beneath camouflage netting and low-hanging branches. Joe helped load the last of the Molotov's, his hands steady despite the gravity of what lay ahead. The weight of each bottle was a grim reminder of the destruction they were about to unleash.

The small flotilla pushed off into the murky water, outboard engines firing up as they began their journey downstream. The night air was cool against their skin, carrying the scents of the river and the faint whiff of smoke from distant fires. Crickets chirped in the darkness, oblivious to the tension that gripped the human intruders.

As they rounded a bend, the first glimpses of the Colonel's docks came into view. Torchlight flickered off the water, illuminating the silhouettes of the boats moored there. Joe felt his heart rate quicken, adrenaline surging through his veins. He took a deep breath, steadying himself for what was to come.

Captain Rodriguez raised a hand, signaling for everyone to slow their approach. They drifted closer, hugging the shadows along the riverbank. The vulnerable boats loomed larger now, their outlines sharp against the night sky. The gentle lapping of water against the hulls seemed unnaturally loud in the stillness.

As they neared their targets, Rodriguez raised his fist, signaling for the engines to be cut. The boats drifted silently towards the Colonel's fleet, carried by the river's gentle current. The only sound was the soft gurgle of water and the occasional creak of wood.

Joe squinted through the darkness, taking in the scene before them. A wry smile crossed his face as he leaned towards Rodriguez. "Look at that. I'm happy to see the Colonel doesn't know his history."

Rodriguez looked puzzlingly at Joe. "What do you mean?"

"All those boats clustered together. Reminds me of Pearl Harbor. All of our planes were grouped together. The Japs hit one and they all went up in flames. Same here, this is gonna be a milk run." Joe's voice was barely above a whisper, but the confidence in his tone was unmistakable.

Rodriguez nodded grimly, his eyes scanning the shoreline for any sign they'd been spotted. The docks were eerily quiet, with only a few guards visible in the dim light. Satisfied, he gave a sharp nod. "Now," he whispered.

In unison, the resistance fighters lit their Molotov's. The soft hiss of burning rags filled the air as they took aim. Joe's arm cocked back, muscles tense. He released, watching the bottle arc through the night sky, a fiery comet heralding destruction.

The first cocktail smashed against the hull of a patrol boat, erupting in a brilliant orange fireball. More followed in quick succession, shattering windows and splashing across decks. Within seconds, the night was alive with crackling flames. The acrid smell of burning fuel and melting plastic filled the air.

Chaos erupted on shore. Shouts of alarm rang out as the Colonel's men scrambled to respond. The fire spread rapidly, leaping from boat to boat like a hungry beast. Thick, black smoke billowed into the sky, obscuring the stars and casting an otherworldly pall over the scene.

A massive explosion rocked the docks as the flames reached a fuel cache. The shockwave rippled across the water, nearly capsizing Joe's boat. He steadied himself, grimly surveying the destruction. The heat from the inferno was intense, even from their position on the river.

"Keep going," Rodriguez barked. "Don't let up."

His face was illuminated by the dancing flames, determination etched in every line.

Joe's team moved methodically, targeting the remaining vessels with practiced efficiency. Each throw sent another boat up in flames, further crippling the Colonel's fleet. The air was filled with the sound of shattering glass and the roar of the growing inferno.

From the shoreline, sporadic gunfire erupted as some of their guerrilla allies provided cover. Bullets whizzed overhead, pinging off metal and splashing into the water. The sound kept the Colonel's panicked forces pinned down and unable to mount an effective defense.

As the last of the Molotov cocktails found their mark, Captain Rodriguez raised his arm. "That's it! Fall back!" His voice was hoarse from shouting over the din of the battle.

Joe gunned the engine of his boat, the sudden roar shattering the night. Around him, the other vessels sprang to life, their motors growling as they peeled away from the inferno. They sped downstream, leaving chaos in their wake. The cool wind whipped at their faces, a stark contrast to the heat of the flames they'd left behind.

Whoops and hollers erupted from the resistance fighters. "We did it!" someone shouted, their voice barely audible over the engines and the crackling flames behind them. The excitement was palpable, a release of tension after the high-stakes operation.

Joe chanced a glance over his shoulder. The Colonel's docks were an inferno, a wall of fire stretching along the riverbank. The flames reached skyward, casting an eerie orange glow across the water. Black smoke billowed upwards, blotting out the stars. It was a scene of apocalyptic destruction, a testament to the power of their small band of fighters.

They didn't slow until they'd put several miles between themselves and the destruction. Finally, Rodriguez signaled for them to pull over to a secluded inlet. The boats glided into the shadowy cove, hidden from prying eyes by overhanging trees.

As the boats clustered together, Joe could see the fierce grins on his comrades' faces, illuminated by the pale moonlight. Captain Rodriguez's eyes gleamed with satisfaction, reflecting the silver light of the moon.

"Initial assessment?" Joe asked, his voice gruff. He could still taste the smoke in the back of his throat.

Rodriguez nodded. "Better than we could have hoped. I'd say we took out at least eighty percent of their fleet. Maybe more." There was a note of pride in his voice, tempered by the knowledge that their war was far from over.

A cheer went up from the group, quickly hushed by Joe's raised hand. "Let's not get ahead of ourselves. This is a big win, but the Colonel won't take it lying down." His words were a sobering reminder of the challenges that still lay ahead.

"Agreed," Rodriguez said, his tone serious. "We need to be prepared for retaliation. But for now, let's get back to base and regroup. We'll plan our next move in the morning." He began issuing quiet orders, organizing their withdrawal.

As they set off again, Joe felt a mix of emotions wash over him. Pride in their success, relief that they'd all made it out unscathed, and a grim determination for the battles yet to come. He knew the Colonel would be furious, his wrath terrible to behold. But for the first time in months, Joe felt a flicker of hope. Maybe, just maybe, they could turn the tide in their favor.

The boats slipped silently through the dark waters, carrying their victorious crews back to safety. Behind them, the glow of the fire still lit up the night sky, a beacon of their defiance against the Colonel's tyranny. As they journeyed home, Joe allowed himself a small smile. Tonight, they had struck a blow for freedom, and the echoes of their actions would resonate far beyond the banks of the Withlacoochee river.

CHAPTER THIRTY

Claire spotted Maria sitting alone in the courtyard, her face pensive as she gazed off into the distance. Deciding to offer some company, Claire made her way over, her footsteps crunching on the gravel path.

"Mind if I join you?" Claire asked, gesturing to the empty space beside Maria on the bench.

Maria looked up, a small smile tugging at her lips. "Not at all. Please, sit."

As Claire settled in, she let out a soft chuckle. "What a night that was the other night with Jack's moonshine, huh?"

Maria groaned, shaking her head. "Don't remind me. I haven't seen that much drunkenness' since college."

Their laughter echoed across the courtyard, a rare moment of lightness in their often grim reality. As their mirth subsided, they fell into comfortable small talk, discussing the day's chores and the latest news from their scouts.

"How's the garden coming along?" Claire asked,

genuinely interested. She'd seen Maria spending a lot of time there lately.

Maria's face lit up. "It's doing better than I expected. The tomatoes are coming in nicely, and I think we'll have a decent crop of beans soon."

As they chatted, Taylor and Alicia approached, carrying baskets of freshly laundered clothes.

"Room for two more?" Taylor asked, setting her basket down.

Claire scooted over, making space. "Always. We were just talking about the garden."

Alicia perched on the arm of the bench, her eyes bright with curiosity. "I've been meaning to ask if I could help out there. I used to have a little herb garden back... before."

Maria reached out, patting Alicia's knee. "Of course, sweetheart. We could always use an extra pair of hands."

The four women fell into easy conversation, sharing stories and laughs as the afternoon sun warmed their faces. For a moment, they could almost forget the dangers that lurked beyond their walls, finding solace in each other's company.

As the conversation lulled, an awkward silence settled

over the group. Claire fidgeted with a loose thread on her shirt, while Maria's gaze drifted back to the horizon.

Taylor cleared her throat, breaking the silence. "Nice day, isn't it?" she offered weakly.

Claire nodded, her smile not quite reaching her eyes. "Yeah, can't complain about the weather."

Alicia exhaled. "Yeah it's a beautiful day for sure."

The unspoken fears hung heavy in the air - concerns about food supplies, the constant threat of raiders, and the uncertainty of their future. But beneath it all lay a deeper worry, one that Maria finally gave voice to.

"I wonder how Joe and the others are doing," she said softly, her eyes meeting each of theirs in turn. "It's been days since they left."

Taylor's breath caught in her throat. She'd been trying not to think about it, but now the worry came flooding back. "Jake..." she whispered, her voice trembling.

Claire reached out, squeezing Taylor's hand. "They're tough. I'm sure they're fine."

But Taylor's mind was already racing. What if something had happened to Jake? What if Parker had to grow up without a father? The thought made her chest tighten with fear.

Unbidden, a memory surfaced - their last moment together before Jake left with the rest of the team.

They stood by the gate, Jake's pack slung over his shoulder. Parker clung to his leg, her little face scrunched up in confusion.

"Daddy go?" she asked, her bottom lip quivering.

Jake knelt down, scooping Parker into his arms. "Just for a little while, kiddo. I'll be back before you know it."

He looked up at Taylor, his eyes filled with a mix of determination and worry. "Take care of our girl," he said softly.

Taylor nodded, fighting back tears. "Always. Just... come back to us, okay?"

Jake pulled her close, Parker sandwiched between them. "I promise," he whispered fiercely.

The memory faded, leaving Taylor with a hollow ache in her chest. She blinked back tears, focusing on Maria's concerned face.

"They'll come back," Maria said, her voice firm with conviction. "They have to."

Maria's words hung in the air, heavy with unspoken emotion. She took a deep breath, her fingers twisting nervously in her lap. "I... I have to confess something," she said, her voice barely above a whisper.

The other women turned to her, concern etched on their faces. Claire leaned in, placing a gentle hand on Maria's arm. "What is it?"

Maria's eyes glistened with unshed tears. "I'm terrified of losing Joe," she admitted, her voice cracking. "We've only just started to... to explore what we could be together. And now he's out there, facing who knows what dangers. I think the worst part is the not knowing, the waiting, the wondering."

Taylor's expression softened, understanding dawning in her eyes. She knew all too well the fear of losing someone you love.

Maria continued, her words tumbling out in a rush. "I feel so selfish even thinking about this. With everything that's happening, all the challenges we face... how can I be worried about my love life?"

She let out a bitter laugh, shaking her head. "People are struggling to survive, and here I am, fretting over whether I'll ever get another chance to be with the man I've fallen in love with."

Alicia reached out, squeezing Maria's hand. "It's not selfish," she said softly. "It's human."

Claire nodded in agreement. "We all need something to

hold onto, especially now. There's no shame in that."

Maria looked at them gratefully, but the guilt still weighed heavily on her shoulders. "I just... I can't help feeling like I'm betraying everyone by focusing on my own happiness when there's so much at stake."

Taylor leaned forward, her gaze intense. "Maria, listen to me. Finding love, holding onto it... that's what gives us the strength to keep going. It's not a betrayal. It's hope."

Maria's breath hitched, a tear finally escaping down her cheek. "I'm just so scared," she whispered. "What if he doesn't come back? I would be so lost and…"

The words hung unfinished, but they all understood. The fear of lost opportunities, of words left unsaid, was something they all grappled with in this uncertain world.

Claire took a deep breath, her eyes meeting each of the women in turn. "Something just dawned on me," she began, her voice thoughtful. "Taylor, you've been married for a while now, but the rest of us are all in really brand new relationships. Maria and your dad are basically a new relationship. Me and your brother just met not that long ago. And little Alicia over here has the hots for Sam in a big way. So they're just starting out as well."

She paused, her gaze softening. "But I think it would be hard either way if we lost them. Taylor has memories and so much history with Jake, not to mention a beautiful little girl together. If Jake were gone it would be tragic. But if any of our fellas were gone, while we may not have all the history, I think we would feel the loss of what could have been."

Claire shook her head, a rueful smile on her lips. "I'm sorry, I didn't mean to be so depressing."

Maria reached out, squeezing Claire's hand. "No, you're right," she said softly. "And I think we've all been thinking it. Worrying about it." She straightened up, a determined look in her eyes. "Let's make a pact to support one another, no matter what."

With a resolute nod, Maria extended her hand, palm down. One by one, the others placed their hands on top of hers - Claire's calloused fingers, Taylor's steady grip, and Alicia's slender hand. They formed a stack, a physical representation of their bond and shared commitment.

CHAPTER THIRTY ONE

Joe leaned in close to Rodriguez, his voice low and urgent, his eyes darting around to ensure they weren't overheard. The lines on his weathered face deepened with concentration as he spoke, the scent of gun oil faintly detectable on his clothes. "I've noticed something while watching the Colonel's operations. Something that might give us an edge. It's a small detail, but it could be our ticket to turning the tables on that bastard." He paused, his calloused fingers drumming softly on the table between them.

Rodriguez's eyebrows raised, his interest piqued. He leaned in closer, his weathered face etched with curiosity, the scar on his left shoulder visible beneath his worn t-shirt. The silver cross around his neck glinted in the dim light as he shifted. "What have you seen, Joe? Don't keep me in suspense. Every little bit helps in this godforsaken situation we're in." His dark eyes locked onto Joe's, intense and focused.

"The Colonel's been using messengers to deliver written orders to his men in the field," Joe explained, a glint of excitement in his hazel eyes. He tapped his temple knowingly, a habit he'd developed over years of strategizing. The stubble on his chin rasped against his fingertips as he stroked it thoughtfully. "Old school, but effective in a world without phones or radios. It's like we've gone back in time, using tactics from a century ago. Reminds me of stories my grandpa used to tell about World War one and two."

Rodriguez nodded slowly, considering the implications. His mind was already racing with possibilities, years of military training kicking into high gear. The muscles in his jaw tightened as he clenched his teeth, deep in thought. Joe continued, his voice barely above a whisper, his breath warm in the cool air between them, "I think we should ambush one of these couriers and replace him with one of our own men. We could send some new orders of our own. Throw a wrench in their operations, maybe even gain some valuable intel in the process." His eyes gleamed with a mix of determination and mischief.

The Captain's eyes widened, a mix of surprise and admiration crossing his face. He absently fingered the silver cross hanging around his neck as he processed the idea, a habit he'd picked up in his years of service. "Do you really think that could work?" he asked, leaning forward, his voice matching Joe's hushed tone. The scent of coffee on his breath mingled with the musty air of their makeshift meeting room. "It's risky, but damn clever. We'd be playing with fire, but sometimes that's what it takes. And what would our replacement orders be? We'd need to make them believable." His brow furrowed as he considered the potential pitfalls.

Joe's face broke into a sly grin, the kind that reminded Rodriguez why he'd come to trust this man so quickly. There was a cunning behind those eyes that the Captain had come to respect, a shrewdness born of years of survival in tough conditions. "How about we have them deliver us a few trucks full of supplies, Cappy? Food, weapons, maybe even some of that fancy whiskey the Colonel's always sipping on. What would you like? We could use a morale boost around here, and nothing lifts spirits like a full belly." He rubbed his hands together, the calluses on his palms rough against each other.

Rodriguez let out a hearty laugh, quickly muffling it with his hand. His dark eyes danced with amusement, a welcome change from their usual stern gaze. The lines around his eyes crinkled with genuine mirth. "Joe, I'd love a two-inch thick steak with a baked potato covered in butter and sour cream. Hell, throw in a cold beer while you're at it." His eyes twinkled with mirth, a rare sight these days. The thought of such a meal made his stomach growl audibly. "Maybe we could even score some fresh fruit. I can't remember the last time I tasted anything that wasn't from a can or scrounged from the wild."

Chuckling, Joe shook his head, his own mouth watering at the thought. The memory of juicy steaks and cold beers seemed like a distant dream in their current reality, a reminder of the world they'd lost. "That sounds damn good, but we better not push our luck. We don't want to tip our hand too soon. We'll start small, see how it goes. If we're successful, who knows? Maybe steak dinner will be on the menu sooner than we think." He patted his belly ruefully, thinking of the meager rations they'd been subsisting on.

They quickly huddled together, hunched over a crude map of the area spread out on a rickety table. The map was a patchwork of different papers, held together with tape and covered in scribbled notes and markings. Their fingers traced potential routes as they plotted out a plan to intercept the courier on his route and how they'd take him out. The faded ink and worn creases of the map spoke to how often it had been consulted in their ongoing struggle against the Colonel.

As they discussed the details, both men knew the risks involved. One wrong move could blow their cover and bring the Colonel's wrath down upon them. The weight of their responsibility to their community hung heavy in the air between them. They weren't sure if they'd be able to recreate the Colonel's orders convincingly enough to fool the recipients, but they agreed it was worth a try. The potential payoff was too good to pass up, even if the danger was considerable.

As they finished their planning, Joe and Rodriguez shared a look of determination. This could be the break they'd been waiting for, a chance to strike back at the Colonel and his oppressive regime. With a firm handshake, they sealed their pact, ready to put their daring plan into action. The calloused skin of their palms pressed together, a testament to the hard work and struggles they'd endured. In that moment, a spark of hope flickered between them, fragile but persistent, like a candle flame in the darkness.

Joe crouched low in the dense undergrowth, his weathered hands gripping his rifle with practiced ease. The forest was eerily quiet, save for the occasional rustle of leaves in the breeze and the soft chirping of distant birds. Rodriguez lay beside him, eyes sharp and focused on the narrow dirt path cutting through the woods, his body tense with anticipation.

"Remember," Joe whispered, his voice barely audible above the gentle rustling of the foliage, "dispatch him quickly and quietly. We can't afford any mistakes."

Rodriguez nodded solemnly, signaling to the rest of their team scattered among the trees and bushes. The wait was excruciating, each minute feeling like an eternity as they strained their ears for any sign of approach, their senses heightened by the adrenaline coursing through their veins.

Suddenly, a twig snapped in the distance, breaking the oppressive silence. Joe's muscles tensed instinctively, his finger hovering near the trigger as he steadied his breathing. The sound of labored breathing grew closer, accompanied by the soft thud of footsteps on packed earth and the occasional crunch of leaves.

A figure emerged from around a bend in the path, moving at a steady jog that belied the weight of his cargo. The courier wore a nondescript outfit, chosen for its ability to blend into the surroundings, but the bulging satchel at his side gave him away instantly. Joe held his breath, waiting for the perfect moment to strike, his eyes never leaving their target.

As the courier passed their position, Joe gave a sharp, piercing whistle that cut through the air like a knife. In an instant, their team sprang into action with well-rehearsed precision. Two men burst from the bushes, their movements swift and silent as they tackled the surprised courier to the ground. One of them quickly ran a blade across the young man's neck, ending any chance of resistance or alarm.

Joe reached down and snatched the satchel from the courier's waistband, his movements quick and efficient as he immediately began rifling through its contents. His eyes lit up with excitement as he pulled out a sealed envelope, its pristine condition a stark contrast to the violence that had just unfolded. "This is it," he muttered, turning it over in his hands to examine every detail. "Let's see what the Colonel's up to this time."

Joe tore open the envelope with barely contained eagerness, his calloused fingers careful not to damage the contents despite his haste. He unfolded the paper inside, revealing elegant cursive handwriting that flowed across the page like a work of art.

"Damn," Rodriguez muttered, peering over Joe's shoulder with a mixture of curiosity and disdain. "Even his penmanship's pretentious. Guy can't do anything without showing off, can he?"

Joe's eyes scanned the message, a grin slowly spreading across his weathered face as he absorbed the information. "Well, well," he said, his voice tinged with satisfaction. "Looks like our little party at the marina had quite an effect. The Colonel's not happy."

Rodriguez raised an eyebrow, his interest piqued.

"What's it say exactly?"

Joe cleared his throat and read aloud, his voice low and tinged with amusement that he couldn't quite hide. "To Sergeant Carter: Rebels have attacked the marina, destroying several of our boats. This is a significant setback to our operations. You are to move your group of twenty-five immediately to the river two miles west of the marina. Intercept all boat traffic and seize every vessel possible. Kill any rebels encountered. We cannot allow them to gain the upper hand."

A chuckle escaped Rodriguez's lips, the sound a mix of pride and joy. "Destroyed their boats, huh? Bet that ruffled the Colonel's fancy feathers something fierce. I can just imagine him pacing around in that ridiculous white suit of his, fuming."

Joe nodded, his eyes twinkling with mischief and a hint of pride. "Oh, I'd pay good money to see his face when he got that news. All those pretty boats up in smoke, his plans going up with them. Must've been quite a sight."

The two men shared a quiet laugh, savoring this small victory against the Colonel's forces. It wasn't often they got such clear confirmation that their actions were having an impact. Joe carefully folded the letter and tucked it into his shirt pocket, patting it once for good measure.

Joe turned to his men, a glint of mischief in his eyes that they had come to recognize as the precursor to one of his more daring plans. "Alright, fellas," he said, his voice filled with anticipation. "Anyone here think they can recreate the Colonel's fancy handwriting? I've got an idea that might just cause some real chaos in their ranks."

The group exchanged glances, some shuffling their feet nervously at the prospect of forging an official document. After a moment of hesitation, one of the Guardsmen stepped forward, clearing his throat. "I'm pretty good with cursive writing, sir," he offered, a mix of pride and apprehension in his voice. "Used to practice calligraphy as a hobby, believe it or not."

Joe clapped him on the shoulder, a grin spreading across his weathered face. "Well, aren't you full of surprises? You're elected then, my friend. I can write in cursive, but my handwriting is chicken scratch compared to the Colonel's flowery script."

They quickly pulled out some paper and a pen from their gear, the chosen Guardsman settling himself on a nearby log. He poised the pen over the paper, looking up at Joe expectantly, ready to begin their act of deception.

"What should I write, sir?" he asked, his hand steady despite the gravity of what they were about to do.

Joe paced back and forth, stroking his beard thoughtfully as he considered their next move. The rest of the team watched in silence, knowing that whatever plan was forming in Joe's mind had the potential to cause significant disruption to the Colonel's operations.

"Alright, let's copy the Colonel's style to a T," Joe finally said, his voice filled with determination. "Start with 'To Sergeant Carter' at the top, just like he did. We want this to look as authentic as possible."

The Guardsman nodded, his hand moving smoothly across the paper as he mimicked the Colonel's elegant script with surprising accuracy. The rest of the team watched in fascination as the forged letter began to take shape.

Joe's smile widened as he continued dictating, his plan unfolding with each word. "Tell our good Sergeant Carter to load two trucks immediately. One full of food and medicine – make sure to emphasize it's our emergency reserves – and the other filled with weapons and ammo. Bring them east to the boat ramp on county road four eighty four on the Rainbow river. It's a secured area where you will be contacted by another group to transfer the supplies. Stress the urgency of the matter."

Rodriguez chuckled, shaking his head in admiration of Joe's audacity. "I like it. Hit 'em where it hurts – their supplies. Clever."

"What the hell," Joe said, his eyes twinkling with mischief as inspiration struck. "Let's push our luck a little, just for fun. Might as well go all out if we're doing this."

He turned back to the Guardsman, who was diligently transcribing every word with meticulous care. "Add this: 'Also, please include two cases of that fine Kentucky bourbon that I do enjoy so much in the transport. These trying times call for a little comfort, and your efforts will be greatly rewarded, Sergeant. The success of this mission is crucial to our cause.'"

The group stifled their laughter, imagining the confusion and chaos this forged order would cause among the Colonel's ranks. It was a bold move, but if it worked, it could deal a significant blow to their enemy's resources and morale.

"Now," Joe instructed, his tone serious despite the audacity of their plan, "forge his signature at the bottom. Make it look as fancy and pretentious as possible. The Colonel never misses a chance to show off, even in his signature."

The Guardsman nodded, his hand moving with practiced ease as he crafted an elaborate signature that would make even the Colonel proud. The flourishes and loops were a work of art in themselves, perfectly capturing the essence of their pompous adversary.

Joe took the completed letter, holding it up to admire their handiwork in the dappled sunlight filtering through the trees. "Perfect," he declared, a note of satisfaction in his voice as he folded it carefully and slid it into an envelope. "This ought to keep the Colonel's men busy for a while, and if we're lucky, they'll deliver us a nice cache of supplies, as well as a little something to celebrate with."

Joe looked at the now lifeless courier and called for Sam.

Sam stepped up next to Joe. "Yes sir?"

Joe looked down and shuffled his feet. "You're about the same size as this guy. Are you willing to put on his clothes and deliver this message?"

Sam stood at attention. "It's a little creepy, sir, but sir, yes sir."

Joe nodded, his expression a mix of pride and concern. "Alright, let's get you suited up then. We don't have much time."

The team worked quickly, stripping the courier's body and helping Sam into the clothes. Joe supervised the process, his keen eyes missing nothing as he ensured every detail was perfect.

"Remember," Joe said as Sam adjusted the courier's jacket, "you're just delivering a message. Keep your head down, don't engage in conversation if you can avoid it. Get in, drop off the letter, and get out. We'll be nearby if anything goes wrong."

Sam nodded, his face set with determination. "Understood, sir. I won't let you down."

Joe placed a hand on Sam's shoulder, giving it a firm squeeze. "I know you won't, son. You've got this."

As Sam prepared to leave, Rodriguez approached, holding out the courier's satchel. "Don't forget this," he said, his voice low. "It's got some other papers in it. Might help sell the act if anyone gets nosy."

Sam took the satchel, slinging it across his body. He took a deep breath, steeling himself for the task ahead. "How do I look?" he asked, attempting a weak smile.

Joe stepped back, giving Sam a once-over. "You look good enough to shoot," he said firmly. "Now get going. We'll be right behind you, watching your back."

With a final nod to his team, Sam set off down the path, his posture and gait carefully mimicking that of the courier they had observed earlier. Joe watched him go, a mixture of pride and worry etched on his weathered face.

As the team began to pack up, preparing to put their audacious plan into motion, Joe couldn't help but feel a surge of pride. It was risky, sure, but sometimes you had to take big swings to make a difference. And if there was one thing Joe Kelly was good at, it was making waves in the Colonel's carefully ordered world.

CHAPTER THIRTY TWO

Sergeant Carter barked out orders to his men in their encampment on the outskirts of Dunnellon. The late afternoon sun cast long shadows across the makeshift camp as the soldiers scurried to obey, their boots kicking up small clouds of dust. The air was thick with tension and the acrid smell of gunpowder from earlier drills.

"Philips, we need more firewood, we don't know how long we're gonna be out here. Make sure it's the dry stuff, none of that green wood that'll smoke us out and give away our position. And while you're at it, check the perimeter for any weak spots in our defenses," Carter growled, his voice gruff from years of shouting commands.

"Jones, make sure those trucks are secure. Double-check the locks and camouflage netting, and for God's sake, make sure the fuel tanks are topped off. We can't afford to be caught with our pants down if we need to move out quickly," he continued, his eyes scanning the camp for any signs of slacking.

"Guerrero, get the next guard shift out there, those

guys have been out there nearly four hours now, give 'em a break Sam. And tell 'em to stay alert, we've had reports of rebel activity in the area. I want eyes on every approach, got it? If so much as a squirrel farts in these woods, I want to know about it."

As everyone went about carrying out their orders with practiced efficiency, a lone man came jogging up to the encampment. Sweat glistened on his brow and soaked through his shirt as he navigated the uneven terrain, stumbling slightly on loose rocks. His chest heaved with exertion, and his eyes darted nervously around the camp. Out of breath, he approached Carter and said, his voice slightly ragged and gasping, "New orders from the Colonel, sir."

Carter looked over the man, his eyes narrowing as he took in the unfamiliar face, scrutinizing every detail of the newcomer's appearance. His hand instinctively moved closer to his sidearm, a habit born from months of constant vigilance. "You a new man? I haven't seen you before. Where's Johnson? He's been our regular courier for months. Last I heard, he was fit as a fiddle and twice as reliable."

Sam, still bent over and out of breath, his hands on his knees, replied between gulps of air, "Yes sir, the regular courier was killed by rebels. Ambush on the north road. It was... it was pretty bad. Bodies everywhere, sir. Barely made it out myself." He straightened up, wincing slightly as if nursing an injury, and handed Carter the envelope containing the fake orders, his hand trembling almost imperceptibly. The paper was slightly crumpled from his tight grip, a small bloodstain visible on one corner.

Carter took them, his calloused fingers running over the sealed flap, feeling the texture of the paper. His eyes lingered on the bloodstain, a grim reminder of the dangers that lurked beyond their camp. "What's your name, soldier? And how long have you been with us? I like to know every man under my command, especially in times like these."

Sam, finally beginning to catch his breath, the color returning to his face, answered, wiping sweat from his forehead with a grimy sleeve, "Byrd sir, PFC Byrd. Just transferred in last week from the eastern sector. Still getting my bearings around here. It's been a hell of a week, if you don't mind me saying, sir."

Carter stood in silence as he read the orders, his brow furrowing deeper with each line, the creases in his weathered face becoming more pronounced. The setting sun cast an eerie orange glow across the camp, deepening the shadows on Carter's face and making his expression even more ominous.

Sam held his breath, praying the sergeant wouldn't

question them. He could feel his heart pounding in his chest, hoping the nervousness didn't show on his face. His fingers twitched at his sides, itching to reach for the concealed weapon he carried, just in case. The weight of the gun pressed against his lower back, a constant reminder of the danger he was in.

Carter shook his head, his weathered face a mask of confusion and disbelief. His fingers clenched the paper tightly, knuckles turning white. "What the hell. The Colonel is losing it. Byrd, is he in his right mind? These orders... they don't make any sense. It's like he's playing some kind of twisted game. We're supposed to be protecting people, not... this."

Sam stood straight at attention, his posture rigid and voice steady, though his insides churned with anxiety. Sweat trickled down his back, and he fought the urge to fidget under Carter's intense gaze. "The Colonel is my commander, sir, and his orders are not for me to question. I'm just the messenger. We all have our roles to play in this new world. The Colonel... he sees things we don't, sir. Has plans we can't always understand."

Carter looked shaken, his usual air of confidence wavering, a flicker of doubt crossing his eyes. He ran a hand through his graying hair, leaving it standing on end. "Yeah, yeah, of course. I don't disagree. I was just wondering how things were going back in town. It's been a while since we've had any real news. Are the civilians still cooperating? Any more... incidents? Last time I was there, things were getting pretty tense."

Sam, still at attention, replied, his voice hesitant, choosing his words carefully, "There have been some setbacks, sir, and there have been some uhm... incidents. The Colonel's methods can be... unconventional at times. But he assures us it's all for the greater good. For a better future." He paused, swallowing hard before continuing, "Some folks, they don't see it that way, of course. But the Colonel, he has ways of... persuading them."

Carter, with a look of concern etched across his face, said, his voice lowered, leaning in closer to Sam, "Go on private, at ease. You can speak candidly. We're all in this together. What's really going on back there? I've got men here with families in town. They deserve to know the truth."

Sam eased his stance, his shoulders relaxing slightly, but remained on guard. His eyes darted around, making sure no one else was within earshot. "Well, to be frank sir, several officers that didn't follow the Colonel's orders to his specifications have been severely... uhm, well, I'll just say... disciplined. It's been pretty tense back at HQ. The Colonel doesn't tolerate any deviation from his vision. There's been talk of...

examples being made. Public ones."

Carter stared at Sam, a flicker of fear crossing his eyes before he masked it with a forced look of determination. His jaw clenched, a muscle twitching visibly. "Well, make sure the Colonel knows Sergeant Carter will not let him down. These orders will be carried out to the letter. No matter how... unusual they might seem. We're soldiers, and soldiers follow orders, right? That's what separates us from the animals out there."

Sam stood at attention once again and saluted crisply, his movements precise and practiced. A bead of sweat rolled down his temple, catching the last rays of the setting sun. "Yes sir, I will let him know immediately. The Colonel will be pleased to hear of your loyalty. He values men who can follow orders without question. Men like you are the foundation of the new world he's building."

Carter turned to his men, his voice booming across the camp, carrying a hint of tension that hadn't been there before. The soldiers stopped what they were doing, heads turning towards their commander. "Everyone gather around. We've got new orders. There's work to do, and it's not going to be easy. But we're soldiers, and we follow orders. That's what separates us from the chaos out there. Let's move! And remember, the Colonel is counting on us!"

As the men scrambled to gather, murmurs of confusion and concern rippled through the ranks. The atmosphere in the camp shifted, a palpable sense of unease settling over the soldiers like a heavy blanket. In the distance, a lone wolf howled, its mournful cry echoing through the gathering darkness.

Sam hurried back down the path, his boots crunching on the gravel as he made his way to the rendezvous point. His heart still raced from the encounter, adrenaline coursing through his veins, but a sense of relief washed over him as he spotted Joe and the rest of the team waiting in the shadows of the dense foliage. The tension in the air was palpable as they anxiously awaited his report, their faces a mixture of concern and anticipation. The humid Florida air clung to his skin, making his clothes stick uncomfortably as he approached the group.

Joe stepped forward, his weathered face etched with concern, his eyes scanning Sam's face for any sign of trouble. The lines around his eyes deepened as he searched for clues in Sam's expression, his hand instinctively resting on the holstered pistol at his hip. "How'd it go?" he asked, his voice low and gravelly, barely above a whisper, the words almost lost in the ambient sounds of the surrounding wilderness.

Sam took a deep breath, steadying himself and wiping a bead of sweat from his brow with the back of his hand. He could feel his pulse still pounding in his ears, the rush of blood drowning out the chirping of nearby crickets. "It worked," he replied, a hint of disbelief in his tone. "Carter bought it, hook, line, and sinker. I couldn't believe it myself. For a moment there, I thought we were done for. My palms were so sweaty, I was afraid I'd drop the fake orders."

He quickly recounted the details of his encounter with Sergeant Carter, describing the man's initial suspicion, the tense moments as he read the fake orders, and his eventual acceptance of the ruse. Sam's hands moved animatedly as he spoke, reliving the nerve-wracking experience. His fingers trembled slightly, a testament to the stress he'd been under, and he could still taste the metallic tang of fear in his mouth.

"Carter seemed shaken by the orders," Sam explained, his voice low and urgent, leaning in closer to the group. The others instinctively huddled around him, their faces illuminated by the dappled moonlight filtering through the canopy above. "He questioned them at first, his eyes narrowing as he read through the document. I could see the gears turning in his head, trying to make sense of it all. But when I hinted at the Colonel's harsh methods, dropping subtle references to past incidents, he fell in line pretty quick. The color drained from his face, and he said he'd follow the orders to the letter, no matter how unusual they seemed. I could see the fear in his eyes, like a cornered animal. He even started to sweat, I don't think the good Sergeant Carter will let us down, not after I put the fear of the Colonel in him."

Joe's face broke into a grin, the tension in his shoulders visibly easing as he processed Sam's words. The creases around his eyes softened, replaced by a glimmer of hope. "Sounds like you did great, Sam," he said, pride evident in his voice. He gave Sam's shoulder a reassuring squeeze, the gesture conveying more than words could. "I think we might just pull this off after all. Your performance was crucial. You've given us a real shot at this. I knew we could count on you when the chips were down."

Rodriguez nodded in agreement, a glimmer of hope in his eyes as he patted Sam on the back, his hand lingering for a moment in a gesture of camaraderie. "Nice work, man. You had us worried for a minute there. We were all on edge, wondering if you'd make it back in one piece. I think I aged ten years waiting for you to return. My hair might even be graying now," he added with a nervous chuckle, running a hand through his dark locks.

Joe clapped Sam on the shoulder, his voice filled with renewed determination and a spark of excitement. His eyes gleamed with a mix of pride and anticipation, a fire rekindled within them. "Alright, team. Let's get over to that spot on the Rainbow River and get set up for their arrival. We've got a narrow window to make this work, so let's move. Every second counts now. We can't afford any slip-ups at this stage. Remember, we're not just fighting for ourselves, but for everyone depending on us back at the compound."

The group gathered their gear with practiced efficiency, double-checking weapons and supplies. Magazines were checked and straps were tightened one last time. The air buzzed with a nervous energy as they prepared to move out, the weight of their mission settling heavily on their shoulders. As they moved out, Sam fell into step beside Joe, still processing the intensity of his encounter with Carter. The weight of their mission hung heavy in the air, almost tangible in its presence, like a thick fog surrounding them.

"You okay?" Joe asked, noticing Sam's pensive expression and the slight tremor in his hands. His voice was low, concern etched in every syllable, his eyes searching Sam's face for any signs of doubt or fear.

Sam nodded, a small smile tugging at the corner of his mouth as he met Joe's concerned gaze. "Yeah, just glad it worked. For a moment there, I thought he was going to see right through me. My heart was pounding so loud, I was sure he'd hear it. I kept expecting him to call my bluff at any second. It was like being back in basic training, facing down the drill sergeant, only with much higher stakes."

Joe chuckled softly, his eyes crinkling at the corners, a warmth spreading through his features. The sound was reassuring, a reminder of lighter times amidst the gravity of their current situation. "That's the thing about good plans, Sam. They work because we make them work. You did your part, and you did it damn well. It's not just about the plan, it's about the people executing it. Now let's go do ours and finish what we started. We're in this together, and together, we'll see it through. Remember, we've faced tough odds before and come out on top. This time won't be any different."

CHAPTER THIRTY THREE

S abrina Alvarez strode purposefully into the compound, her face etched with tension and exhaustion. Her crew followed close behind, their expressions mirroring her concern and weariness from the grueling mission. The weight of their discovery hung heavily in the air, palpable even before a word was spoken. Maria and several National Guardsmen quickly gathered around as Sabrina began her report, the urgency in her demeanor drawing them in like moths to a flame. The atmosphere crackled with anticipation and dread.

"We went south to Groveland," Sabrina said, her voice low and urgent, barely above a whisper. She glanced around, ensuring no unwanted ears were listening, her eyes darting to the shadows as if expecting enemies to materialize at any moment. "Looking for supplies, any sign of the Colonel's men. But what we found..." She trailed off, shaking her head, her eyes distant as if reliving the horrific scene they had stumbled upon. A shudder ran through her body, visible even to those standing a few feet away.

"What?" Maria pressed, leaning in, her warm brown

eyes filled with worry and a hint of fear. Her hand instinctively reached out to touch Sabrina's arm, offering silent support. "What did you see, Sabrina? How bad is it?"

"Uniformed men patrolling the streets," Sabrina continued, her voice tight with tension, her fingers unconsciously tracing the scar on her eyebrow. The nervous gesture betrayed her unease more than her words ever could. "They were everywhere, armed to the teeth. It was like a scene from a nightmare, only this time, we couldn't wake up."

Corporal Dixon's brow furrowed deeply, his jaw clenching as he processed the information. The lines on his face seemed to deepen with each passing second. "So the Colonel's men have taken Groveland? They've expanded their territory that far south? Christ, that's closer than we thought."

Sabrina's dark eyes met Dixon's, a flicker of fear visible in their depths. She took a deep breath before answering, steeling herself for the impact her words would have. "No, sir. These weren't the black uniforms of the SS-SA. They were green. A deep, military green. Like nothing we've seen before. It was... unsettling, to say the least."

Dixon's face twisted in confusion, his mind struggling to process this new, alarming information. His hand instinctively moved to the holster at his hip, as if preparing for an immediate threat. "Green uniforms? What the hell? Are you sure about this? Could it be some new faction we haven't encountered yet?"

"Solid green," Sabrina confirmed, her voice steady despite the tremor in her hands. She clenched them into fists to hide the shaking, her nails digging into her palms. "With a patch on the shoulder. A very specific patch that I recognized immediately. It's not something I could ever mistake or forget."

Maria's eyes widened, her breath catching in her throat. The color drained from her face as the implications began to sink in. "A patch? What kind of patch? What did it look like, Sabrina? Don't keep us in suspense. We need to know what we're up against."

Dixon's expression darkened, a shadow passing over his face as the implications began to sink in. His voice was gruff when he spoke, laced with a mixture of frustration and growing dread. "I take it by the look on your face it wasn't an American flag patch. Or anything we'd recognize as friendly. Spit it out, Alvarez. We can't dance around this."

Sabrina swallowed hard, her throat suddenly dry as sandpaper. She could feel the weight of everyone's gaze upon her, the air thick with tension. "No," she said softly, the word barely audible in the tense silence. She paused, steeling herself before continuing, knowing her next words would change everything. "It was a Cuban flag. Clear as day, right there on their shoulders."

The words hung in the air, heavy with implications and unspoken fears. A collective gasp rippled through the group, followed by a stunned silence that seemed to stretch for an eternity. Dixon stared at Sabrina, disbelief etched across his weathered features. His hand gripped his rifle tighter, knuckles turning white. "Are you absolutely sure?" he demanded, his voice rising with each word, echoing in the stillness. "You're certain it was a Cuban flag? There's no room for error here, Alvarez. This isn't something we can afford to be wrong about."

Sabrina met his gaze unflinchingly, her chin lifting slightly in defiance. Her voice was steady, filled with a quiet certainty that left no room for doubt. "Corporal, I grew up in Miami. My grandparents were Cuban refugees who fled Castro's regime, risking everything for freedom. They told me stories about that flag, what it meant to them, how it changed from a symbol of hope to one of oppression. If there's one thing I know without a shadow of a doubt, it's a Cuban flag when I see one. I'd stake my life on it. Hell, I'd stake all our lives on it."

Dixon exhaled slowly, running a hand through his

graying hair. The gravity of the situation seemed to age him before their eyes. "Well, I'll be damned. It could answer some questions about the grid going down. The Cubans or more likely the Russians might be behind it. Maybe the Chinese and North Koreans are in on it as well. I don't know that we'll ever really know for sure, but this is a game-changer. Everything we thought we knew just got turned on its head."

He paced back and forth, his boots scuffing the dirt as his mind raced through the possibilities. The others watched him, tension mounting with each step, the air thick with unspoken fears and questions. "If the Cubans are here, if they had anything to do with the grid going down or not, the Russians can't be far behind if they're not already here as well. This could be the start of a full-scale invasion. God help us all. We're looking at a whole new level of threat here, folks."

Dixon's fist clenched at his side, knuckles white with tension. His voice was a low growl when he spoke again, filled with a mixture of anger and determination. "Damn it all to hell! This changes things in a big way. Fighting off these rogue groups is tough enough, but trained armies, that's a whole other ball game. We're talking about a potential war on our own soil. One we're not prepared for in the slightest. We've been so focused on surviving day to day, we never even considered this possibility. Now we're facing an enemy with resources, training, and God knows what kind of weaponry. We're going to have to completely rethink our strategy if we want to have any hope of surviving this."

CHAPTER THIRTY FOUR

C aptain Rodriguez surveyed the area with a critical eye, his years of military experience evident in his meticulous assessment. His gaze swept over the terrain, taking in every detail from the overgrown parking lot to the dense treeline, noting potential cover and lines of sight. He mentally cataloged each vantage point, his mind already formulating tactical scenarios and contingency plans. The fading sunlight cast long shadows across the landscape, creating pockets of darkness that could conceal friend or foe alike. "This is a perfect ambush spot, Joe. Excellent choice," he said, nodding appreciatively, his voice low and filled with professional admiration. A slight smile tugged at the corner of his mouth, recognizing the strategic brilliance of the location. His fingers unconsciously tapped against his thigh, a habit from his days of combat readiness. Joe's face bore a grim smile, a mix of pride and determination playing across his weathered features. The lines around his eyes deepened as he squinted against the fading light, his expression a testament to the weight of their current situation. His calloused hand absently rubbed the stubble on his chin, a nervous tic he'd developed in recent months. "That's why I picked it, Cappy. Jojo and I spent a lot of time at that restaurant right there," he said, gesturing to the abandoned building with its faded sign, paint peeling and windows boarded up. Memories of happier times flashed through his mind, a stark contrast to their current reality. He could almost hear the echoes of laughter and the clink of glasses from years past, now replaced by an eerie silence. "The wooded area gives us cover, and the river cuts off their retreat. Once they get here, they're sitting ducks." His hand unconsciously tightened on his rifle as he spoke, the weight of the coming confrontation settling over him like a heavy blanket. The cold metal against his palm was a grim reminder of what lay ahead, sending a shiver down his spine that had nothing to do with the cooling evening air.

Rodriguez's eyes glinted with approval, a spark of tactical excitement lighting up his face. His posture straightened, years of military training kicking in as he assessed the battlefield. The muscles in his jaw tightened as he ran through various scenarios in his mind, considering every possible outcome. Without hesitation, he began deploying the group, positioning each member strategically to create an inescapable kill zone. He moved with practiced efficiency, his low voice issuing clear, concise orders, each word carrying the weight of years of combat experience. His hands gestured precisely, indicating exact positions and fields of fire, occasionally pausing to make minute adjustments to someone's stance or line of sight. The air was thick with tension as they settled into their hiding spots, weapons at the ready, fingers resting lightly on triggers. The rustle of clothing and the soft crunch of leaves underfoot gradually faded as everyone found their positions, melting into the landscape like ghosts. The occasional glint of metal from a rifle barrel or a watch face was the only indication that the area was anything but deserted.

Time seemed to stretch endlessly as they waited, the only sounds the gentle rustle of leaves in the breeze and their own measured breathing. The minutes ticked by, each second feeling like an eternity, the anticipation building like a coiled spring ready to snap. The sun dipped lower on the horizon, casting long shadows across the landscape, painting the world in shades of orange and purple. The air grew cooler as twilight approached, sending a shiver down their spines that had nothing to do with the temperature. The chirping of birds gradually gave way to the first calls of nocturnal creatures, nature oblivious to the human drama about to unfold. Finally, the low rumble of engines broke the silence, growing steadily louder. Two trucks appeared on the horizon, their headlights cutting through the gathering gloom as they pulled into the restaurant's cracked and weed-choked parking lot, tires crunching over broken asphalt. The sound echoed in the stillness, seeming unnaturally loud in the tense silence. The vehicles' engines sputtered and died, leaving behind an oppressive quiet broken only by the soft pinging of cooling metal.

Sergeant Carter and his men jumped out, their boots crunching on the gravel as they lined up in formation. Carter paced back and forth, his anxiety palpable as he awaited the group the Colonel had promised. His eyes darted nervously from side to side, unaware of the danger lurking just yards away. The tension in his shoulders was visible even from a distance, his hand repeatedly checking his sidearm as if to reassure himself of its presence. Sweat glistened on his forehead despite the cool evening air, betraying his unease. His men shifted restlessly, their discomfort evident in their rigid postures and darting glances. The occasional whisper passed between them, quickly silenced by a sharp look from Carter. The atmosphere was electric with anticipation and fear, the men clearly on edge in this exposed position.

Suddenly, the air exploded with gunfire, shattering the eerie calm. Joe and his men opened fire with deadly precision, their shots finding their marks with ruthless efficiency. The crack of rifles and the staccato bursts of automatic weapons filled the air, echoing off the abandoned buildings and reverberating through the trees. The ambush was swift and merciless, a perfectly orchestrated symphony of destruction. Muzzle flashes lit up the growing darkness, briefly illuminating the grim faces of Joe's team, their expressions set in stone as they carried out their grim task. The air filled with the acrid smell of gunpowder and the metallic tang of blood, a sensory assault that seemed to heighten the chaos of the moment.

In a matter of seconds, it was over. The parking lot fell silent once more, now littered with the bodies of the Colonel's men. Wisps of gun smoke drifted lazily through the air, mingling with the acrid smell of cordite that burned their nostrils. The last echoes of gunfire faded away, leaving behind a ringing silence that seemed almost as loud as the battle itself. Carter and his squad had been caught completely off guard, cut down before they could even reach for their weapons. Their lifeless forms lay scattered across the asphalt, a testament to the brutal efficiency of Joe's team. Blood seeped into the cracks of the old parking lot, a stark reminder of the violence that had just unfolded. The metallic scent of blood mixed with the gunpowder, creating a nauseating cocktail that hung heavy in the air. In the distance, a flock of birds took flight, startled by the sudden violence that had shattered the peace of the early evening. The last rays of sunlight caught their wings as they wheeled away, nature's silent commentary on the human carnage below.

Rodriguez barked orders to his men, sending them to verify each body with military precision. As the group emerged from their hiding spots, the full extent of the carnage became apparent. The parking lot was a grim tableau of death, bodies sprawled across the cracked asphalt in various states of repose. The acrid smell of gunpowder still hung in the air, mingling with the metallic scent of blood and the faint, sickly-sweet odor of decay beginning to set in under the hot Florida sun.

"Jojo, check the trucks for keys," Joe called out, his voice cutting through the eerie silence that had descended upon the once-bustling restaurant.

His son jogged over to the vehicles, quickly returning with a nod. "Yep, Dad. Keys are still in both ignitions. Looks like they didn't have time to grab them before all hell broke loose. Tanks are nearly full too."

Jojo stood silently for a moment, his gaze fixed on the restaurant. Memories washed over him like a bittersweet tide – happy customers at outdoor tables, their faces sun-kissed and carefree; hours spent with his dad at the covered bar overlooking the Rainbow River, their laughter mingling with the gentle sound of flowing water and clinking glasses. Those moments felt like a lifetime ago now, a stark contrast to the scene of carnage before him.

Turning back to the scene before him, Jojo's expression shifted. An idea sparked in his mind, a flicker of inspiration amid the chaos. He approached his father and Rodriguez, his steps hesitant but purposeful, boots crunching on broken glass and spent shell casings.

"Dad, Cappy. I have an idea," he said, his voice hesitant, almost apologetic, as if he were ashamed of the thoughts forming in his head.

Rodriguez walked over, curiosity in his eyes. "What's up, Jojo? You look like you've seen a ghost. Hell, given what we've just been through, I wouldn't be surprised if you had."

Jojo looked down, struggling to voice his thoughts. His fingers fidgeted with the hem of his shirt, a nervous habit he'd had since childhood. "I don't know how you'd feel about this, hell I don't know how I feel about it myself, but I was thinking, uhm..."

Joe squeezed his son's shoulder reassuringly, his calloused hand a familiar comfort. "Spit it out, son.

We're all ears. After what we've just been through, I doubt anything could shock us now."

Taking a deep breath, Jojo met their eyes, his gaze steady despite the unease in his voice. "I know this sounds kinda ghoulish, but I was thinking maybe we could take these bodies and pose them in some of these chairs sitting at tables, maybe a few sitting at the bar, some down at the tables by the river. We might even be able to find some cocktail glasses and plates and stuff in the restaurant to set out and make it look like they're still... you know, enjoying themselves. Like nothing ever happened."

Joe and Rodriguez exchanged stunned glances, a mix of shock and grudging admiration in their eyes. "Why the hell would we do that, son?" Joe asked, his brow furrowed, but his tone more curious than judgmental. "That's some pretty dark stuff you're suggesting."

"Like I said, I know it sounds ghoulish and creepy," Jojo explained, his expression grim but determined. "But think about the psychological factor it would have on the rest of the Colonel's men. Imagine them coming here, expecting to find their comrades, only to see... this. It could really mess with their heads, maybe even demoralize them. Make them think twice about following the Colonel's orders."

Joe and Rodriguez looked at each other again, this time

with slow smiles spreading across their faces. The gears were turning in their minds, weighing the potential impact of such a macabre display against the moral implications of desecrating the dead.

Rodriguez chuckled, patting Jojo on the back with unexpected enthusiasm. "I'm game if you are, Joe. And you're right, your boy is a goddamn genius. Twisted, but genius. This kind of psychological warfare could give us a real edge."

Joe laughed, pride evident in his voice and the way he looked at his son. "Yes, he is. Actually, just a chip off the old block. I guess all those strategy games we used to play are finally paying off, huh? Who'd have thought those late nights playing board games would come in handy in the apocalypse?"

CHAPTER THIRTY FIVE

Pernell approached the Colonel's cabin with apprehension and dread, his heart pounding in his chest like a trapped bird. He hesitated for a long moment before raising his trembling hand to knock on the weathered wooden door, its paint peeling in the relentless Florida sun.

The Colonel's deep, commanding voice bellowed from within, cutting through the silence like a knife. "Enter," he barked, the single word dripping with authority.

Pernell slowly opened the door, wincing at the protracted creak of the rusty hinges, and stepped inside. The musty scent of old leather, bourbon, and stale cigar smoke assaulted his nostrils as he entered the dimly lit room, his eyes struggling to adjust to the gloom.

The Colonel, an imposing figure even when seated, set his crystal glass of bourbon on his polished mahogany desk with a soft clink that echoed in the tense silence. His piercing blue eyes, cold as a winter sky, locked onto Pernell's face, searching for any hint of good news. "What is it, Bobby? Good news, I hope," he drawled, his tone deceptively casual.

Pernell took a deep breath, feeling the weight of his news settle heavily on his shoulders like a lead blanket. He swallowed hard, his throat suddenly as dry as the dusty Florida roads. "I'm afraid not, sir," he managed to croak out.

The Colonel's expression darkened like storm clouds gathering on the horizon as he picked up his glass once again. He swirled the amber liquid thoughtfully before taking a deliberate sip, savoring the burn. "What now, Bobby?" he asked, his voice deceptively calm, a predator toying with its prey.

Pernell stiffened, his body rigid with tension, every muscle coiled tight as a spring. He forced the words out, each one feeling like a jagged stone in his mouth. "It's Carter and all of his men, sir. They're dead. We found them east of town by the Rainbow River, their bodies left like discarded trash."

The Colonel's eyes flashed dangerously, a bolt of lightning in a thunderstorm, as he glared at Pernell. He rose from his chair in one fluid motion, his pristine white suit a stark contrast to the growing storm on his face. "How could that be?" he snarled, his carefully cultivated charm evaporating like morning dew. "I ordered him to move west on the Withlacoochee and garner us more boats. What in tarnation was he doing out east?"

Sweat began to form on Pernell's brow, trickling down the side of his face like rainwater down a window pane. He resisted the urge to wipe it away, not daring to move under the Colonel's intense scrutiny. "I have no idea why they went east, sir. There's more," he added, his voice barely above a whisper.

The Colonel's face contorted with rage, his carefully cultivated mask of control slipping like sand through an hourglass. "More? More? What more, Bobby?" he demanded, his voice rising with each word, filling the small cabin with his fury.

Pernell fidgeted in his stance, fighting the urge to take a step back, to flee from the storm brewing before him. He licked his dry lips before continuing, tasting salt and fear. "Whoever took them out also left a message, sir. A warning, I think."

The Colonel moved around to the front of his desk with predatory grace, each step measured and deliberate. He drew his face closer to Pernell's, close enough that Pernell could see the flecks of grey in his neatly trimmed goatee and count every line etched by time and ambition. "What kind of message, Bobby?" he growled, his breath hot on Pernell's face.

Pernell could smell the alcohol on the Colonel's breath as he spoke, mingling with the scent of expensive cologne and barely contained rage. He fought to keep his voice steady as he replied, each word feeling like it might be his last. "It's a message to you, sir. I think it would be best if you came to see it for yourself, sir. It's... it's not something I can easily explain."

The Colonel reached for his glass once more, his movements deliberate and controlled, a stark contrast to the chaos in his eyes. He downed the remaining bourbon in one quick gulp, the muscles in his throat working as he swallowed. Setting the empty glass down with a sharp clank that made Pernell jump, he fixed Pernell with a steely gaze that could have frozen Hell itself. "Lead the way, Bobby," he commanded, his voice low and dangerous.

The Colonel's pristine white suit seemed to glow in the dim light of the cabin as he strode towards the door, his polished shoes clicking against the hardwood floor like a ticking clock counting down to doomsday. His face, usually a mask of calm control, now twisted with a mixture of anger and curiosity, a dangerous cocktail that Pernell knew could explode at any moment. He paused at the threshold, adjusting his black string tie with practiced precision, his long fingers moving with surprising delicacy for a man capable of such violence.

"Well?" he snapped, his blue eyes boring into Pernell with an intensity that made the younger man flinch, feeling like a bug under a magnifying glass. "Don't just stand there gawking like a slack-jawed yokel. Move!"

Pernell jumped as if stung, nearly tripping over his own feet in his haste to obey. He fumbled with the door handle before managing to yank it open, stepping out into the oppressive Florida heat that hit him like a wall. He led the way out of the cabin, acutely aware of the Colonel's imposing presence behind him, feeling the weight of the older man's gaze on his back like a physical touch. The gravel crunched under their feet as they made their way to a waiting truck, the sound seeming unnaturally loud in the tense silence, each step bringing them closer to a revelation neither truly wanted to face.

As they climbed in, the Colonel's movements were fluid and graceful, belying the storm brewing beneath his carefully cultivated exterior. He settled into the passenger seat, his posture ramrod straight, hands folded neatly in his lap like a Southern gentleman at church. His eyes stared straight ahead, focused on some unseen point in the distance, perhaps seeing the future he had planned now crumbling before him.

"Drive," he commanded, his voice low and dangerous, carrying the promise of retribution. The single word hung in the air between them, heavy with unspoken threats and the weight of lives already lost.

Pernell started the engine with shaking hands, his

fingers fumbling with the keys before finally bringing the old truck to life. He gripped the steering wheel so tightly his knuckles turned white, a stark contrast to his sun-bronzed skin. The vehicle lurched forward, kicking up a cloud of dust as they sped towards the Rainbow River, leaving behind the relative safety of the camp and heading towards an uncertain future.

The weight of unspoken threats hung heavy in the air between them as they drove, the Colonel's silence more terrifying than any words could have been. Pernell found himself holding his breath, afraid that even the sound of his breathing might shatter the fragile calm and unleash the Colonel's wrath. The Florida landscape flew by outside the windows, a blur of green and brown, but neither man noticed, both lost in their own thoughts of what awaited them at the end of this journey.

As the truck neared the Rainbow River, the Colonel's eyes narrowed, spotting a large gathering of townspeople and his SS-SA men in their signature black uniforms. The crowd huddled together, their attention fixed on something beyond, an air of unease palpable even from a distance. The sun cast long shadows across the scene, adding to the ominous atmosphere. A gentle breeze rustled through the nearby trees, carrying with it the faint scent of the river and an undercurrent of something more sinister.

The vehicle rolled to a stop, gravel crunching beneath its tires like brittle bones. The sound echoed in the eerie stillness, a stark contrast to the usual bustling activity of the area. The Colonel stepped out, his pristine white suit a stark contrast to the somber atmosphere, the fabric seeming to glow in the fading light. He adjusted his string tie and straightened his plantation-style hat before striding towards the commotion with purposeful steps, his voice cutting through the air like a whip, sharp and demanding.

"What the hell are you all gawking at?" he barked, his southern drawl more pronounced in his agitation. His piercing blue eyes scanned the crowd, daring anyone to meet his gaze.

At the sound of his voice, the crowd parted like the Red Sea, their faces a mixture of fear and reverence. Some bowed their heads, while others shuffled nervously, desperate to avoid drawing attention to themselves. The sudden movement revealed the macabre scene that had captivated their attention, a tableau of horror that seemed almost surreal in the tranquil riverside setting.

The Colonel's steps faltered, his carefully constructed mask of control slipping for a moment as he took in the grotesque sight before him, his mind reeling to comprehend what his eyes were seeing. His hand instinctively reached for the antique silver pocket watch in his vest, a habit he'd developed when faced with unexpected situations.

His men, once loyal soldiers proud in their black uniforms, now sat lifeless at various tables, drinks clutched in their stiff hands as if frozen in time during a moment of revelry. Their eyes, once alert and ready for action, now stared blankly into the distance, a haunting reminder of their sudden demise. Three more were propped up on bar stools, a mockery of a night out drinking, their glassy eyes staring into nothingness. Carter, the man once in charge of this group of men, leaned against a nearby tree, his unseeing eyes staring into the distance, a look of surprise eternally etched on his face. His hand still rested on his holstered weapon, a futile attempt at defense frozen in time. Two more bodies occupied kayaks, tied securely to the dock as if waiting for a leisurely river trip, the gentle lapping of the water against the vessels a cruel counterpoint to the grim scene. Their paddles lay across their laps, ready for an excursion that would never come.

The Colonel's piercing blue eyes darted from one grisly sight to another, his mind struggling to process the scene, to make sense of this brazen attack on his people, his authority. A shiver ran down his spine, a feeling so foreign that it took him a moment to recognize it as fear, an emotion he thought he'd long since banished from his psyche. He clenched his fists, his manicured nails digging into his palms as he fought to regain his composure.

Then he saw it. The message. Two large pieces of drywall propped up against the bar, their stark white surfaces marred by crimson letters that seemed to pulse in the dying light. The first read: "My dear Colonel, your world is shrinking." The second continued: "We have unfinished business see you soon." The words were a challenge, a promise of more violence to come. The handwriting was bold and confident, each letter meticulously formed, mocking the Colonel's own penchant for fine penmanship.

The Colonel's breath caught in his throat as he realized the gruesome medium used for this communication. Blood. His men's blood. The metallic scent of it hung heavy in the air, mixing with the earthy smell of the river. It was a potent cocktail that spoke of death and defiance, a clear message that someone out there was not afraid to stand against him and his empire. He swallowed hard, his Adam's apple bobbing visibly, as he fought to maintain his composure in front of the watching crowd.

The Colonel's voice wavered, an unfamiliar tremor in his usually commanding tone. "Bobby, tell those men to clean this mess up immediately. Then get me back to the cabin." His hands, normally steady as a surgeon's, trembled slightly as he smoothed down his lapels, a nervous tic he thought he'd long since conquered.

As Pernell strode off to relay the orders, the Colonel turned on his heel, his pristine white suit a stark contrast to the grim scene behind him. He made his way back to the truck, his steps lacking their usual confidence, more of a shuffle than his typical purposeful stride. Sinking into the passenger seat, he stared straight ahead, his jaw clenched tight enough to crack teeth. The leather upholstery creaked under his weight, the sound unnaturally loud in the oppressive silence.

Pernell returned, sliding into the driver's seat with a grunt. The engine roared to life, breaking the eerie silence that had settled over the area like a funeral shroud. They drove back to the Colonel's cabin, the silence between them as heavy as a coffin lid. The familiar landscape seemed alien now, twisted by the knowledge of what had transpired.

Upon arrival, the Colonel burst through the cabin door, making a beeline for the liquor cabinet. His hands shook visibly as he poured two large glasses of bourbon, the bottle clinking against the rims. He thrust one at Pernell before taking a hefty gulp from his own, the amber liquid sloshing against the glass and nearly spilling over. A drop escaped, trailing down the side of the tumbler like a tear.

The Colonel swirled the bourbon in his mouth, savoring the burn before swallowing. It scorched a path down his throat, a welcome distraction from the cold fear settling in his gut. His piercing blue eyes, usually so confident and calculating, now held a hint of fear as he locked gazes with Pernell. The look of a man who had just glimpsed his own mortality. "It's Kelly, Bobby," he said, his voice barely above a whisper.

Pernell took a measured sip from his own glass, his brow furrowed deep enough to plant crops in. "How can you be sure, Colonel?" he asked, his gravelly voice laced with concern.

"You saw what it said," the Colonel snapped, his voice rising to a near shout. "Unfinished business." He began to pace, his polished shoes clicking against the hardwood floor like a metronome counting down to disaster. "There's an old quote, 'Vengeance is a monster of appetite, forever bloodthirsty and never filled.' This is vengeance for the death of his mother. This is a man on a mission." He paused, turning to face Pernell, his face a mask of grim determination. The fear in his eyes had hardened into something more dangerous - resolve.

"He's coming for me. It's personal." The Colonel drained his glass in one long swallow, as if trying to wash away the bitter taste of his own words.

CHAPTER THIRTY SIX

As Joe, Rodriguez, and the rest of the group arrived back at their camp on the river, they began unloading the two trucks Carter had delivered. The next few hours were spent in focused silence, burying caches of supplies and weapons. The work was grueling, but necessary, each man acutely aware of the importance of securing their resources. Sweat dripped from their brows as they dug deep holes in the soft earth, carefully placing their precious cargo and covering it with layers of soil and foliage. The humid Florida air clung to their skin, making the task even more arduous, but they pressed on, knowing the safety of their group depended on their diligence.

When they finally finished, Joe called everyone together. His voice was weary but resolute as he addressed the group, the setting sun casting long shadows across their faces and painting the sky in hues of orange and pink. "I hate what we did today, but I also feel maybe it will benefit us all in the long run. I can't help but think of President Truman having to make the decision to drop atomic bombs on Japan. Don't get me wrong, I know this pales in comparison to that, but in some ways it's very similar."

Joe paused, his eyes scanning the faces of his companions, taking in their exhausted but determined expressions. The weight of their actions was evident in the slump of their shoulders and the creases in their brows. "He knew by using extreme force it might just shorten the war and save many allied lives in the long run. Today what we did, while repugnant to us all, may have helped to shorten this war with the Colonel. Hopefully we put the fear of God into many of his men. Hopefully they might just lay down their arms and walk away from his tyranny. I want nothing more than to save lives on both sides. I want this to end."

His voice softened as he continued, the weight of his words hanging heavy in the air, "That being said, let's take a moment to reflect on those that perished today at our hands."

The group bowed their heads, a heavy silence falling over the camp. The weight of their actions hung in the air, each person grappling with the moral implications of what they'd done. Some closed their eyes tightly, while others stared blankly at the ground, lost in their own thoughts. The chirping of crickets and the distant call of a whip-poor-will seemed to underscore the gravity of the moment.

After a moment, Joe spoke again, his tone lighter,

attempting to lift the somber mood. "Alright everyone, we just got some food from the Colonel as well as some fine Kentucky bourbon. Let's enjoy ourselves tonight, but not too much booze fellas, we still need to stay alert." He managed a small smile, hoping to ease the tension that had settled over the group. The mention of food and drink seemed to breathe some life back into the weary faces around him.

As the men began to disperse, the sound of running footsteps caught their attention. Jake came bursting into the camp, breathless with news. He approached Joe, Jojo, Sam, Rodriguez, Dave, and Miguel, his eyes wide with excitement and his chest was heaving. Twigs and leaves clung to his clothes, evidence of his hasty journey through the underbrush. "They found our little display that we left behind for them," he panted, bracing his hands on his knees as he caught his breath.

Jojo leaned in, eager for details, his hand resting on Jake's shoulder. The others gathered closer, forming a tight circle around Jake. "What happened? Tell us everything."

Jake, still catching his breath, replied, his words coming out in short bursts, "They were pretty stunned. I think it really affected their men. You should have seen their faces - pure shock and disbelief. It was like they'd seen ghosts."

Joe smiled, a glimmer of hope in his eyes, the lines around them crinkling slightly. "Then maybe it was worth it. Maybe we've finally gotten through to them." His voice carried a mix of relief and cautious optimism.

Jake, now breathing easier, straightened up and continued, his voice gaining strength, "There's more. They brought the Colonel himself to see it. Joe, he was visibly shaken. Joe, he's scared. I could see it. Hell, everyone could see it. After he left, everyone there was talking about how terrified the Colonel looked from what he saw. It was like watching a man's entire world crumble before his eyes. His hands were shaking, and I swear I saw him stumble as he walked away. The men were whispering among themselves, and I could tell some of them were starting to doubt him."

Joe smiled and looked around at his group, his eyes gleaming with a mixture of hope and determination. The fading sunlight cast long shadows across their faces, highlighting the weariness and resolve etched into their features. "Jake, that is very good news," he said, his voice carrying a hint of excitement. "Now all we need to do is to push them just a bit further and the Colonel's army might just crumble."

The group exchanged glances, a spark of renewed energy passing between them. Rodriguez nodded slowly, his hand resting on the grip of his holstered pistol. "What's our next move, Joe?" he asked, his voice low and steady.

Joe rubbed his chin thoughtfully, considering their options. "We need to capitalize on this momentum," he mused. "The Colonel's men are starting to doubt him. If we can exploit that weakness, we might be able to end this without any more bloodshed."

Jojo stepped forward, his brow furrowed in concentration. "What if we could get a message to his men directly? Something to fan the flames of their doubt?"

Sam nodded in agreement, his eyes lighting up with the idea. "We could use leaflets or maybe just more calling cards like we did today with the drywall."

"That's good," Joe said, his voice gaining enthusiasm. "We need to make them see that their leader isn't invincible. That he's just as frightened as they are."

Miguel, who had been listening silently, spoke up. "Kilroy was here."

Jake's brow furrowed, his confusion evident. "Say what? What is Kilroy?"

Joe's eyes lit up with recognition, a smile spreading across his weathered face. "Brilliant, Miguel. Yes, that could work."

Jake shook his head, still perplexed. "What could work? Who is Kilroy?"

Joe turned to Jake, his voice taking on a patient, almost teacher-like tone. "During World War Two, soldiers would leave their mark. It was a drawing of a cartoon character with the words 'Kilroy was here' underneath it. Again, it's a fear tactic. It makes your enemy think you're everywhere."

Jojo let out a chuckle, his eyes gleaming with mischief. "I think we should update it to modern times, something like 'Kelly was here.' We already learned from interrogating Jenkins that the Colonel has an irrational obsession with you, Dad."

Joe turned to Rodriguez, his eyebrow raised in question. "What do you think, Cappy?"

Rodriguez stroked his beard thoughtfully, considering the idea. After a moment, he nodded slowly. "I think if nothing else, it might just drive the Colonel to the edge of insanity. Let's do it."

Joe nodded, a plan starting to form in his mind. "Alright, let's put our heads together and figure out the details. We've got them on the ropes, and we can't let up now."

CHAPTER THIRTY SEVEN

The Colonel sat in his dimly lit office, a glass of bourbon trembling in his weathered hand. The amber liquid swirled softly in the glass as he raised it to his thin lips, taking a long, slow sip that burned its way down his throat. His mind replayed the horrors he'd witnessed earlier that day, each gruesome detail etched into his memory like a macabre tapestry. The bodies, the blood, the acrid smell of gunpowder - it all swirled together in a nauseating kaleidoscope of violence. He could still hear the whispers of his men and of the townspeople that stood watching the scene before them. The weight of his decisions pressed down on him, a suffocating blanket of guilt and responsibility.

As the night wore on, exhaustion finally overtook him, seeping into his bones like a heavy fog. He drifted off to sleep, slumped in his high-backed leather chair behind the imposing mahogany desk. Hours later, he jolted awake with a gasp, disoriented and stiff, his neck aching from the awkward position. Rubbing his bleary eyes with the heels of his palms, he stumbled to his bed, collapsing onto the plush mattress without bothering to change out of his sweat-stained white suit. The silk sheets offered little comfort as he tossed and turned, haunted by nightmares of blood-soaked fields and accusing eyes.

Morning light streamed through the gaps in the heavy velvet curtains, rousing the Colonel from his fitful slumber. He sat up with a groan, his head pounding like a jackhammer, and made his way to the front door. The floorboards creaked beneath his feet, each step a reminder of the weight he carried.

"Get me Pernell. Now," he barked, his voice hoarse from sleep and bourbon. The words echoed in the empty hallway, a testament to his isolation.

Minutes later, a sharp knock at the door announced Pernell's arrival. The Colonel waved him in impatiently, his piercing blue eyes fixed on his subordinate with an intensity that could melt steel. The tension in the room was palpable, thick enough to cut with a knife.

"How many men did Kelly take out at the Rainbow River?" he demanded, cutting straight to the chase. His fingers drummed an impatient rhythm on the desk, betraying his agitation.

Pernell cleared his throat nervously, his Adam's apple bobbing. "Twenty-five men, sir. Plus Carter. Twenty-six in total," he reported, his voice steady despite the tension in the room. He stood ramrod straight, hands clasped behind his back, the perfect picture of military discipline.

A slow, unsettling smile spread across the Colonel's face, transforming his features into something almost inhuman. "Perfect," he purred, the word dripping with malice. "For every one of ours, two of theirs shall die. Like a deck of cards - round up fifty-two townspeople and bring them to the square. We'll make an example of them." His eyes gleamed with a cruel satisfaction, a predator savoring the hunt.

Pernell hesitated, shifting uncomfortably from foot to foot. His conscience warred with his loyalty, the internal struggle visible in the tightness around his eyes. "Colonel, we need to go after those responsible, not innocent townspeople. This will just entrench these people against us even more than they are now. It could backfire spectacularly." The words tumbled out, each one a risk.

The Colonel's eyes flashed dangerously as he turned to face Pernell, his smile vanishing in an instant. The temperature in the room seemed to drop several degrees. "Bobby, this will bring Kelly out into the open. He's watching us, mark my words. Make sure you advertise the fact that these people will soon be executed. Trust me, Joe Kelly will reveal himself. He won't be able to stand for people dying because of his actions. He'll try to play the hero and save them, and we'll be waiting for him like a spider in its web." His voice was low and menacing, each word carefully enunciated.

Pernell stood at attention, his face a carefully constructed mask of professionalism, but his eyes betrayed a flicker of doubt. Sweat beaded on his forehead, betraying his inner turmoil. "And Colonel, what if Kelly doesn't show? What then?" The question hung in the air, heavy with implications.

The Colonel's smile returned, wider than before, a predatory gleam in his eye that sent a chill down Pernell's spine. "Then we have fifty-two fewer dissenters to worry about. A win-win situation, wouldn't you agree? Now go and round up a group of troublemakers. And Bobby," he added, his voice dropping to a menacing whisper that seemed to suck the air from the room, "make sure you throw in a few women and children in the mix as well. That ought to light a fire under our friend Joe's ass. Understood?" The casual cruelty in his tone was chilling, a stark reminder of the monster that lurked beneath his charismatic exterior.

Pernell stiffened, his jaw clenching almost imperceptibly as he fought to keep his expression neutral. The internal struggle was visible in the tightness around his eyes, the slight tremor in his hands. He snapped a crisp salute, his hand trembling ever so slightly. "Understood, sir," he replied, his voice tight with suppressed emotion. The words tasted like ash in his mouth, a bitter reminder of the line he was about to cross.

CHAPTER THIRTY EIGHT

T he early morning sun crept over the horizon, casting long shadows across their makeshift campground. The air was thick with the lingering scent of last night's celebration, a bittersweet reminder of their recent victory and the daunting challenges that lay ahead. A gentle breeze rustled through the palmetto trees, carrying with it the promise of another sweltering Florida day and the faint, musty smell of the nearby river. Joe stood before the assembled group, his weathered face etched with determination and the lines of countless sleepless nights. He held up a crude sketch, the paper crinkling slightly in his calloused hands, worn from years of hard labor and recent combat. The men before him, a mix of family members and loyal allies forged in the crucible of their struggle, leaned in with curiosity and anticipation, their eyes fixed on the makeshift diagram that could be their next masterstroke against the Colonel's regime.

"Alright, men," he called out, his voice carrying across the quiet morning, tinged with a hint of his native Florida drawl. "Take a good look at this. I think we've got something here that could really shake things up."

The drawing was simple but effective - a bearded man, bearing a striking resemblance to Joe himself, peering over an imaginary wall, with the words "Kelly is Coming" scrawled beneath in bold, uneven letters. It was a clever take on the classic Kilroy graffiti, tailored to their current situation and imbued with a touch of Joe's dry humor. The image captured the essence of their resistance movement, a potent blend of wit and defiance in the face of overwhelming adversity.

A ripple of laughter and cheers spread through the group as they caught sight of the image, the tension of their circumstances momentarily forgotten. Some nudged their neighbors, pointing out details they found particularly amusing or meaningful. A few of the older men nodded in appreciation, recognizing the historical reference. Joe allowed himself a small smile, the corners of his eyes crinkling with genuine pleasure at their reaction. It was good to see them in high spirits, despite the gravity of their situation and the losses they'd endured.

"We need some artists," he continued, his voice growing serious as he brought their attention back to the task at hand, the smile fading from his face. "Who here thinks they can recreate this image with some consistency? We need it plastered everywhere, as close to the Colonel's headquarters as we can manage without getting caught. I'm talking walls, fences, abandoned buildings - anywhere it'll catch people's eyes and get them talking."

Joe's eyes, sharp despite his years, scanned the faces before him, noting the mix of excitement and apprehension that played across their features. He could see the wheels turning in their minds, weighing the risks against the potential impact of such a bold move. Some of the younger men fidgeted, eager to prove themselves, while the veterans among them exchanged knowing glances, fully aware of the dangers such an operation would entail.

"I won't lie to you," he said, his voice low and grave, each word measured and deliberate. "This could be very dangerous work. We'll be operating right under the Colonel's nose, in the heart of his territory. But it could also be incredibly effective. This is psychological warfare, gentlemen. We're not just defacing property; we're sending a message. We're letting the Colonel and his followers know that we're not backing down, that we're watching them, and that their days are numbered. We're also instilling some hope into the people of Dunnellon. Hope of something coming, the knowledge that they are not alone in their fight against the Colonel"

He paused, letting the weight of his words sink in. The air grew heavy with tension as each man considered the implications of what Joe was proposing. The chirping of birds and the distant hum of insects seemed to fade away, leaving only the sound of breathing and the occasional creak of a shifting foot. Then, with a deep breath that seemed to fill his entire frame, Joe asked, "Any volunteers?"

The response was immediate and overwhelming, a testament to the loyalty Joe had inspired and the cause they all believed in. Every man in the group raised his hand, their faces set with grim determination. Some even stood up straighter, chests puffed out with pride at the chance to contribute to the resistance in such a meaningful way. A few of the men exchanged fist bumps or clasped each other's shoulders, drawing strength from their shared resolve.

Joe felt a lump form in his throat, his eyes misting over at this display of unwavering loyalty and raw courage. It was moments like these that reminded him why he fought so hard, why he believed they could overcome the seemingly insurmountable odds stacked against them. These men, his brothers in arms, were the reason he pushed on when exhaustion threatened to overwhelm him.

"That's why I love you guys," he said, his voice thick with emotion, a rare display of vulnerability from their usually stoic leader. He cleared his throat, quickly regaining his composure, not wanting to dwell on sentiment when there was work to be done. "Alright, let's get to work and start putting this plan into action. Remember, safety first. We need to be smart about this. No unnecessary risks. We're in this for the long haul, and I need every one of you to make it back."

The men broke into smaller groups, their movements purposeful and efficient. Some huddled together, discussing strategies and planning their approach in hushed, excited tones. Others began sketching practice versions of the image on scraps of paper, comparing techniques to ensure consistency. A few of the more tactically-minded members pored over crude maps of the area, identifying potential target locations and plotting the safest routes in and out.

The air buzzed with nervous energy and determination, a palpable sense of purpose uniting them all. As Joe watched them work, moving among the groups to offer advice or a word of encouragement, he felt a glimmer of hope ignite in his chest. They might be outgunned and outnumbered, facing an enemy with seemingly limitless resources, but they had something the Colonel's forces lacked - heart. And in that moment, surrounded by the quiet intensity of his men preparing for their next move, Joe Kelly believed that might just be enough to turn the tide.

CHAPTER THIRTY NINE

As darkness descended on Dunnellon, the quiet streets erupted into chaos. Pernell, his face a mask of grim determination tinged with barely concealed anguish, led the Colonel's men through the neighborhood. The sound of splintering wood and shattering glass filled the air as they kicked in doors, their boots heavy on creaking floorboards. The smell of fear permeated the night, mixing with the dust kicked up by the frantic activity and the lingering scent of dinner leftovers from hastily abandoned homes. A dog barked frantically in the distance, adding to the cacophony of destruction. Somewhere, a baby wailed, its cries piercing through the din.

"Get out here, now!" a soldier bellowed, dragging a terrified family from their home. His voice cracked with a mixture of authority and barely suppressed guilt. The family stumbled onto their porch, blinking in confusion at the sudden upheaval of their quiet evening. The father's hand instinctively reached for his wife, seeking some semblance of comfort in the chaos. Their young daughter clung to her mother's leg, eyes wide with incomprehension and fear.

Men were wrenched from their wives' arms, children screamed for their parents, their high-pitched wails cutting through the chaos. Mothers clutched infants to their chests, trying to shield them from the violence. The soldiers moved with brutal efficiency, their faces impassive as they carried out their orders, though some couldn't help but avert their eyes from the scenes of family separation. One young recruit turned away, his Adam's apple bobbing as he swallowed hard, his fingers trembling slightly on his weapon. Sweat beaded on his forehead, despite the cool night air.

A teenage boy, his eyes wild with fear and anger, lunged at the soldier restraining his father. "Leave him alone!" he shouted, spitting in the soldier's face. Flecks of saliva glistened in the dim light of a nearby torch lamp. Without hesitation, the soldier swung his rifle, the butt connecting with a sickening crack against the boy's skull. The teenager crumpled to the ground, blood pooling around his head on the dusty street, seeping into the parched earth. His father let out a guttural cry of anguish, struggling against his captors with renewed vigor, veins bulging in his neck from the effort. The boy's mother screamed, a sound of pure, primal grief that seemed to hang in the air long after it faded.

House after house fell to the raid, doors hanging off hinges and windows reduced to jagged shards. Personal belongings littered front yards – a child's teddy bear, a family photo album, remnants of lives abruptly shattered. A woman's wedding ring glinted in the dirt, lost in the struggle. By the time they finished, thirty-one men, fifteen women, and six teenage boys had been rounded up. Pernell watched from the sidelines, his throat tight and his hands clenched into fists at his sides. A single tear escaped, tracing a path down his weathered cheek as he witnessed the injustice unfolding before him, powerless to intervene. He could taste bile rising in the back of his throat, the acid burning as he fought to maintain his composure. The weight of his complicity pressed down on him like a physical force.

The captives were herded like cattle, stumbling and frightened, toward a fenced-in area on the outskirts of town. Some tripped on the uneven ground, only to be roughly yanked back to their feet by impatient guards. The chain-link fence loomed ominously in the gathering gloom, its metal links glinting dully in the fading light. Guards took up positions around the perimeter, their weapons at the ready, fingers resting uneasily on triggers. The air was thick with tension and the metallic scent of gun oil. A cold breeze swept through, carrying with it the distant sound of crickets, a surreal backdrop to the unfolding nightmare. The rustling of leaves seemed to whisper accusations of betrayal and cruelty.

As the gate clanged shut with a finality that echoed through the night, a woman's anguished cry pierced the darkness. "Why are you doing this? What have we done?" Her voice was raw with desperation and disbelief. She clutched at the fence, her knuckles white with the force of her grip, the metal links leaving imprints on her palms. Her eyes, wide and pleading, searched the faces of the guards for any sign of mercy or explanation.

A guard nearby let out a cruel chuckle, though his eyes betrayed a flicker of unease. "You're all being charged with being subversives," he sneered, his voice dripping with false bravado. "By order of the Colonel." The name hung in the air, a specter of fear and oppression that seemed to smother any remaining hope. A collective shudder ran through the group of captives, the Colonel's reputation for ruthlessness well-known throughout the region. In the distance, a lone coyote howled, its mournful cry a fitting soundtrack to the despair that had descended upon Dunnellon. The night seemed to grow darker, as if the very stars were averting their gaze from the injustice below.

Pernell trudged up the worn wooden steps of the Colonel's cabin, his boots heavy with the weight of the night's events. The old planks creaked and groaned beneath his feet, echoing in the still night air like mournful sighs. He paused at the door, steeling himself before knocking, his hand hesitating for a moment before rapping sharply on the weathered wood.

The sound seemed to reverberate through the quiet darkness, announcing his arrival with an air of finality.

"Enter," the Colonel's voice called from inside, smooth as silk but with an undercurrent of steel that sent a shiver down Pernell's spine.

Pernell stepped into the dimly lit room, the thick scent of cigar smoke and expensive whiskey hitting his nostrils. The Colonel sat behind his massive oak desk, a crystal glass of amber liquid in hand. His pristine white suit seemed to glow in the warm lamplight, a stark contrast to the deep shadows that clung to the corners of the room like reluctant spectators.

"Report," the Colonel said, his piercing blue eyes glinting with anticipation and a hint of something darker, more predatory.

Pernell swallowed hard, his throat suddenly dry as sandpaper. "It's done, sir. Thirty-one men, fifteen women, and six teenage boys. They're in the holding area now, just as you ordered. We... we had to use force on some of them, but no casualties."

The Colonel's face split into a wide grin, revealing perfectly white teeth that gleamed in the low light. He set down his glass with a soft clink and steepled his fingers, leaning back in his high-backed leather chair with an air of supreme satisfaction. "Excellent work, Bobby. You've done well, very well indeed. Come morning, I will address the town. We'll draw Joe Kelly out of hiding like a moth to a flame. He's a sappy sentimentalist, you see. That will be his downfall."

The Colonel chuckled, a sound that sent chills down Pernell's spine and made the hairs on the back of his neck stand up. It was a laugh devoid of warmth, filled instead with cruel anticipation. "He won't be able to help himself, Bobby. That bleeding heart of his will compel him to try to save those people. But we'll be ready for him, yes we will. We'll be rid of the Kelly problem once and for all. It's high time we showed everyone who truly runs things around here."

Pernell felt his stomach churn, a mixture of guilt and fear roiling within him like a turbulent sea. He hesitated, then spoke, his voice barely above a whisper, cracking slightly with the weight of his words. "Sir, are you really prepared to kill those innocent people? They've done nothing wrong. They're just trying to survive like the rest of us. Some of them... some of them have children."

The Colonel's eyes hardened, all traces of mirth vanishing from his face, replaced by a cold, calculating look that made Pernell wish he could take back his words. "Bobby, my boy," he said, his voice low and dangerous, "I am prepared to do whatever needs to be done to remove any obstacle that stands in our way. Right now, Joe Kelly is that obstacle. He's a thorn in my side, in our side, Bobby." He picked up his glass, swirling the amber liquid thoughtfully. "After all, you can't make an omelet without cracking a few eggs, now can you? It's a simple matter of necessity. Unlike Mr. Joe Kelly, I am unencumbered with such trivial things as feelings of guilt or misplaced compassion. In this new world, such weaknesses will only get you killed."

The Colonel leaned forward, his eyes boring into Pernell's with an intensity that made the younger man want to look away. "Remember, Bobby, we're building a new order here. A better world. And sometimes, that requires making hard choices. Sacrifices must be made for the greater good. Joe Kelly and his ilk are relics of the old world, clinging to outdated notions of morality. We can't afford such luxuries anymore Bobby. Do you understand?"

Pernell stood at ease, his posture betraying a hint of tension. "Yes Colonel, I understand but it's a dangerous game of chess you're playing here."

The Colonel's eyes lit up, a spark of genuine interest flickering in their icy depths. "Chess, now that's a game I love. A game for kings and generals. A game of endless strategy." He leaned forward, his voice dropping to an almost conspiratorial tone. "Do you play, Bobby?"

Pernell's eyebrows rose in surprise, caught off guard by the sudden shift in conversation. "I've played a few games in my days, Colonel."

A slow smile spread across the Colonel's face, transforming his features into something almost boyish. He sat back in his chair and opened the top drawer of his desk, removing a chessboard and a small velvet bag containing chess pieces. The board was a thing of beauty, made of polished ebony and maple wood, each square perfectly inlaid. The pieces, as he began to set them up, were carved from ivory and onyx, their details exquisite.

"Sit down, Bobby," the Colonel said, gesturing to the chair across from him. "Let's have a game, shall we?"

Pernell hesitated for a moment, his eyes darting between the Colonel's face and the chessboard. The absurdity of the situation wasn't lost on him – here they were, discussing kidnapping and potential murder one minute, and now setting up for a friendly game of chess. But he knew better than to refuse. Slowly, he lowered himself into the chair, watching as the Colonel's nimble fingers arranged the pieces with practiced ease.

"White or black?" the Colonel asked, his tone light, almost playful.

"I'll take black," Pernell replied, his voice barely above a whisper.

The Colonel nodded, rotating the board so the white pieces were on his side. "A bold choice, Bobby. Always letting your opponent make the first move. But remember," he paused, picking up a white pawn and moving it forward two spaces, "in chess, as in life, the one who moves first often has the advantage."

CHAPTER FORTY

T he Colonel awoke before dawn, his routine as meticulous as ever. He stood before the mirror, meticulously grooming himself, ensuring every hair was in place and his white suit was impeccably pressed. His appearance was his armor, a symbol of control in a chaotic world. He adjusted his string tie, smoothing out any wrinkles, and polished his shoes until they gleamed. With practiced precision, he trimmed his mustache and dabbed on a touch of cologne, a luxury he allowed himself even in these trying times. As he finished, he paused to study his reflection, his piercing blue eyes staring back at him with an intensity that could unnerve even the bravest soul.

As the sun peeked over the horizon, casting a warm glow across the landscape, he strode confidently to the town square of Dunnellon. The gathered crowd watched him with a mixture of fear and curiosity, their eyes following his every move. Some whispered among themselves, while others stood stock-still, afraid to draw attention. He ascended the makeshift podium, his presence commanding attention, his piercing blue eyes scanning the faces before him. The crowd fell silent, anticipation hanging heavy in the air. Even the birds seemed to quiet their morning songs, as if nature itself recognized the gravity of the moment.

"Good people of Dunnellon," he began, his voice smooth as honey, with a hint of a Southern drawl. "I come to you today with grave news. Your loved ones are being held for acts of subversion against our community." A ripple of murmurs swept through the crowd, growing louder with each passing second. Mothers clutched their children closer, while men clenched their fists at their sides. "They will face trial tomorrow, and if found guilty, execution will follow the day after." The Colonel's words hung heavy in the air, like a storm cloud threatening to burst. He allowed himself a small, satisfied smile as he watched the fear spread through the assembled townspeople. The tension was palpable, a collective shudder running through the crowd as they processed the implications of his announcement.

He paused, letting the weight of his words sink in, his eyes never leaving the crowd. "However, however there is hope. If Joe Kelly, the misguided leader of this resistance movement, were to turn himself in, I might be persuaded to show mercy." His eyes scanned the crowd, searching for any sign of recognition or guilt. Some people shifted uncomfortably, averting their gaze, while others stared back defiantly. "I know you're listening, Mr. Kelly. Come on down, turn yourself in, and spare these fine men, women… and children." He emphasized the last word, his voice dripping with implied threat. The tension in the square was palpable, a collective breath held in anticipation of what might come next. The Colonel's gaze lingered on a group of young children, his implication clear to all who witnessed it.

Satisfied with his performance, the Colonel stepped down, a smug smile playing on his lips. He began shaking hands with his men, basking in their admiration and reverence. They nodded respectfully, some even offering words of praise for his leadership. But something caught his eye, wiping the smile from his face and replacing it with a look of confusion. A flicker of unease passed across his features, so brief that only the most observant would have noticed it.

He approached a white picket fence, his steps measured and deliberate. There, drawn in crayon with childlike strokes, was a crude sketch of a bearded man peeking over a wall. Beneath it, the words "Kelly is Coming" were scrawled in uneven letters. The Colonel's eyes narrowed as he studied the drawing, his mind racing. He traced the lines with his finger, as if trying to decipher some hidden meaning in the childish scribbles. His jaw clenched, a muscle twitching beneath the surface as he fought to maintain his composure.

The Colonel's face contorted with rage and fear, his carefully cultivated composure crumbling. He whirled around, shouting, "Who made this? I want to know now! Who made this?" His voice echoed across the square, causing several people to flinch. Children began to cry, and parents tried to quiet them, fearful of drawing the Colonel's wrath. His eyes, usually so controlled, now darted wildly from person to person, searching for any sign of guilt or defiance.

Silence fell over the crowd, thick and oppressive. As he scanned their faces, searching for any sign of guilt or complicity, he noticed another drawing tacked to a nearby tree. His eyes darted around, spotting three more scattered about, each one a mockery of his authority. The crude drawings seemed to taunt him, challenging the very foundation of his power. His breath came in short, angry bursts, his nostrils flaring as he struggled to regain control of his emotions.

His face flushed with anger, a vein throbbing at his temple, he turned to Pernell. "Meet me in my cabin in fifteen minutes," he snarled before storming off, his white suit a stark contrast to the darkness of his mood. His usually measured stride was now hurried and uneven, betraying the turmoil within. As he walked, his hands clenched and unclenched at his sides, his knuckles white with the intensity of his grip.

As the Colonel departed, the townspeople watched in stunned silence, unsure of what to make of this uncharacteristic display of emotion. Once he was out of sight, they began to whisper among themselves, their hushed conversations filling the air with a nervous energy. Some cast furtive glances at the drawings, while others huddled closer together, seeking comfort in numbers. A few brave souls even dared to smirk, taking a small measure of satisfaction in seeing their tormentor so rattled. The air buzzed with a mixture of fear and excitement, as if a spark had been lit in the collective consciousness of Dunnellon.

Pernell remained, his eyes moving from face to face, watching as the citizens of Dunnellon huddled together, their whispers growing more animated by the second. He could feel the tension in the air, thick enough to cut with a knife, and wondered what this new development would mean for their community. His hand rested on his holstered weapon, a silent reminder of the power he still wielded, even as doubt began to creep into his mind. He scanned the crowd, trying to gauge the mood, wondering if this small act of defiance might be the first crack in the foundation of the Colonel's carefully constructed regime.

Pernell approached the Colonel's cabin, his boots crunching on the gravel path that wound through the compound. The Florida air was thick with humidity, and cicadas chirped incessantly in the surrounding trees. Sweat beaded on his forehead, trickling down the back of his neck as he made his way up the path. He hesitated for a moment, wiping his sweaty palms on his pants, before rapping his knuckles against the solid wooden door, its surface weathered by countless Florida summers and scarred by the occasional tropical storm.

"Enter," the Colonel's voice barked from inside, sharp and commanding even through the thick oak. The words seemed to reverberate through the still evening air, causing Pernell to flinch involuntarily.

Pernell pushed the door open with a creak and stepped into the dimly lit room. The air inside was heavy with the scent of cigar smoke and leather, mixed with a faint hint of bourbon. The Colonel sat behind a large oak desk, its surface polished to a high shine that reflected the warm glow of the antique lantern. A chessboard, its pieces gleaming in the low lamplight, was already set up before him, the black and white squares a stark contrast to the rich, dark wood.

A slow smile spread across the Colonel's face, his eyes twinkling with an intensity that made Pernell's skin crawl. The lines around his eyes deepened, giving him an almost predatory look. "Come in Bobby, come in. Sit yourself down." He gestured to the high-backed leather chair opposite him, its brass studs catching the light. "Why don't you take white this time. Shake things up a bit."

Pernell's brow furrowed in confusion, his mouth working silently for a moment. His eyes darted from the Colonel to the chessboard and back again. "Huh?"

The Colonel's eyes gleamed with an almost manic energy, his fingers drumming a staccato rhythm on the desk. The sound seemed to fill the room, echoing off the wood-paneled walls. "You play white, I said. I like to switch it up and play the game from both sides. It's good practice, keeps the mind sharp. The difference between playing white and black is night and day, Bobby. Two completely different strategies. Like life itself, wouldn't you say? One side always moving forward, the other always reacting, but both equally important in the grand scheme of things."

Still puzzled but knowing better than to argue, Pernell lowered himself into the chair. The leather creaked beneath him, cool against his sweat-dampened shirt. He reached out and moved his king's pawn forward two spaces with a soft click, the sound oddly loud in the quiet room.

As the Colonel countered with his own king's pawn, sliding it across the board with practiced ease, he continued to ramble, his voice taking on a dreamy quality. His eyes seemed to look beyond the board, as if seeing some greater strategy. "I love this game Bobby, I truly do. I find it invigorating, relaxing, and it helps me to think out clear strategy in real life. It exercises the mind, sharpens the wits. In these troubled times, a man needs all the mental acuity he can muster. The world out there is a chessboard, Bobby, and we're all just pieces moving according to rules we don't fully understand."

Pernell remained silent, his face a mask of concentration as he moved his queen's knight to protect his pawn. The piece felt cool and heavy in his hand, a stark contrast to the oppressive heat of the room. Sweat trickled down his back, making his shirt cling uncomfortably to his skin.

The Colonel's eyes never left the board, drinking in every move with an intensity that bordered on obsession. His fingers hovered over the pieces, twitching slightly as if itching to make his next move. "Ahhh, you're playing the Vienna Game, Bobby. I can't wait to see what variation you might take. You

are a worthy adversary, make no mistake. You could
have won last night, but you blundered. You took
your queen out too early, left yourself exposed. I like
aggression Bobby, but patience is a virtue. Remember
that. In chess, as in life, timing is everything. One wrong
move, one moment of impatience, and everything can
come crashing down."

As the night wore on, they played game after game.
The room grew hazy with cigar smoke, curling in lazy
spirals towards the ceiling, and Pernell's eyes began
to burn with fatigue. The pieces blurred before him,
black and white merging into a confusing gray. But the
Colonel seemed tireless, his enthusiasm never waning.
With each victory, his voice rang out with the same
triumphant phrase: "Check and Mate, Bobby." He
savored each win as if it were his first, his face alight
with a fierce joy that sent chills down Pernell's spine.
The words seemed to echo in the small room, a constant
reminder of the Colonel's dominance both on and off
the board.

CHAPTER FORTY ONE

The Colonel's eyes fluttered open, squinting against the harsh morning light that streamed through the plantation-style windows. His head throbbed mercilessly, a dull ache that pulsed behind his eyes and threatened to split his skull. He groaned, pushing himself up from the plush leather armchair where he'd fallen asleep, his joints creaking in protest. "Damn chess," he muttered, his voice rough with sleep and bourbon. His mouth felt like it was stuffed with cotton, his tongue thick and unwieldy as he tried to form words. "I love the game so much but I need to learn when enough is enough."

He stumbled across the room, his usually graceful movements replaced by an unsteady lurch that would have shocked his followers. The antique credenza loomed before him, a beacon of hope in his foggy state. His fingers, usually so nimble and sure, fumbled with the ornate crystal decanter, nearly knocking it over in his haste.

The bourbon sloshed into the cut-glass tumbler, its rich amber hue catching the morning light and sparkling like liquid gold. He lifted it to his nose, inhaling deeply, letting the aroma fill his senses. The rich, oaky scent filled his nostrils, promising sweet relief from the pounding in his head.

Without a moment's hesitation, he tipped his head back and drained the glass in one long, practiced swallow. The liquor burned a fiery path down his throat, settling warm and comforting in his belly. He closed his eyes, savoring the sensation as it spread through his body, chasing away the cobwebs of sleep and hangover.

"Ahh," he sighed contentedly, a small smile playing at the corners of his mouth. "A little hair of the dog. Just what the doctor ordered."

Feeling marginally more human, the Colonel turned to face the full-length gilded mirror that dominated one wall of his private study. His reflection stared back at him, disheveled and rumpled in a way that would have horrified his devoted followers. This simply wouldn't do at all.

With practiced movements honed over years of meticulous self-presentation, he straightened his crisp white suit jacket, smoothing out the wrinkles with firm strokes. His fingers, steadier now, deftly retied his signature black string tie, adjusting it until it sat just so against his starched collar. He ran a silver-backed comb through his thinning white hair, taming the unruly strands into submission.

Finally satisfied with his impeccable appearance, the Colonel strode purposefully to the front door of his private quarters. He paused, hand on the brass doorknob, taking a deep breath to center himself. His public persona – the charismatic leader, the visionary savior – slid into place like a well-worn mask, covering any lingering signs of weakness or humanity.

He stepped outside onto the wraparound porch, blinking in the bright Florida sun that beat down mercilessly. Two of his most trusted men stood at attention on either side of the door, awaiting orders from their revered leader.

"Bring the prisoners to the town square," he commanded, his voice strong and clear despite the lingering effects of the previous night's indulgence. The soft drawl that usually colored his speech was crisp and authoritative now. "It's time for their trial. Let's show these non-believers what happens to those who defy the will of the Sunshine State Sovereign Alliance."

The fifty-two prisoners shuffled into the town square, their faces drawn and haggard, eyes sunken with exhaustion and fear. Chains clinked with each weary step as armed guards, their faces set in grim determination, flanked them on all sides. The crowd that had gathered fell silent, a palpable tension hanging in the air like a thick, oppressive fog. Children clung to their parents' legs, sensing the gravity of the moment.

The Colonel ascended his raised podium with measured steps, his pristine white suit gleaming in the harsh Florida sun. He surveyed the assembled masses, his piercing blue eyes scanning faces both familiar and strange, lingering on those who dared to meet his gaze. A bead of sweat trickled down his temple, but he remained otherwise unperturbed by the sweltering heat.

"My dear friends," he began, his voice carrying effortlessly across the square, rich with a honeyed Southern drawl. "These prisoners stand accused of sedition against the SS-SA. A most serious charge, I'm sure you'll all agree. One that strikes at the very heart of our community."

Murmurs rippled through the crowd like waves on a stormy sea, growing louder until shouts erupted from various corners of the square.

"They did nothing!" cried a woman, her voice cracking

with emotion.

"What did they do?" demanded a gruff-voiced man, his fists clenched at his sides.

The Colonel raised a hand, silencing the outcry with a simple gesture. The crowd fell quiet so quickly it was as if someone had flipped a switch. "The evidence has been presented to me, and it is overwhelming. I judge these people as guilty." His words hung heavy in the air, each one a blow to the hope of the accused and their loved ones.

More shouts rose from the agitated spectators, a cacophony of anger and disbelief. The Colonel's face hardened, his genial expression slipping for just a moment, revealing a flash of cold fury beneath the mask of Southern charm.

"Now, now. Settle down," he admonished, his tone deceptively gentle, like a parent scolding a misbehaving child. "I am not an unreasonable man. I know these people were led to their traitorous actions by one man. They are good people, led astray by Joe Kelly, like sheep following a false shepherd."

He paused, letting his words sink in, his eyes roaming the crowd. "If Joe Kelly were to turn himself in, or if one of you good people were to bring him to me, I might be so inclined to show mercy to these misguided individuals. The person who brings Joe Kelly to me would also be rewarded handsomely. A new home, perhaps, or extra rations for a year."

The Colonel's eyes glittered dangerously, like shards of ice catching the sunlight. "If not, their sentences will be carried out tomorrow at noon. Sharp." He emphasized the last word, letting it hang in the air like a threat.

A woman's voice rang out from the back of the crowd, trembling with fear and desperation. "What is the sentence?"

The Colonel's lips curled into a smile that didn't reach his eyes, a predator's grin that sent shivers down the spines of those who saw it. "My fellow townspeople, sedition is a very serious offense. It undermines everything we've built here, everything we've struggled and sacrificed for. The only punishment for such a crime can be death." He said it almost casually, as if discussing the weather rather than the lives of fifty-two people.

Gasps and cries of dismay erupted from the crowd, a chorus of anguish and shock. Sobs could be heard, and angry mutters, but no one dared to speak out loudly against the Colonel's decree. The Colonel seemed to savor the moment, drinking in the fear and despair like a fine wine, before gesturing to his men with a lazy flick of his wrist.

"Take the prisoners back to their holding area," he commanded, his voice cutting through the chaos like a knife. "And remember, good people of our fair town, you have until noon tomorrow to make things right. To save your friends and neighbors. To prove your loyalty to our cause." With that, he turned and strode off the podium, leaving the crowd to wrestle with their consciences and their fear.

CHAPTER FORTY TWO

Joe, Rodriguez, Jojo, and Sam watched the scene unfold before them from the cover of the woods beyond the square. The tension was palpable, each man's face etched with concern and grim determination. The air seemed to crackle with the weight of their shared anxiety, the leaves rustling softly around them as they crouched in the shadows. The distant sounds of the camp — muffled voices, the occasional clanking of metal — only served to heighten their sense of urgency. Rodriguez turned to Joe, his voice low and urgent. "Joe, the Colonel just put a bounty on your head. We need to take some precautions." His eyes darted back and forth between Joe and the square, assessing potential threats. His hand instinctively moved to the holster at his hip, fingers brushing against the cool metal of his sidearm.

Joe looked down, his shoulders sagging under the weight of responsibility. The lines on his face deepened as he contemplated their dire situation. "Maybe I need to give myself up," he said, his voice barely above a whisper. "I can't let him execute those people." His hands clenched and unclenched at his sides, betraying his inner turmoil. The thought of innocent lives being lost because of him was almost too much to bear.

Jojo's head snapped up, his eyes flashing with a mixture of fear and determination. "You can't do that, Dad," he insisted, his voice tight with emotion. "You can't trust that the Colonel will let them go even if you do turn yourself in." He reached out, gripping his father's arm as if to physically hold him back from such a rash decision. The mere thought of losing his father sent a chill down his spine.

Sam and Rodriguez nodded in agreement, their faces set in grim lines. The four men exchanged meaningful glances, each understanding the gravity of their predicament. The bond between them, forged through shared hardships and unwavering loyalty, was evident in their silent communication.

Rodriguez leaned in, his voice dropping even lower. "We need to come up with a plan," he said, his tactical mind already working overtime. "Maybe we can get those people out before tomorrow." His fingers tapped against his thigh, a nervous habit that betrayed his intense focus. Years of military training kicked in as he began to mentally map out potential strategies.

Joe's expression hardened, his eyes scanning the faces of his companions. The weight of leadership settled heavily on his shoulders as he considered their options. "Look, guys, I get what you're saying," he began, his voice heavy with the burden of responsibility, "but I don't see any way we can free those prisoners overnight. Did you see all the guards around them?" He paused, taking a deep breath before continuing, his gaze fixed on the distant square. "I just know one thing for sure. I could never live with myself, my own conscience, if those people died and I just stood by." The conviction in his voice was unmistakable, a testament to his unwavering moral compass.

The four men fell silent, the weight of Joe's words hanging in the air between them. Each understood the gravity of the situation and the impossible choice they faced. The distant sounds of the camp seemed to fade away as they grappled with the enormity of their dilemma, the fate of innocent lives hanging in the balance. The air felt heavy with the burden of their decision, as they stood on the precipice of a choice that could change everything.

As night fell over the camp, Pernell strode purposefully towards the Colonel's quarters. His face was a mask of calm, betraying none of the tension that coiled within him like a tightly wound spring. The soft glow of lanterns cast long, eerie shadows across the compound, providing ample cover for the clandestine movements of his loyal soldiers. A cool breeze whispered through the trees, carrying with it the faint scent of pine and the promise of change.

Pernell rapped sharply on the Colonel's door, his knuckles echoing in the stillness of the evening like a drumbeat of impending confrontation. The Colonel's voice, smooth as honey but laced with venom, called out. "Enter." The word hung in the air, heavy with unspoken authority.

Pernell stepped inside, his posture rigid and formal, every muscle taut with suppressed anticipation. The Colonel sat behind his ornate desk, a glass of amber liquid glinting in his hand like liquid gold. His piercing blue eyes, cold and calculating, fixed on Pernell, searching for any sign of deception or weakness.

"Sir," Pernell began, his voice steady as a rock in a turbulent sea, "I wanted to report that the prisoners are secured for the night. Extra guards have been posted, and we've taken every precaution to ensure they won't escape before tomorrow's... proceedings." He stood at attention, hands clasped behind his back, the very picture of a dutiful soldier, while his mind raced with the weight of his true intentions.

The Colonel's thin lips curled into a satisfied smile, a predator's grin that never quite reached his eyes. "Excellent work, Pernell. I knew I could count on you." He took a sip from his glass, savoring the burn of the liquor as it slid down his throat. "We can't afford any slip-ups, not with Joe Kelly still out there. These executions will send a clear message about the consequences of defiance." His words dripped with malice, each syllable a testament to his ruthlessness.

Pernell nodded curtly, fighting to keep his expression neutral, a battle waging behind his stoic facade. "Of course, sir. Everything will be ready for tomorrow." The lie tasted bitter on his tongue, but he swallowed it down with practiced ease.

As Pernell left the Colonel's quarters, he allowed himself a small, grim smile, a crack in his mask of obedience. What the Colonel didn't know was that even as they spoke, Pernell's most trusted men were quietly neutralizing the other guards around the prisoner compound. Months of careful recruitment and cultivation of loyalty were finally bearing fruit, a harvest of rebellion ripening in the dead of night.

In the shadows of the camp, Pernell's loyalists moved with practiced efficiency, like a well-oiled machine designed for stealth and precision. They subdued the unsuspecting guards with swift, silent takedowns - a chokehold here, a carefully administered sedative there. The air was thick with tension, broken only by the occasional muffled thud of a body hitting the ground.

The fifty two prisoners, huddled together in fear of their impending fate, watched in confusion as their captors were replaced by unfamiliar faces, their eyes wide with a mixture of terror and bewilderment.

One of Pernell's men, a grizzled veteran named Lovell, approached the prisoners. His face was a roadmap of scars and experience, each line telling a story of survival. "Listen up," he whispered urgently, his voice barely audible above the pounding hearts of the captives, "We're here to protect you. Stay quiet and do exactly as we say. Your lives depend on it." His eyes, filled with a fierce determination, scanned the group, silently pleading for their cooperation.

The prisoners exchanged bewildered glances, hope and suspicion warring on their faces like battling armies. But as the night wore on and no harm came to them, they began to understand that their fortunes had unexpectedly shifted. The air of despair that had hung over them like a shroud began to lift, replaced by a fragile, tentative hope. In the darkness, a spark of rebellion had been ignited, and its light was spreading, ready to engulf the camp in the flames of change.

CHAPTER FORTY THREE

Shortly after the sun rose, Sam sprinted up to where Joe Kelly slept, gently shaking him awake with an urgency that belied the early hour. The cool morning air nipped at his skin as he stood over Joe's sleeping form, his breath coming in short, excited bursts. Dew clung to the grass around them, glistening in the first rays of sunlight that filtered through the trees. Joe stirred, his eyes blinking open, still heavy with sleep. The world around him slowly came into focus as he fought against the lingering tendrils of slumber. "What's up?" he mumbled, trying to shake off the fog of sleep that clung to his mind like cobwebs. He could hear the distant chirping of birds beginning their morning songs, a stark contrast to Sam's urgent demeanor.

Sam shifted his weight from foot to foot, a mix of excitement and urgency in his voice. His fingers twitched at his sides, betraying his impatience. "Sir, uhm Joe, you gotta see this. It's important. Really important." His eyes were wide, darting between Joe and the direction from which he'd come, as if afraid the sight might disappear if they didn't hurry.

Still groggy, Joe rubbed his eyes with the heel of his palm, sitting up slowly. The blanket pooled around his waist as he tried to focus on Sam's face. "See what? What's happening, Sam? Is everything alright? Are we under attack?" His mind raced through potential scenarios, each more dire than the last, as he struggled to fully wake up.

Joe got up, stretching his stiff muscles, and grabbed his trusty rifle out of habit. The familiar weight of the weapon in his hands helped ground him as he followed Sam. He found Jojo, Jake, Miguel, Dave, and Rodriguez all waiting for him, their faces a mix of anticipation and barely contained excitement. The early morning light cast long shadows across their features, adding to the air of mystery. A cool breeze rustled through the leaves, carrying with it the scent of damp earth and possibility.

Joe looked at them, confusion etched deeply on his weathered face. His eyes darted from one person to another, searching for clues. "What's going on, guys? Why's everyone up so early? Is there something I should know about?" He noticed their barely suppressed grins and relaxed slightly, realizing that whatever was happening, it likely wasn't a threat.

Jojo smiled, a mischievous glint in his eye. He bounced slightly on the balls of his feet, unable to contain his excitement. "You just need to see this, Dad. Trust me, words can't do it justice. It's something you've got to witness for yourself. It'll blow your mind." His enthusiasm was infectious, and Joe felt a spark of curiosity ignite within him.

Intrigued and slightly concerned, Joe followed the group through the dense woods until they reached an area overlooking the town square. The leaves crunched beneath their feet as they made their way through the underbrush, the anticipation building with each step. The morning mist still clung to the lower branches, giving the forest an ethereal quality. As they emerged from the treeline, Joe's eyes widened, his jaw dropping at the incredible sight before him. He blinked rapidly, unsure if he was still dreaming, the sudden brightness momentarily dazzling him.

The town square was completely transformed, almost unrecognizable from the day before. Every available surface was covered in drawings - posters, banners, and makeshift signs of all sizes and colors. They hung from buildings, were taped to windows, draped across fences, and even spread across the ground in a sea of paper and ink. Some bore the now-familiar drawing of the bearded man peeking over the fence, while others simply displayed the words "Kelly is Coming" in various fonts and styles. The sheer volume of artwork was staggering, creating a kaleidoscope of color and hope that stretched as far as the eye could see. The morning sun caught the edges of the papers, making them shimmer and dance in the light breeze.

Joe couldn't believe what he was seeing, his mind struggling to process the sheer scale of it. He rubbed his eyes, certain he must be hallucinating. "You guys outdid yourselves," he said, shaking his head in disbelief. "How the hell did you get that many drawings posted overnight? It must have taken hours. Did you even sleep?" He turned to his companions, searching their faces for an explanation.

Rodriguez chuckled, shaking his head with a grin. His eyes sparkled with amusement as he watched Joe's reaction. "Joe, we didn't. We were only able to put up maybe ten or twelve of those pictures before calling it a night. We're good, but we're not that good." He gestured towards the sea of artwork, his expression a mix of pride and wonder.

Joe turned to them, his brow furrowed in confusion. The gears in his mind turned as he tried to make sense of what he was seeing. "What? Then how the hell did this happen? Where did all of these come from? It's like the whole town exploded with artwork overnight. Did we miss something?" He ran a hand through his hair, still struggling to comprehend the magnitude of what lay before them.

Sam gazed on the spectacle before them, his voice filled

with awe and a hint of pride. He gestured broadly at the sea of artwork, his hand trembling slightly with emotion. "As best as we can figure, it was the townspeople of Dunnellon. They must have seen our few posters and decided to join in, creating their own versions throughout the night. They took our idea and ran with it, Joe. They made it their own." His words hung in the air, heavy with the weight of their implications.

Joe let out a low whistle, his eyes scanning the sea of artwork that seemed to stretch endlessly before them. The morning sun caught the edges of the papers, making them glow like beacons of hope. "There must be hundreds of them, maybe even thousands." A tear fell unbidden from his eye as he took in the overwhelming sight, his voice thick with emotion. He cleared his throat, trying to regain his composure. "I am truly in awe of these people. They are fighters, every last one of them. This... this is something special. Something I never could have imagined." He stood there, surrounded by his companions, as the full impact of what they were witnessing washed over them. In that moment, Joe felt a surge of hope unlike anything he'd experienced since the world had changed. The people of Dunnellon had spoken, and their message was clear: they were ready to stand and fight.

CHAPTER FORTY FOUR

T he Colonel stirred in his makeshift quarters, the early morning light filtering through the threadbare curtains. He stretched, his joints creaking in protest, and donned his pristine white suit with practiced efficiency. As he adjusted his string tie in the mirror, he allowed himself a small, satisfied smile. Today was the day he'd cement his control over Dunnellon, and he could almost taste the sweet victory on his tongue.

He strode out of the building, ready to survey his domain. The moment he stepped onto the porch, his smile vanished, replaced by a look of utter disbelief. His eyes darted from building to building, taking in the sea of posters and banners that covered every available surface. The once-bare walls of shops and homes were now a cacophony of color and defiance.

"What in tarnation?" he muttered, his soft drawl tinged with confusion and growing anger. The Colonel blinked rapidly, as if hoping the scene before him would disappear like a mirage.

The Colonel's fists clenched at his sides as he read the words "Kelly is Coming" repeated over and over again.

His face flushed red, veins bulging at his temples as rage consumed him. The carefully crafted image of control he'd built began to crumble around the edges.

"Johnson!" he bellowed, his voice echoing across the square, startling a flock of pigeons into flight. "Get your sorry behind over here this instant!"

A young man in an ill-fitting black uniform scrambled up, fear evident in his eyes. He nearly tripped over his own feet in his haste to reach the Colonel. "Y-yes, Colonel?" he stammered, sweat beading on his forehead.

The Colonel's voice was dangerously low, barely containing his fury. His piercing blue eyes bored into Johnson's skull. "Would you care to explain to me why my town looks like it's been wallpapered by a band of rebellious kindergartners? Did we suddenly decide to host an arts and crafts fair without my knowledge?"

Johnson swallowed hard, his Adam's apple bobbing nervously. "I... I don't know, sir. It wasn't like this last night. We had patrols out, but..." he trailed off, realizing excuses would only make things worse.

The Colonel's eyes narrowed to slits, his jaw clenching so tight it was a wonder his teeth didn't crack. "Well, I'll tell you what we're going to do about it." He straightened his jacket, his movements precise and controlled despite his anger. The contrast between his calm exterior and the storm raging within was chilling. "Bring the prisoners to the square. Immediately."

Johnson hesitated, his face paling. "Sir? You mean for..."

"Execution," the Colonel finished, his voice as cold as ice. "It's high time we reminded these people who's in charge. We'll make an example of those who dare to challenge my authority."

As Johnson scurried off to carry out his orders, the Colonel surveyed the square once more. His lip curled in disgust at the hopeful messages surrounding him. He pulled out a fine white handkerchief, dabbing at his forehead with deliberate motions, as if he could wipe away the very notion of resistance.

"Kelly is coming," he muttered mockingly, his voice dripping with disdain. "We'll see about that. By the time I'm done, they'll wish they'd never heard that name."

The sun climbed higher in the azure Florida sky as a restless crowd gathered in the town square of Dunnellon, their faces a complex mixture of fear, defiance, and barely suppressed anger. The Colonel stood atop the hastily constructed wooden podium, his pristine white suit gleaming in stark contrast to the grim scene unfolding before him. The crisp linen seemed to absorb and reflect the harsh sunlight, creating an almost ethereal glow around his tall, thin frame. To his left, a line of prisoners knelt in the dirt, their hands bound tightly behind their backs with rough rope that chafed their wrists.

The Colonel cleared his throat, the sound carrying easily in the tense silence. His piercing blue eyes, cold as a winter sky, scanned the crowd methodically, seeming to make contact with each person individually. When he finally spoke, his voice carried effortlessly across the square, dripping with barely contained fury and disappointment.

"My dear citizens of Dunnellon," he began, his southern drawl more pronounced than usual, honey-sweet yet laced with venom. "I must say, I'm deeply disappointed in y'all. Truly, profoundly disappointed. Here I am, working tirelessly day and night to bring order and prosperity to our little slice of paradise, to create a haven in this godforsaken world, and how do you repay me? How do you show your gratitude?"

He paused dramatically, letting the silence stretch uncomfortably like a rubber band ready to snap. A few people in the crowd shifted nervously, their eyes darting to the ground, to their neighbors, anywhere to avoid the Colonel's penetrating gaze. The air seemed to thicken with tension, making it difficult to breathe.

"With disobedience," he finally spat the word like it was poison on his tongue. "With this childish, foolish display of rebellion." He gestured contemptuously to the posters still plastered around the square, his long fingers splayed in disgust. "'Kelly is coming,'" he mocked, his voice rising to a near shout. "Well, let me tell you something, and you'd best listen good. Joe Kelly ain't nothing but a washed-up nobody, a has-been, a man who couldn't protect his own family if his life depended on it, let alone an entire town. He's a relic of a world that no longer exists."

The Colonel's hands gripped the edges of the podium so tightly his knuckles turned white, the veins in his forearms standing out like cords. His carefully cultivated image of genteel charm was slipping, revealing the ruthless anger beneath. "You've made your choice, clear as day, plain as the nose on your faces. You've thrown your lot in with a man who ain't even here, who probably don't give two hoots about any of you. A man who, if he even exists anymore, is likely cowering in some hole, waiting for the world to right itself. And for that foolish, misguided choice, there will be consequences. Severe consequences."

He straightened up slowly, deliberately, adjusting his black string tie with exaggerated care. The motion seemed to calm him somewhat, allowing him to regain a measure of his composure. When he spoke again, his voice was quieter, but no less menacing. "Since y'all have chosen to back Joe Kelly, to pin your hopes on a fantasy, no mercy shall be shown. Not to these prisoners," he jerked his thumb towards the kneeling figures, who flinched at the motion, "and not to anyone else who dares to challenge my authority or the new order we're building here."

His eyes narrowed to icy slits as he scanned the crowd once more, seeming to memorize each face, each potential troublemaker. "Let this be a lesson to all of you. Burn it into your minds. There is no hope coming over the horizon. There is no white knight, no savior riding in to rescue you from the harsh realities of this new world. There is only me, only us, and the sooner you accept that, the better off you'll be. The kinder I'll be inclined to be." His lips curled into a mirthless smile. "And trust me, my friends, you want me to be kind."

As the Colonel's chilling words hung in the air, a commotion rippled through the crowd. People shifted uneasily, murmuring and gasping as a figure pushed his way forward. Joe Kelly emerged from the throng, his weathered face set in grim determination. He strode towards the podium with purposeful steps, hands raised high in surrender, the sun glinting off his salt-and-pepper hair.

"That's enough, Colonel," Joe called out, his voice carrying across the square with a slight Southern drawl. "I'm here now. You've got me. Let's end this madness."

The Colonel's eyes widened in surprise, then narrowed with cruel delight. He watched as Joe approached, a predatory smile spreading across his thin lips, his fingers drumming an eager rhythm on the podium.

"Well, well, well," the Colonel drawled, his soft voice somehow reaching every ear, "if it ain't the man of the hour himself. Joe Kelly, in the flesh. I must say, I'm impressed by your bravery... or is it foolishness?"

Joe stopped at the base of the podium, looking up at the Colonel. His hazel eyes met the Colonel's piercing blue gaze unflinchingly. "I've surrendered peacefully," he said, his voice steady despite the tension evident in his squared shoulders. "Now make good on your promise. Show mercy and release these prisoners. That's all I'm asking."

A tense silence fell over the crowd as they waited for the Colonel's response. The air seemed to crackle with anticipation. For a moment, it seemed as if he might consider Joe's request, his head tilted slightly as if weighing the options. Then, without warning, he threw his head back and laughed - a high, unnerving sound that sent chills down the spines of those gathered and echoed off the surrounding buildings.

"Oh, Joe," the Colonel said, wiping a tear from his eye with a pristine white handkerchief, "you simple, naive fool. Did you really think it would be that easy? That you could waltz in here and play the hero?"

Joe's jaw clenched, the muscles working beneath his stubbled skin, but he remained silent, his eyes never leaving the Colonel's face.

The Colonel's voice dropped to a menacing whisper, though it still carried to every ear in the square. He leaned forward, his hands gripping the edges of the podium. "Your punishment, Joe Kelly, will be to watch each and every one of these fifty-two prisoners die. Then and only then, after you've witnessed the consequences of your foolish rebellion, will you be executed. Perhaps then you'll understand the true nature of this new world."

A collective gasp rose from the crowd, followed by muffled sobs and angry mutters. Joe's face paled, the color draining from his sun-weathered cheeks, but his eyes burned with a fierce defiance that seemed to radiate from his very core.

"You're a monster," he growled, his hands clenching

into fists at his sides. "This isn't about survival or building a new world. This is about your ego, your twisted desire for power."

The Colonel smiled, revealing teeth as white as his immaculate suit. He spread his arms wide, as if embracing the crowd. "No, Joe. I'm just a man who understands the world we live in now. And in this world, mercy is a luxury we can no longer afford. Kindness is weakness, and weakness gets you killed. It's time you learned that lesson, once and for all."

CHAPTER FORTY FIVE

The Colonel stepped back from the podium, his eyes glinting with a potent mixture of triumph and anticipation. He snapped his fingers sharply, and immediately his men sprang into action with practiced precision. They moved swiftly through the crowd with ruthless efficiency, roughly grabbing the prisoners and dragging them forward, ignoring their protests and pleas.

"Line 'em up!" barked one of the Colonel's lieutenants, a burly man with a shaved head and a jagged scar that ran across his cheek like a cruel smile. His voice carried the unmistakable authority of someone used to being obeyed without question.

The prisoners were unceremoniously shoved into a ragged line facing the crowd, their faces a kaleidoscope of emotions - terror, defiance, and resignation etched deeply into their features. Some stumbled, barely able to stand after days of harsh confinement and brutal mistreatment. Their bodies bore the visible marks of their ordeal - bruises, cuts, and hollow eyes that spoke of sleepless nights and constant fear. Others, drawing on some hidden reserve of strength, held their heads high, meeting the eyes of their friends and family in the crowd with silent, heartbreaking goodbyes.

Joe Kelly watched the scene unfold helplessly, his face contorted with a potent mixture of anguish and barely contained fury. He made a sudden, desperate move towards the prisoners, but two of the Colonel's men, anticipating his reaction, swiftly grabbed his arms, holding him firmly in place with iron grips.

"Now, now, Joe," the Colonel chided, wagging his finger in mock disapproval. His voice dripped with false concern, a veneer of civility masking the cruelty beneath. "You'll have the best view in the house. Wouldn't want you to miss a moment of this... educational experience. After all, it's important for everyone to understand the new order of things."

The Colonel turned back to the crowd, his voice ringing out across the square with practiced charisma. "People of Dunnellon, I want you to look closely. Burn this image into your minds. These men and women before you thought they could defy me, defy us. They foolishly believed they could cling to the old ways, the weak ways that led to the collapse of civilization." He paused dramatically, letting his words sink in, his eyes scanning the crowd to gauge their reactions. "But there are consequences to such foolishness, such disobedience. And today, you will all bear witness to those consequences."

A woman in the crowd suddenly cried out, her voice raw with desperation as she reached for one of the prisoners - her son, barely more than a boy with fear-widened eyes. A guard reacted swiftly, roughly shoving her back with the butt of his rifle. She collapsed to her knees, sobbing uncontrollably, her anguish a palpable thing that seemed to hang in the air.

The Colonel continued, his voice taking on an almost regretful tone, though his eyes remained cold and hard, betraying the falseness of his sympathy. "I take no pleasure in this, truly. But for us to survive, for us to thrive in this new world, we must be strong. We must be unified in purpose and action. And those who would threaten that unity, who would sow discord and rebellion, must be... removed. It's a harsh necessity, but one we cannot shy away from."

He turned to his men, who stood at rigid attention behind the line of prisoners, weapons at the ready. Their faces were impassive masks, trained to show no emotion in the face of what they were about to do. With a deliberate nod, the Colonel gave the order, his voice carrying clearly across the now-silent square: "Carry out the sentences."

The guards raised their weapons in unison, a motley arsenal of old hunting rifles and scavenged military hardware that glinted dully in the sunlight. The prisoners tensed visibly, some closing their eyes tightly, as if by doing so they could shut out the reality of their impending fate. Others stared defiantly at their executioners, determined to face death with whatever dignity they could muster in their final moments.

As the guards' fingers tensed on their triggers, a commanding voice cut through the tense silence.

"Stand down! Lower your weapons, now!"

The unexpected order froze everyone in place. Heads swiveled to see Pernell striding forward, his face set in grim determination. The guards hesitated, their eyes darting between Pernell and the Colonel, unsure whose authority to follow.

"I said stand down!" Pernell barked again, his voice brooking no argument.

Slowly, reluctantly, the guards lowered their weapons. A collective exhale seemed to ripple through the crowd, the tension palpable but slightly lessened.

The Colonel's face contorted with rage, his carefully cultivated mask of genteel civility cracking. His eyes, usually cold and calculating, now blazed with fury as he rounded on Pernell.

"What is the meaning of this, Bobby?" he snarled,

dropping the folksy drawl he typically affected. His hands clenched into fists at his sides, knuckles white with barely contained anger. "You dare countermand my orders?"

Pernell met the Colonel's gaze steadily, not backing down an inch. The two men stood face to face, the air between them crackling with tension. The crowd watched in stunned silence, hardly daring to breathe as this unexpected drama unfolded before them.

Pernell locked eyes with the Colonel, his gaze unwavering and resolute. The air around them seemed to crackle with an almost palpable tension as he spoke, his voice low but firm, each word carrying the weight of long-held convictions.

"This has to stop, and it has to stop now," Pernell declared, his jaw set with determination. "Your once righteous vision has turned into something twisted and corrupt. You've lost control and you've lost perspective, you've been blinded by your own ambition."

The Colonel's face contorted with unbridled rage, his carefully cultivated mask of gentility shattering. But before he could unleash his fury, Pernell pressed on, his voice steady and unyielding.

"You taught me a valuable lesson while playing chess, Colonel," he continued, a hint of irony coloring his words. "Patience is a virtue. You were correct and I have been patient." A ghost of a smile flickered across Pernell's face, a grim acknowledgment of the path that had led them to this moment. "Now, please allow me to teach you another lesson from chess, Colonel. Never underestimate your opponent. Overconfidence is a killer, and you've grown far too sure of yourself."

In one fluid motion, honed by years of practice and preparation, Pernell raised his gun. The barrel now pointed directly at the Colonel's forehead, unwavering and deadly in its precision. The crowd gasped collectively, the sound a mixture of shock, fear, and morbid anticipation. The air itself seemed to hold its breath, waiting for the inevitable.

"Check and mate... Colonel," Pernell pronounced, his voice carrying a finality that echoed through the square.

The Colonel's eyes widened in disbelief, his carefully crafted facade crumbling in an instant like a house of cards. For the first time since Pernell had known him, real, unadulterated fear flashed across the older man's face as he realized the magnitude of his miscalculation. The tables had turned, and he now found himself on the losing side of the game he thought he controlled.

"No, BOBBY!" he cried out, his voice cracking with desperation, all pretense of power and control evaporating in the face of his imminent demise.

The sound of a single gunshot shattered the tense silence, echoing across the square with a deafening finality. The bullet struck true, hitting the Colonel squarely between the eyes with deadly accuracy. For a moment, he stood there, frozen in time, a look of utter shock and disbelief etched onto his face. Then, like a marionette with its strings suddenly cut, he crumpled to the ground, his once-imposing figure now nothing more than a lifeless heap on the dusty earth.

CHAPTER FORTY SIX

Pernell turned to face the troops, his gun still warm in his hand, the acrid smell of gunpowder lingering in the air. His voice carried across the square, steady and resolute, cutting through the tense silence that had fallen over the assembled soldiers and citizens. The weight of what he'd just done hung heavy in the atmosphere, but there was no turning back now.

"Stand down, all of you. The Colonel... he lost his way. Got carried away with his own power. That's not what I signed up for, and I bet it's not what most of you signed up for either. We didn't come here to be tyrants or oppressors. We came here to make a difference, to help people, not to rule over them with fear and intimidation. You all know these prisoners have done nothing wrong. This was all a perverse plan the Colonel came up with to draw out Joe Kelly."

He paused, letting his words sink in. The soldiers exchanged uncertain glances, their weapons lowered but still at the ready, fingers hovering near triggers as they processed this sudden shift in allegiance. Some looked relieved, others confused, and a few seemed downright angry.

"When we started this journey, we all agreed to make a better world. To fix the problems of the past, to build something worth fighting for. But somewhere along the line, the Colonel forgot that. He started believing he was above us all, that he knew better than everyone else. He made this about his glory, not about a better world for all of us. He became the very thing we swore to stand against. And I'm sorry I couldn't stand by and watch it happen any longer."

Pernell's gaze swept across the assembled troops, meeting each pair of eyes in turn. His voice grew stronger, more impassioned, fueled by the conviction of his words. "If any of you disagree with me, feel free to shoot me where I stand. I won't hold it against you. But if you agree, if you remember why we started this in the first place, I beg you to join together to build a better world. One that's fair for everyone, not just those at the top. One where we work with communities, not against them."

He took a deep breath, his chest rising and falling visibly. The tension in the air was palpable, but he pressed on. "I'm not looking to be in charge. I don't think any one man should be. That's why I knew what the Colonel was doing here was wrong. These people never did anything to deserve this. The Colonel just wanted to intimidate everyone, using us as his pawns in some twisted game of power. And I, for one, am done being a pawn."

Gesturing towards the citizens of Dunnellon, who stood watching with a mixture of fear, hope, and defiance, Pernell continued, his voice ringing out clear and strong, "These people have resisted and fought tyranny at every turn. I applaud them for that. Actually, I am in awe of their strength and courage and I am filled with shame that I and all of us let things get this far. Their strength and determination are exactly what we need to rebuild this world. I suggest that the people of Dunnellon have earned the right to elect the people who represent them going forward, and I encourage them to do just that. It's time we put power back in the hands of the people, where it belongs. No more dictators, no more self-proclaimed saviors. Just people working together for a common good."

Turning to his men, he ordered, his voice ringing with authority, "Release the prisoners. All of them. No exceptions. They're not our enemies, they're our neighbors. It's time we started treating them as such."

As the confused soldiers began to comply, some moving quickly while others hesitated, clearly torn between their ingrained obedience and this new paradigm, Pernell approached Joe Kelly. "Release him too," he instructed, watching as the ropes were removed from Joe's wrists.

Looking Joe in the eye, Pernell's voice softened, taking on a note of genuine regret. "I am truly sorry, Joe. I never should have let things get this far. I had high hopes for the Colonel and his original vision. I really thought we were building something good, something lasting. I was blind to what he was becoming. I should have seen it sooner, I should have acted sooner. That's on me, and I'll have to live with that."

Joe stood before him, his face a mix of emotions - anger, relief, and a grudging respect. His voice was gruff when he spoke, tinged with the weariness of a man who'd been through too much. "You have nothing to apologize for," he said, rubbing his wrists where the ropes had dug into his skin. Then, unexpectedly, a hint of a smile played at the corners of his mouth. "Well, maybe there is one thing you could apologize for."

Pernell furrowed his brow, confused by this sudden shift. He braced himself, wondering what recrimination was coming his way. "And what's that?" he asked, ready to accept whatever Joe threw at him.

Joe's smile widened as he replied, a glint of dark humor in his eyes, "I wanted to be the one to put a bullet in that man's head. You stole my thunder, Pernell. I've been dreaming about that moment for weeks, and you went and did it yourself. That's just not fair, man."

Pernell's lips curved into a small, rueful smile. "I can

understand that, Joe, and I do apologize for stealing your thunder. It wasn't my intention to deprive you of that moment. I heard about your mother, and for that I apologize as well. That never should have happened, not to someone like her. I am truly, deeply sorry for your loss. It's a tragedy that weighs heavily on my conscience."

Joe looked down, his jaw clenching as he tried to keep the tears at bay. His voice was thick with emotion when he spoke, barely above a whisper. "Pernell, I appreciate your words, and even more I appreciate your actions here today. You seem like a good man caught up in a bad situation, trying to do the right thing. I'm glad you had the courage to stand up against this tyrant. It couldn't have been easy, given your position."

He took a deep breath, steadying himself, his hands clenched at his sides. "I propose an alliance, a partnership of sorts. If you can get your men together on the same page, rally those who share your convictions, I think together we could be a formidable force for justice in this broken world. I trust you, and I trust your judgment. I invite you and any of your men that feel the way you do to join us for a mutual cause. You know where we are. After you get things settled here and figure out who is trustworthy and who isn't, I invite you to come to us. We could use men like you."

A tear rolled down Pernell's weathered cheek, leaving a glistening trail. "That means a lot to me, Joe. More than you could know. After all that has happened, that you can still be so gracious tells me everything I need to know about you and the kind of man you are. I have several men that feel the same way I do, good men who've been waiting for a chance like this, and I'm sure there are many more just waiting for someone to take a stand. Give me a week or so, and I'll bring an army of men to your compound that have the same vision of peace and justice." He paused, a hint of hesitation in his voice, his eyes searching Joe's face. "Just one thing I ask in return, Joe. It's not much, but it would mean the world to me."

Joe looked him squarely in the eyes, his gaze steady and open. "What's that, Pernell? Name it, and if it's in my power, it's yours."

Pernell grinned, a touch of his old charm returning to his face. "All I ask is that you call me Bobby. It's what my friends used to call me, before all this. I'd like to hear it again."

Joe smiled, a genuine warmth spreading across his features. He grasped Pernell's - Bobby's - hand in a firm handshake, the grip of two men sealing a pact. Then, in a moment of shared understanding and newfound camaraderie, the two men embraced in a brief but heartfelt hug, the kind shared between brothers-in-arms.

When the two men released from their embrace, Joe looked at Bobby, his eyes twinkling with a mix of mischief and seriousness. "Since you've asked something of me, Bobby, I'll make one request of you too."

Pernell's eyebrows rose, curiosity etched across his face. "Certainly, what?"

Joe's lips curved into a smile, the lines around his eyes crinkling. "Please don't show up at our compound with those damn black SS-SA uniforms."

Pernell threw his head back and let out a hearty laugh, the sound echoing across the square. It was a genuine, unburdened laugh, one that seemed to shake off the last vestiges of the oppressive regime they'd just toppled. "That, my friend, is a deal."

The two men clasped hands once again, their grip firm and resolute. The handshake sealed more than just an agreement about uniforms; it represented a new alliance, a fresh start built on mutual respect and shared values.

Around them, the square buzzed with activity. Soldiers were releasing prisoners, some with hesitation, others with obvious relief. The citizens of Dunnellon watched warily, hope and disbelief warring on their faces as they tried to process the sudden shift in power dynamics.

Pernell turned to survey the scene, his shoulders squared with newfound purpose. "We've got a lot of work ahead of us," he mused, running a hand through his hair. "Rebuilding trust, reorganizing our forces, establishing a new order that actually serves the people."

Joe nodded, his expression thoughtful. "It won't be easy, but nothing worth doing ever is. We'll face it together, one step at a time."

CHAPTER FORTY SEVEN

Rodriguez, Jojo, and the rest of his men emerged from the dense treeline, their boots crunching on the undergrowth as they approached Joe and Pernell. The tension in the air was palpable, a reminder of the precarious situation they had just navigated. The smell of damp earth and pine needles filled their nostrils, a stark contrast to the adrenaline still coursing through their veins.

Rodriguez fixed his gaze on Joe, his expression a mixture of relief and lingering concern. His eyes, sharp and alert, scanned the area for any signs of lingering danger. "That was touch and go there for a minute," he said, his voice low and gravelly, barely above a whisper. "I had my snipers trained on both the Colonel and his execution squad, as well as Pernell here. We were ready for anything. One wrong move, and it could have been a bloodbath."

Pernell, his face etched with gratitude and a hint of residual fear, extended his hand to Rodriguez. His fingers trembled slightly, betraying the adrenaline still coursing through his system. "Thank God you didn't have to use those snipers," he said, his voice slightly shaky, relief evident in every word. "I can't even imagine how that could have played out. The carnage... it would have been devastating."

Rodriguez clasped Pernell's hand firmly, his grip strong and reassuring. The calloused skin of his palm spoke volumes about the hardships he'd endured. "No, thank God you saw the Colonel for what he really was in time to save a whole bunch of people," he replied, his tone conveying both respect and admiration for Pernell's decision. "It takes real courage to stand up to a man like that, especially when you're in his inner circle."

Joe turned to Rodriguez, his eyes bright with purpose and a newfound sense of hope. The lines around his eyes crinkled as he spoke, a testament to the weight of leadership he carried. "I've invited Bobby and any of his men he feels have the same outlook, the same moral compass that we share, to join us at the compound," he explained, his voice carrying a note of hope for the future. "I think it could be a real turning point for us. We need good people, and from what I've seen, Bobby and his men fit the bill."

Rodriguez nodded approvingly, a small smile playing at the corners of his mouth. His mind was already whirring with tactical possibilities. "That would be a great asset," he agreed, already considering the strategic advantages of such an alliance. "More manpower means better security, more efficient resource gathering. It could change everything."

Jojo chimed in, his voice eager and curious, his posture straightening as he addressed Pernell. "Agreed. Pernell, how many men do you think you can trust enough to join you? We need to know what we're dealing with here. Every person counts in this new world, but we can't afford to bring in anyone who might compromise our safety."

Pernell rubbed his chin thoughtfully, his brow furrowed in concentration. The weight of responsibility was evident in his expression. "I've got well over a hundred men that I would trust with my life," he said after a moment, his eyes distant as he mentally tallied his loyal followers. "We'll spend the next week, maybe two weeks vetting everyone thoroughly to find out how many more. It's crucial we get this right. One bad apple could spoil the whole bunch, as they say."

Jojo let out a low whistle, his eyes widening at the number. The implications of such an influx of people were staggering. "Dad, that's a lot of people," he said, turning to his father with a look of concern. "How are we even gonna be able to house that many men? Not to mention feed them? This could stretch our resources pretty thin. We're talking about potentially more than doubling our population overnight."

Joe turned to Jojo and Rodriguez, his face set with determination. The gears in his mind were visibly turning, working out logistics and possibilities. "That's a great question, son, but I think with the additional manpower, a lot of building can get done pretty quickly," he explained, his mind already racing with plans. "We can set up temporary shelters while we work on more permanent structures. Plus, we'll need to step up the hunting and fishing to provide more food until some of that cattle is ready to butcher. It'll be a challenge, but I believe we can make it work. We've overcome worse odds before."

Pernell looked stunned, his jaw dropping slightly. His eyes lit up with a mixture of disbelief and excitement. "You've got cattle?" he asked, his voice filled with awe. "Real, live cattle? In this day and age?"

Jojo smiled, a touch of pride in his voice. He stood a little straighter, clearly pleased by Pernell's reaction. "We do indeed. We've been careful to keep them hidden and protected. We need to be careful not to over-harvest it for now, but along with the chickens, I think it will be something your men will enjoy. It's been a game-changer for us. Fresh meat and milk... it's like a taste of the old world."

Pernell now let out a low whistle of his own, shaking his head in amazement. His eyes shone with newfound hope, the prospect of such abundance clearly overwhelming. "That is a game changer," he agreed, his voice filled with wonder. "I look forward to getting there and seeing it all for myself. It's been so long since I've seen anything like that. The Colonel... he never cared about long-term sustainability."

Joe spoke up, his voice firm but fair. His eyes locked with Pernell's, conveying the seriousness of his words. "Just remember, the men who you bring will all be expected to work," he said, wanting to make sure everything was clear from the start. "There is plenty to do. We'll need new buildings for them to sleep in. Security needs to be maintained and expanded. We've got the start of a garden that needs to be expanded significantly. The animals need to be tended to as well as guarded. The list never ends. So make sure anyone you bring is aware this is no free ride. They will be expected to contribute their fair share. We're building a community here, not running a charity."

Pernell straightened his stance, his posture radiating determination and respect. He met Joe's gaze unflinchingly, his voice steady and resolute. "Joe, I wouldn't have it any other way," he said firmly. "If you find any of my men not pulling their weight, let me know and we'll deal with them together. I want this to work. We all need this to work. After what we've been through with the Colonel, we understand the value of a fair and just community."

Joe shook Pernell's hand once more, his grip strong and resolute. The two men stood there for a moment, the weight of their agreement hanging in the air between them. "That's all I can ask for, Bobby," he said, a glimmer of hope in his eyes. "Let's make it work. Together, we might just be able to build something truly special here. A place where people can not just survive, but thrive. A beacon of hope in this dark world."

CHAPTER FORTY EIGHT

J oe and his men spent the remainder of the day loading up all the supplies they had originally brought and all the supplies they had gathered into their vehicles, preparing for the return trip home. The sun dipped low on the horizon, casting long shadows across the makeshift camp as they worked tirelessly. Jojo and Rodriguez hefted crates of canned goods, their muscles straining under the weight, while Jake and Dave helped organize the medical supplies they'd scavenged, carefully cataloging each item.

"Easy with that one," Joe called out as he saw Jojo struggling with a particularly heavy box, its contents shifting precariously. "Here, let me give you a hand." He jogged over, his boots kicking up small clouds of dust, before grabbing the other end of the crate.

"Thanks, Dad," Jojo grunted, his face flushed with exertion and a sheen of sweat on his brow. "I swear these things get heavier every time we do this."

Joe chuckled, his own breath coming a bit harder as they maneuvered the crate. "Maybe you're just getting soft, kiddo. Spending a little too much time in the chow line, eh?"

Jojo rolled his eyes, but there was a smile playing at the corners of his mouth. "Yeah, yeah. Keep talking, old man. We'll see who's soft when we're done with all this heavy lifting."

When they had finally finished, the sun having long since disappeared behind the horizon, they went back to their basecamp to get a good night's rest before returning home. The campfire crackled merrily, casting a warm glow over the tired but satisfied faces of the group. Joe ladled out bowls of hot stew, the rich aroma filling the air as he passed them around the circle.

"Man, nothing beats a hot meal after a long day's work," Jake said, inhaling deeply before digging in with gusto. "I swear, Joe, your campfire cooking gets better every time."

Rodriguez nodded in agreement, his mouth already full of the hearty stew. Jojo sat a little apart from the others, his posture still slightly tense, but Joe noticed he seemed more relaxed than he had been earlier, the lines of worry on his face softening in the firelight.

As they sat around the campfire eating and enjoying this rare moment of relaxation, Joe had a thought that made him pause mid-bite. He lowered his spoon, his brow furrowing slightly as he considered the idea that had just struck him, its potential unfolding in his mind.

Joe cleared his throat, drawing the attention of the group. "Rodriguez, I've been thinking," he began, his voice low but clear over the crackling fire and the soft clink of spoons against bowls. "Something's been bothering all day. I hate leaving behind all these boats we've gathered. Been studying this map, and it looks like we could actually sail these boats down the Withlacoochee as far as Lake Panasoffkee."

Rodriguez raised an eyebrow, intrigued by the proposition. "Go on," he said, leaning forward, his stew momentarily forgotten.

"It ain't home," Joe continued, his fingers tracing the route on the worn map spread across his knee, "but it's less than twenty-five miles from there. Would it be silly if we got those boats that far? Maybe we could trailer them back over to the Harris Chain of Lakes?" His eyes lit up as he spoke, enthusiasm creeping into his voice, painting a picture of possibility. "I mean, they would be a valuable asset. Think about it - security patrols, fishing, transport, recon. We'd have eyes and access to places we've never had before."

Rodriguez's interest was clearly piqued, his meal all but forgotten. "Let me see that map," he said, reaching out with an eagerness that belied his usual stoic demeanor.

Joe handed him the map, watching intently as Rodriguez studied it, the firelight dancing across the paper's creased surface. The captain's finger traced down the Withlacoochee River, his brow furrowed in concentration as he mentally calculated distances and potential obstacles. For several long minutes, the only sounds were the crackling of the fire, the soft rustling of the map, and the distant call of a night bird.

Finally, Rodriguez looked up, a glimmer of excitement in his eyes that Joe hadn't seen in a long time. "I see what you mean, Joe. Yeah, that would be fantastic." He nodded slowly, his mind clearly working through the logistics, weighing risks against rewards. "We would just need to get our hands on a trailer or several trailers that could haul those pontoon boats, but I don't see that as a big problem considering how many marinas are around Lake Harris and that entire area."

He handed the map back to Joe, a determined smile spreading across his face, erasing years of worry and hardship. "Let's do it. It's ambitious, but it could change everything for us."

Joe stood before the group, his weathered face illuminated by the flickering campfire, casting deep shadows that accentuated the lines of experience etched into his features. The men's chatter died down as they turned their attention to their leader, sensing the importance of what was to come.

"Alright, fellas," Joe began, his voice carrying a mix of excitement and determination that immediately captured everyone's attention. "We've got ourselves an opportunity here that's too good to pass up. One that could make a real difference in our lives back home."

He gestured towards the map spread out on a nearby crate, its edges curling slightly in the heat from the fire. "Rodriguez and I have been looking at this map, and we've realized we can sail these boats we've gathered down the Withlacoochee River as far as Lake Panasoffkee."

A murmur of interest rippled through the group, men leaning in to catch a glimpse of the map. Joe continued, his eyes scanning the faces around him, gauging their reactions. "Now, I know what you're thinking. That ain't exactly home. But it's less than twenty-five miles from our place. That's a hell of a lot closer than where we are now."

Jojo leaned forward, his brow furrowed in thought, the firelight casting deep shadows across his face. "What's the endgame here, Pop? What are we really looking at?"

Joe's face broke into a grin, his enthusiasm infectious. "Well, son, if we can get those boats that far, we might be able to trailer them back to the Harris Chain of

Lakes. Think about it - we'd have boats for security patrols, fishing, transport, recon. It'd be a game-changer for us. We'd have access to resources we've never had before, ways to protect ourselves we've only dreamed of."

Rodriguez chimed in, his voice carrying the weight of experience and the authority of command. "It's a solid plan. We'd need to get our hands on some trailers that can haul those pontoon boats, but with all the marinas around Lake Harris, that shouldn't be too much of a problem. We've overcome bigger challenges before."

Joe nodded, his gaze sweeping across the group once more, taking in their thoughtful expressions. "So, here's where you come in. We need volunteers for this mission. It won't be easy - we're talking about navigating a river you don't know, in boats we've just acquired. There are risks, no doubt about it. But the payoff could be huge for our community. This could be the difference between just surviving and really living."

He paused, letting his words sink in, the crackling of the fire filling the silence. The faces around him were a mix of excitement, apprehension, and determination. "So, who's with us? Who's ready to bring these boats home and change the game for our people?"

CHAPTER FORTY NINE

J oe and his men began to stir at first light, anxious to get back home. The camp bustled with activity as they packed up their gear, the air thick with anticipation and the scent of strong coffee. The crackle of a dying campfire mingled with the rustle of sleeping bags being rolled up and the metallic clink of cooking utensils being stowed away.

"Let's move, people," Joe called out, his voice carrying across the campsite. "Daylight's burning." He ran a hand through his salt-and-pepper hair, squinting against the rising sun as he surveyed the organized chaos around him.

They loaded up in their vehicles, a mismatched convoy of trucks and SUVs, and made their way to the boats they had hidden in a cove a short ride south of their camp. The morning sun glinted off the water as they arrived, casting long shadows across the shoreline. A gentle breeze carried across the river, a reminder of the vast expanse of water they were about to traverse.

Joe watched as the volunteer captains and crews boarded each boat, his chest swelling with pride at their determination. Each vessel was methodically loaded with extra fuel, rations, and maps, the men working with a quiet efficiency born of shared purpose. The occasional grunt of effort or muffled curse punctuated the otherwise focused silence.

"Alright, listen up," Joe addressed the crews, his voice carrying over the lapping of waves against the hulls. He stood tall, his weathered hands resting on his hips as he spoke. "You've got two days to make it to the south side of Lake Panasoffkee. That's where we'll meet you."

He paused, making eye contact with each captain, his hazel eyes intense and unwavering. "We're gonna do our damnedest to secure some trailers for transport. But if we can't, we'll still be there. We'll figure out how to get these boats home one way or another." The set of his jaw conveyed his resolve, a silent promise to see this mission through.

Joe's gaze swept over the assembled men, a mix of determination and concern etched on their faces. Some shifted nervously, while others stood stock-still, hanging on his every word. "You've got your maps, you've got your supplies. Trust your training and trust each other. Any questions?"

The crews shook their heads, ready to embark on their mission. Joe nodded, satisfied, his expression a mixture of pride and concern. "Alright then. Good luck and

Godspeed. We'll see you boys in two days."

As the boats began to pull away from the shore, Joe watched them go, a knot of worry and hope tightening in his chest. The success of this mission could change everything for their community. Now, all they could do was wait and hope. He stood there, feet planted firmly in the sand, until the last boat disappeared from view, the weight of responsibility settling heavily on his shoulders.

Jojo stepped up behind his father. "Dad, you ready to hit the road?"

Joe turned to his son, his weathered face softening. "I most certainly am, son. I most certainly am. We've got loved ones back home that need some huggin'."

Jojo chuckled, a warm smile spreading across his face. "Dad, I think we could all use some huggin' right about now."

The two men shared a moment of understanding, the weight of their mission and the longing for home reflected in their eyes. Joe clapped a hand on Jojo's shoulder, giving it a firm squeeze.

They walked to the convoy of vehicles, their boots crunching on the gravel. The air was filled with the sound of engines starting up, a mechanical chorus signaling their imminent departure. Joe and Jojo approached their truck, the sun's glare reflecting brightly off the metal hood.

Joe paused, his hand on the door handle. He took a deep breath, inhaling the crisp morning air. "You know, son, Claire and Maria are gonna have a fit when she sees how scraggly we've gotten."

Jojo ran a hand over his stubbled chin, grinning. "Speak for yourself, old man. I think I'm pulling off this rugged look pretty well."

Joe snorted, shaking his head as he climbed into the driver's seat. Jojo hopped in beside him, adjusting his faded tan beret.

The convoy began to move out, a line of dust-covered vehicles snaking its way along the rough road. Joe and Jojo sat in comfortable silence for a while, the familiar rumble of the engine beneath them.

As they drove, the landscape slowly changed around them. Dense forests gave way to open fields, the morning sun casting long shadows across the land. Every now and then, they'd pass the skeletal remains of abandoned buildings, stark reminders of the world they'd left behind.

Jojo broke the silence, his voice thoughtful. "You think the boats will make it okay?"

Joe's hands tightened slightly on the steering wheel. "They've got good men at the helm. If anyone can do it, they certainly can."

The convoy inched along the winding roads, every mile feeling like ten. Joe's knuckles were white on the steering wheel, his eyes constantly scanning the surroundings for potential threats. Jojo sat beside him, rifle at the ready, his posture tense and alert. The air in the vehicle was thick with tension.

As they crested a hill, the compound finally came into view. A collective sigh of relief seemed to ripple through the entire group. Joe felt a weight lift from his shoulders, but he knew better than to let his guard down completely. Years of experience had taught him that the last stretch of any journey was often the most dangerous.

The vehicles rolled through the gates, and immediately a crowd began to form. Excited voices filled the air as people rushed to greet their returning loved ones. Joe and Jojo climbed out of their truck, their eyes searching the sea of faces. The smell of home - a mix of wood smoke and fresh-baked bread - washed over them, a stark contrast to the acrid scent of gunpowder that had filled their nostrils for days.

Suddenly, Taylor burst from the crowd, her face alight with joy. She threw her arms around her father and brother, pulling them into a tight embrace. "I'm so glad you made it back safe and sound," she said, her voice thick with emotion. Her grip was fierce, as if she feared they might disappear if she let go.

Joe held his daughter close, savoring the moment. The warmth of her embrace seemed to melt away the tension of the past few days. "Where's Jake? Is he okay?" Taylor asked, concern creeping into her voice.

"Yes, he's fine. We're all fine," Joe reassured her, his hand gently stroking her hair. He could feel her relax slightly at his words.

Taylor pulled back slightly, her brow furrowed. "And the Colonel?" Her voice was barely above a whisper, as if speaking the name too loudly might summon the man himself.

A smile tugged at Joe's lips. "The Colonel is no longer a worry. Justice has been served." He left out the gory details, knowing there would be plenty of time over the coming days to share the entire story with the group.

Taylor's face lit up with relief as she tightened her hug. "That is very good news, Dad." Her words were muffled against his chest, but the relief in her voice was palpable.

As the reunions continued around them, a cacophony of laughter and tears, Joe spotted Maria making her way through the crowd. Their eyes met, and suddenly nothing else mattered. They came together in a fierce embrace, their lips meeting in a passionate kiss that seemed to make up for all the time they'd been apart. Joe could taste the salt of her tears, mingled with his own.

When they finally broke apart, Maria's expression turned serious. Her eyes, which had been shining with joy moments before, now held a shadow of worry. "Joe, we need to talk."

Joe's heart sank at those words. He tried to lighten the mood with a joke, hoping to dispel the sudden tension. "Those words are never good sweetie. Please don't tell me you've fallen in love with someone else while I was away."

Maria chuckled, shaking her head. "No, absolutely not, nothing like that. But I do need to share some disturbing information with you." Her voice was low, meant for his ears only.

Joe looked skyward, heaving a sigh. The weight of leadership settled back onto his shoulders like a familiar, unwelcome burden. "Dear God, can't we just have a breather before the next crisis?" He turned and called out, "Rodriguez, get over here. Apparently, there is no rest for the weary."

As Captain Rodriguez approached, his face set in its usual mask of calm professionalism, Joe, Maria, and Rodriguez walked away from the crowd, seeking a quiet place to talk. The joy of reunion was tempered by the weight of whatever news Maria had to share. Joe couldn't help but wonder what new challenge they would have to face, even as the sounds of celebration continued behind them.

CHAPTER FIFTY

M aria's brow furrowed deeply as she glanced between Joe and Rodriguez, her eyes filled with concern. "Wait here a few minutes, please. I want you to hear this directly from the source. I don't want to risk getting any details wrong or misrepresenting the situation. I'll be right back, I promise."

Joe and Rodriguez exchanged worried looks as Maria hurried off, her footsteps quick and purposeful. The celebratory atmosphere around them seemed to fade into a distant hum, replaced by a palpable tension. The two men stood in uneasy silence, their minds racing with possibilities of what news could be so urgent.

Several minutes later, which felt like an eternity to the waiting men, Maria returned with Sabrina and Corporal Dixon in tow. The serious, almost grim expressions etched on their faces did nothing to alleviate Joe's growing sense of unease. He felt his heart rate quicken, preparing himself for whatever news was about to be delivered.

Maria nodded solemnly to Sabrina, her eyes conveying a mix of concern and encouragement. "Go ahead,

Sabrina. Tell Joe and Rodriguez exactly what you found during your mission."

Sabrina took a deep, steadying breath, her shoulders visibly tensing as she prepared to speak. She quickly recounted her group's scouting mission into Groveland, her voice trembling slightly as she described the shocking sight of Cuban troops in the area. Her words painted a vivid picture of foreign soldiers moving through familiar streets, a jarring juxtaposition that sent chills down Joe's spine.

As Sabrina finished her account, Corporal Dixon stepped forward, his posture rigid with military bearing. His face was etched with concern as he explained how he had personally led another scouting mission to Groveland to verify Sabrina's alarming information. "I can confirm it's true," he said, his voice low and urgent, tinged with a hint of disbelief. "There are indeed Cuban troops present in Groveland. Based on our observations, we estimate their numbers to be at least between fifty and one hundred men, possibly more."

Joe felt his stomach drop at the news, a cold weight settling in his gut. He glanced at Rodriguez, seeing his own shock and concern mirrored in the Captain's eyes. The implications of this information were staggering, threatening to upend everything they had worked so hard to build and protect.

Dixon continued, his tone grave and his words measured. "But the situation could be even more dire than we initially thought. If they've managed to penetrate this far north, there's no telling how many more Cuban forces might be present further to the south. We could be looking at a much larger invasion force than we initially anticipated."

The implications of this information hung heavy in the air between them, like a storm cloud threatening to burst. Joe's mind raced with potential scenarios and strategies, each more daunting than the last. The brief moment of peace and accomplishment he'd felt upon returning home now lay shattered at his feet, replaced by a renewed sense of urgency and danger. As he looked at the faces around him, Joe knew that their fight for survival had just entered a new, even more perilous phase.

Rodriguez's face darkened as he turned to Joe, his voice low and grave. "Joe, you know what scares me more than the Cubans being less than twenty or so miles away? It's that the Cubans are backed by the Russians. That scares the hell out of me. We're not just dealing with a local threat anymore; we're potentially facing a global power."

Dixon cleared his throat, stepping forward. "Sir, I had

the same thought. We did a thorough scouting all around Groveland, then moved east to Clermont and further east to Winter Garden just outside of Orlando. We found no other Cuban troops and never saw any Russian troops. It's possible their presence is limited, but we can't rule out a larger force hiding somewhere."

Joe ran his hand through his hair, his brow furrowed in thought. "Well, thank God for that at least, but we have to assume at the very least there are more Cuban forces out there. I would imagine they would have come up from the keys and into Miami." He paused, shaking his head. "I don't know, it doesn't add up. I would think the Cuban population in Miami would have unleashed holy hell on them. The city's got a huge Cuban-American community; they wouldn't just roll over for an invasion force."

Dixon looked at Joe, a thoughtful expression on his face. "Maybe they thought the same way and completely bypassed Miami. It's possible they're trying to avoid stirring up that hornet's nest, at least for now."

Joe reached up and smoothed his beard, considering the idea. "That's a thought. You may be right. Which would mean the people in Miami wouldn't even know that the Cubans have landed here. Which also means if they were to find out, the Cuban troops' rear flank is heavily exposed." He nodded slowly. "I mean, it's all conjecture at this point, but it is a glimmer of hope. We need to get some people down to Miami and see if we can rally some troops to flank the Cubans from the south side, and we'll have to do whatever we can from the north side. It's a long shot, but it might be our best chance at turning the tide."

Maria's voice was filled with worry as she interjected. "Joe, you can't be serious. We can't take on an army with the people we have here. It's suicide! We're talking about trained soldiers with heavy weaponry. Our group is mostly civilians with hunting rifles and handguns."

Joe turned to Maria, his expression softening. "You're right, sweetie, but we have help on the way. We found a good man among the Colonel's forces and he is bringing an army here in the next couple of weeks. We just need to hang on and gather as much intel as we can as to the numbers we're up against. I know it's risky, but we can't just sit back and let them take over. We've got to fight for our home, for our future."

Rodriguez nodded, a grim smile playing at the corners of his mouth. "Looks like we have a plan then. It's not perfect, but it's a start. We'll need every advantage we can get, and dare I say it."

Joe turned to Rodriguez, curiosity in his eyes. "Say what, Cappy?"

Rodriguez's grim smile widened slightly as he replied, "Back into the fray, just like old times. Let's hope we're as lucky this time around." His words carried a weight of experience, hinting at battles fought and won in the past, and the sobering knowledge of what lay ahead. "I dare say, here we go again Joe."

AFTERWORD

I want to thank you once again for taking the time to read my book, and I truly hope I was able to entertain you for a bit.

It is a series, so there is definitely more to come.

I want to take this opportunity to invite you to visit my website and let me know what you think about this book as well as the series.

It would mean a great deal to me to be able to interact and get your thoughts for the future of this series. You can not only interact but also join my newsletter to get all the latest on new releases and behind the scenes info on this series and others that will be coming in the near future.

If you're so inclined you can find my site at:

BrunoBrennan.com

The entire "Blood is Thicker" series can be found here:

https://www.amazon.com/dp/B0CVFWCWS5